UNSTRUNG

UNSTRUNG

Danielle Leneah

Donnelly Bootcamp Series

Book Two

Boettcher-Tuufuli Publishing LLC

ISBN: 978-1-7325461-3-4

Printed in the United States of America

First Edition: March 2019

10 9 8 7 6 5 4 3 2 1

Dedication

To all my family and friends we have lost this last year; I dedicate this book to you.

Acknowledgments

Publishing these books have been my dream. Thank you to everyone who continues to support me in my journey.

A big thanks to Krystlynne who continues to push me and remind me that there is still more to do. It is easy to get side tracked, and your emails are a reminder that I need to get back to work. Your thoughts and opinions mean the world to me. Thank you for everything you do for me!

Thank you to all my family and friends who have been helping me along the way. Whether it is helping with everything outside my book world or everything in it, it is greatly appreciated. To my husband and kids, I love you, and thanks for putting up with my craziness, especially when release day gets close.

Finally, to all my fans. You guys have been great. Thank you for continue to push me. Even when it is just asking 'when is the next one coming out," it pushes me to continue doing what I love. Thank you, thank you, thank you!

UNSTRUNG

PROLOGUE

When is enough, too much? How much can one person endure before they completely shut down? No one should have to go through what I went through in my childhood – no one. It's the kind of thing that breaks people to even listen to, but I survived.

The first half of my life was good, great even. I had my best friends Jeff and Patrick, and my brother, Evan. Every day was spent being an average kid on the streets of Chicago. We were naive and ignorant of the horrors of life around us. Most kids stay that way until they reach their teen years, and most never know the horrors I went through. For me, a trip to summer camp opened my eyes and showed me how cruel the world could really be. It changed my life, it changed me, and nothing after that would ever be the same.

Spending the second half of my life closed off and living in fear of the touch of others, I didn't think it could get any worse, but I learned to survive. It wasn't ideal, and my ways of coping didn't always keep me out of trouble, but I refused to give up. My secret was buried deep, really deep, right where I wanted it and always planned to keep it.

Unfortunately for me, fate had other plans. After an unlucky series of events, I ended up at the Donnelly Bootcamp in Cle Elum, Washington. It was a last chance camp for juvenile delinquents, in a tiny hick-town buried in the mountains of Eastern Washington. It was where I came face-to-face with the only person ever to find their way behind my walls.

At first glance, Aerick was nothing but a piece of eye candy – something Donnelly had an abundance of. His body was fit for a god, but that was where his charming attributes ended. He was hard, demanding, full of himself, a complete prick – or so I thought. Keeping with my serious amount of bad luck, I drew his attention immediately.

His intentions in the beginning were nothing short of his own asshole need to know everything. I'm not sure at what point it changed for him, but something happened between us. Whether it was his victory in learning my secret, or the need to conquer another part of me, something grew between us. I had an undeniable pull toward him which only grew with his touch.

His touch. Just the thought of someone touching me would normally put me into a panic attack, which usually would result in some form of violent reaction from me, but with him it was different. From the first moment his fingers came into contact with my skin, an eruption of longing and need exploded in me. It was nothing short of an addiction. I fell for him quickly and thought the feeling was mutual. He seemed to want me just as much as I wanted him. I was wrong.

It turns out Aerick and the camp psychologist, Liz, had a thing too. I was just a distraction to him. Just when I thought my life was turning around for the best, I got knocked back down into reality. Everything I had feared and struggled against since meeting him all came crashing down when I found Liz all over him while Aerick just stood there like it was an everyday occurrence. From the look of things, it probably was.

It was just game for him. There had been a nagging in the back of my mind warning me it was too good to be true, but after years of loneliness and isolation I ignored all reasoning. There were several times I started to give in to my internal struggle to push him away, but he pulled me back to him.

I even hid it from my best friends Jeff and Patrick, who by some miracle ended up here with me. A part of me knew this wouldn't end well, and I knew they would have told me that much. If they weren't here with me right now, nothing would keep my thoughts from wandering to the most unspeakable parts of my mind.

I'm trying to stay strong, to survive this, to survive being knocked back into my own personal hell.

CHAPTER ONE

(Wednesday July 8th)

I LIE HERE in bed unable to sleep, even though it is only four-fifty and I've already been awake for an hour. In a strange turn of events, it isn't because of my nightmares. Every time my eyes close, his ocean deep eyes are staring back at me and I can't stand it.

When I do manage to fall asleep, it's into a bizarre dream where I'm chasing him but can never catch up. It always ends with me waking up, out of breath and dripping in sweat. I've spent a lot of my spare time the last few days just lying here in bed with the music blaring in my ears, so I don't have to think about how fucked up shit is right now.

At night, when I don't have the benefit of my music, my thoughts are often consumed with curiosity of who might visit. Sunday night, Aerick came into the dorm in the middle of the night. I wasn't sleeping, but assumed he thought I was. He leaned against my desk for a few minutes, just staring at the floor beside me, before moving my hair out of my face and running his finger down my jaw line. The heat of his touch ran through my entire body but I stayed as still as possible, not wanting to speak to him; it's better this way. After his visit, I started making sure I lay facing away from the camera. If he is bold enough to come in here in the middle of the night, nothing would be stopping him from watching the cameras.

It's weird how I feel so lost and hurt after only being with him for such a short time. A little pathetic really, falling so hard for him so fast, but it's so hard to shake the monstrous weight lodged in the pit of my stomach. I go about each day as if things are okay, but it's all a show. I feel nothing on the outside, and I'm a twisted mess on the inside.

His daily actions are a conundrum all in themselves. He's tried several times to talk to me, but I cleverly find ways to almost never be alone. Aerick has reverted to full-on instructor mode but I constantly catch him sneaking glances at me. Sometimes he looks confused and other times I think there is hurt in his eyes. Although I have no idea why; this was his doing and I really don't care. *He can go play with his little toy, because I refuse to be one.*

The alarm goes off and I drag myself up to get dressed before making my bed. Even though I'm ready well before everyone else, I wait for the others in the dorm before I go outside. Jeff has become almost attached at the hip. He knows something is wrong, despite my facade, but he doesn't bother asking me why and gives me space when I ask. His calming presence makes it just a little bit easier, but he's becoming increasingly concerned about me. Last night he asked me if it was something like *that summer* at camp. I quickly insisted it was nothing like that, but I'm not sure if he believes me anymore. As much as it hurts to think about, I need to find a way to spend more time away from him.

We go through our workout doing the routine we've done for the last few days. Instead of running with Aerick, I now run with Jeff. Our PT doesn't seem to be as much of a chore anymore. My body is now accustomed to the exercise, but I've been trying to push myself even harder, letting the pain push away any other emotions that try to break through. Somewhere in my mind, I also know that it keeps Aerick from being able to say something while we work out.

Before I even realize, our workout is over. I go back inside and lie on my bed to listen to my music. I've caught up on all my school work and managed to get some of this week's assignments done already. Anything to keep my mind busy and off him. 'Buried Beneath' comes on my music player and my eyes fixate on the ceiling as I clear my head before my mind can roam any further.

Jeff nudges me to tell me it is breakfast time and we set off for the mess hall. "Is she okay today?" I hear Patrick ask Jeff quietly as we walk. Jeff just shakes his head 'no'. It's apparent now that Patrick has noticed too. Not that I'm completely surprised or anything. I've reverted to being more jumpy when people touch me, even when it's them. The only thing to be thankful for is that I'm not always reacting with violence.

As I sit down between them and pick at my food, Aerick is nowhere in sight. It's a good thing because I don't want to see him anyway. *Damn hypocrite.* He was gone from dinner last night, too! All that crap talking about how eating is so important and then he skips multiple meals.

My stomach already feels heavy, making the food in front of me even more unappealing, so I sit there pushing my food around on my plate until Jeff mutters to me. "You need to eat or I'm taking you to Luther." My anger appears in a heartbeat; I can't believe he would even consider that. "You haven't been eating enough. I know you don't want to explain, but you have to eat."

My frustration dies away and I let out a heavy sigh, partly because he's right. I give in, eating my eggs and potatoes. When I finish the small plate I've gotten myself, he gives me a half smile. *So glad I have his approval,* I think sarcastically. At least it will quell him for now.

It is my day to clean up after breakfast and I'm glad when Jeff stays to wait for me to finish without me having to ask. It's the best way to not have to walk back alone, but today, even that isn't enough to protect me. As we are leaving the mess hall, Aerick stops us.

"Nadalynn, I need to speak with you."

Jeff tenses beside me and my eyes look anywhere but at Aerick. "Well, I don't want to talk."

"You can't avoid me forever, you know." A tingling sensation runs down my spine and, not even looking at him, I know it's because he has that cold, intense stare focused right on me.

My fingers wrap around Jeff's wrist, trying to ground myself, before looking up at Aerick. Letting my composure break, I allow all my irritation and anger to show. "Watch me!" I pull Jeff out the door and to his credit, he never flinches at the death grip I have on his wrist as we walk across the field.

"I fucking knew it!" Jeff suddenly burst out. "He did something to you, didn't he? I swear on my mother's good name I'm going to kill him."

My feet pull to a stop, making Jeff turn to look at me. "Jeff, it isn't what you think."

He looks across the field from where we just came. "Really? Then why don't you clarify what the hell that was, because it sure in hell didn't sound like an instructor requesting to talk to a cadet."

The words are stuck in my throat and I can only shake my head. His frustrations from the past few days break free and he continues, almost shouting at me.

"Nadi, I've always been around to protect you, and really, I don't mind, but I can't help you if you shut me out. I've been patient the last few days, but I see you slowly deteriorate back into that little shell of a girl that hides behind me and it kills me to see you like this. I care so fucking much about you and I feel utterly helpless because I don't know what to do. You need to tell me what the hell is going on, dammit!" He lowers his voice, letting out a sigh. "Please, please let me help you."

I'm pulled deep into his eyes and they are so full of anger, hurt, and sadness. This is not what I want. He is my best friend and now my misery is his. *Fuck!* I put my hand on his cheek and look into his eyes.

"Jeff, I care for you deeply, you know that. You are my best friend and I'm so sorry this is hurting you, but there are some things you cannot protect me from. There are things I need to work out on my own. I can't explain this to you because honestly, I'm not quite sure how to, but I do know this is something I have to fight on my own. Please let me deal with this, okay?" I kiss him on the cheek and leave him standing there frozen as I walk into the dorm.

My heart is even heavier as I lie down, turning my music up to the highest level and putting in my earbuds to drown out my thoughts. Jeff walk in a few minutes later. He pauses at the end of my bed, staring at me for a moment, before he stalks off toward the bathroom.

Patrick jars me out of my blank state when it is time to go. Jeff walks next to me, but he seems upset still and doesn't talk to me. I'm not sure how, but I need to fix this between him and I, because as selfish as it sounds, I need him. He is the only thing keeping me tied down.

When we get into class, both Paulo and Aerick are standing at the mats. Paulo proceeds to tell us that today we are doing our defensive test, in which we will each be fighting the instructor. He tells us all to work on our weight training and we will be pulled out individually. *Great*. Well, Aerick was right about one thing: I can't avoid him forever.

I follow the others over to the weights and start my arm exercises. Paulo and Aerick split up, each one going to a set of mats in the gym. I'm grateful when Aerick pulls Mike and then Huck first. I'm hoping by some miracle that he will just skip over me, or that Paulo will call on me instead.

"Nadalynn, you're up." His voice echoes around me. Of course I couldn't be that lucky. On a positive note, he sounds like the Instructor Aerick. Maybe he will just keep this professional. I slip my gloves on and step on the mats. Something like concern crosses his face for a moment but he quickly recovers. "Ready?" he asks and I nod.

"Let's just get this over with." Rolling my shoulders, I put my hands up, trying to focus on all the different defensive moves we have learned. We circle for a moment and I attempt the first punch to his face. We are supposed to be protecting ourselves, not the other way around, and he seems a little surprised at my swing, but easily moves out of the way.

"I really need to talk to you." *So much for keeping it professional.*

The closest people to us are Paulo and Patrick, but they're far enough away not to hear us. "Well, I don't want to talk." I try to hit his side and he spins out of the way, glaring at me as he lightly taps his glove against my unprotected shoulder.

"Nadalynn, I need to know what hell I did wrong."

A small laugh escapes my mouth. "I'm really surprised you haven't figured it out. Maybe you're not as smart as I thought." He makes a lame attempt to hit my arm, but I move quickly, mimicking his move from a few moments ago. He smacks his hands together in frustration as he gets back into position. I'm not sure if it is from our conversation or the fact that he missed.

"Then maybe I'm a fucking idiot, because I am completely at a loss here." He lets down his guard just a little. I capitalize, hitting him in his ribs, not holding back; I hear him grunt as his lips press together.

"I'm serious, I don't know. Did I hurt you Sunday?" he asks as his eyebrows pull together. *How can he not know?*

He is not protecting himself again and I take the opportunity to kick him in his ribs. It feels so good so release some of this tension and I'm feeling braver.

"Yes, you did." My face hardens, as his turns to concern and sadness. My fist shoots out again, but he grabs my arm. Spinning me, he wraps it around me, pinning my arm to my chest with his, and pulling my back against his chest.

"Dammit, and you couldn't talk to me about it?" he hisses in my ear. "I told you to tell me if it was too much for you. You seemed fine when I left you back there." *Seriously!* That is what he thinks I am talking about. Maybe he really thinks *I'm* the idiot!

My anger hits a boiling point. I turn my hip slightly, grabbing his arms with my free hand so he can't let go. I quickly kick my feet in the air, then swing them back down hard, catching him off guard and throwing him over my hip. He goes down, hitting the mat with a loud thud. "That's not what I was talking about!" I snap at him. He lies there stunned, staring into my irate eyes.

"Nice job Nadi, about time someone put him on his ass," Paulo chuckles and I turn to see him still standing on his mat looking at us.

Aerick jumps up quickly, putting on a good show and trying to act like nothing just happened. He looks at me pissed and confused for a minute, then clears his emotions. "Good job cadet. You can go back." His cold tone indicates I've just hurt his pride. *Serves him right!*

* * * *

Aerick hasn't said another word to me, even during our hike this afternoon. I stuck to the middle of the group knowing he would be out front leading the group, but that didn't keep him from looking back at me with this odd expression that I can't figure out. He has to realize at some point that I saw his little rendezvous with his plaything.

We finish up evening PT but my body is still tingling with pent up anger. Aerick goes inside the dorm and I decide to go to the gym to use the punching bags. Aerick and Paulo usually go right after dinner so it's unlikely he will show up in there. I let Jeff know I'm going to the gym and he nods before heading off without me. He's still giving me the cold shoulder, making things that much worse.

Inside the gym, the gloves are on and within a minute I'm

taking out my day on the punching bag. Today has been so frustrating and I'm not sure what to make of Aerick's reaction to what I said. My body starts to get into a rhythm as my earphones blare 'Trenches' by Pop Evil. The song ends just as the door opens; Aerick walks in with Paulo on his heels.

Shit. Why are they in here so late? Aerick's expression changes to shock as his eyes land on me, which is unusual. Typically, he always knows where I am; or I was fairly certain he did.

For a moment I'm not sure if I should stay. As far as I know, he still doesn't want anyone to know and it isn't like he is going to say anything in front of Paulo, so I continue. He comes over to the bag next to me and starts hitting it. He hasn't put gloves on and my mind is screaming at me to leave. Pulling out my earbuds and removing my gloves, I walk past him, heeding my internal warnings.

"Running again?" he asks me in a low voice as he hits the bag harder.

The words are out of my mouth before I can stop them. "I'm not running."

"Really? Because that is what it seems like to me. You can't deal with something, and you run. You know, there is seriously something wrong with you."

How dare he! All my anger, irritation and sadness return with vengeance as I turn toward him. "Screw you! I'm not the asshole."

He huffs as he squares his shoulders to me. "Oh, is that what I am? How is that? Because you have made up some stupid shit in your head convincing yourself I did something I didn't?"

So now he's calling me delusional? "I didn't imagine what I saw Aerick. It was plain as fucking day, you prick," I say, trying to keep my voice down because Paulo isn't far away.

He closes the small distance between us. "And what the hell did you think you saw? Because I'm pretty sure I left you satisfied coming down off your orgasm... and the next time I saw you, you were pissed!" He doesn't raise his voice but his face is full of anger.

Apparently, I have to spell it out. "Well I am pretty sure I didn't imagine Liz all up on your shit. Maybe you should make sure she follows your rules next time."

His eyebrows pull together and the anger drains from his face. "You saw that?"

That's right, asshole! "Yes I did, and I'm not a fucking toy for you to play with when you get bored with your little hoe. So you can leave me the hell alone and run to her with your sexual frustrations."

My feet turn to leave but he grips my wrist pulling me back so that I am inches from his chest. "Nadalynn, wait. You don't understand."

It hurts so much looking into his eyes. Not the normal ache of anxiety that blooms from the closeness of others, but another painful ache. "I understand just fine. You want to fuck her, that's just fine. You're a grown-ass man, but you're not dragging me along for the ride." Tears are threatening to spill and he looks confused.

"Babe please, let..." I slap him with all my strength across the face, not letting him finish.

"Don't! Just, don't! We're done here." Pulling my wrist out of his shocked grasp, I turn and walk out the door.

"I fucking knew it," Paulo bellows behind me, but I can't listen to anything else.

I sprint back to the dorm. Grabbing some clothes quickly, ignoring the curious looks from the others, I hurry to the shower. Adrenaline keeps my tears at bay until I'm under the water and then I can no longer stop them. I promised myself I wouldn't cry over this anymore, but hearing him confess to being there – even though I already knew it – is like a punch in the gut. *This is so unfair!*

I'd finally found someone I could have a real, physical relationship with, and he turns out to be a bastard that can't keep it in his pants. My silent cries roll down my cheeks until there's nothing left. The cold water finally forces me to wash up and get out. With a few calming breaths, I dress and go in to face the boys.

Jeff looks worried and it only intensifies when he sees my face. Slowly, I sit and face him. He is my best friend and deserves the truth, but in this moment I'm too raw; I need some time.

"Hey, I'm sorry for earlier, and you're right. You are my closest friend, my best friend, and you deserve to know. You've seen me through some of the worst times in my life and you will always have a special place in my heart. Please just give me a few days and I will explain it all to you. I promise."

He smiles and moves next to me, patting me on the leg. "I can do that that."

The lights go out. Jeff kisses me on my temple as he gives me a side hug. "Goodnight," he says sweetly and goes to get in his own bed. I grab my earbuds and turn on the music. I'm so tired and exhausted, sleep takes me as I listen to the first song that comes on – of course the song relates ever so well to my situation.

"I never thought I'd feel this, guilty and broken down inside..."

CHAPTER TWO

I HAVE MIXED feelings on whether I should pretend to be sick or something to get out of this trip. Luther informed us last night at evening PT that today, we will be leaving on our hike to the Lookout Tower. He explained it's a half-day hike to get up there, in which we would be leaving after lunch today and hiking back down in the morning.

They sure don't give us much notice when we venture out. I suppose that keeps us from planning our escape or something. My schedule only lists my educational classes today, which is fine by me. A small break from our routine. Better yet, a break from a certain person. Aerick has backed off a little since Wednesday and stop trying to talk to me all the time, but I still catch him looking over at me a lot, deep in thought.

Unfortunately, I have been suffering from a serious lack of

sleep, especially after Wednesday night. I fell asleep fast Wednesday, but I awoke several hours later when I felt Aerick's fingers moving my hair out of my face and him running his fingers along my jaw. It startled me, but I held still, not letting him know he woke me. After a minute, his lingering fingers left my face and his footsteps moved to the end of my bed, but no further. I chanced peeking up and he was sitting on my clothing chest at the end of my bed with his head in his hands. He just sat there for almost two hours before he got up and left, giving me one last look. I assume he finally realized I'd figured out his game and gave up, because he hasn't been in our dorm since – at least when I'm in there.

Bringing a little more closure to the situation, I let another part of him go yesterday morning after PT. I was getting out a clean shirt when I found his sweater that was still in my clothing chest. There really isn't any reason to keep it now that we aren't together, so I decided to return it. He and Brand had walked toward Luther's office when I came inside, and I made the decision it would be better to do it while he wasn't around. Walking into the instructors' dorm, I hesitated. Paulo was there, and after a second of debating, I pushed down my anxiety and pushed myself to just do it.

Paulo pretty much knew already, and I was just returning something; no big deal. I quietly explained and set his sweater on the bed. My mind immediately flashed back to the times Aerick and I had spent just sitting on that bed. Watching him relaxed and sprawled out next to me. It's where he got me to confess my darkest secret, then he held me, comforting me as my feelings flooded to the surface.

I'd begun to think after the bonfire that he actually felt bad for hurting me when he got me to tell him those things. Now I'm not so sure that's entirely true; maybe he just said that to get closer to me. *It's easier to take advantage of some who is broken.* As I was leaving, Paulo had tried to say something, but when I gave him a dirty look and shook my head, he dropped it.

Jeff, Patrick and I head to our Health class and I'm mostly on autopilot. I've made a big effort to be polite to Tia, although it's probably not going to keep me out of the bottom this week since I walked out on my counseling session. Still, it's not fair to be taking out my anger on Tia. She's actually the one that has remained nice to me despite my bitchy and withdrawn attitude.

Jeff nudges me when we get to class and smiles, trying to cheer me up. He's been giving me the few days I've requested and deserves an award for his patience with me. I allow my lips to turn up slightly, grateful that he is there for me. I've played it out over and over in my head how I'm going to tell him, but I'm still stumped. Divulging my private life isn't my strong suit and, even with him, this is going to be difficult – partly because I'm embarrassed about what happened, but I know he will not be patient forever.

Before I know it, we begin our second class and discuss the lookout that we are hiking to. Tia cleverly ties it into the progression of technology. Apparently, back in the old days, there were large towers in the mountains. Men would live in these towers, watching for fires, so they could alert people when there was danger. The one we are hiking to is one of those that is still standing and has been restored. *Sounds like an awfully lonely life to me.*

Normally, this is the kind of stuff I would love to learn about and would dive into further, finding out as much as possible, but not now. All my drive to do or learn anything is completely absent. As we finish up the class, Tia lets us know we have thirty minutes to get ready and be back out to the stage, telling us that we're only to bring a change of clothes, pajamas, and a jacket; everything else will be provided.

As we exit the classroom, there is a flurry of activity going on. It seems like everyone is working on our prep for the hike. There are black hiking backpacks that are lined up in front of stage, but there are more packs than there are cadets. I'm curious to know how much of the staff is actually going with us, given how many bags are sitting there.

Jeff pulls my arm because I have slowed to a crawl, and I pick it up. Inside, everyone is moving around busily getting their stuff. "Wonder if we all share the same tents?" Mike says. *Lord, I hope not!* The last thing I want to do is sleep close to him. In fact, I'm not sure how I would do in such a confined space with all of them.

"Ha! I wonder if they will let us bunk with one of the girls," Huck speaks up.

I force out a laugh to cover my disgust, "And who would you want to be sharing one with?"

He smiles at me. "Wouldn't you like to know?" I roll my eyes at him and shake my head at his ridiculous thought – or so I hope it is ridiculous.

Crap. I forgot to ask Tia if I could bring my iPod. I silently weigh my options of having to go into the instructors' dorm and risk having to ask Aerick or decide not to take it. I'm about to spend the next twenty-four hours in close proximity to everyone, including Aerick, with little chance to get away. *I'm going to need it.* I chance it, hoping Brand is in there. It's a pain in the ass having to ask permission to do anything around here.

Of course, my luck is non-existent. Paulo and Aerick are both in there, but Aerick's back is turned to me as he leans over his desk, tapping away at his tablet. I've had a bit of a hard time looking Paulo in the face after he heard Aerick's and my conversation. I only did it the other day because for my sake I needed to shut down that conversation before it started; but I am not going to ask Aerick, so I turn toward Paulo.

"Uh, Paulo, is it alright to bring my iPod?" Out of the corner of my eye, I see Aerick spin around at the sound of my voice. Paulo looks at me, then at Aerick, who nods at him, before looking at me. He gives me a dejected smile and then turns back around. *Damn, why does he have to look so miserable?*

"Sure, that's fine." Paulo gives me a strange look and I'm suddenly very uncomfortable.

"Thanks," I say retreating as quick as possible.

Okay, that wasn't so bad. Maybe things will start getting a little easier. I grab all my stuff and go out to the stage. Brayden starts handing out the backpacks and gives us a marker to write our names on the tape that has been placed across the top. Once everyone is outside and has a backpack, Luther comes out to the stage.

"Alright, cadets. This hike will last for the rest of this day and the first half of tomorrow. Your instructors will be escorting you up to The Lookout. This is a traditional hike and you will be stopping to see several things on the way up. There is an awesome waterfall and the Old Oak that is still standing, things like that. You will stay the night at the Lookout Tower and then you will be taking the shorter trail back down. As always, do not stray away from the staff or your trackers will activate. Terrie and Jake are going to be joining you on this hike as support. I hope everyone enjoys your hike and I'll see you when you get back." He smiles at all of us, but his body language indicates he is nervous.

Aerick moves up onto the stage. "Everyone, go ahead and take a seat. Andi will be handing out your lunch; you have ten minutes to eat and to get your stuff put in your bag." Andi hands me a brown lunch bag with a sandwich, a protein bar and a water. This just may be the most unimpressive meal since we've arrived. "Everyone has been given a backpack that you can put your personal stuff in, but it also contains supplies that we need. Everyone will pull their own weight on this hike and I won't tolerate any complaining. Some of these trails can get a little dangerous, so listen and pay attention to where you're going. Things will not go well for you if I have to report back bad news to Luther." Aerick has a completely straight face but Paulo ruins the seriousness when he tries to hide his smile. "Keep close to us and we should get along just fine. You've got nine minutes and then on your feet."

There are a few groans of irritation from those around me, but most seem happy about this little get away. *Not me.* I stay quiet and do as we're asked.

✻ ✻ ✻ ✻

A little over eight hours later, we finally make it. My feet feel like one giant blister and I'm so grateful we are finally here. We stop as Brand starts talking about the tall wood lookout tower in front of us and its history in the area. The tower looks a little rickety and the chipped, water-logged beams show its age. My eyes follow the stairs up to the top; it's a long way up. I crane my neck all the way back just to look at the top.

When he finishes his speech we all drop our packs, following Aerick, Paulo and Trent as they take us up to the top. I laugh a little seeing that Brand isn't coming with us. With his fear of heights, he must really loath this trip. On the hike up there were tons of cliffs we walked next to. Then we had to cross a bridge that was just a thick wire to walk on and two more thick wires on either side to hold on to. The drop below was probably thirty or forty feet. Brand tried his best not to show his fear, but his face was white as a ghost.

It's torture trying to climb all these steps after we've just hiked for eight hours, but as we get to the top, it is completely breathtaking. There is a platform walkway with two rails running around the entire building. Inside is a small room with glass windows going all the way around. It is sparsely decorated with a bed, desk, old instruments, and other oddball stuff. I go out to the walkway and the sun is just starting to set. Looking down, it's clear why Brand stayed down below. He may have a heart attack being up this far. From up here, there is a view of the whole ridge and the valley below. It's a magnificent sight, seeing it lit up by the dying sun.

"It's really beautiful up here this time of day," Aerick says, coming up next to me and looking out at the valley. I nod my head, not sure what to say. We stand there in silence for a minute, just taking in the sinking sun. He glances at me and then turns around, walking back to the group that is still investigating the room inside.

After everyone has happily investigated everything up top, our group heads back down, where Brand has pulled out all of the tents and is setting them in two tight rows. He explains that there will be two people per tent, and how we need to set them up. They are pop-up tents and we set them up together with the staff tents, placing theirs in a large box around us. They do not let us sleep co-ed, much to Huck's dismay. Aerick and Terrie are the only ones that get their own tents. Aerick because he is in charge and Terrie because she is the only woman staff member.

It seems Terrie was required to come in case we get hurt, which turned out to be a good thing for me. There was one close call on our way up and the thought of what almost happened sends a shiver down my spine. Huck, Mike, Jeff and I were hiking right behind Aerick as we walked up the narrow path with a steep ridge to one side. I really hadn't been paying attention to the guys. I was busy listening to my music, focusing too hard on the next step in front of me; mostly to keep myself from staring at the man only a few feet in front of me.

Apparently, Mike had shoved Jeff, who stumbled against me. Not expecting it, I fell sideways toward the ridge. My hands flew out trying to stop myself from falling and I was able to grab a branch of the tree on the edge, but my pack was heavy and my feet were barely keeping their grip on the edge as I leaned out over it. Before I could scream that my feet were slipping, Aerick was grabbing me around my waist, and pulled me back to safety. The terror in his eyes was clear as day, but it quickly turned to relief.

He stared into my eyes just a moment longer than he really should have before he released me, and then he turned and ripped Mike a new one. *Poor Mike.* Aerick can be a little scary sometimes. It was probably lucky for Mike that I was fine, other than a deep cut on my hand that Terrie cleaned and wrapped. Really, I was the lucky one; if that tree hadn't been there, I would have fallen at least fifty feet down the ravine.

By the time we get all the tents set up and our sleeping bags inside, Aerick and Paulo have the fire built in the pit. Aerick tells us we get the rest of the evening to relax and Jake hands out bags of M&Ms to snack on. They are so delicious after eating the Meal-ready-to-eat pouch, or as they are better known, the MREs, that we stopped and ate for dinner on our way up.

I look up into the sky, half paying attention to the guys as they goof around, seeing if they can throw candy into each other's mouths. A smile tugs at my lips as they tease each other. *Boys!*

Conversations flow easily around until Leena suggests we play Twenty Questions. My mind instantly screams 'no,' but I'm not putting damper on our evening, and being the only one to say no will only bring more attention to me, so I stay quiet. Jokingly, Royce suggests we take off clothing if we don't want to answer, but Aerick puts a quick stop to that, looking at me when he says 'absolutely not'; so we just play.

Leena starts: "Mike what is the craziest thing you have ever done?"

"Stole a car." He shrugs, not even fazed, and continues. "Tara, are you a virgin?"

Wow, way to turn that one quickly. She looks at him, shocked. "Seriously?"

"Come on, it's just a question." The others encourage her answer as her face reddens.

She breaths deeply. "Fine, yes."

Mike's eyes get big, a smirk playing across his lips. "Wow,

really?"

Tara shakes her head. "Yes, not that it's any of your business. Patrick, do you have a girl back home?"

His face is suddenly flush. "Yes."

His answer moves my discomfort for this game to the background of my mind as I sit up a little straighter, looking to him. I didn't know that. I wonder who it is, but then his eyes snap up to mine.

Shit. "Nadi." My stomach drops and I look down at my hands. "Out of pure curiosity, who was the first guy you kissed."

Crap. Definitely not something I want to admit in this group. My eyes glance up quickly to Jeff and then back at my hands before I realize what I'm doing.

"I knew it. I freaking knew it! Jeff, I told you I would find out eventually."

I look over at Jeff, a little confused. "You never told him?"

He looks at me annoyed. "No, although he has tried for years to get me to say it. He only had his suspicions. You let that one out of the bag." He looks at Patrick, pissed. "For the record, it was at camp when we were thirteen, out on the docks, not before, not anywhere else. I kissed her, she kissed me back, and nothing else happened. So drop it, now!" Patrick puts up his hands in defense and Royce laughs. Makes me curious to know what exactly was discussed about me between them in the past. There is an awful lot of when, what, and where that could have come up, but more than that, I don't like not knowing what those conversations were.

My face must be as red as a tomato right now. Out of the corner of my eye I see Aerick get up, walking toward the lookout tower and lean against it so I can no longer see his face in the spreading darkness, just his outline.

"Um, yeah okay." I try to change the direction of our conversation. "Brand, what were you in here for?"

He looks at me incredulous, "I'm not playing this game!" A few others chime in with 'come on' but he refuses.

"Fine, Huck, is there someone here that you like?" It seems like he does and I really want the attention off my admission.

"Yep," he says, rapidly throwing out another question to someone else.

We keep going for a little while longer. Thankfully everyone leaves me alone after they discover there are a few crushes amongst our group. Everyone trying to get names out of each other provides the perfect distraction. After a while, we end up back to just having random conversations and it isn't long before people start heading off to bed after such a long day.

Most people have gone to bed, including Jeff and Patrick, when Paulo waves me over to the edge of the fire. I wanted to go to bed when they did but I'm wide awake.

"What's up?" I ask him warily.

"Can I show you something? I promise it isn't anything bad." I laugh a little to hide my discomfort and shrug.

"Okay." He turns and we go over to the tower and start climbing the stairs. As we go up I am a little nervous, and curious at the same time, but then again, I really don't think Paulo would do anything bad. We get to the top and he turns around.

"Please don't be mad, okay?"

I look at him confused as he steps aside, letting me pass, and I see Aerick standing out on the walkway looking up at the sky. I immediately turn on my heels, trying to walk past Paulo down the steps, but he puts up his hand. I stop, but only because I can't get past without touching him.

"Just give him five minutes. Please."

I look to Aerick and then back to him again. Reigning in my anger, I let out a heavy sigh. "Fine, five minutes." Paulo smiles and starts going back down. I hesitate a moment, trying to work out if I should just quietly follow Paulo back down, but I don't. With the old creaky wood steps in the quiet night, it isn't likely I would go unnoticed anyway. Instead, against my better judgment, I turn and go out to the walk way.

"Hey," he says nervously. *Since when does he get nervous?* "Can we sit and talk for a few minutes?"

I roll my eyes because I 'm already here and it isn't like I can just leave. "Apparently I have already agreed to that," I mumble, mostly to myself.

His hand reaches out to grab my wrist, but I pull it back. He looks down, his lips pressing in a thin line, and motions to the floor. I sit down mostly because this talk was inevitable unless we want to spend the rest of our time here irritated and avoiding each other. He sits next to me, leaving a little space between us. It's irritating that my body just wants to scoot over next to him despite how I feel about him right now.

I let my head tilt up at the stars to distract myself; it's so beautiful out here. I've never seen so many stars in my life, and being up here where it's so dark and high up off the ground, it is almost like I'm floating in the sky. If it wasn't for the extremely uncomfortable discussion I'm guessing we are about to have, this would be incredible.

"I'm not really sure where to start," he says finally, after sitting in awkward silence for a few minutes.

"Aerick, you don't need to justify your actions to me. I saw it and that's all there is; end of story." My voice is quiet and small as I play with a string on my shirt.

"But it isn't." He pauses as he seems to be collecting his thoughts. "The thing is, I haven't had many normal relationships. In fact, I have only had one other relationship that was purely exclusive, and just so you know, my relationship with her did not end because I cheated on her. All my other relationships were with women who knew it was an open relationship. They all knew I'm not good with emotional attachment. As you now know, one of those open relationships was with Liz, although that was mostly out of convenience."

My blood is beginning to warm with irritation. "Aerick, I really don't want to listen to this shit. What you do with your life is your business." I take a deep breath, hoping he just stops.

"Wait, please hear me out. What you saw the other day – you

only saw part of the conversation. I honestly didn't know what you were so upset about at first. Then when you told me, I went back and looked. The cameras were still on since they are only off when Liz is actually in session." He hands me his tablet and it shows both classrooms on two different cameras. I look at him, not sure what he wants. "Watch it, please."

He reaches over and clicks the play button, not giving me a chance to say no. Giving in, my frustrated eyes watch. I see myself enter on one half of the screen in one room, and Aerick is on the other half in the room next door, walking over to lean on the desk. My eyes are glued to the screen and it isn't any better watching it instead of only hearing it:

Aerick is picking at his nails as I watch Liz walk up to him. I see it all over again and my anger starts to boil the more I watch.

"Dammit, Liz, I told you I don't do this shit at work." His voice rings out and I see myself rush out of the room on one side of the screen.

"What is the matter, Aerick? You don't want me anymore? Because that would be a first?" she says sarcastically.

"Actually, I don't. I'm in a relationship with someone and I plan on being with just her."

She laughs, still not moving back from him. "Since when do you do monogamous relationships?" She drags her finger down his chest and Aerick looks a little irritated.

"Since I met her," he snaps and gets up, causing her to move back as he goes and stands against the wall.

"Wow. You're serious?" *What a stupid bitch.*

"Yes Liz, I'm serious. This little thing that we had, it's done. Got it?" He says firmly, looking her in the eyes, and she has the decency to look embarrassed.

"Um, okay. If that's what you want, then so be it. So are we still friends, or are you not interested in that either?" she asks quietly, biting her lip.

"Yes, I want to be friends, but this girl is, I don't know – different. I want to try to give our relationship a chance and I don't want my past fucking it up."

She gives a fake laugh, "Okay, strictly friends, I get it. Do I get to know who it is?" She seems a little hurt for someone that was just an occasional fling.

He gets a worried look on his face. "Not right now; maybe later, alright? I got to go, I'll talk to you later." He pushes off the wall and leaves the room.

Damn. He did tell her, and I didn't stay around to find out. I kind of feel like an ass now, but not completely. He really shouldn't have let her get up on him like that before he said something.

"When I realized you only saw the first part of that conversation, I figured out why you were so upset. I wanted to explain but it took me the last few days to figure out if I should. I told you that this would probably end up with you being hurt and that is not what I wanted. It's like a punch in the gut knowing I hurt you and I 've been thinking if maybe it would be better for you, if I just let you go, so you can have a relationship with a normal person. When I came back to my room yesterday and my sweater was sitting there, I knew you had given up on me. I thought I had resolved it in my head to let you be, but then today turned everything upside down." He stops to take a deep breath and he looks back at the sky.

"First you almost fell over that ledge and I thought I was going to have a heart attack. I don't think I've ever been so scared in my life. It took all the restraint I could muster to not kill your little friend." He takes another deep breath. "Then we were sitting around and you guys were playing your game. When you admitted Jeff was your first kiss it pissed me off because I don't want to think about anyone else kissing you. The only person's lips that should touch yours are mine."

He looks down into my eyes. His face is lit just enough by the moonlight to see the softness and need in his eyes. It is a look I have only seen a few times and only when we're alone. "Nadalynn, I want you back – I need you back. I need to know you're mine." He looks down and slides something into my hands.

"What's this?" I turn the box over a few times confused.

He gets a small smile on his face. "A peace offering. Even if you deny me, you should have it anyway. I bought it for you."

My nerves surface in my hands, causing the box to rattle slightly. *When did he by this for me? Why would he buy me anything?* The deep-blue velvet covering the box feels so soft in my fingers.

"Open it," he requests in a whisper as he pulls at his lip. He must be nervous, too. I open it and my eyes grow wide and my mouth drops open.

Wow. The white gold pendant necklace shines in the moonlight. Two dolphins chase each other in a circle around a beautiful black stone with blue floating in it. Inside the cover, in fancy writing, it says, '24k White Gold and Genuine Rare Black Opal'. My words catch in my throat; this is one of the ones I had run my hand over at the fair. It was so pretty but I was completely put off by the five-hundred-dollar price tag, knowing I could never afford something like that. *How did I not see him buy this?* This is way too much; I can't keep this.

"Aerick, this was really expensive. I can't accept this."

"Don't worry about the money. I know you like it. You had that far off look in your eyes while you stared at it. You love dolphins and you love blue. I don't see how anything could better suit you."

I look up at him, impressed again at how observant he has been. He looks so young and caring, a rare sight for him. "Please, even if you don't want to be with me, take this – it's yours." He gives me a sad smile and then looks back down.

I reach up and pull his face back up so I can look in his eyes. All my anger, irritation, and sadness from the last few days has dissolved completely away. I look deeply in his eyes, hoping he can sense everything I feel as my heart is being pulled to him. "Thank you." I pull him down and kiss him gently on the lips.

He seems a bit surprised at first, but doesn't resist, and after a moment his lips turn more desperate like he is afraid he might never touch mine again. All the longing and need instantly reappears as he pulls me to him.

He breaks our kiss in need of air and puts his forehead to mine. "Nadalynn, I'm sorry, please forgive me. Please, be with me." His words hit hard and there is no more denying him. My lips find his again.

"Okay," I mumble through my swollen lips and he deepens our kiss. I want him, I need him. His worry has been replaced with lust as he holds my face to him. He pushes me back, gently lowering my body to the floor as he positions himself next to me. I feel cold hands slide under my shirt. The feeling of his hands on me again is amazing, sending shivers all over my body.

He pushes my sports bra up, releasing my breasts, and his hand gently begin to massage each of them. His lips leave my mouth and he kisses me down my neck as he twist and pulls at my nipple. It resonates down between my legs and as I let out a moan, I feel his smile on my neck.

He pushes my shirt up, exposing me to the chill of the night, which is replaced by his warm mouth. I pull his hair, trying not to moan again. He hums, still sucking on my nipple, causing me to squirm under him. His hand roams across my stomach, making his intentions clear. Moving his hand down further he unbuttons my pants with ease and slides his hand into my pants, stopping once he reaches my underwear.

I ache for him to touch me there. He brings his mouth back to mine. "Can I?" he begs me. Words elude me at the intense feeling I'm lost in, so I crush my lips to his, answering wordlessly.

He slides his fingers into my folds and pushes one finger inside me as I gasp at the amazing feeling. A foreign tug starts to build almost immediately as I feel him harden against my leg and he slides in another finger. The pleasure is incredible.

"Always so wet for me." He bites at my neck. "Did you miss me?"

"Hmm," is all I can manage.

"I think I owe you something." I have no idea what he is talking about, but I'll take it as long as he doesn't stop. He pulls his fingers out of me suddenly and he moves his head down as he slowly begins kissing down my stomach. He looks at me with a sly smile as he begins to pull my pants off, kissing down my legs as he peels my pants down and deftly removes my boots. When he has them off he runs his fingers up and down my thigh slowly. Staring in my eyes, he put his hands on the top of my panties, silently asking for my permission. I nod ever so slightly and he doesn't hesitate, quickly and expertly removing them. His breath quickens as he looks at my newly uncovered skin and he sucks in his bottom lip, biting it.

He moves back up so he is over me, but he still has all his clothes on. He leans down to kiss me and I hold the back of his neck as he pushes his very swollen self against me, only the fabric of his pants separating us. I push myself up to relieve my insane

36

ache. His lips bite my earlobe as he moans in my ear and then whispers to me, "I always keep my promises." He begins kissing down my jaw, then down my neck. I try to remember what promise he is talking about, but as his mouth moves down to my breast again, I lose all concentration.

When he continues down, sucking and kissing, across my stomach, realization hits me. What he said as he left me behind the mess hall. I feel the hard ball on his tongue as he sucks on my stomach. *He's going to do this right now?* He pauses, looking up at me, biting his barbell with a devious smile, and I almost lose it before he has even done anything. He moves down, kissing my thighs and when he reaches the apex, I moan louder than I mean to. He looks at me with a very satisfying look.

"You are going to have to quiet down or I'll have to stop." He continues and I can no longer watch. I look up into the sky, lost in the intensity. I breathe in sharply as I feel his tongue on me for the first time. My back arches and his arm wraps around my leg and his hand spreads across my stomach, holding me down. I'm having a hard time trying to stay quiet as he wraps his other arm around my other thigh, pulling my legs further apart. His tongue moves magically, up and down along my most sensitive part, over and over, teasing my entrance and my nub until it is unbearable.

"Aerick I am going to..." This is even more intense than our last encounter; it's almost too much.

"I'm counting on it." His voice is so low and rough.

"Nadalynn, it's okay babe, let go." His tongue enters me and he hums, sending vibrations through my whole body – I can't stop it. My orgasm rips through me like it's going to tear me in half. I have to cover my mouth with both hands to stay quiet. He continues relentlessly, sending aftershocks through my body as he holds me down, making me absorb them.

When I finally come back down from where ever I just went, my heavy eyes open. He's leaning over me, running his fingers along my face. "Hey, you," he says with a cheeky smile. I only smile back, still not sure how I could even describe the level of incredible I am feeling.

"That was absolutely incredible," he says, mirroring my thoughts as he bites his lip again and then kisses me. I expect him to stop but he doesn't. I can feel the desire and longing in his kiss.

It only takes a few minutes before I feel the ache again. *Geez, how can I still want more?* Feeling bold, my hands move to undo his belt and his body becomes tense. I quickly undo his button before he can stop me and slide my hand in his pants over his boxers. As I begin to massage him, he relaxes.

"Fuck!" he says as I feel a shiver go through his body. "Nadalynn I really want you right now, so if you don't want this..." He swallows thickly as I grab him harder. "If you don't want this, I need you to stop right now." There is no conviction behind his words; he doesn't want me to stop.

I continue without a second thought; he lets out a feral growl and I intensify the pressure. "Are you sure?" he asks, and I squeeze him tight in my hand again. "Ah fuck." He grabs my hand, pulling it out of his pants and pushes it above my head. My questioning eyebrows pull together.

He kisses my nose. "You are going to make this end before it even begins." He smiles and lets go of my hand, moving his hand down between my legs and begins to tease my already sensitive nub again. His slides his fingers into me again. "God, I love that you are so wet for me. I need to get you close. This is going to be much quicker then I prefer." He moves his lips to my neck as he begins to slide his finger in and out slowly, his thumb circling my most sensitive spot, building up the pull that is quickly becoming familiar.

My head is tilted back and my eyes are closed as he continues to push me higher, kissing, sucking and biting my neck, my jaw, my breast. He suddenly stops and I assume he can no longer help himself. He moves rather quickly doing something but I don't open my eyes. There is a distinct sound of a wrapper tearing and a second later he is leaning over me. My legs are pushed apart with his own, positioning himself at my entrance. Warmth suddenly engulfs my entire front as I realize he has removed all of his clothes. "Babe, look at me."

I comply, staring up into his bright eyes, feeling just a little nervous with what we are about to do. His eyes are deep, reaching far within me, and are so full of lust. "Are you sure you want this?" he asks me one last time.

I move his lips down to me. "Yes," I whisper, and kiss him

gently before he pulls back to look at me. A triumphant smile spreads across his lips and he pushes into me quickly and then stops as I close my eyes, gasping at the shocking feeling.

"Fuck! You're so tight." His voice is so low and rough, driving me crazy. With his size, it is painful, but at the same time there is a satisfying relief to the ache that was there. His forehead is on mine and he gives me a minute to get used to him – or maybe he is trying to control himself. His breaths have gone erratic.

He tugs back slightly to look at me. "You okay?" I swallow loudly and nod my head, focusing on his beautiful eyes. He starts moving slowly, watching me as he does. The feeling is so foreign, but it feels so incredibly good and I can't help lifting my hips to meet his as the pull inside me gets stronger and stronger. His speed picks up and I am so close. I don't know if I can handle another orgasm and I try to hold it in.

"Dammit Nadalynn, let go!" he growls as he slams into me hard, pushing me over the edge as another orgasm rips through me, even more relentless than the first one. His lips crush to mine to quiet my screams and he quickly follows, causing him to groan into my mouth as we ride out our orgasms together.

When my thoughts finally come down out of the clouds, he is still inside me, hovering over me, trying to catch his breath, resting his head on mine. "You really are the most amazing woman."

I smile and put my hand on his cheek. "You're pretty amazing yourself." He slowly pulls out of me, rolling onto his back, and we stare up at the stars for a few minutes until our breathing has evened out.

A breeze hits my naked lower half, sending a shiver through me. He props himself up on his arm, looking down at me with a smile. He grabs something next to him. "Move your legs apart." I looked at him, scrunching my eyebrows, but do as he asks. He sits up and in his hand is his tank top. He looks at me with a smile and gently wipes me up. I am so sensitive down there that it sends shivers up and down my body. "Fuck, Aerick."

He laughs a little. "That a girl." He leans down, giving me a quick chastising kiss. "Put your pants back on before I decide I can't wait to take you again." The thought makes me blush and I sit up to dress.

When I put my hand down, there is fabric under my hand. I look down and see that I had been lying on his sweater. *How did that happen?* I wonder, but in retrospect I'm grateful, as my backside would have been cold and uncomfortable against the rough wood walkway. I glace sideways, seeing him remove the condom, and even no longer hard he is still pretty impressive. I can't believe that was just in me. "See something you like?" he smirks when he sees me look at him.

I bite back my smile, embarrassed that I just got caught looking at his manhood. He grabs my chin, giving me another quick kiss before he grabs his pants, standing up and sliding them on quickly. I stand and do the same.

When we are fully clothed again – minus Aerick's tank top,

which he has tucked into his back pocket – he wraps his arms around me and I nuzzle into his bare chest. "Can we stay up here for a bit longer? The stars are so beautiful."

"Sure," he says with a chuckle as he takes my hand and turns back toward the wall where his sweater is. He grabs it and the box next to it. He puts his sweater on and embarrassment hits me again as I think that we just had sex on that sweater. He sits down with a smile; obviously he knows what's going on in my head.

"Come here." He pulls my arm down and I sit between his legs with my back to his chest. He opens the box he picked up and takes out the necklace. He opens the clasp and wraps it around the front of me and pushes me up a little so he can clasp it around my neck. His lips nip at my shoulder before pulling me back against him. "Keep it hidden under your tee shirt if you wear it. Cadets aren't supposed to have jewelry," he warns. The chain is thick and long, and the pendant falls just above my breast.

I pick it up and look at it closely. "It really is beautiful, thank you."

He kisses the top of my head. "It's fitting that you are wearing it, then." My heart swells. This man has no idea how incredibly sweet he can be when he wants to. I stare up at the stars with his arms wrapped around me.

After a bit I have to shift. Now that I have come down off my high, the dull ache between my legs is becoming more noticeable. "You feel okay?" He must know it is the reason for me moving.

"Yeah, I'm okay. Just a little... sore."

His mouth brushes my ear. "Not to be an ass but I am actually pretty happy about that." He chuckles. "It's normal the first few times to be a little sore. I guess I'll have to give you a few days before we do that again."

I want to laugh at his presumption, even if he is right. "And how exactly do you know that was my first time?"

He runs his fingers along my collarbone. "Well, I had a hunch before, and after when I cleaned you up, there was a little blood. Dead give-away," he laughs.

Oh my God! I cannot believe he just said that. I slap his leg, "Jerk. That is not funny!"

"Hey, don't be mad! I am incredibly honored and happy to be your first." He sits up just a little so he can kiss my shoulder. "I would love to give you a lot more firsts here in the close future." His sexy, low voice resonates right between my legs. I turn my head and grab his neck, pulling his lips to mine. As our kiss deepens, so does my need for him. I twist my body so I'm facing him and kiss down his jaw to his neck. "Fuck, babe, you gotta stop."

That is the last thing I want right now. "Why?" I almost whine, looking away irritably.

He pulls my chin back up so I can see his eyes. "For one, I need you to be able to walk back to camp tomorrow and it is already going to be pretty uncomfortable. Second, I don't have another condom. Believe it or not, I didn't plan for this to happen tonight."

I laugh, "Really? Then why did you have one at all?"

He smiles and stands up, pulling me with him. "Well, after you damn near jumped me the night of the bonfire, I've made it a point to carry one at all times."

I raise an eyebrow. "If I remember correctly, you were all too happy about that."

"That I was. Come on, we should head back down." He tucks my necklace in my shirt and wraps his arms around my waist, pulling tight against him. We stay that way for a few minutes before he reluctantly pulls away. He slides the box in my pocket before taking my hand and we start toward the stairs. "And princess, don't wear any tank tops for the next few days." *Huh?* I decide to drop it for now.

When we get to the bottom the only person that is still up is Paulo. Aerick turns to me before we get near the tents and fire. "You should probably go to bed." He gives me his signature smirk as we part; I move to go to my tent, giving him a shy smile.

He moves toward Paulo, who spots him when he nears the pit area. As I'm getting into my tent with Tara, Paulo's whisper breaks the silence. "You know that grin on your face is a dead giveaway." I bite my lip. *Shit – he knows what we just did.*

"Fuck off, man. You have no idea what you are talking about." Aerick keeps his voice low and I barely hear him.

"So how was it?" Typical males, can never keep their mouths shut.

"Seriously? We are not having this conversation right now." *Thank God.* I really don't think I could ever look Paulo in the face if Aerick did tell him. I relax into my sleeping bag, absolutely exhausted, and fall asleep listening to their whispers.

CHAPTER THREE

(Sunday July 12th)

I WAKE UP early to the crisp cool air and birds chirping. My body is still exhausted, but my body's internal clock has adjusted to waking at five in the morning. The time on my watch shows exactly five. Everyone must still be asleep, because there is no other noise, but my body is aching to stretch. I step outside my tent and the light is just over the horizon. I slip on my sweater to cover the goosebumps that have risen on my arms. Aerick is sitting on a log with his ear phones on next to the fire. He has a big grin on his face as he just stares into the roaring fire.

As I begin to walk I realize how sore and tired my lower half is. His eyes spot my movement and he immediately stands up as he removes his headphones. "Good morning."

"Morning," I smile back and go sit down on a log next to where he just was.

"You want some coffee?" he asks, and I nod. Coffee sounds awesome. He pours me a cup from the pot on the fire and hands me a tin mug. "Sorry, no milk or sugar." I shrug, indifferent to the idea of black coffee. He pours himself a cup as well and sits down next to me. "How do you feel this morning?"

"Honestly, tired and sore." His grin gets bigger and I roll my eyes. I mean that is sore too, but my legs also are sore from our long hike yesterday. "You know, Paulo was right. That grin is a dead giveaway," I laugh quietly.

"Well no one is up now," he whispers, leaning in to kiss my neck. "Besides, he has no room to talk. He wasn't waiting up for me last night. He was waiting for everyone to go to sleep so he could sneak into Terrie's tent."

I stare at him in shock. "What?"

He chuckles. "They've kind of had a thing for a while but they don't want the others to know. It's why I wasn't entirely opposed to him knowing about us. I keep my mouth shut about them and he will keep his shut about us. It may actually come in handy like it did last night." I look away, trying to hide my blush.

"Why would they care if someone knew?"

He shrugs. "Paulo is pretty private; well mostly, but they also would lose privileges. There is a reason Tia and Andi are not on this trip. Luther wants us to make sure we focus on you guys."

The distinctive sound of a zipper pulls my attention to a nearby tent. Paulo emerges from the tent that is supposed to be Terrie's. He looks at me like a deer caught in headlights. I try to hide my grin as he walks over to us. "Morning." He grabs out a cup and pours himself some coffee. "Did you get any sleep Aerick?"

"Yeah, I slept really good for a few hours, but you know me, my body is wired to be up by four-thirty every day." He tries to hold in his smile when he says the first part and my eyes immediately divert to the ground.

"You know, Nadi, if you don't want people to know, you really need to work on that blushing thing." His bluntness is shocking; no wonder he and Aerick get along. My cheeks heat a few shades redder.

"Paulo, don't be an ass," Aerick tells him, trying to hold in a smirk but failing miserably. "Hey, you mind if we go up in the tower for a few minutes before everyone starts to wake up?"

Paulo nods his head and Aerick stands, grabbing my hand. "Come on, the sunrise here is incredible. We'll be back in fifteen," he tells Paulo as he pulls me toward the tower.

"Too many stairs, too early," I whine, having a hard time making it back up.

"Come on, you can do it." We make it to the top and walk out to the outside. It's amazingly beautiful. There are a few clouds and the sun is throwing stunning shades of pink, blue, and purple on them. Aerick stands behind me, hands around my waist we look out over the valley.

The air here is so clean; I draw in a deep breath. "I love this. It's so beautiful and perfect."

"That it is."

"You know, I never got around to apologizing last night."

He huffs behind me. "For what exactly?"

Just say it... "Well, granted I was pretty pissed at you for letting Liz do what she did, which was not okay, even if you eventually pushed her away – but I should have given you a chance to explain. I don't let people in, but I let you in, and then I felt betrayed. My instincts were to block everyone out again. I'm sorry I overreacted."

He is quiet for a minute. "Forget it, Princess, let's just put it behind us." I nod. "Are you really okay about last night? I mean, I know it was kind of a big deal, being your first time." I roll my eyes at his shaky tone. Being self-conscious doesn't suit him.

"You're kidding right?" He stays quiet and I turn toward him. "Let's see, my first time was out under the stars with an unbelievably sexy, smart, sweet man, that nearly drove me insane with pleasure." I pause as he licks his lip. "I really don't see how it could have gotten any better."

He smiles at me. "Glad you think so highly of me." He kisses me gently and I wrap my hands around his neck so he cannot pull back. I want him.

He pulls me tighter against him and I deepen our kiss, but when I bite his lip he growls at me. "Stop that shit, it's like an instant wake up call to my dick." His bluntness knows no bounds.

"Good to know," I mummer on his lips.

"Babe, I am serious. Trust me, you're going to want a few days to recover. I'd much rather the next time be pleasurable for you, not painful."

I bite my lip and look at him with wanting eyes. "You mean I have to wait a few more days?" He sighs, adjusting his pants and I assume he is getting frustrated at his inability to control the growing bulge in his pants. I can't help being proud about that. He kisses me one more time before pulling back with a sigh.

"You are going to be the death of me."

"Well, hopefully not anytime soon."

He lips turn up slightly and he grabs my hand. "We better get back down there before everyone wakes up." Right before we begin our descent, he turns to me with his face very serious. "Next time I fuck up or do something to upset you, please talk to me – don't shut me out. I want to be honest with you and I want you to be honest with me. If there is something wrong, tell me." I'm an idiot. We could have resolved this a long time ago if I would have talked to him.

I smile up at him. "Yeah, okay." He gives me one last kiss and we head back down.

Paulo is still the only one awake. "That was quick." My neck heats up and Aerick punches him in the shoulder. "Dude, I was joking!"

Aerick shakes his head. "Yeah well, enough of the jokes." A quiet giggle escapes me. They're pretty funny but Aerick only seems irritated at my encouragement.

We sit down, drinking our coffee and Paulo and I talk about

his life before camp. He tells me about his life back in Samoa, describing the beautiful scenery on his home island and their way of life. Joseph had told me little about it too. Apparently, Samoans have some anger issues, because Paulo reveals to me that he was here back in the day for assault.

By seven, everyone has gotten up and we eat our MRE breakfast. Today's isn't as bad as last night's dinner and I actually really like the trail mix. We pack up everything and are ready to go by eight. As we get ready to leave, Aerick steps to the front of the group and speaks up.

"Alright, we will be taking a quicker trail to get back down to camp, but the trail can get very steep in places, so be extremely careful. I do not want a repeat of yesterday." He looks at the guys that were messing around yesterday. "And you," he looks toward me. "Keep one of your earbuds out of your head so you can hear what's going on."

Okay, Mister Bossy. He is definitely in 'instructor mode'. I nod and Jeff shoves at my shoulder lightly with a smirk. Aerick's face darkens slightly before he hurries and turns around. "Let's go!" he shouts over his shoulder.

When Aerick said steep, he wasn't downplaying it. At one point, the path is only a few feet across, with drop-offs on both sides. My legs are killing me and the soreness between them isn't helping my cause. I have to hold on to the trees that line the path and to Jeff to keep my footing. When Aerick looks back he seems irritated that I'm holding on to Jeff, but honestly, he needs to get over it. I'd much rather hold him, but that is not a possibility, and Jeff is my friend. He needs to get used to that; I'm not giving up my friends over jealousy.

Jeff is acting a little strange during our hike back. He keeps a smile on his face, but something is bothering him. There's no way he knows about Aerick and I. We were really careful to make sure no one would know. All morning we sat apart and he has been good at keeping the smile off his face. I'm starting to wonder if Jeff is getting impatient with the explanation I owe him. I still don't know how to explain it, and I'm not sure if I should now that Aerick and I have worked things out.

Finally, the bridge that goes over the river into the main camp comes into view. My entire body is spent. Aerick informs us that we need to go sit by the stage. Luther comes out and does his normal Sunday morning routine. Unfortunately, my day is ruined when the list shows me in the bottom three.

This really sucks. I am so frustrated with myself. That is it, no more getting in the bottom, no matter how much people piss me off. The only bright side is that we only have two meals today. Luther tells us to report to Brayden right after our lunch clean up.

More than anything, I really just want to take a shower and lie down. The lack of sleep is weighing on me and Aerick was right, the hike down was quite uncomfortable between my sore legs and the soreness from last night's after-dark activities. Luther tells us to leave our packs and dismisses us giving us ten minutes to put our stuff away before we have to get to the mess hall for lunch.

My feet drag walking into the dorm with everyone else. The schedule on my desk shows that our counseling sessions are only fifteen minutes today and there is no evening PT. *Thank goodness for small favors.*

While putting my dirty clothes in my bag, I pause with my underwear I wore yesterday. I silently debate whether to throw them away. When I changed this morning, there was indeed blood on them. The indication that he had taken my virginity. Then again, I have no idea how to get rid of them without people noticing them in our communal garbage cans. I make a snap decision to let them be washed and see if it comes out. Maybe whoever does the laundry will think I was on my period. I hang my bag for the laundry quickly before we walk to lunch.

"What did you do this time?" Royce ask as we walk across the court yard.

"Walked out on my counseling session. She was kind of pissing me off. It was that or hit her in her face."

He laughs, "Wow. Good thing I've never pissed you off, but I know what you mean; she gets on my nerves too." That seemed to hit a soft spot with him.

"Who is up for a game this evening."

I turn to see Huck walking up behind us. "Are you crazy? I'm not doing anything but sleeping. Well, except cleaning up after you slobs," I grumble irritably and he laughs at me.

"We aren't that bad!" I roll my eyes. Maybe not one, but when you have twelve guys using the same bathroom… I don't even want to think about it.

"I'm in," Royce says as we go inside to eat.

* * * *

I wake up in the late afternoon. Everyone is gone, except Jeff, who is sitting next to me on my bed. He looks pissed, just staring in front of him. *Something's wrong, very wrong.* I sit up.

"You okay?" I ask. For once it's me asking him and not the other way around.

"I guess you would say that." My eyes scrunch together as he turns on the bed to face me. "You want to tell me what has been going on?"

I'm taken aback by his attitude. "Not particularly. Is there a reason you are suddenly getting so pushy?"

He grunts and shakes his head. "Let's just say there are no reasons to try to hide it from me anymore." *What the hell?*

"Jeff, I don't know what you think you know, but I am fairly certain it isn't true."

The anger rises in his glare. "That's funny, because these are plain as day." He reaches up, pulling the neck of my shirt down and exposing my skin. There are two dark marks just above my breast.

Shit. I swat his hand away giving him a dirty look. "So what, you are looking down my shirt now?" There is no way he just saw those, my shirt covered them pretty well.

"Actually, I came in here to check on you. To think, I was

concerned about you, and your shirt was all twisted, exposing them for everyone to see." He seethes. "Then again, it was pretty clear what you did last night when you were walking around this morning. You know, before today, I really thought he was just being a prick to you, not that you were actually *with* him. But apparently, despite the fact that he has been a fucking asshole to you, causing you unimaginable emotional pain, you go and open your legs to him anyway." His words infuriate me and anger boils over the top along with hurt.

My hand flies across his face before he can say anymore. He is dumbfounded, looking just as shocked as I feel that I actually did that, but it does nothing to diffuse the anger inside me. "Fuck you!"

Scrambling to my feet, I hurry out of the dorm, leaving him sitting on my bed. I can't look at him right now – or anyone. My thoughts scream for privacy, but with no shoes on, I settle for going back behind the dorms where Aerick and I spent the night of the bonfire. With a loud sigh, I slide down the wall, putting my elbows on my knees and my hands behind my head, trying to calm down.

Fuck! Can't shit just be good and stay that way? I'm so mad at him for saying that, even if there is truth to it. Aerick has caused me all kinds of emotional pain and Jeff was the one that was there for me. He always has been.

But there is no reason why he has to be so upset, and even though I'm sure he doesn't want to see Aerick hurt me again, this is my life. Going about it the way he just did wasn't right. He doesn't get to make those decisions. I clench my teeth and bang my head back against the wall a couple times, hard, in frustration.

"Stop!" Aerick's authoritative voice stops me from continuing. He walks over to me and sets my boots next to me.

"Let me guess; you saw that."

He squats down and looks in my eyes. He looks a little frustrated, or maybe angry, I can't tell which.

"I did." He grabs my hand, the one that smacked Jeff, and turns it over. It actually stings a bit now. He smirks and kisses my palm. "I have been on the receiving side of that before and it doesn't feel too good." I pull my hand out of his and bite the inside of my cheek.

"Sorry, Aerick, but I really want to be alone right now."

He presses his lips in a line and nods. "I know. You seem to like to be alone when you are mad. Here." He hands me my iPod. "Figured you might want that too." He runs his hand along my jaw and stands up. He looks a little irritated, but I hope he understands. It's my way of working shit out in my head. Kind of ironic that Aerick and Jeff's roles have reversed.

"You have counseling in twenty-five minutes, be on time." He turns to leave but stops and looks back to me. "And no more hurting yourself." I nod once, looking down at the ground as he turns once more and leaves.

I slide on my boots and put my earbuds in, turning up my music, singing the words in my head, *"Crawling in my skin..."*

By the time I have to go to my counseling session, the music has mostly calmed me down. My nerves are in my throat having to see Liz again and it's important to make it through this without overreacting.

"Hello Nadi," she says, and I give her a tight smile. Even though he told her to back off, I still don't have to like her. "Are we feeling better today?"

I shrug my shoulders, not giving anything away. I sit for a few minutes tapping my toe on the ground but she obviously isn't going to let me out without an answer. "Maybe a little, but I'm working through a lot of shit right now. Stuff I do not want to talk about."

She gets a frustrated look on her face. "Okay, so what would you like to talk about, if we had to talk about something?"

"I'm not sure." Nothing we talk about could equate to anything good.

She thinks about that for a second. "Okay, last time you said you like to exercise and listen to music when you are mad. Can you tell me what kind of music you like?"

Apparently, the same kind as you. I think about my answer for a long minute; the more I draw this out, the less time there will be to answer other, less desirable questions. "Rock and alternative, mostly. Things like Linkin Park, Theory of a Dead Man, and Three Days Grace."

She smiles, "Really? Did you know all three of those bands just played a venue not too far from here, yesterday? I actually went." *Yes, I am aware, you damn twit.*

"Yeah, I heard about some music festival this weekend. Did you go with someone?" Mostly I'm curious to see if she took someone else.

Her cheeks turn a light shade of pink. "Well actually, my really good guy friend had to cancel so I went alone, but I met up with some friends." Huh, it's becoming a lot more apparent that she is more hooked on Aerick than he played it out to be – or maybe he really is blind to it; hopefully it is the latter of the two.

"So, you told Aerick that I cut our session short last week." Trying to get her to talk, so I don't have too.

"Yes, I did. He is very good at his job and I thought he might be able to talk some sense into you." I know exactly what she means by 'very good' and she isn't talking about as an instructor, though he does have a reputation for that as well.

My anger starts to rise again. "Well, next time just let me be. When I want to be alone, I want to be alone and nothing anyone says or does will change that."

She writes something down. "You know Nadi, I am here to help you. Learning to work through your problems is important. Learning your triggers and then finding ways to deal with them in the proper way is important. The current way you deal with them is obviously what landed you here." Her preaching is old and irritating. She is no Miss Perfect. I look at the clock.

"Well, that is nice and all but there is only one way you can help me, and I am not interested in telling you what it is." *Like, stay the fuck away from Aerick.* "My fifteen minutes are up; can I leave now?"

She looks ruffled as I stand. "Um, sure. I'll see you next week." Not giving her another chance to talk, I exit the classroom, heading around the back to avoid the others. It's a little gratifying making it through the session without incident.

As I make it behind the cabins I hear a quiet yet heated argument. "You don't fucking scare me." *Jeff?*

"I am telling you, you better keep your mouth shut." *Aerick? What the hell?*

"Why are you even doing this? It isn't like you could possibly have feelings for her. She doesn't need this shit. She's been through more than you could possibly imagine." *Always trying to protect me.*

"Oh, trust me, I know exactly what she needs, and for the record, I do know." Aerick's irritation is showing in his voice. *Crap.* This is the last thing I need right now.

"She told you?" Jeff's voice is barely above a whisper. He knows I've never told anyone.

Aerick is quiet for minute. "Yes, as much as she could. She confided in me – she trusts me." His voice is cocky and it's laughable because that isn't exactly why I told him. He kind of pulled it out of me.

"Well, I guarantee she didn't tell you everything. I seriously doubt she could ever sit through explaining some of that shit. The things that bastard did were horrible. I was there, and I was the one who saw the bruises he left on her. I'm the one who comforted her night after night as she cried herself to sleep. Me! Just like I did when you brought all that shit back to the surface. I knew there was a reason her dreams had gotten so bad again. It was because of you, and I'm not going to sit here and watch you fuck her over and then leave." I don't think I have ever heard Jeff so angry in my life. He seems positively murderous right now.

"Oh, don't worry Jeff," Aerick menacing voice gets quieter. "I will fuck her in all sorts of ways you couldn't even imagine. What's the matter, jealous?" I hear the distinct sound of a fist hitting flesh and then a struggle.

I hurry around the corner that I've been inching my way toward. They are between two cabins and Aerick has Jeff pinned to the wall of one. "Stop!" I say as forcefully as I can without yelling. I don't want to draw anyone over to us. Aerick looks at me with shock. He lets Jeff go, taking a few steps back until he is against the other wall. He looks down, obviously pissed he was just caught. I notice a small cut on his lip. It must have been Jeff that hit him. Jeff's actions mirror Aerick's and he looks just as pissed.

"Both of you just stop, right now." I take a deep breath, collecting my thoughts before I continue. "Jeff, I am a grown ass woman and I can make my own decisions. You don't have to like them, but you will respect them, or you can consider our friendship done. And Aerick, you need to leave him alone. He's right, he has seen me though some fucked up shit and if you care about me, even a little, you will respect that. Jeff won't say shit, so lay off. This shit is done right now or you both can stay the hell away from me!" Jeff stares at me with surprise, while Aerick looks at the ground with a proud smirk on his face. He glances up at me, but right now I don't want to be here with either one, since they insist on acting like over-bearing cavemen.

I turn around, shaking my head in disbelief at the situation and continue walking the way I was going, but Aerick's voice carries behind me "I told you! She is stronger than you think." He says it with pride and I hear him run up after me.

I half wonder what the hell they said before I walked up on them. Aerick grabs me around my waist, successfully stopping me, and I don't struggle. "Babe, come on, wait."

"Aerick. He's just looking out for me. You didn't need to do that."

He chuckles, "Do what? Your little friend hit me. He's lucky I didn't lay his ass out. The only reason that didn't happen is out of respect for you."

I turn in his arms to face him. "Well, maybe next time you should let me deal with him."

He bites the inside of his lip. "Yeah, about that, I would prefer you let me. That boy has it bad for you."

I shake my head. "I'm not going through this with you. He is a good friend. He was there for me when things were – bad. He has spent so much time since then trying to protect me from bad shit. I won't stop being his friend, so you can get that out of your head right now. He's a friend, that's it."

He's quiet for a minute as the wheels turn in his head. "Okay. But he'd better keep it strictly friends."

Men! Taking a deep breath, I calm my nerves a bit. "Besides, look what happens when you try to deal with it." I pull at his chin and he licks the cut on his lip as his lips turn up.

"Well, I think you should nurse it back to health for me." He walks me back until I am up against the cabin. I wrap my arms around his neck, trying not to smile at his corny line, but it is so cute.

"Really? Is that what you think?"

He kisses me. "Yep." He kisses me again. "You know, if you're upset, I have the perfect tool to work off some of that frustration." He kisses me again, but this time doesn't stop. He deepens our kiss and I start to ache. He kisses down my neck and when he bites lightly, it sends a shock through my body.

There is no way we are doing this right here, right now. "Didn't you say we should wait a few days?"

He smiles against my neck, "Hmm hmm."

"Well then, you should stop before I don't care who comes out here."

He brings his lips back to mine. "You should know by now, that wouldn't stop me."

I sigh. "Come on Aerick, I don't want you to get in trouble."

He finally pulls back and looks at me with that smirk. "Demanding." He kisses my forehead. "Alright Princess, I'll be good." He steps back. "It's dinner time, you should go. I got to run inside for a second." I nod and he smiles, walking away.

"Oh, and Aerick." He turns to look at me with a raised eyebrow. "Don't think I don't know what you were doing just now." He was hoping Jeff would come back around that corner and see us. The thing with having a lot of guy friends is you learn exactly how they think.

He gets that signature smirk on his face. "I'm sure I have no idea what you are talking about."

"Sure you don't." He turns and keeps walking. *This man.*

I turn toward the mess hall and head to dinner. I don't know how I am going to deal with these two. They are both so frustrating. On top of that, I am going to have to figure out a way to spend some time with Aerick. Something tells me these little meetings are going to be few and far between. I'm already starting to regret stopping Aerick.

CHAPTER FOUR

(Thursday July 16th)

Aerick POV

ELEVEN, TWELVE, THIRTEEN, fourteen...

I try to concentrate on my pushups, but I am failing miserably. I have already restarted counting three times. Every time I try to concentrate my mind flits back to her. These last few weeks have been such a fucking emotional roller coaster.

The day of the festival, she surpassed any expectation I ever had for her, or any woman for that matter. Jumping off that basket with her in my arms was the biggest rush I've ever had. The shock of feeling her push off first left me in awe of her.

Being all mixed up about how to manage work and her, and Paulo being on to us, had me pushing her away that week. It made me feel like shit seeing her mope around because of me. I think that was one of the reasons I bought her the necklace. When she had looked at it, she had such longing in her eyes. It was expensive but when she ended up taking that jump with me, I knew there wasn't anything I wouldn't do to make this girl happy.

Shit. I did it again. I start again. *One, two, three, four...*

It was even more amazing when she let me work her over behind the mess hall. It wasn't my original intention, although I'd been extremely worked up after seeing her strip on the video, wearing little other than my sweater. What I wouldn't do to have her come crawl into my bed with just my sweater on.

Her boldness threw me off again as I teased her. Just the thought of her only in my sweater made me lose it. Not wanting to be a complete ass and take her for the first time right then, I decided to test the water first. *Damn, she was so fucking responsive, so wet.*

It sent me into a bit of a panic when she did a complete one-eighty after that. I sat for hours trying to figure out what the hell was going on in her mind, going crazy that I couldn't figure it out. I'd already been so frustrated when we walked into the gym and she was there punching at a bag. The anger inside me exploded. I had to know what the hell was going on and the nice way didn't work. All it did was confuse me even more. So, I used the one thing that would push her over the edge, other than my charm. I used her anger – it worked perfectly.

The smack to my face hurts like hell; not physically or anything. It wasn't like that was the first time my face was met by a woman's hand. I'm a pretty straight-forward kind of guy and some women don't like finding out they were merely a one-night stand. No, when she smacked me it was like being punched in the gut, reaching something way down inside me. I still don't quite understand my feelings for her, but the more time I spend with her, the more my need for her grows.

It's almost irritating how much I felt like shit when I was debating whether or not to let her go. She was right to be pissed at what she saw. In the end I pushed Liz away, but she was right, it was wrong to let it get that far. At the time, I was merely trying to keep my relationship with Liz intact. She is one of my closer friends despite our occasional 'no strings attached' rendezvous.

Nadalynn really does deserve better than me. I'm truly fucked up. It only occurred to me after watching it, how wrong it was. My damaged past will never allow me to love her the way she deserves. Sitting on the chest at the end of her bed, war raged in my mind, debating what to do. In the end, I resolved to leave her alone. As much as I still wanted her, the right thing to do was to let her go. Finding my sweater on my bed, it was clear she had given up on me, and that I did the right thing.

Or so I thought. Things were fine until she almost fell over that cliff. It was only then that I realized I did not want to spend another day without her. It no longer mattered to me how selfish I'm being. All that mattered was she should be mine and only mine, which was my intentions when I sent a text to Paulo and asked him to bring her up. He text me back with that 'you sure' bullshit, but I had made up my mind to try at least once to get her back.

For a moment, when she said 'okay,' I thought it was the most exciting moment of my life. I wanted her so much, needed her so much, and she let me take her there on the lookout tower. It really was one of the most extraordinary moments of my life.

Just the memory of seeing her lit by the moon, mostly naked and completely lost in the pleasure I was so expertly providing. And feeling my pleasure being pushed even higher as I entered her, she was so tight around me. It was difficult not coming within seconds, but I managed and when her orgasm hit, clamping around me even tighter, I couldn't hold on any longer. I don't think I've ever come so hard in my life. *Fucking amazing.*

Shit. I am hard now and my fucking arms hurt. I have no idea how many pushups I have done. I really need to find some time to be alone with her for more than a few minutes. To fulfill that need to feel her around me again. I gave her a few days to recover but every day that goes by, my want, my need for her grows and I'm going insane. I've always been 'asshole Aerick' but now I am becoming 'crazy asshole Aerick.'

Shaking my head, it's clear yet another cold shower for the umpteenth time this week is necessary. I quickly get my stuff and get in. Most of the cadets are out in the court yard so hopefully I don't run into them. It does look a little odd when I'm taking showers so early in the evening.

I finish and get dressed; Paulo should be coming in anytime to get me for our evening workout at the gym. I am putting my clothes away when he gets here. Trent had come in while I was in the shower to take over dorm duty.

Paulo comes walking in. "Hey man you ready?" I grab my iPod and headphones, and give him a quick nod. He smiles as he sees my freshly showered appearance. I sigh, and we head out the door.

"Another cold shower huh? You ain't getting it enough from your girl?" I give him a cold stare. "Dude, I'm just saying. You need my help getting her alone, just let me know. Lord knows you have helped me and Terrie out plenty of times."

I shake my head. "Yeah well, it's easy when all I have to do is make sure her roommate doesn't show up, and make sure you're not needed. It's as simple as asking Ayla out for drinks, which she is always up for some beer and pool. I, on the other hand, have to worry about cameras, not having a private bedroom, and keeping people from noticing that she's not around. Then on top of all that, trying to keep her quiet wherever we go."

He laughs, "So she's a loud one huh?"

Fuck. Yes, she is. How many times did I have to cover her mouth or remind her to be quiet? I'm looking forward to being able to work her over without keeping her quiet. I can't help but smile. "I'm not having this conversation with you. You already know more than enough, and I don't intend on taking another fucking cold shower."

Loud shouts make their way out of the gym. I look at Paulo and see that it isn't just me, we both take off running. I swing the door open almost too hard only to see Joseph is on the top of Jeff, hitting him over and over, while Leena looks on, shouting for both of them to stop. Jeff isn't even fighting back, though he's conscious.

What the fuck? I grab Joseph by his arms and throw him hard back onto the floor in front of Paulo and step in between them.

"What the fuck is going on here?" I look at both of them getting to their feet, then look to Leena, but she avoids my gaze. I'm guessing this had to do with her even, though it's surprising being I've never really seen Jeff show interest in anyone other than Nadalynn. It has only been the last few days that he's been hanging out with these two more and more. It didn't bother me since he isn't hanging with Nadalynn as much, but I thought they were all friends.

I look to Joseph, irritated that I'm still without an answer. "I asked you a question cadet. What the hell is going on?"

"Why don't you ask that little sneaky bastard?"

I raise my eyebrow at his tone. With my earlier sexual frustrations, my anger pops off fast and I get in his face. "You better watch how you talk to me cadet or I will lay your ass out right here and now. I don't fucking care the reason." His face pales in fear and I feel a little better. I change targets and move the few steps over to Jeff.

"What is this, cadet?"

He looks at me with cold eyes, no doubt still pissed at me. "I don't know what you are talking about Aerick, *sir*. We are in the gym and we were merely sparing. It just got a little heated," he says sarcastically, giving me a sly smile. "Just two guys who aren't afraid to deal with shit like men!" I hear the double meaning in his words. *Little prick.* He has no idea.

I turn back toward Joseph, "That true cadet?" He is still pissed but nods his head.

Fucking headstrong idiots, fine! It's always the same thing, 'what happens on the streets, stays on the streets.' I know they aren't going to tell me but they don't need to: I have a pretty good idea what is going on and I have cameras.

"Fine, since you two seem to have so much extra energy, you can work it out by doing an extra thirty-minute run before evening PT for the next week." I see Joseph shake his head, pissed as ever, but Jeff just keeps his eyes pinned on me.

Nadalynn and Patrick catch my eye, standing just inside the door, and I have no idea how long they have been there. "Paulo, escort these two back to their dorms. You two are to be confined to your own dorm for the rest of the night, and if I have to pull you two apart again you'll be sorry." Paulo grabs each by an arm and hauls them toward the exit.

Nadalynn stops them, looking at Jeff's face with concern. He took quite a few hits to the side of his face. "Jeff, what the hell is going on with you?" she asks with worry splashed across her face.

He laughs at her. "It isn't my business who you are fucking with, just like it isn't your business who I'm fucking with." He pushes past her, dragging Paulo forward and out the door.

Damn, I just want to lay him out, seeing him treat her like that. Her eyebrows pull together and she looks over to me. I can only shrug my shoulders. She shakes her head and walks, out followed by Patrick and Leena.

I pull out my phone and log into the security cameras, rewinding them to lunch to see what started this. It would be easier if I had my tablet, but this will have to do. I see all three go to their afternoon classes, which they had together today. They sit together in the first class with Tia; them they go to knife throwing. Things seem normal until part way through class, when Jeff steps behind Leena and helps her with her stance. He runs his hand up her side slowly before positioning her arm in the right spot and then tells her to throw it. She does and hits the target.

Huh, not bad, other than that his intentions are clear as day. Then he whispers something in her ear and she gets red. With a sly smile on his face he goes back to stand next to her, and Joseph, who is on the other side of him, gives him a dirty look.

They go to dinner and she sits between the two. Things seem normal until Joseph gets up, going into the kitchen for clean-up duty. The other two get up and leave together. Jeff leads Leena out the door and over to the gym. When they get inside, he grabs her around the waist and starts kissing her. She seems pretty eager herself, so I can rule out that this was forced.

He sticks his hand down the front of her pants, asking her if she wants 'a real man'. I laugh but quickly stop when she says yes. In just a few seconds, he pulls her pants down, unbuckles his own, turning her around leaning her over the table, and inserts himself in her.

Fucking hell! I was sure that Joseph was pissed because Jeff made a move on Leena, but it never crossed my mind that he actually fucked her. Not to mention the way he just took her over the table like that; it reminds me of myself. I've done it, not because I liked the girl, but because I was desperately in need of a release. I fast forward the video, not wanting to sit here and watch this shit, but try to make sure she doesn't fight it at any point. After a few minutes, I press play as I see Joseph walk in. Leena is moaning Jeff's name as he finishes off.

"Are you kidding me, you little fucking prick? She's mine."

Jeff laughs, buckling up his belt, and Leena quickly pulls up her pants, clearly embarrassed.

"Well, I guess you should take better care of her, so she doesn't have to come to me to be sated." Joseph's hands ball into fists as he grows more and more pissed.

"How could you do this to me?" he asks Leena, but she has no response.

"Don't blame her, sometimes they just need a real man." Jeff gets that smile and Joseph loses it.

I know that smile – that cocky, I-got-it-and-you-didn't smile. The same one I gave him the other day when he found me and Nadalynn. I'd actually set it up on purpose. Jeff likes Nadalynn, and it was my way of getting a bit of revenge while showing him she is mine. After our little heated exchange, he started spending more time on the side of the cabins to avoid her. He also started to become quite cold towards her, which would have been fine with me, except it was hurting her. Seeing the pain in her eyes made me want to hurt him as much as he was hurting her. Then yesterday the perfect opportunity arose when I saw him sitting back there as I went to check on my girl. My plan formed quite quickly and worked out to perfection.

Flashback

I wait for her to finish clean-up and catch her as soon as she comes out of the mess hall, getting her to follow me around the back of the buildings, toward the cabins. She gives me a knowing smile and it's a turn-on knowing she wants it just as much as me. She follows me to the second-from-last cabin where I know he will hear us, but where we will still be hidden from the cameras.

I can't help myself any longer. My hands pin her against the wall and my lips press hungrily to hers her letting her know I want her now. "Fuck, I have missed you." I whisper on her lips.

Her happy grin is replaced by lust. "The feeling is mutual." Gently turning her face to the side, I kiss her jaw down to her neck. I'm already hard and my body is screaming for me to take her right now, but time isn't on my side.

Besides, that might push the little boy over the edge. I kick her feet apart and pin the side of her body against the wall with my own, letting her feel my growing arousal against her hip. She moans, and it clear she wants this too.

I kiss her deeply; she bites my bottom lip, sending a shiver straight to my already hard dick, making it swell more. "Ah fuck, babe," I say, loud enough for him to hear, although he has to have heard her moans. She leans her head back, closing her eyes as I continue to kiss her neck and unbutton her pants. I look over just as he looks around the corner, confused.

Perfect timing. I slide my hand down her pants and as my fingers reach her nub, I circle it, getting a very satisfying moan out of her. As my eyes find his, pure anger spreads across his face. I don't stop; I continue down her folds, sliding first one finger in and then a second. *Fuck, she is so wet for me.* It's hard to concentrate.

"Aerick," she moans as she pulls my hair hard and I want to take her right now. I need to get her off as fast as possible because I'm not sure how long my self-control will hold out. I start moving my fingers faster, in and out, in and out, using my thumb to tease her nub. Jeff is still staring at us and I get a sly smile on my face - that smile, satisfied my message is getting across. *SHE. IS. MINE.*

But I want him to hear it for himself, "Does that feel good, Princess?" I ask still smiling at Jeff.

"Yes." She can barely talk, and pride builds in me.

"Do you want me?"

Her breaths are getting staggered, "Yes." She's close.

I pull her tighter, rubbing my dick against her, trying to get a little relief as it's getting uncomfortably swollen. "Only me?"

His eye shoots to her lips. "Yes." She is barely audible as she is so close and I can feel her begin to tighten. I don't know how it is possible, but he looks even more pissed, and I'm satisfied he got the message.

"Then come for me babe, let go!" I say with a growl because I want so much to have my dick in her right now and with that I feel her orgasm hit hard around my fingers and I tighten my grip around her, putting my head to hers, trying to control myself. I continue moving my fingers and she rides out her orgasm, gripping my neck painfully tight and moaning my name. I have to cover her lips with my own for a moment as it peaks, to keep anyone else from hearing her.

I lick my lips with a proud grin on my face as I look up at Jeff and feel her begin to relax, completely exhausted. If looks could kill I would be dead a hundred times over. For a second, I think he is going to say something, but he just turns and walks away.

End Flashback.

Fuck. I am hard again, thinking about her. I adjust myself in my pants before anyone walks in. I really need to do something about that. I have a plan for Sunday, but I don't know if I can wait that long.

I can't believe Jeff gave Joseph the same look I gave him, and wonder if he did it on purpose so Joseph would kick his ass. Jeff didn't fight back, but the cut he left on my lip from the other day proves he packs a hard punch, and if he isn't scared of me, he wouldn't be scared of Joseph. I wonder if I pushed the little piss-ant too far.

Paulo walks in, shaking his head. "Nadi wants you to meet her out back." I really wish she wouldn't do that. That is the second time this week she's asked him to do that. It's not like I haven't seen her at all. In fact, we've had several make-out sessions back there, in addition to my little show for her friend. It's not the whole meeting up with her part. I just don't like anyone knowing we're back there. But I'm sure she is upset with what just happened and she's worried about the little shit.

"Hello?"

I look up at Paulo as I get pulled out of my thoughts of her. "Huh?"

He shakes his head, "Did you figure out what the fight was about?"

I smile at him as I'm sure he will get a kick out of this. "Oh yeah. This kid is fucking nuts." I rewind the camera to right before they walk into the gym and hand him my phone.

"I'm going to check on her. That little shit's one of her close friends." He nods his head as he presses play and I head out the door.

She is waiting for me in a spot that the cameras don't reach and making me smile that she has been memorizing the blind spots in the cameras. "Hey, you okay?" I ask, trying to sound a little concerned. She gives me that, 'what do you think' look. "Okay, stupid question."

"Do you know what the hell that was all about?"

I bite my lip. I'm not sure how well this is going to go over. I look her in the eyes, hoping I can distract her. "Yes," I say in a low voice as I put my hands on her waist, pulling her shirt up slightly so I can touch her, skin to skin. She closes her eyes for a second. I take the opportunity to kiss her and it works for a minute, until she stops me.

"Stop trying to distract me and talk," she says against my lips. I pull back a little looking into her eyes. *So demanding!*

"I really don't think you want to know." I already know she isn't going to give up, but it doesn't hurt to try.

"My best friend just got his ass kicked when I know he could do damage of his own and yet the other guy doesn't have a scratch. Now what the hell happened?"

I shake my head and let out a sigh. Well, she asked for it. "It appears your little friend just fucked another guy's girl, and the other guy happened to walk in on them."

She stares at me like I have two heads. "Jeff wouldn't do that. He probably just wanted you to think that."

She can be so naive sometimes. "Sorry to burst your bubble, Princess, but your little friend has quite the bad boy in him." She rolls her eyes at me and it is so fucking cute. Even when she is being difficult I'm drawn to her. "I pulled the camera footage. Joseph caught Jeff and Leena."

She looks down, shaking her head. "What the hell is wrong with him?" *How does she not see this shit?* Even without me pushing him yesterday, he is clearly pissed that I'm with her and not him. He's been a prick about it ever since he found out.

It was him that stopped me the other day by the cabins. Getting in my face, telling me to leave her alone. He had a lot of balls standing up to me like that. Telling me that she is not strong enough to have some prick like me break her heart. Obviously, he was mistaken. I don't want to break her heart, and she is stronger than he thinks. I told him that much and she proved it when she came around the corner and put her foot down. I couldn't keep the pride off my face and I made sure to rub it in his face before I walked away. But seriously, she is completely blind to his feelings for her.

I pull her chin to bring her eyes back to my own. I hate when she is upset like this. "Hey. He's a big boy and he can make his own decisions. Just as you have requested of him."

She's still struggling but sees reason. "I just don't like seeing him like this. He has been there for me so much."

Urgh. She cares for him. Much more that I prefer, but she is right. He was there for her when she needed him. I'm glad she had someone to help her through such dark times. I only wish it could have been me. *Shit, why can't shit just be simple?*

I kiss her softly and then wrap my arms around her, pulling her to my chest. All I want right now is to sit and hold her in my arms. The quicker the next few months go by, the better, because I'm already tired of trying to hide our relationship.

"I'm going to go check on him," she says quietly, not moving from my chest.

"Okay. You going to be alright?" It's irritating that she is choosing to leave to go see him.

She smiles up at me, "As long as I have you, I'll be just fine."

This woman. She is ridiculously sweet. I feel that weird pulling in my chest again, but I quickly push it back.

"Well, in case I don't see you later – sleep well." I give her one last kiss and she turns and leaves.

Damn, I feel so fucking emotional watching her walk away. The only thing that is going to make this better is to have some uninterrupted time with her. *Control, Aerick. I need to get my shit under control.* I take a few deep breaths and go back to the gym to face Paulo.

In the gym, Paulo's at the punching bag, so I grab a pair of gloves and my headphones and go join him. "How's your woman?" he says quietly.

I shrug. "Frustrating as ever."

He laughs. "Well, don't expect that to change, man; that's women. I have to hand it to her little friend. That boy's got a set on him."

My eyes throw daggers at him. I need to figure that shit out, but for now I just need to get everything out my head. Scrolling through my play list, I select Skillet's 'Monster' and turn it up loud before punching away.

* * * *

I'm a little disappointed I didn't get to kiss her again before lights out. Today was a crazy day and having that one moment of Zen would have done wonders. Once back in the dorms, I pulled the cameras to see if she was able to talk to Jeff. She really did try but he just told her, 'It's no longer your concern'.

He's really starting to piss me off. It isn't her fault that he has absolutely no sense. He should have told her he had feelings for her a long time ago. I mean, of course I'm glad that he didn't, but this is his fault, not hers, and it isn't fair for him to just be a dick to her. She moped around the rest of the night until lights out. She got into bed, turning toward the camera, giving me a sweet smile before saying 'good night' to everyone, including me.

I turn off my side light. Might as well get to sleep, then at least I can dream about her. I shut my eyes, seeing her smile on the back of my eyelids and fall fast asleep.

✳ ✳ ✳ ✳

I'm startled awake by Nadalynn's blood curdling scream. Me and Paulo jump up and sprint through the door, just to come to an abrupt stop two steps in. *Oh, fuck! What did I do?*

CHAPTER FIVE

(Friday July 17th)

IT'S TOO EARLY! The clock reads two in the morning, but the large glass of water I drank before falling asleep is now sitting uncomfortably in my bladder. Giving in, I get up and head for the bathroom.

This floor is too damn cold. This is exactly why I like to wear socks to bed. I mentally kick myself for not putting some on before getting into bed, but I was too wound up to think straight.

The door pushes open easily and I stop dead in my tracks.

No, this isn't happening,

This can't be happening,

This has to be a dream,

An unimaginable, horrible dream!

Tears instantly begin flowing from my eyes as they land on Jeff lifeless body slumped against the wall, blood pooled at both wrists, and a razor next to him on the floor.

"NOOO!" I shriek before clamping my hands around my mouth, utterly shocked at the scene before me.

My head begins to violently shake back and forth. "No, no, no this isn't happening, this isn't happening!" Everything moves slow motion as I rush over to him, pulling him against me. "Wake up Jeff, please wake up!"

Aerick skids to a halt in front of me. His pained eyes find mine. "Aerick, do something please! Please don't let him die. Please, please, do something, please!"

I can't lose him, *God, please no.* Aerick is trying to pull me away but I can't, I can't let him go.

"Dammit, Paulo, grab her." Strong arms wrap around me, pulling me a few feet away, and stay so tight it's impossible to move. My eyes close to block out the scene in front of me, but the same bloody image is burned into the back of my eyelids. I open my eyes as Aerick ties towels around Jeff's wrist. *Blood, there is so much blood!*

"Brand, we need a fucking ambulance now," Aerick shouts as he feels Jeff's neck for a pulse. Brand sprints out of the room, nearly knocking over Luther, who is rushing in.

"Fuck! Aerick?" Aerick looks up at him, grim.

Don't say dead, please don't say dead!

"His pulse is weak." *What does that mean?* I try to scream but nothing comes out.

"Get these guys out of here now!" Luther shouts. *Jeff! Jeff wake up!* Trent starts bellowing for everyone to go back to the dorm and Paulo starts moving back, with me in his arms.

"NO! NO!" My voice finally breaks through. *They can't take me away from him.*

NO! I struggle with all my might. *Let me fucking go!* My voice eludes me again as Paulo drags me further away. *Jeff!*

I throw my feet up as hard as I can, swinging them back down with everything I have, and Paulo goes over the top of me. I run to Jeff, grabbing a hold of him again. I can't leave him. He can't leave me!

"Jeff... I need you. Wake up, please wake up." I hold on to his chest and cry. "This isn't fair. You made me promise... you made me swear and now I'm still here, I kept my promise... you don't get to leave me now. You have to wake up, dammit, wake up!"

"Terrie – it's about fucking time. Aerick, get her the hell out of here," Luther demands as he tries to pull me away.

Aerick grabs me hard and pulls me away. I kick and scream but he is too strong. "Let me fucking go!" I scream as he drags me through his dorm and out the door toward our spot. "I don't want to leave him. He needs me, take me back!" I scream, trying so hard to get away.

"Ow – fuck, goddammit. Nadalynn, stop fucking struggling!" Aerick barks.

He is behind me and I can almost get out of his grip. "I can't leave him, let, me, go!" My elbow meets his side, and I hear his sharp intake of breath.

He grabs both my arms, crossing them over my chest, pinning them there with his own. He backs up against the wall, sliding down and taking me with him, wrapping his legs around my own. I'm caged in, but I can't stop. He's my best friend, my rock, the only reason I'm still here on this earth. *I can't lose him. I need him.* I try again to get out of his grasp.

"Baby stop, please, stop. He'll be okay, just stop," he pleads into my ear, "Please, just stop." The sadness in his voice shatters my already broken heart – I stop struggling.

"Babe, I need you to be strong. Jeff needs you to be strong." The softness of his voice is calming, and my mind moves back to reality, as the tears fall harder.

"Why?" I ask through my shaky cries. He releases my legs and crosses his as he pulls me sideways to cradle me in his arms, holding me tight against him. My tears fall onto his bare chest, and the sirens of the ambulance beginning to echo through the night make me sob even harder.

I can't believe he did this. *Why would he do this?* He was always there for me. Why wouldn't he let me be there for him? He finally has come back into my life and now I might lose him again. I hadn't realized until now how much I missed him being there to help me, to comfort me. He always pulled me out of my dark place, made me feel strong, reminded me that I could make it through anything.

There's commotion from the EMTs as they enter the dorm and leave almost as quickly, shouting out commands to each other.

God, please let him be okay. Please Lord don't take him from me.

The love of my best friend is only rivaled by my brother and I feel like I'm about to lose part of me. Nausea hits me like a ton of bricks. Jumping up quickly out of Aerick's arms and going to the tree line, I fall to my knees just before I expel what little bit of food was in my stomach. Aerick is behind me in a second. One of his arms wraps around my waist for support while the other pulls my hair back out of the way.

Aerick tenses as footsteps come up from behind us. "Is she alright? Is she hurt?" Luther's sullen voice inquires as I continue to dry heave, nothing left in my stomach.

"She seems to be okay, but that was one of her closest friends and finding him like that must have been traumatizing. I think it may be a good idea for Terrie to give her a Valium." Aerick is in instructor mode but there is the smallest hint of worry laced in his voice.

Luther is quiet for a moment and then sighs. "When she's done, take her to the infirmary and Terrie will have it waiting. Let her sleep it off in there, but I would like you to stay with her. I don't want a repeat, and after what she just did to Paulo, Terrie would be no match for her."

I hear him walk away and my body starts to relax. Aerick's arm is the only thing keeping me upright, as I have no energy left. "You done?" he asks quietly, and the worry in his voice is painfully clear now that Luther has left. I nod my head.

He pulls me up to stand and I turn, trying to bury my face in his chest. I want to crawl under a rock and die. He wraps his arms around me.

"This is my fault," I cry.

"How the hell is this your fault?" he asks, shaking his head.

"I should have been a better friend. He has been distant and I haven't been there for him. After all the times he was there for me, I let him do this to himself." My tears return harder after admitting my thoughts.

He pulls me back, looking into my eyes. "Hey, this is in no way your fault, so quit that shit now. You have been a good friend to him. He had issues that he was dealing with and he tried to take the easy way out. Don't blame that crap on yourself. He's grown and there is no reason he couldn't resolve that crap another way."

My eyes cast down and he pulls me back against him. That's the point. My problems weren't his either, but he stuck with me, never letting me hit rock-bottom. Something I was unable to do in return. *I failed him.*

I don't want to ask, but the nagging pull to know isn't going to go away. "Is he going to die?" My voice is barely audible.

Aerick's quiet and for a second, I don't think he is going to answer me, or maybe he didn't hear me. Then he tightens his grip on me and speaks barely above a whisper. "I don't know."

My legs feel like jello and I begin to slump in his arms as a new set of tears cascade down my cheeks. Aerick leans down, picks me up under my knees, and kisses me on my head. "Come on babe. Let's get you inside where it's warm."

It's only then I realize I'm only in my shorts and tee shirt with no socks or shoes. It doesn't matter though, I'm numb on the outside. On the inside I feel like my stomach is being twisted into a thousand knots. He walks us across the court yard with me in his arms and into the infirmary where Terrie is sitting at her desk.

"Take her into the room." He does and sits down on the edge of the bed with me still on his lap, releasing my legs. "Here, I gave her two. She needs to take them with water, and I have shot of Zofran for the nausea. Luther says she was vomiting."

I hear them talking but my mind keeps circling back to Jeff. Seeing him there in a pool of blood, pale, and not responding to any of my pleas. The tears come faster again. "Nadalynn, please hold still while she gives you this shot, okay?" I make no move to answer or acknowledge them. She pushes the needle in and pushes on the plunger, but I don't feel it.

"Give her a few minutes for it to kick in so she is able to keep the pills down. Need anything else?"

"She needs some clean clothes, and a wash rag or something to clean up." His voice is flat, he's trying to hide his feelings from Terrie.

"Sure, let me go next door." Aerick doesn't move, just holds me in his arms, and I'm grateful.

She returns a few minutes later. "I got her a clean shirt, some sweats, and socks. Do you want to step out so I can help her?" I grab him harder. *Please don't leave.* Aerick tenses and hesitates before answering her. "It's okay, you can do it if you want, and you can sleep in here with her. It's probably better for her anyway." Aerick stiffens again. "You don't have to pretend, Paulo told me. I'll keep your secret. The camera isn't on and I will keep people out." Then she leaves the room, shutting the door.

I want to sleep but there is a never-ending stream of tears and every time I close my eyes there's blood. Aerick grabs the pills and water on the side table. "Here, take these, it will help." My mouth willingly opens as he feeds me the pills and gives me a drink – I swallow them quickly without question.

Aerick turns and sets me on the edge of the bed, grabbing the pack of wet wipes Terrie brought in with my clothes. I hold in the threatening whimper, as he cleans the blood off his arms and hands. *Jeff's blood.*

He pulls off my shirt and blood-soaked shorts. Quickly he pulls a clean shirt over my head, and to his credit doesn't stop to admire my lack of clothing. There is no lust in his eyes, just sadness.

He kneels down, using the wipes to clean the dirt and blood off my legs and feet. The weight of the night builds in my chest as he drops each blood-soaked wipe into the garbage can. He slips on my socks and slides my sweats on, pulling on my arms to stand me up, so he can move them the rest the way up. I move by his guided actions but I'm dazed, staring at his hands deftly working, as the tears fall.

He looks up, drawing my eyes to his. "It is killing me to see you like this, babe. What can I do?" He lays his head on my stomach and wraps his arms around me.

I need him, that's it. I just need him. "Just don't let me go," I whisper.

He looks up at me with such understanding and longing. He stands and hugs me tightly. "I'm not going anywhere. I'm yours."

My heart swells momentarily and as much as I have been fighting it, I know I love him. It is completely illogical, way too fast, and the stupidest time to think it, but it's the truth. My head is starting to get a little fuzzy and I feel unbalanced.

Aerick tenses a bit and looks down at me. "Come on, time for you to lie down." I listen to him, getting into the bed and moving back toward the wall as he follows, lying next to me. He pulls me to lie on his bare chest and I gratefully comply. His kiss presses on the top of my head as we wrap our arms around each other, tears still pouring from my eyes. Not just because of my fear for my friend but also of the fear that one day I might lose Aerick too.

My body relaxes as my head gets more and more cloudy, but I fight the tiredness, afraid of what I may see. I'm no stranger to bad dreams and they bring a sense of dread. Aerick runs his hands through my hair and I hear the rhythmic beats of his heart. It's calming. "Be brave," he whispers to me as he kisses my head again and I reluctantly let the darkness take me.

* * * *

When I wake, I'm half lying on Aerick over his chest. I glance up at him, surprised that we are in the same bed together – my head is still a little fuzzy. Then I remember why I am here, and the sadness hits me hard.

Jeff! I feel the tears threatening to spill again. I need to be strong, brave. I am suddenly aware of how warm Aerick is below me. His breathing makes his chest rise and fall at a steady pace. My hand glides over his stomach and the ache between my legs begins as my need for him hits me. I look at my watch and it is already six in the morning. Aerick never sleeps in, and I very much intend on taking advantage of being in the same bed as him. I remember last night, finally admitting to myself that I love him, and while I can't tell him just yet, I can definitely show him. Show him my love, show him my thanks for comforting me last night, and show him my need to forget the outside world right now.

My hand slides into his pajama pants and I start to massage him. It doesn't take long for him to harden under my grip as my hand moves up and down his impressive length. I hear him moan lightly as he pushes his hips up. I shoot up and crush my lips to his as my hand continues. This is what I need: him, right now. He seems shocked for a second but then kisses me back, just as desperate, and his hand slides under my shirt.

I moan into his mouth at his touch. It feels so good. I kneel up beside him without breaking our kiss so I can pull down my pants and underwear. Using my legs and feet, I manage to get them the rest of the way off. He pauses in surprise.

"Are you sure?" he mumbles on my lips.

"Aerick, I need you... now." After debating it for just a second, I feel him take something out of his pocket and lift his hips, pulling down his pants to his thighs. My ache gets worse knowing my relief is only moments away, and I'm impatient. I shove his pants down he rest of the way as he kicks them off, and then crawl back up to straddle him.

He looks at me with a raised eyebrow and I bite my lip. He smiles, handing me a condom. I looked at him, confused; I have never done this before.

He smirks, quickly explaining how to put it on properly. I open the package and do as he says, taking my time to do it right. His eyes close and he tilts his head back as I do it. "God your hands feel amazing," he tells me, and I can't help the smile that spreads across my face. I finish and scoot forward, positioning him at my entrance. "Slow, babe. I don't want this to be over too soon."

I slowly start to lower myself, but the feeling is overwhelming, and I drop quickly down, letting him fill me with pleasure. His fingers dig into my hips almost painfully. "Fuck. Nadalynn!" It is such a turn on hearing him talk to me like that. My body fights to move but he doesn't let me. "Wait, just a second." His breathing is erratic. As it starts to slow a bit, I am aching to move, and he finally begins to move my hips forward and back as he lifts me up and down. He feels so deep in me and I quietly moan his name.

He continues to move me as the pull inside me builds. He is big, filling every part of me. After a few minutes, he lets go of my hips as I continue moving in the same pattern he was guiding me. My breathing begins to stagger as I lose myself in pleasure. He sits up, pulling my shirt off and then my bra. I'm completely naked above him as he begins kissing and caressing my body. I moan again as his mouth finds my breast, pushing me even closer to the inevitable.

"Quiet," he reminds me, and I grab his hair, pulling hard, trying to stifle my moan as he lets out his sexy growl that resonates in his chest. He grabs my hips again and begins to move me faster. I am so close but I don't want this to end. It feels so incredible, I never want it to end.

His grip tightens and he moves me even faster. I can't hold on much longer. "Come for me babe!" And that is it, my orgasm rips through me and Aerick wraps one of his arms around me tightly as he continues to move my hips. His lips crush to mine to hide our moans as his orgasm follow mine.

When we both finally stop moving, he pulls me forward to lie on his chest as he lies back, still inside me. That was just what my body needed. He runs his fingers up and down my back. The simple action makes my heart swell as a single tear escapes my eyes and falls to his chest.

"Hey, it's okay. He is going to be okay. Terrie came in a little while ago; he is stable, and they were able to stop the bleeding. They had to give him some blood, but he is going to be okay. I'm sorry I didn't wake you to tell you, but you had been through so much, I just wanted you to rest." I tighten my grip on him, hearing the thoughtfulness and compassion in his voice. I know my heart is his, but it's too soon to tell him, the feelings are so strong it scares me.

"It's not that, but thank you for telling me."

He must sense my hesitation as he rolls onto his side, placing me on my back so he can look into my eyes. "What is it?" He runs his fingers down my jaw. "You can tell me anything. You know that, right?" His eyes are soft and he looks so young. It's the Aerick no-one but me gets to see.

"The feelings I have for you scare me," I tell him honestly.

Several things cross his eyes quickly and he gently kisses me, before resting his forehead on mine. "Me too. Me too." I'm surprised; that is not what I expected to hear, but it warms my heart.

He lies back and removes the condom before pulling me to lie on his chest again. It's amazing feeling his nakedness against my own as he runs his fingers through my hair. I just want to stay in this bubble forever.

Someone bangs on the door. *No such luck.* Terrie talks through the door when she turns the handle and it doesn't open. "Aerick, you have about ten seconds before Luther gets in here."

"Shit" Aerick says, mirroring my thoughts.

Aerick jumps out of bed quickly, pulling his pants back on and grabbing a cleanly folded shirt I hadn't seen on the table next to the bed. I pick up my shirt that is lying next to the bed, putting it on without my bra, but I don't see my pants. "Just pull up the blanket and lie down and pretend to be asleep."

I see him kick my pants under the bed as he unlocks the door and sits in the chair. I do as he says, turning to face the wall so Luther doesn't see my flushed face. Aerick has time to take about two deep breaths before Luther opens the door quietly.

"Morning, Aerick."

"Luther." *How can he calm down like that?*

"How is she?"

"She was pretty traumatized. Terrie had to give her a double dose. She's still out cold."

"I have been reading the boy's counseling file. Seems these two grew up together and, other than the last few years, they were very tight due to some childhood trauma she suffered. Liz hasn't been able to get what it was out of either of them. By the looks of her last night they must be really close. That took a whole lot of adrenaline for her to put Paulo on his ass like that. How about you? Did she get you at all?"

"Yeah, my ribs and chin are a little sore, but nothing bad."

"She's definitely a fighter." He's quiet for a moment. I'm tempted to turn and look to see if he is staring at me, but I don't. "I am excusing her from this morning's activities. When she wakes, make sure she gets some food. I need you to make sure she is okay before we let her go back to a normal routine."

"Sure. What about Jeff? Any word?"

"Yes, I just spoke with the hospital psychologist that was on call. They say he's okay and that they don't think he is a further threat to himself. They are releasing him to our custody this evening with orders to watch him closely for the next few days.

Ayla and I will be leaving around six this evening to go get him up in Ellensburg. We will keep him on bed rest in here for a few days before we ease him back into the group.

"I'm also having Liz come up tomorrow for a few days to have a few extra sessions with him, and anyone else that may need it. I need you to set up shifts to keep twenty-four-hour surveillance on him until I am sure he won't do it again. Brayden and Jake can help out, too." He stops for a second, letting out a deep sigh.

"He is really lucky she found him when she did. Any longer and he probably wouldn't have made it. I want to thank you, too, Aerick. Your quick actions getting pressure on the wounds and getting the ambulance right away played a big part, too." Aerick doesn't say anything. "I really hope we can help these two," Luther says quietly. "Alright, make sure you get some rest, too. It won't hurt the others to take on classes by themselves today. PT is just getting over and I have some calls to make. Let me know if there are any more concerns."

"Will do."

Luther leaves, quietly closing the door, and I turn over. Aerick smiles at me and then gathers my clothes from under the bed and I quickly dress under the covers. Aerick chuckles, but I'm not as confident when it's not in the heat of the moment. I sit up and he sits down beside me, giving me a big hug. "I told you he would be alright. You need to lie down and get some rest."

I look up at him. "Will you stay with me? I'm afraid to sleep."

He kisses the top of my head. "Of course."

There is another knock at the door and both Paulo and Terrie come in. Paulo smirks at Aerick holding me and I try to pull back, but his grip tightens, not letting me move out of his arms. "Here, dude. Thought you might like some shoes. How you doing, sweetie?" His smile turns to me.

"Better, thank you."

"I need to check her vitals and check her head. Aerick, if you don't mind unwrapping yourself from her for a few minutes."

"My head?" I have a bit of a headache, but after crying all night I wasn't surprised.

"Yes, your head, apparently you are awfully strong and head-butted Paulo over here." Looking at him, there is a hint of a small bruise on his cheek. I don't remember doing that, and I'm instantly ashamed. I look down at my hands and start fiddling with them.

Paulo laughs, "Don't worry, it takes a lot more than that to hurt me." He smiles brightly at me, easing my feelings.

"Alright, alright." Aerick stands up beside me. "Hey, Paulo. Can you stay here with her for a few minutes?"

"I'm just fine by myself," I say, embarrassed that he thinks I need someone to look after me.

He grins widely and kisses me on the cheek. "Don't take it like that. Luther wants one of us guys with you while you're here. Apparently, he thinks you're dangerous because of your impressive display kicking this guy's ass last night." He nods to Paulo and Paulo punches him in the arm.

"Shut up, dick! Yeah, I will stay with her, but hurry up. I'm hungry and I can smell breakfast from here. Some of us actually went to PT this morning."

Aerick smirks as he looks down at me. "I'll be back in a few, behave." I give him an exaggerated eye-roll before he turns and leaves.

Paulo looks at Terrie. "Man, he's got it bad. I don't think I 've ever seen him this way." She shakes her head in agreement as she starts taking my vitals. I am intrigued by their thoughts. Terrie starts pushing around on my head until she hits a tender spot. "OW!"

"Sorry. Have you been experiencing any dizziness or nausea since last night?" She shines a light in my eyes.

"Not since last night." *At least not the dizziness she's thinking of.*

She clicks off the light and writes on my chart. "Alright, let me know if you have any new symptoms, alright? I will get you some Ibuprofen as I'm sure you have a nasty headache."

I hate pills. "I don't need any. I'll be fine."

Her brows stitch together, "Are you sure? It's just plain, over-the-counter medication."

"I'm sure." I've always tried to stay away from taking anything. Living around drugs all your life is an eye-opener; well, for me, anyway. I've seen and heard it all.

"Alright. I will be just outside if you need me."

She goes out and sits at her desk as Paulo sits in the chair across from me. I scoot back and cross my legs. "Sorry about last night." Paulo always seemed pretty nice. He didn't deserve to be on the other end of my meltdown. "I really didn't mean to hurt you."

He laughs. "Don't worry about it. I don't blame you. Sometimes we can't control our actions." He looks down at his hands and then out the door like he's nervous. "You know, I'm serious what I said about Aerick. I've known him for years and I have never seen him take interest in anyone. Girls have always thrown themselves at him, but he just pushes them off like they're nothing. It's different with you. He really has fallen head over heels for you." I smile at the thought. "I know he is difficult sometimes, but just try to be patient with him. He's a bit hard-headed"

"You think?" I say with a grin but get more serious. "Okay, I will."

Aerick walks back in with a backpack, clean clothes on, and a tray of food. "Thanks, man."

Paulo stands up. "No problem. I will leave you to it."

Aerick hands me a toothbrush and toothpaste. Gratefully I go over to the sink and brush my teeth; my mouth tastes awful. I see him watching me in the mirror and I can't figure out his expression. When I sit back on the bed he gives me some toast and a small bowl of oatmeal. I take it and he picks up his own as we eat in a comfortable silence. I'm kind of hungry after getting sick last night, and the food hits the spot.

I'm finishing up my oatmeal when Terrie comes in, handing

a few pills to Aerick. He hands them to me with a small bottle of apple juice. "Come on. I know you don't want to, but take them for me. That is a nasty bump on your head."

I shoot a dirty look out the door and then back at him before taking them. As much as I hate to admit it, my head is still pounding. Satisfied, Aerick sits across the top of the bed and I lie on his lap. "Get some sleep."

I stare at the ceiling, thinking of the past few hours. Aerick promises me I'll get to see Jeff tonight, so I can only lie here waiting. He begins running his fingers through my hair, causing my body to relax. I'm still, exhausted so I gladly comply to his request, closing my eyes and falling fast asleep.

✳ ✳ ✳ ✳

I end up sleeping until just after two. It is amazing I slept for so long. My head is still laying on Aerick's lap and I'm impressed he sat there for so long. He is working on his tablet, but his attention is on me as soon as he realizes I'm awake. He tells me I can go back to the dorm. He has excused me from classes for the day and PT is optional. I want to get up and stretch, so I put on my shoes that he grabbed, and he walks me back.

Once inside, my mind begs for a shower and to get into clean clothes, but I'm extremely nervous to go into the bathroom. Trying to push the feelings away, I gather my stuff. Aerick notices my nervousness as he walks with me in there. I stop a few feet inside, looking down at where Jeff had been. The blood is gone but the image is permanently etched in my mind.

The tightening in my chest begins to build until I feel Aerick's hands on my shoulders and he whispers in my ear, "He's okay. Be strong babe. You can get past this." He is right, and after a few deep breaths, I calm down and proceed into the shower. When I look up Aerick bites on the bottom of his lip, clearly wishing he could join me. Stupid cameras. I give him a smile and close the door.

I decide to participate in PT, although I take it easy. None of the instructors seem to mind and the exercise releases some pent-up energy, but now all I can do is wait. I look at my watch, growing impatient. It's just after eight and I know Jeff is back. Aerick walks in and I sit up quickly. "Nadalynn, come with me," he says with no emotion. I'm off my bed in a second and at his side. He turns, and I follow him out the door.

"I convinced Luther to let you see him, but he is still sedated, so this is going to be quick. You can visit again tomorrow when he's awake. I'll make sure Terrie knows it is okay."

I want to hug him so bad. "Thank you. Aerick. For everything. I don't think I could've made it through this without you."

He glances sideways and there is a glimpse of happiness in his eyes. "Anything for you," he says, his lips turning up slightly as he tries to hold in his smile. "I really wish I could kiss you right now."

I smile, feeling the same way. "Ditto."

When we walk in, Terrie and Trent are in there. Trent is sitting on the couch in the corner, doing something on his tablet. "Go ahead and go in. He is sedated so he won't be waking up tonight," Terrie tells me. I glance through the door and I can see the bed.

"It's okay. You can do this," Aerick whispers behind me.

I take a deep breath and go in. He looks so young and untroubled sleeping in the bed. My eyes wander down to his wrist where I see the bandages hiding the cuts. I feel tears swell in my eyes, but I keep them from spilling over. I swallow down the lump in my throat and go sit next to him.

How could things be so bad for him that he would resort to this? After everything I have been through, he is the one that tries to end his life. He is the one that always preached to me that it wasn't the way out. How there were people in this world that would miss me and how I couldn't do that to them, that it would be selfish. Then he did it and tried to leave me and Patrick, and I have no idea why – but I will. I will find out.

I take another deep breath and try to calm my heart that has begun to beat too fast. I shake my head, resolved to be a better friend, and stand up. "I'll be back tomorrow." I know he doesn't hear me but feel I need to say it out loud. I lean down, giving him a kiss on the cheek, and leave the room.

Aerick is leaning against the wall, looking at the ceiling, deep in thought. He gives me a small smile.

"I can come back tomorrow?" I question Aerick but Terrie answers.

"Yes. The sedatives should wear off by morning and I will not be giving him more." I nod my head at her. I smile at Aerick and walk out the door as he follows.

We stop a few steps outside and he looks at me. "You okay?" His eyes are guarded.

"I'll be okay, I feel a little better now that I've seen him. Kind of makes it more real that he is okay."

"Alright, well I have a meeting with Luther. You okay to walk back?"

I let out a laugh, feeling better than I have all day. "I'm fine, Aerick. I'm sure I'll manage by myself, but I don't know. I may trip over a stick and who will be there to catch me?"

His smile grows at my sarcastic words and he lets out a chuckle. "That's my girl. I'll see you in the morning. Sleep well."

I shine him one last smile before turning to walk back to the dorm. Everything in me is much more relaxed. Seeing Jeff sleeping there was like a weight lifting off my shoulders. Almost like I didn't believe he was okay until he was right in front of me.

The moment I step back into the dorm, I'm bombarded with questions.

"He's okay. He is sleeping right now but he should be awake tomorrow," I quickly get out to stop the questions.

"Can we go see him tomorrow?" Tara asks.

"Um, you would need to ask. I'm not sure if they are allowing everyone in, but I don't see why not. Now, if you guys don't mind, I really just want to sleep."

Patrick comes up and gives me a hug. "He's strong. He'll bounce back."

He's so sweet. Although Jeff and I have always been closer, I care for him a great deal as well. "Oh, and I brought you your homework, it's on your desk."

I laugh. "Geez, thanks. You know, some flowers would have sufficed."

He lets out that mousy little grin. "Sorry, fresh out of flowers." I smile and lie down with my iPod. I'm not really tired, but it's better than talking right now. I turn up the music and try to clear my mind of everything.

CHAPTER SIX

(Saturday July 18th)

PT THIS MORNING is dragging. My mind is consumed with the need to go see Jeff. The minute Aerick tells us we are dismissed, I head for the infirmary.

Terrie smiles at me as soon as I get through the door. "Hey Nadi." Paulo is sitting on the couch but the door to the room is shut.

"Is he awake?" I ask cautiously. I've been waiting for this all morning.

"Yes, he is. Go on in and visit until breakfast. Please keep in mind he needs to stay calm and stay in bed." I nod in understanding and quietly open the door. He is sitting up against the headboard reading a book.

"Hey," I say softly, testing out the waters. He looks at me, but his face shows not emotion.

"Hi."

Okay, so he isn't too happy. Obviously, or he wouldn't be here. I cautiously go sit next to him on the bed as his face stays guarded. There were so many things I wanted to say to him, so many questions to ask; but now that I'm here, I don't care – I'm just glad he is still here. My emotions take me over and I lay my head on his chest and wrap my arms around him.

He freezes, and for a second it crosses my mind I've made a mistake, but then he relaxes and hugs me back, putting his chin on my head.

"Don't you ever fucking do that to me again."

He huffs under me and I just know he is shaking his head at me. "Yes ma'am," he says sarcastically.

"I'm serious, Jeff. I don't know what I'd do if I lost you. I need you."

He doesn't answer, and I sit back up. There is sadness in his face. "I don't think that is true anymore, Nadi. You've found someone that makes you happy and it isn't me. You don't need me anymore."

He looks down, playing with the edge of the blanket, and I begin to get angry and hurt at the same time. "How could you say that, Jeff? After everything we have been through, everything you have helped me through. How could you possibly think I didn't need you anymore?" He keeps quiet and my anger continues to grow. "Jeff, who did I seek out all those nights at camp?"

"Me," he says quietly.

"And who did I sneak out to see when my nightmares were too much?"

He looks at me for just a moment. "Me."

"You have always protected me, Jeff. From my thoughts, from my dreams, from other people, even from myself. Do you think I will ever forget everything you have done for me?"

He breaths deeply. "I guess not."

I grab his hand, being careful not to touch his wrist. "Then how in the hell can you think I don't need you anymore?" He pulls his hand out of mine and I suck in the emotional punch to my gut.

"Your boyfriend seems pretty content on helping you with all your future needs."

"Seriously, Jeff. He's my boyfriend. What him and I have will never be what you and I have. You're my best friend, and the things you have helped me through can never be replaced. I can go off, fall in love, maybe get married one day, but there is always going to be a special place in my heart that will be eternally yours. I love you and I don't ever want to lose you." He is staring at me, shocked and I can't help the tear that escapes my eye just at the thought that he could have died. He snaps out of his shock after a second and his face turns apologetic.

"Fuck, don't cry, please. Come here." He pulls me back against his chest. "I'm sorry. I swear I'll never do that again; okay?" I let him hold me for a minute before I sit back up, a little calmer.

"So, do I get to know what the hell you were thinking? You know you're a fucking hypocrite, right?"

"How the hell am I a hypocrite?"

"You don't remember?" He looks at me and shrugs his shoulders while shaking his head. "Hello, the night at the docks when you kissed me?"

He gets a half smile on his face. "Oh, I remember the kiss."

"Geez, fucking guys. Do you remember why I snuck out to the docks in the first place?"

His chagrined face falls. "Oh, yeah."

"Exactly. I told you I didn't want to live anymore, and you told me that it was the cowards' way out and that I wasn't a coward."

His face stays focused on the blanket. "How do you know I'm not a coward?" His voice is so quiet.

"You're fucking kidding me, right? It took all the balls in the world to kiss me after that. You're lucky I didn't kick your ass!" That got a smile out of him.

"If I remember correctly, you did kiss me back." He peeks up at me with a sly smile.

"Hey, enough of that! You know it isn't like that between us. I love you, but I am not in love with you."

He breaks our eye contact and takes in a deep breath. "Yep, I know that. Just promise me that you won't forget me now that you have your new boy-toy."

I smack his arm as my face heats up with embarrassment. "He is not a toy, and of course I won't forget you. Couples fight, you know. I'll always need my best friend to comfort me. Promise you will always be there for me?"

He gives me a sad smile that I don't quite understand and after a deep breath he pulls me back into a hug. "Promise."

Terrie comes in. "Hey, time for you pain meds. Nadi, they have started breakfast."

Satisfied he is more content, I get up, giving him a smile. "I will come visit later." He gives me a genuine smile that gives me that last bit of relief to know he'll be okay. "Terrie, are the others allowed to visit?"

"Sure, as long as you guys are on free time." I squeeze Jeff's hand and leave for breakfast, more refreshed.

When I get in the mess hall, everyone is already there, and I take a sit next to Aerick. It doesn't escape my attention that Patrick didn't move down and sit where Jeff normally does. This has been hard on him too, but he refuses to express it on the outside.

I smile at him. "Hey Pat, Terrie says you guys can go visit on your free time." I say it loud enough that everyone hears, since others had asked too.

Patrick lets out a relieved sigh. "Thanks, I'll go see him later."

✳ ✳ ✳ ✳

As we're on our afternoon hike, I'm walking beside Aerick but being careful to not be too close, even though I really want to. We walk in a comfortable silence most of the time, just taking in the beautiful scenery. We both seem to love just being out in nature.

When we start nearing the camp again, Aerick breaks the

silence, talking very low to only include us in the conversation. "I saw the video from your visit with Jeff this morning."

I look at him with a raised eyebrow – not that it should be a surprise. He gives me an apologetic look and shrugs his shoulders. I kind of had a feeling he would, knowing he has to review most of the video that is taken to be sure we're not up to anything against the rules.

In truth, I've been waiting to see his reaction, not sure how he felt about me hugging and telling Jeff I loved him. I just hoped that he listened to all of it and understands he is just my best friend that I deeply care for. The love I have for Jeff is nothing like the love I have for Aerick. "You love him?" His voice is guarded.

"As a very close friend, yes, but that is it." I glance at him, trying to show him I am completely serious. He nods his head slightly, obviously still deep in thought.

We get back to camp and walk into the court yard. "Have a good class," he says as we part ways, but he seems bothered still, so I try to reassure him with my smile.

I want nothing more than for him to understand. I want to tell him I love him, but in a completely different way than the way I love Jeff; to assure him that my heart is his, but I am afraid to tell him so soon. *I'm afraid.*

* * * *

In my technology class, I sit next to Huck, who gives me a tight smile. Everyone is still being careful around me and it's starting to grind on my nerves. I made a scene, I get it, but everyone pussyfooting around me is irritating. I'm fine, now my best friend is okay. Everybody needs to go back to fucking normal already before I go crazy.

I'm still worried about Aerick. He seemed to be bothered a lot by what he saw, and I'm worried he is going to let it come between us. It's nothing, really. I hope we can move past this quickly. I loved being wrapped in our bubble. I really hope we can find time to be together again. Yesterday was incredible and I could see how our life could be together once I am out of here.

We get out of class and I resolve to go see Jeff again before dinner. He has to be bored as hell sitting in that room all day. Maybe if I can convince them he is okay they will let him out sooner. The thought of being able to hang out with him makes me feel better. Just talking with him this morning, he seemed to be feeling better. He just needed to be reminded that there are people around him that really care about him. Although the true cause of his actions has yet to be revealed to me.

I walk in the building and Terrie is sitting at her desk, but none of the guys are on the couch. She must see the confusion on my face. "Aerick's in with Jeff."

For a moment, I wonder why. He doesn't particularly like Jeff, especially because he thinks he likes me. "Everything okay?" I ask, a little guarded.

"Oh, yeah. They've just been talking for a while. Hey, I have run and give this report to Luther. Can you tell Aerick I'll be back in a few?" I nod my head and she gathers up her paperwork. "You can go on in, I really doubt they are talking about anything heartfelt." She laughs a little as she walks out.

I debate whether or not to go in, but I really only have a limited amount of time before dinner. I lean against the wall next to the closed door to see if they are talking.

"Fuck, I knew it was bad, but didn't realize it was that bad for her." I hear Aerick say. Please tell me they are not talking about me. I'm yet again eaves-dropping, which is becoming a bad habit.

"If I see that fucker again, I will probably go to prison for murder. I thought about doing it a couple of times during that summer, but she made me promise I wouldn't do anything. She was scared out of her mind. He threatened to kill her several times. Beat her up pretty bad a few times, too, but he never left marks that her clothes didn't cover and only left permanent marks once. He found her in my room one night, crying and curled up on my lap. He dragged her out by her hair and locked me in my room. By the time someone let me out the next morning I found her curled up in the corner of her room. Two of the belt marks broke the skin and bled pretty badly. I cleaned them up, but they ended up scaring."

I was having a hard time breathing. It hurts just sitting here listening to this, but I am frozen in place. Why the hell is he telling Aerick this? "In the shape of an 'x', just to the right of her spine," Aerick says, sounding so sad. I don't want him to hear this shit.

"You've seen it?" Jeff sounds a little shocked.

"Um, no. I've felt it. I ran my fingers over it several times

111

wondering where she got it."

Oh my God, no! I didn't want him to know about that. My eyes blur.

"Oh," is all Jeff says back.

"Hey man, sorry, I don't mean to throw that in your face."

"Well, it's not the first time." *What the hell does he mean?*

"Yeah, about that. That's why I originally wanted to talk to you. We just kind of got side-tracked. You know she makes it hard for me to focus these days. Anyway, I am sorry about that day you caught us behind the cabins. I let my male ego get out of control. I knew you were there, but I had no idea it was going to upset you so much."

He did what? When the fuck did this happen?

"It's alright, I'm the one that was being nosy. I just love her so fucking much, it really hurt to see her with someone else."

"Was that it? Is it was made you do this?"

I stop breathing. "I don't know, maybe a little, but not really. It's just, I've loved her for so long, and I figured that one day she would realize it and that we would be together. Even though she had pulled away from me because I started dealing, I still watched over her all the time. But being here, I slowly started to see that it wasn't ever going to happen. I mean, what you guys have, I've never seen her like that, not even with me. She's happy with you, not guarded, never afraid, bolder, stronger.

"She has been on an emotional roller coaster and for someone who rarely lets her emotions get to her, other than her anger, I know you must mean a whole lot to her. That is why I decided to let her go. I want her to be happy, that's all I ever wanted for her. She deserves that, after everything she's been through, but I can't pretend it doesn't affect me or hurt me. After all these years it was just too much for me and when I saw you doing that to her, it just kind of pushed me over the cliff I was already hanging over. I tried to take the easy way out of the pain and I figured it would be easier for her if I wasn't around."

I can't control the tears that are falling down my face as I figure out what they are talking about. The day behind the cabins, when Aerick was so insistent on me telling him I was his. Jeff was watching and Aerick knew it. He made me say that on purpose to prove his point to Jeff. He did it knowing Jeff loved me.

I didn't even see it. I never knew he felt so strongly. This is all my fault. Mine and Aerick's, we pushed Jeff to this. How could I do this to him? I slide down the wall with my head in my hands. I am so fucking stupid. How couldn't I have I known he loved me like that?

The door opens suddenly and Aerick is there pulling me up off the ground. "Babe, what's wrong? Are you okay? How long have you been here?" Jeff is at my other side in an instant. I don't know how to process this, I am so mad at both of them.

I look at Aerick through my tears. Before I realize it, I slap him hard. "How dare you! You did that and made me say those things just to hurt him. To fulfill your own fucked up need to make sure he never made a move on me. Even though you obviously saw he would never do it. You are one fucked up son of a bitch." He stands there frozen from shock and I turn to Jeff.

"And you – you selfish asshole, should have just grown some balls and told me how you fucking felt about me instead of just waiting around for me to figure it out and then be mad when I fall in love with someone else!"

I go to turn around and Jeff grabs my arm; I yank it away quickly. "Stop. If you know what's good for you then you'll leave me alone." I look at Aerick. "Both of you." My feet move before my brain does.

"Don't, dude. Give her some time, trust me," Jeff says as I walk out the door, not looking back.

I want to be alone and I'm really fucking pissed that there is nowhere to go that he can't find me. I go back to the fire pit in the back field and sit on the ground behind the logs so they mostly hide me from the camp. Here we go again: shit in my life can never be happy. My screwed up past always coming back to bite me in the ass.

I'm so tired of this. Jeff was right, I've been on an emotional roller coaster since I met Aerick and I hate it. How could he be so fucking cruel to Jeff? I don't care how much Jeff likes me, there was no reason to put him through that.

And Jeff, all these years that he pretended that his love for me was merely as a close friend. He said he loved me – he actually loves me. My actions pushed him to try to end his life. How do I ever feel better about that? How do I ever apologize for putting him through so much pain and hurt?

All I know is I need to calm down and think about this with a clear head because right now I just want to stand up and walk right out of this camp, not caring what happens. I grab my iPod out of my pocket and turn up my Linkin Park to clear my head.

* * * *

I have to get up to go to PT I skipped dinner which I 'm sure Aerick is probably mad at me for but he wisely left me here to cool off. I'm really not in the mood to be around people but I am trying not to get into trouble this week. So I just go.

Brand and Trent are the only ones there. I still don't know what to say to Aerick, or even if I will be able to for that matter. The one thing I do know is that Jeff deserves an apology. I've put him through so much and it's leaving me a heaviness in the pit of my stomach. He doesn't deserve this. Although, him keeping his true feelings from me was kind of a dick move.

I push though our work out harder than I probably should, but it works to push off some of the irritation built up inside me. By the time we are done, I feel a little better and I'm ready to face Jeff.

Inside the infirmary, Paulo is sitting on the couch with Terrie. "Hey sweetie," he says once he sees me, and I have a feeling he knows what happened earlier. The door to Jeff's room is open. I nod at Paulo and walk into the room, closing the door behind me and leaning on it. I look straight forward at a spot on the wall but sense that Jeff is looking at me.

"Hey, you feel better now?" he asks me.

I shrug my shoulders. "A little. More confused than ever." I look down. "I am so sorry I hurt you, Jeff." I try to hold back the tears that are already threatening to spill. It's really irritating that I'm struggling to hold it in. I have cried more in the last few weeks than I have in five years.

"Hey, stop it. It's not your fault I'm a dumbass. Come here." He pats the bed next to him. I hesitate for a second and then slowly sit on the bed, looking down at my lap. He grabs my chin, forcing me to look at him.

"You're right, I should have told you and it isn't fair for you to blame yourself over this. You finally found someone that you can be happy with. I have seen you with him and I know you really love him."

"Jeff, I don't know if I love him."

He laughs a little. "Well, I am pretty sure you already told me that you do."

I look at him confused. "I didn't say that."

He shakes his head. "You told me that I couldn't get mad that you fell in love. It's true, I can't get mad, and it's true that you love him. I see it, just like I can see that he loves you. Although, like you, he's stubborn and doesn't want to admit it." My heart jumps at that thought, but I don't know if it is true as much as I wish it is. Jeff continues, "Yes, I am hurt, but I really want you to be happy, and if I have to settle for being your friend then that's what I am going to do, because I don't want to lose you completely."

116

I'm so overwhelmed by his words, I lean over and hold him.

He lets out a heavy sigh. "I love you Nadi, and as long as you're happy, I'm happy." Words elude me, so I just nod my head. "I wanted to tell you I'm sorry, too."

Pulling back from him, my eyebrows pull together. "For what?"

It's his turn to attempt to hide the shame on his face. "Aerick told me you were the one that found me. He said you completely lost it. I had to beg him, but he finally let me see the camera footage. I'm so sorry, Nadi. I never thought in a million years you would have taken it that hard." He looks at me with a shimmer in his eyes. "I'm so fucking sorry, all the things you've been through, you should've never had to see that. I should've never done that to you. I was so stupid. I swear on everything, I will never do that again. Just please, forgive me." I pull him into a hug again, heartbroken at the hurt in his voice, and just stay there, holding him tight.

"Stop, it's done. It's finished. Let's just move forward," I tell him, and he kisses the top of my head.

I pull back and smile at him. "Now that I have cried for the fiftieth time in the last forty-eight hours, I really need a shower."

He laughs and holds his nose. "Yeah you do!"

I smack his arm. "Shut up. No, I really do just need a hot, relaxing shower."

His face gets serious. "You should really go talk to him. He was pretty upset when you left. He punched that solid oak desk

117

out there pretty hard. I'm pretty sure he did some damage to his hand."

I look toward the door, shaking my head. He really shouldn't do shit like that. "I don't know if I can. What he did to you, Jeff, was pretty messed up, and he pulled me along on his little fucked up scheme."

"Oh no you don't. He did that shit to me, and we have worked it out. Nadi, he loves you, you love him. You are not going to use me as a reason to hide from your happiness. You deserve it. I want you to be happy. If that means I have to put up with him, then that is what I'm going to do; but you have to forgive him. Here, he wanted me to give this to you." He hands me a folded piece of paper. "Now go talk to your new boy-toy. Then take a damn shower."

I allow myself to smile at him, but it doesn't clear up with what I'm going to say to Aerick. I give him a hug and a kiss on the cheek. "See you later." I go outside and take a deep breath. I unfold the small piece of paper and read it.

I'm shit at telling you how I feel,
since music seems to be the way to your heart,
maybe it can do a better job.
'Cold' by Crossfade.
Forever yours, A.

I swallow back the implications of his last sentence. I pull out my iPod, not sure if it has the song. I can't think of it off the top of my head. I find it, but I don't remember put this on here. Shaking it off, I put my earbuds in, sit on the step and turn it on.

Looking back at me, I see that I never really got it right, I never stopped to think of you... What I really meant to say, is I'm sorry for the way I am... I never really wanted you to see, the screwed-up side of me that I keep, locked inside of me so deep... I never meant to be so cold...

I listen to it twice. I want so much to be mad at him, but the feeling is quickly fading. I'm not perfect, how the hell can I expect him to be? Yeah, what he did was fucked up, but Jeff is right – Aerick apologized and Jeff forgave him. He knows he screwed up.

I think about what Jeff said. Does he really love me? I know I have fallen in love with him, but that is different. I've never been with anyone else, and he is an incredible man – but me, I'm just a broken girl. In the back of my head I was pretty convinced that this would never be serious for him. He told me himself, he doesn't know how to love. There is no way someone like me could hold down a man like him.

But I do know he cares for me, even if it's only a little, and if I can have him for even a little while, then it is worth it. I do love him and maybe my love for him can hold us together. All thoughts aside, I need to see him. He's probably in the gym. That is his go-to place – but... the cameras.

I get up and go back inside. "Paulo, are you able to disconnect the camera in the gym for a few minutes?" He looks at me like I am crazy. "I need to talk to him and I would rather he doesn't get in trouble, assuming that is where he is."

He looks a little nervous. "Um, that records my name and I will be questioned as to why." He gives me an apologetic smile.

"I'll do it. Jake owes me a favor. I can only do it for fifteen minutes before it alerts Luther," Terrie says, like it's an everyday request.

"Thanks."

"It's worth it. He really cares about you. You know that, right?" I just nod my head and go to the gym.

My nerves really don't hit me until I'm right outside the door. I take a deep breath and go inside. Of course, he is at the punching bag and he is shirtless, completely drenched in sweat. He must have been here the whole time. I'm happy to see at least he put gloves on, but he is concentrating so hard he doesn't see that I've come in. I start to walk toward him and notice he is not hitting very hard with his left hand. That must have been the one he hit the desk with. He really shouldn't do that shit. As I walk up behind him, he slows his jabs almost to a stop. He must sense me.

I can hardly breathe, and I lose all the words that were in my mind. I reach up and place my hands on his back; he flinches, making my stomach drop. Shit. I go to drop my hands.

"Please put them back." His voice is so sad and rough. I do as he asks, unable to deny his request. "I didn't know if I would ever get to feel your hands on me again." He is breathless, and I can feel his heart pounding a hundred miles an hour. "Nadalynn, I..."

My heart breaks hearing his sorrow. "Aerick stop, please." He turns around slowly and looks at me. His eyes show me the only apology I need. "I know, you're sorry, I'm sorry. Please, can we just put this behind us?" I want this wall between us to be gone.

He looks at me for a second, then closes his eyes and shakes his head 'no'. My stomach falls again. This is not going to be over this quickly. He falls to his knees, sitting back on his heels, pulling me down with him so I am straddling his legs. He puts his head on my chest and wraps his arms tightly around me. "I don't deserve you," he whispers and I want to cry, suddenly understanding that he shook his head in disbelief instead of denying my request. I take a deep breath, holding him to me, laying my head on top of his.

When he finally looks up at me, he kisses me so soft and tenderly as if I might break. I deepen our kiss, allowing our tongues to dance around each other and lose myself feeling him against me again. We finally break apart to catch our breaths.

"Hey, as much as I would love to stay right here with you all night, there are cameras in here," I say breathlessly.

"I don't care anymore. Besides, it's too late, they just saw us anyway."

I pull back a little, frowning at him. "You don't mean that, and no they didn't. Terrie gave us a fifteen-minute window. I don't want you to lose your job, I know you love it. I can't be the cause of that."

He smiles at me. "If it means I get to keep you it would be worth it." He kisses me again so softly. Damn, he can be so fucking sweet sometimes. "And for the record, I wouldn't necessarily lose my job. At least, I don't think so." I smirk at him and peck him on the lips before I stand up, taking a step back. He isn't having none of that. He stands and grabs my waist, pulling me back to him.

"How did I get so lucky?" He bites the inside of his cheek.

I'm unable to suppress my laugh. "I was saying the same thing about you." He rolls his eyes. "Our time is about up, and I really need a shower."

He pulls me in by my shoulders one more time to give me a kiss. When he pulls back I see the lust appear in his eyes. "What I wouldn't give to be able to join you." I smile, about to respond, when the door opens and Liz walks in. Aerick drops his hands quickly and looks back at me. "Just keep in mind what I just told you" He looks at me, giving a wink that she can't see.

I successfully play it cool. "Oh, I intend to." I turn and walk out the gym, satisfied by the shock that crossed his eyes so quick I almost didn't notice it. I was careful not to look at Liz, because I was afraid she would look past the facade I had put on.

I go back and take a shower before crawling back into bed. Today has been exhausting.

CHAPTER SEVEN

(Sunday July 19th)

I FEEL THE smack across my back and I bite down hard on the pillow. I know if I scream he will keep going. It hurts so much more this time. 'You fucking little slut. What were you doing in his bed?' He says it quietly so no one can hear, but he is mad and I can smell the strong stench of alcohol.

Another smack, and I don't know how much more I can take. I didn't break his rules, I'm not even sure why he is doing this. I thought I was okay going to see Jeff. He never comes back once he has left for the night. Oh God, please let him stop. I feel something warm running down my back. I reach back and touch my back but he hits my hand away. 'I said fucking stay still, you little hoe.' He hits me again. There's blood on my hand, and I am afraid he is going to kill me. 'Now take your pants off and turn over.' I hurry before he hits me again. 'Spread your legs, I want to see what you were going to give him.' He smacks my thigh with his belt when I don't go quick enough. I do what he says and close my eyes tight, I don't want to see him touching himself and I pray he doesn't make me this time. I sing in my head, blocking out his voice and trying to forget the pain that I am feeling. 'Wake up!' I feel him shaking me. 'Wake up!' I can't do this anymore. I swing out, punching him.

"Ow, fuck!" *Aerick?* I open my eyes and I feel my face soaked in tears. Aerick stands in a blur above me, holding his mouth. *Shit.* I sit up quickly, still trying to catch my breath. "Oh Aerick, I'm so sorry." I must have been dreaming.

"I'm fine. Are you okay? You were sobbing. I thought you were awake at first."

I try to wipe my face. "I'll be fine. It was just a dream. It was just a dream." I wrap my arms around my legs, trying to get the dream out of my head. I really wish Jeff was here. I just stare down at the bed, rocking myself back and forth.

"What can I do?" he asks, so softly I barely hear him, but the sorrow in his voice is clear. He wishes he could comfort me. He looks around at the other beds. Everyone is sound asleep. "Fuck it. I will fix the video." He sits down at the top of my bed. "Come on, lie down, I'll stay until you fall asleep."

"Aerick? I don't..."

He cuts me off. "Just lie down, let me do this for you." I give in for purely selfish reasons. I lay my pillow in his lap, then lay my head down. He begins to stoke my hair and it's so calming. I begin to relax after a few minutes and the feeling on my skin starts to dissipate. I pull his hand down to my mouth and kiss his palm.

He runs his finger down my jaw and I smile. "Night, Princess," he whispers softly and I close my eyes, focusing on the feeling of his fingers in my hair.

✻ ✻ ✻ ✻

Patrick and I are on our way to PT. I feel a little lighter this morning despite my lack of sleep. As usual, Luther is on stage, ready to reveal our rankings. I am fairly certain I am not in the bottom this week. In fact, I worked really hard this week to make sure I would stay out of it. Our rankings appear and I am ecstatic to find that I actually ranked second this week. Even with all the shit going on, I still managed to do well. Luther walks past me.

"Nice display of self-defense the other night," he says quietly. I laugh because it was more like I wanted to kick Paulo's ass, but it is true – I learned to do that in class. Aerick smirks at me quickly before he starts our workout; a smile splays across my face and stays there throughout.

When we finish, Steven and I are called up to the stage to pick our prize for being in the top two for the week, while everyone else is dismissed. Aerick hands the list to Steven first who picks a thirty-minute Skype chat. Steven says he would like to Skype his girlfriend and gives her name to Aerick so he can get her approved. Then he hands the list to me.

1. No morning PT for one day
2. Pass on 1 instructional class
3. Pass on 2 homework assignments
4. No mess hall duty for 3 days
5. Sports Balls (Basketball/Football/Soccer)

6. PSP*
7. Kindle Reader*
8. iPod (1 gig)*
9. Lunch at The Cottage Café
10. 30 min Skype chat (may not use until day 30+)
*Cadet may only choose 1 electronic item during the four-month camp

What do I want? I read down the list. "If I do the lunch, how does that work?" I'm really hoping maybe Aerick could take me; it would be nice to spend time with him outside of camp again. "Well, two instructors will escort you out of camp to lunch." He winks at me, letting me know he will be one of them.

"I would like to pick that one."

He writes it down. "Alright, I will let Luther know. Steven, once Luther approves this, Jake will set you up in the office whenever you are ready; and I will get your Lunch approved and work out your escorts. I also wanted to let you know they are letting Jeff out this morning. He has shown a significant change in attitude. He should be in the dorms here shortly. You guys are dismissed." I love the 'instructor mode' Aerick. Too bad I don't have as good self-control as he has. It is probably good he does, because it keeps people from being suspicious.

I'm so excited. Not only do I get to leave camp, but Aerick gets to take me out to lunch; and to top it off, Jeff is getting out of the infirmary. I start to wonder if Aerick gets to choose the other person. Of course, my hope is it's with Paulo, because Aerick and I can be more open with him. I walk back to the dorm to get some work done before my afternoon.

126

✣ ✣ ✣ ✣

I head out to the parking lot, excited to get out of here for a while. Jeff came into the dorm a while ago and I was so happy to see him, even though it had only been a few hours. He looked better and it raised my spirits even more.

When I get out front Aerick is leaning against a Ford Expedition with dark tinted windows, twirling the keys on his finger. His tight shirt is showing off his muscular upper body and flat stomach, and he has a half smile on his face as he stares at the ground. Damn he is so hot. He looks up and smiles at me. "You ready?"

That look gets me giddy inside. "Yep, who else is going?"

"I am." Paulo startles me from behind. "Thanks for requesting my presence." He laughs at me and I look at Aerick, confused.

"Oh yeah, I passed on your request that Paulo go with us to make up for kicking his ass the other night."

He laughs. "Hey, if it gets me lunch out at the cottage, she can do it anytime. I can't wait to get me some country fried steak!"

"Come on, let's get out of here," Aerick says, with a nod toward the SUV.

The guys jump into the front seats and I get in the back. As we pull out of the camp, my excitement grows. Aerick turns on his iPod through the bluetooth and Evans Blue comes through the speakers. "Come on, man – can we listen to something else?" Paulo whines.

Aerick smirks, "Nope, I am driving, we play my music.

Besides, majority rules." He looks at me in his review and I can't help but smile that he is listening to the music I downloaded.

We pull up to the little restaurant just as people are getting out of a car next to us. Paulo jumps out quickly, greeting one of the guys. "What's up man? It's been a while."

I get out and Aerick comes to stand beside me as Paulo and his friends come over to our side. "Sup Aerick? Who's this fine little thing you got here?" the guy says to him as he looks me up and down like I am a piece of meat. Aerick tenses beside me.

Thankfully Paulo steps in; he must have noticed Aerick as well. "Oh, this is Nadi, but be careful of this one. She'll put you on ass; trust me." He turns and winks at me and I see Aerick holding back a smile. "Nadi, this outspoken one here is Sean, and this is Eddie and Clara."

I give them a smile and laugh in an attempt to lighten the mood. "Nice to meet you." Sean is still eyeing me.

"I'm starved, let's get some lunch," Aerick says as he puts his hand on my back and turns me toward the door. He silently leads us to a booth against the back wall. Aerick and Paulo sit on opposite sides, so I slide in next to Aerick. Their friends sit next to us in another booth. The waitress comes over, taking our drink orders and giving us menus.

The guys start talking to their friends and I look at the menu. They have a Philly cheese steak, but it is a little expensive. "Um, do we have a price limit or something?" I question Aerick quietly.

"No, I have Luther's credit card, get whatever you want. He's footing the bill on this date," he whispers and smiles at me.

I raise my eyebrow, "So we are on a date, huh?"

"It's the best I could do for now," he laughs.

The waitress comes over and we order our food. Paulo and Aerick both get the country fried steak and Paulo tells me it is the best. "You know this is an extra hour in the gym tonight, right?" Aerick says to Paulo.

"It'll be well worth it." Everyone goes back to talking about the gossip in town. I feel a little left out because I have no idea who or what they are talking about, but the smile never leaves my face because this feels so...normal.

Sean comes back from the restroom and, instead of sitting back down at his table, he sits next to Paulo. "So Nadi, what is your deal? What are you in for?" They must be used to seeing these guys bring cadets here.

"Assault." I shrug my shoulders like it's nothing. Paulo hinted at it already, anyway.

"A fighter, huh? So, do you have a guy out there waiting for you to get back?"

"Um, not really." He is right here next to me, but I am not sure he wants me telling anyone. I look up at him and he seems to be debating something.

"Really?" Sean says, way too eager.

"That's right. Because she has someone right here," Aerick says as he puts his arm across the back of the booth behind me. He must be giving the guy one cold stare because his face suddenly turns pale. I look down to hide my smirk, 'jealous Aerick' is shining through and I like it. Sean gets up and goes to join his own table as the waitress brings our food.

My Philly is delicious. When I'm down to my last few bites of sandwich, Aerick takes the opportunity to steal some of my fries. "Hey, step off my fries." He laughs and bites the inside of his lip and I know his thoughts have turned.

"Here, try a bite of mine, it is the best." I give him a shy smile as he feeds me a bite of his lunch. There is something so fucking sexy in what he just did. I raise my eyebrows at him. "That is delicious. Would you like to try mine?"

"Oh, I would love to," he says as he grabs my hand, bringing it to his mouth. He puts my thumb into his mouth and sucks on it before gently biting it, sending chills right down between my legs. I close my eyes and try not to moan.

I suddenly remember there are people around us and I quickly glance around as my face turns a little red. Paulo is looking down at his plate, trying to hold in a smile, and Sean is staring at Aerick. When I look back at Aerick he has sly smile on his face. "Behave!" is all I can say through the grin on my face.

He leans down to whisper in my ear. "What if I don't want to?" His low, rough voice wakes up the ache between my legs.

"Well, there isn't anything we can do about it here, because we sure aren't doing anything in front of a bunch of people," I say quietly.

"That's what you think." I look at him a little worried. There is no way I am doing anything in front of people.

He chuckles a little. "Follow me." *Seriously?* He has been driving me nuts the whole time we've sat here. He's sitting so close to me, yet he has barely touched me, and it is making me antsy to touch him. "Be right back. I am going to show her where the restrooms are," he tells Paulo and nudges me to get up.

I do, and follow him. The restaurant's dining area is in an L shape and we walk around the corner and to the other end and down a hall to where there are two unisex bathrooms. I pause for a moment and he looks back at me. "A bathroom – really?"

He looks down the hall. He obviously isn't into public displays of affection. Guess I better get used to that. He grabs me by my hips, pulling me to him and surprising me as he crushes his lips to mine. "Baby," I try to reason with him – we are in a damn hallway!

"I need you now, and I am not a patient man." Man, he drives me crazy. He breaks our kiss and pulls me into one of the bathrooms, closing and locking it behind us. "And if that means I need to fuck you in the bathroom, then so be it. Besides, I didn't hear you complain at the fair." His lips find mine again as he pins me against the wall and I can tell he needs me now. It just makes me want him more, like right now, but this is not exactly the ideal place. "That is, unless you tell me to stop?" He rubs himself against me and I can feel he is hard, needing a release. The last thing I want to do is stop, and inspiration hits me.

I spin us so that he is against the wall and flip the light switch.

I don't think I can do this if he is watching me. He finds my face with his hands and kisses me lightly before pulling back. "What are you doing?"

I pull his face down to kiss him again. "Just taking care of my prince." I move my hand down to massage the growing bulge in his pants. "Seems he is very uncomfortable." He moans, leaning his head back. I move both my hands to find his buckle and am able to get it undone quickly. I feel his hands on my arms.

"You know you don't have to do this." I smile at his concern, but I have thought about this before and I want to.

Pushing down his pants down a little, I free him from his confinement and grab him, hard. I'm rewarded with another moan. "I wouldn't do it unless I wanted to."

I slide down, biting his stomach on my way down, and hear his breath hitch. I push my nerves away as they start to show themselves. I massage his hardness for a second before I lick the tip. "Ah," he moans and I feel his body tense. I swirl my tongue around the very top of him several times and then take him all at once into my mouth. "Holy Fuck!"

Exactly the reaction I wanted. I begin moving him in and out of my mouth. He is so big I cannot put it all in. I wrap my hand around his base and massage around it as I pull him in and out of my mouth as deep as I can take him. He moves his hands so they are holding the back of my head and I pick up speed. He gets even harder and I know he's enjoying this. I begin to ache between my legs hearing his moans of pleasure and I suck on him even harder.

He breaths begin to shorten. "Babe, if you don't want me to come in your mouth, stop now." His voice is so rough and ragged I'm about to come without him even touching me. I suck harder, not wanting to stop. "Fuck, Nadalynn!" he cries out as his hands ball up in my hair and I taste him as he comes hard. After a second of thought, I swallow and keep going, allowing his orgasm to work through him.

When I finally release him, he pulls me up to him and gives me a quick, chastising kiss and hugs me tightly as he tries to catch his breath. "Have you ever done that before?" He asks, a little hesitantly, still out of breath.

"No, of course not!"

He switches on the light. "Then where the hell did you learn to do that?"

I hold in the giddiness in my chest. "Aerick, I watch movies, I read books. You can learn a lot." I smile at him. "So, it was to your liking?" By the way he looks right now, I already know.

He grabs my face with both hands, looking me in my eyes. "That was fucking amazing." He kisses me tenderly. "You are amazing." He kisses me again and my heart explodes with happiness at his words.

He steps me back a little as he does up his pants again. I go over to the mirror and see that my hair is all messed up. I use my fingers to straighten out my hair and he walks up behind me. He smiles at me through the mirror and bends down to kiss me on my neck. "You are so beautiful." I look up at him, unable to remove the grin on my face. "Come on, Paulo will start to wonder what is keeping us." I straighten my clothes and we walk out.

As we round the corner I see Paulo laughing with their friends. Aerick stops me as we get to the bar counter. "You want a latte or something?"

That sounds so good. "Yes, I would love one." He leans against the counter between two stools, looking toward the waitress, and she comes down.

"Hey, Aerick, what's up?" she smiles at him, a little too sweetly for my liking.

"Hey, Kate. Can I get my normal?"

She flips her hair back, taking out her pad and pen from her apron. "Sure, Paulo too?" He nods his head. Damn, I wonder if he knows all the girls in town. He is overly attractive, I am sure they all fall over him.

He looks down to me. "What about you?" It takes me a moment to recover from my thoughts. "Um, I will have an iced, venti, non-fat, caramel sauce latte." Aerick raises his eyebrow at me. "What? They have Starbucks in Chicago too, you know." His lip turns up a little.

"That it?" she asks.

He answers her as he looks back toward Paulo and then to me again. "Stay here and wait for our drinks. I'll get the knucklehead." He runs his thumb nail down the side of my thigh and winks at me before walking back toward Paulo. I see him leaning in talking to him and I sit down on the bar stool. Paulo nods his head and they turn to start talking to their friends and I wonder what that is all about.

A guy sits down next to me and shouts down to the waitress. "Kate, can I get my normal?" She nods at him. *Wow. Does she know everyone's order?* "Hey, are you new around here?"

After a minute, I realize he is talking to me as he turns toward me with a smile. "Not really. I'm just visiting for a few months." He looks me up and down.

"Let me guess. Donnelly?" He lets out a chuckle.

"Is it that obvious?"

"Pretty little thing like you in all black? Yep, just a bit." I smile, not knowing what else to say. I glance over at Aerick and he is still talking to Eddie. but I see he is watching me out of the corner of his eye.

"Any plans on sticking around afterward?" I shrug my shoulders. I still have to talk to Aerick about that. "You know, this place can be pretty fun if you know the right people." I look over at him and I see that look in his eye. Man, do these guys not have enough girls around here, or what? "I could take you out and show you a good time if you like." He licks his bottom lip but before I can decline his offer, I feel Aerick behind me, and sit up straighter.

"You okay?" he asks, and I hear him trying to hold back is anger.

I turn the stool around so I am facing him. "Yep, I'm good." He looks at the guy with an evil look before looking back at me,

"Good." He puts his hand to my cheek and bends down, giving me a very hot, passionate kiss, then leans down to my ear. "I love tasting myself on your lips." My face instantly gets red thinking of what I just did in the bathroom and I am completely floored at his boldness. He pulls back to give me his sly smile and drops his hands to my thighs. I'm praying I was the only one to hear that.

Kate interrupts our moment, "One non-fat caramel latte and two caramel mochas. Ready for the check?" Her voice now sounds a bit bitter. I take it she saw that kiss.

Aerick nods his head at her and then turns to the guy. "Hey, Aerick. Who is your little friend here?" the guy tries asking smoothly, but fails miserably. I really wish people would stop calling me 'little'.

"Sorry, Kevin. Didn't mean to be rude. This is my girlfriend, Nadi." My heart quickens at the word 'girlfriend,' but my emotions slow when I see the confused look on the other guy's face.

"Ready, babe?" Aerick asks, moving my attention back to him, and I nod at him, grabbing mine and Paulo's coffee while Aerick grabs his. "Good to see you, man," he says with pride in his voice, obviously happy that he has staked his claim on me. Jealousy is definitely going to be a problem with him.

Paulo comes up behind us and I hand him his coffee. I notice he has a bag of to-go plates. Aerick laces his fingers through my now freed hand, pulling me from the stool toward the register.

Aerick pays, then puts his arm around my waist and we go out to the car. I guess Aerick doesn't have any problems with public displays of affection after all.

"Well that's new..." I hear Paulo mumble behind us. I wonder what he is talking about. Aerick releases me, giving me a smile and a wink. I am saddened by our loss of contact and even more sad that he didn't kiss me again; he won't be able to do it once we are back at camp.

We get in the SUV and head back. When we turn off on a dirt road that is not the way we came, my interest is piqued. "Where are we going?"

"I want to show you something." We drive for a few minutes and then we stop. He looks at me in the review view. "Come on." I wonder what he is up to now.

We get out and he takes my hand, but Paulo is still in the car. "Isn't Paulo coming?"

He shakes his head. "No, he wants to finish the pie he ordered, and he has seen it before." We walk in silence for a few minutes before we begin to descend some wooden steps. We emerge in a round cove with a waterfall cascading over the side. We walk to the end, where there is a round platform.

I lean against the rail and look out; it is so beautiful. The waterfall has to be fifty feet tall and runs down into a pool of water that drains into the river. The mist seems to float and the sun shining in the cove is creating a beautiful rainbow that dances all around. "Wow! This place is incredible."

"We come here sometimes and jump off the top. Technically, it's on the camp's property. The water is pretty deep, and really refreshing on a hot day."

He seems to be willing to talk, so I figure I will take advantage. "So, you seem to know a lot of people around here."

He shrugs his shoulders. "I've been working here for few years, and sometimes we go drink at the local bar at night."

"You guys can do that?"

He laughs. "Yes. After lights out we can go out for a bit, as long as two instructors are at camp. Usually Brand and Trent will go or Paulo and me. Before we were legal, we would meet up with the local kids and go to the bonfires they have out in the woods. The town is pretty small, it doesn't take much to get to know everyone."

I look down at the water. "Guess you've met quite a few girls, too. Kate seemed overly warm toward you."

He pulls my chin up and I see his raised eyebrow. "Are you jealous?"

"No. I'm not really the jealous type, but it is kind of hard to not notice all the girls who throw themselves at you. I am curious how many of their fantasies about you are actually true."

He sighs. "Nadalynn, I am not going to lie to you. Yes, I have been with a lot of them." I try to look down but he places both hands on my face so I can't move it. "Hey, it's not like that. They were just a means to an end. What I have you with, I've never had with anyone. None of them mean anything to me. I swear, you are the only one I want." There is truth and passion in those bight eyes. I nod and he kisses me.

He pulls back and looks out toward the water. "Did you mean what you said to Jeff yesterday?" He seems worried.

"What part?" I said a lot of stuff yesterday.

His voice goes really quiet. "Are you in love with me?"

Shit. Do I tell him? I look down and bite my lip. I don't want to scare him away. My heartbeat picks up and I'm afraid to answer him. He turns toward me again and pulls my face inches from his. "Please tell me the truth."

I look at him, getting lost in his eyes, and swallow the lump in my throat. "Yes."

He closes his eyes and breaths in deeply. This is it, he isn't going to want to be with me. I got too attached to quick.

Suddenly his lips are on mine, so desperate and full of want. I kiss him back, sliding my hands round his neck, trying to pull him closer because I want him, too. He kisses down my neck.

"Please Nadalynn, I need you now," he begs me, and I know I can't say no because I am so desperate to relieve the ache between my legs that is by now getting painful.

"Okay."

"Do you trust me?" he whispers in my ear. I just nod my head, as his lips continue nipping at my neck. He unbuttons my pants and I kick off my boots, knowing what he is doing. He slides down me, pulling my pants and underwear down together. I step out of them. He grabs my hips and stops with his nose at the top of my thighs and breaths in deeply before licking my nub once, sending shock waves through my body. "Hmm, I wish I had time for dessert. Next time, I promise." He smiles up at me and I'm at a loss as to how he can keep shocking me with his actions. He kisses me there one more time before standing up and pulling off his shirt and setting it on the rail.

He kisses me roughly and grabs me under my ass, picking me up. I quickly wrap my legs around him and he walks forward to the rail, setting me on his shirt. I smile as I get what his plans are. I reach down, massaging him through his pants, and he is already hard. I love that I excite him so much, it makes me want him so bad. "Aerick, I want you in me."

"My princess is impatient, is she?" He slides his hand between my legs and quickly inserts his fingers, sliding them in and out. I moan loudly, unable to hold it in. "Fuck, I love that you are always so wet for me." My hands frantically undo his belt for the second time today and release him from his boxers. "We have to be quick," he says.

I grab him hard. "I don't think that is going to be a problem." My voice is all breathy. I am already so close. He kisses me hard and I feel him grab the condom out of his pocket and put in on himself without his lips leaving mine. He grabs my hips and enters me quickly, then stills.

"Fuck, I will never get tired of that feeling." I can't reply, I am too close. He starts moving in and out, slowly at first, then picking up speed. His fingers dig into my skin hard, but I don't care. I lean back just a little, putting one hand on the rail and the other holding his neck, not caring that there is a ten-foot drop behind me. He feels absolutely divine as he pushes me higher and higher. I open my eyes and he is looking at me with pure lust. "Come, baby." He slams into me hard and I can't hold back any longer – my orgasm tears through me. I moan his name loudly and it is enough to push him over too. He grabs me tightly, holding me to him as we come down.

When my breathing evens out a little my head is resting on his shoulder. "I don't think I will ever get enough of you." I grin at his words. He sighs. "As much as I like our little bubble here, we have to get back." I take one more deep breath and unwrap my legs from him. He pulls out of me slowly, watching me. I close my eyes as the aftershocks go through me. When I open my eyes, he has a huge smile on his face. "I love seeing that." He helps me down and I grab my pants to put them on. He turns his shirt right side in and puts it back on, then does up his pants. I could look at him all day. He looks up at me and smiles. "Did you not get enough?"

I get a little embarrassed, but I pull his lips to mine. "It will do for now." I kiss him and he shakes his head.

He grabs my hand and we start back. When we reach the car, he gives me one more tender kiss before we get in. I look at Paulo and he gives Aerick a knowing smile. "Nice walk?" He asks sarcastically. I look down, embarrassed. He knows what we just did. "Yes, it was breath-taking," Aerick says back with amusement in his voice.

"Oh my fucking god, you guys, enough!" I snap at them with a smile, not wanting to hear this. They both laugh. Aerick starts up the car and we drive the short distance to the main camp.

We come to a stop and Paulo turns back to me with a mischievous smile. "Do you want your dessert, or did you get enough at the restaurant?" *Holy Shit. Aerick told him!*

My face turns about five shades of red and Paulo laughs. Aerick punches him in the arm. "Subtle, asshole." He looks at me apologetically in the rear view.

A smile spreads across my face. "You can have it; Aerick's, too. I had my dessert already and Aerick promised to come get his from me later." I lick my lips and wink at Aerick. He looks at me shocked as his mouth falls open; as does Paulo's. "See ya later, boys." I hop out, satisfied.

"Oh damn, dude!" Paulo laughs at him.

✽ ✽ ✽ ✽

I head to my session with Liz. I still can't stop smiling. Lunch with Aerick was just amazing and I can't wait to see him at dinner after this. I walk in and Aerick is in there. He looks up at me and keeps a straight face.

"I will bring these to you when I am done. Thanks, Aerick." The sweetness in Liz's voice is nauseating but Aerick goes to leave and gives me a wink, making me forget my irritation.

Liz and I go over and sit on the couch and greet each other. Of course, she wants to talk about what happened with Jeff.

"Jeff tells me you guys are really close."

I look up at her. "Yes, you can say that. We grew up together. He has always been there for me."

"Luther also told me you found him, and that you took it really hard."

I shrug. "Yeah, I guess so. He is my best friend. I'm sure you could imagine that was pretty hard for me."

She smiles. "Yes, I guess I could. How were you able to calm down?"

Shit. I am not sure how much I should actually tell her. "Aerick took me out of the room."

She looks down at her notes. "And how did he get you to calm down?" Her voice has changed somehow.

I think of how to word this without giving him away. "Um, he basically took me outside and held me down until I calmed down."

She looks up at me. "Why would he hold you down?" She has temporarily lost her composure.

Crap. Think! "I sort of lashed out physically at him, Paulo too. I think I left a few marks behind."

She chuckles. I think her suspicions are gone. "I also noticed you seem different around him compared to others." Nope, she knows something is up.

I shrug, trying to play it off. "I have emotional issues and tend to lash out, he has been showing me how to control them. He told me he used to have the same issues."

"He did, huh? Well I suppose that is what they are here for. To work through your issues. I suppose it helps that he is extremely good looking." I keep a straight face. I know her game now.

I shrug again, keeping a straight face. "Actually, they are all pretty hot, but that's not really what I am here for. I didn't come here to find a boyfriend." But I found one anyway.

"What about Jeff, you ever consider dating him?"

This is my way to get off the topic of Aerick. "I know he likes me. He was actually my first kiss." I give a shy smile and she relaxes a little. She gets me to talk about it and I tell her, leaving out a few details that are none of her business. She has the guts to tell me I should really look into his feelings for me. I think that is a little out of her job description, to be fixing me up with guys.

We finally finish up and I am happy to be done with that, but it still worries me that she has been so observant of Aerick and I. I may have to say something to him. I go outside and find the guys outside kicking the soccer ball around, so I go join them.

Today turned out to be another great day. Lying in bed waiting for lights out, my mind runs through everything that happened today. I still can't believe I told Aerick that I love him, - well, sort of, anyway. He asked, and I said yes. He hasn't run for the hills so I think he is okay with it and I feel so much better that he knows. He also called me his girlfriend today. It was so amazing hearing it come out of his mouth. I've noticed I have become bolder around him. I still can't believe I actually went down on him! I don't know how I had the courage to do that, or say what I said to Paulo.

He was teasing me at dinner when he asked Aerick, 'You going to have dessert after dinner?' I almost choked on my food and they both laughed at me while everyone else just stared at me. It was nice to just joke around, though. As well, I was happy to have both Jeff and Aerick at dinner, both seemingly done with their feud and were even talking to each other.

The lights go out and I close my eyes with a smile on my face, thinking of my boyfriend as I fall asleep.

CHAPTER EIGHT

(Sunday July 26th)

THINGS ARE AWESOME. Considering my current situation, I don't things could be better right now. There haven't been any problems all week, and Jeff is more cheerful these days; our friendship falling back into the normal best-friend mode. Jeff and I talked again about our feelings toward each other on Wednesday. It made me feel a little shitty that I never realized how strong his feelings were for me, but he seems to feel better that he got out the truth. A few times, I've caught him looking at Aerick and I, but it's not like his feelings after so many years are just going to disappear.

Classes this week have gone by smoothly and after two months of being here, workouts no longer bother me. Exercise has never been my thing, but now I understand why people get into it. It seems to give me more energy throughout the day and overall my body feels great. A few times this week Jeff and I even chose to run a few extra laps in the evening. He has always complimented me, but in the last week, when he compliments my newfound toned body, it brings a blush to my cheeks knowing his true feelings.

Mine and Aerick's relationship is finally going smoothly too. Although I haven't had enough nerve to actually say 'I love you,' I did answer his question when he asked. It still sucks to have to hide our relationship, and seriously limits the amount of time we can spend together. Currently, it mostly consists of impromptu meetings behind the buildings to make-out, but last night was really nice.

Instead of the staff's normal drinking night, Paulo and Aerick joined Jeff and me at the monthly bonfire with the other cadets. We talked a lot about ordinary, everyday things and it was interesting getting to find out things about them. As it turns out, Aerick really likes the local sports teams and loves to hike. Aerick told me about wanting to hike the whole length of the John Wayne trail, which would definitely be a memorable experience. Of course, we talked about music, and Jeff was surprised to find out that Aerick likes much of the same music we do. They told us a few crazy stories about the time they've spent here, the funniest being how Paulo was the one that tried to escape and had to learn the hard way not to sneak out. It was so normal to just talk and laugh.

The only thing pulling me down a bit today is that we have

visiting day this evening. It's the only one there is, but several of us don't expect to see anyone. Chicago to Washington is a bit too far for most of our family and friends. Personally, my dad would never take off work and my mom wouldn't come without my dad. My sisters are off doing their own things and my brother has his 'business' to keep up with. It makes me miss home even more knowing they won't be here. Jeff's mom wrote last week and said she didn't have the money to make the trip. He gets letters from her regularly, and after he told her Patrick and I were here, she wrote us a few letters too. She's such a nice woman – always happy and trying to make the best out of crappy situations.

Other than her occasional letter, I haven't heard from anyone, including my family. It's a little depressing, but at least I have Jeff, Patrick, and now Aerick. It isn't so terrible that no one in my family seems to care, and the one that does just has no time. I know Evan is mad at me, but he'll get over it when I'm out.

It will be interesting to see how he reacts to Aerick. I've never really showed interest in guys before, but I have made it clear I don't play for the same team. Although he had blocked a few guys attempting to get close to me, I mostly kept them away.

He doesn't know what happened and I prefer to keep it that way. He'd probably go to every length possible to find him and kill him. My brother doesn't need to ruin his life and possibly end up in prison because of me. He's a good kid and deserves to have a better life than that.

Aerick sits down next to me at breakfast, breaking me out of my thoughts. He keeps a straight face but bumps his knee against me saying hello. "Penny for your thoughts?"

"Just thinking about my life." I try to stay happy.

"Is that a good or bad thing?" Paulo asks with a smirk as he glances from me to Aerick. Paulo sure has gotten more and more friendly with me and the guys, which is nice, but he always has something sarcastic to say and many times it's highly irritating. Aerick says that it usually happens about half way through camp because he gets tired of only having Aerick to talk to.

"Oh, there are the good parts..." I smile, glancing at Aerick, trying not to be too obvious, but then move my eyes back to my food and let out a sigh. "...and then there are the bad parts."

"No family coming today?" Paulo asks, guessing at my souring mood.

I shake my head 'no', "We were hoping to see Jeff's mom, but she can't make it."

"Well then, we will just have to find something to do to have a little fun," he says with a wily smirk.

"Did someone say, 'have a little fun?'" Liz's ice-edged voice breaks through our bubble. She plops down on the other side of Aerick, sipping on a cup of coffee. I give Paulo a questioning look because she never joins us for meals and her sessions don't start for a while. Since I don't dare look at Aerick, Paulo is my go-to person. He gives me a shrug with his eyes and it's clear he is just as confused by her presence.

"We were just talking about hanging out is all," Paulo says

smoothly. Something is off but I'm not sure why.

"Oh, yeah. Are you guys up for hanging out and playing pool tonight? It's been a while."

"Actually, we can't tonight; we went out last night," Aerick explains.

I sit up a little straighter. I didn't know they went out; or maybe he is just making up a reason.

"Speaking of that. I need to find a new drinking partner. These days, Aerick here won't shut up once he's drunk." *So they did go out!*

"Well, that is something new. Since when are you the talkative type?" Liz questions Aerick.

He sends a pissed-off glare at Paulo. "I just have a lot going on right now. I thought I could talk about it with my best buddy here, but obviously he doesn't want to hear it." He's clearly irritated either by the fact that Paulo brought it up, or with the fact that Paulo didn't want to listen to it.

"Well you know, Aerick, I'd love to listen to your problems." Her seductive voice is sickening. My eye catches her rubbing a hand on his leg and his body tenses up beside me. My teeth clamp down on the inside of my cheek and I look at Paulo, trying to reign in my anger. Her advances are obviously unwelcome, but it still pisses me off.

Jeff bumps my arm, pulling my attention to him. "Deep breaths," he whispers to me. My façade must be breaking more than I realize.

"I'm good. Thanks for the offer Liz," Aerick tells her, moving her hand off his leg. She leans over and whispers something in his ear and he swallows hard.

If I don't get out of here now, I'm going to do something stupid. I quickly get to my feet, and Jeff rises with me. "We'll see you guys outside," he says. Thank the Lord he is still trying to protect me. There is no way I could talk right now without giving myself away.

"Oh, hey Nadi, I didn't see you there. You have my first session, don't be late." Aerick's lips press in a tight line as he stares at the food he isn't eating. I grant her a tight nod and turn around before I roll my eyes. Jeff and I head outside before anything else can happen.

"What the hell was that all about?" Jeff asks as soon as we are outside.

I shake my head. "I have no fucking idea. I mean, they had a thing for a while, but he told her he wasn't interested anymore."

Jeff looks at me almost sympathetically. "Don't get mad at me for asking, but are you sure?"

I let out a chuckle, not taking his dig personally. I still haven't told him about 'that' argument. "Yes, I'm sure, I saw him do it." Well, on camera I did, anyway. "But it's weird that she is here so early and she sure is more touchy than normal." My voice is beginning to show my anger.

"Wow, are you getting jealous?"

No! I'm not the jealous type. "Of course not. I just don't particularly like her. She comes off as a bit of a slut if you ask me. He told her he is with someone now; and look how she is acting toward him."

"Maybe she still likes him?" Jeff looks at me to see my reaction.

"Well, too bad for her," I grin at him, not wanting to talk about it anymore. Maybe I'm a little jealous. She's older and way more beautiful. Aerick's good looks obviously draw in the good-looking ones.

"So, what are we doing today?" I try to lighten the mood.

"How about we kick around the soccer ball?" He always knows just what to say. With only a few more assignments to get done, I need something else to occupy the rest of the day.

"That sounds good to me."

When I step into the classroom for my session, Aerick is talking to Liz. *Seriously!* Aerick has a smile on his face until he turns and sees me.

"Thanks for the files, Aerick," she says to him sweetly.

"Sure thing," he says, not looking back at her, probably trying to hide his change in expression.

Liz looks at me and then grabs his arm. "Oh, Aerick?" He stops and turns to face her with his brows scrunched together. She touches his chest with one finger and drags it down to his stomach. "I'll see you later."

Anger instantly boils inside me as a confused look plasters across Aerick's face. He doesn't say anything, just nods at me and leaves. I try to breathe evenly, not wanting her to know that bothered me so much, but when my eyes move back to her, her head is cocked to the side and her eyes are fixed on me. She did that on purpose to see my reaction. Stupid bitch is starting to figure it out. *Crap.* This is only going to get more complicated.

We walk over to the couch and it takes several deep breaths to ground myself. We sit, and she grabs her pen and paper, trying to play it off like everything is normal. "Sorry, that man just drives me wild." I refrain from rolling my eyes and just shrug like it is no big deal.

"I'll let you in on a secret – we kind of have a thing." Her voice is nauseating to listen to, and apparently, she doesn't know Aerick already told me about them. But I have the advantage because I also know there is nothing between them anymore. Granted, it's pissing me off that she is trying to make me mad at him on purpose – or maybe she is just trying to be sure it's me that he is interested in. Either way, it's making me dislike her more and more.

When I fail to react to her petty comments, she changes tactics and starts talking about Jeff again and how maybe he has feelings for me that I don't realize. Again, frustrating as hell because she's a little late on this point. She is the least helpful shrink I've ever seen in my life. I play along with the Jeff conversation just to run out our time.

Our thirty minutes is finally up, and I join the guys who are messing around in the court yard. With the beautiful weather today, it seems like everyone is outside enjoying it. On second thought I should really get my work done first, so I can enjoy the afternoon without worrying about it. I change tracks and head for the dorm to get my homework.

As I'm walking to the door, Paulo stops me. "Nadi, Aerick wants you to meet him behind the cabins."

Out of the corner of my eye, I see Liz is standing across the way watching us. "Tell him, not now."

Paulo rolls his eyes. "What the hell am I? A damn messenger? I'm tired of being in the middle of your lover quarrels." He walks off, taking out his phone, probably to text Aerick.

✳ ✳ ✳ ✳

Liz has been getting on my fucking nerves all day. Every time I turn around, she is nearby. She sat with us for lunch and now dinner. I haven't been able to talk to Aerick all day and it's starting to wear on us both. He's like stone beside me as we eat dinner in an uncomfortable silence.

"So, Liz. You out of here after dinner?" Aerick asks, a little rougher than he usually is toward her.

She seems pretty surprise at his tone too. "Yeah. I thought I'd get some food in my stomach before driving back, was all." She almost sounds saddened. My hand hurries to clear my plate so I can get out of here. I've had more than enough of her today and my need touch Aerick is becoming painful. Being so close to him is making it extremely difficult. Jeff is making small talk but it's no longer helping.

Begging, I look at Jeff and then look out the door. He nods, getting the hint, and stands. "You coming?" he asks, bumping my shoulder lightly, and I gratefully nod my head, letting him lead me out to the courtyard.

We set up a small soccer area so we can play three on three. As we finish, Aerick exits the hall, with Liz following on his heels. She smiles sweetly at him and tells him she will see him soon. Then she runs her hand down his arm and tells him bye.

My face must look murderous because Jeff hisses at me, "Nadi! Knock it off." He turns me back toward him before anyone sees me.

"Is it that obvious that I want to tear her head off right now?"

He chuckles, "Yes. Now stop."

The others trickle out, and those of us not expecting visitors start kicking the ball around. Since there is no PT tonight and there wasn't any last night due to the bonfire, the game will help get out some of my pent-up frustration. I've been avoiding Aerick all day and I am sure he's just as frustrated as me.

Visitors start arriving and it seems like all the staff is on watch duty as they are all spread out around us. The visitors are pretty sparse, but everyone seems to be in a good mood. A woman with two younger girls comes to visit with Tara. Both of Huck and Steven's parents come, and John's dad shows up, which he doesn't seem happy about. When Leena's mom makes her overly dramatic appearance, it's clear why she is the way she is. Her mom seems to be the exact same. She is actually flirting with Luther and Aerick. A bit ridiculous if you ask me, but it's not like

I expected anything less.

My body suddenly spins around to a woman's voice calling Jeff's name. I'm overwhelmed with happiness seeing Jeff's mom moving toward us with bright, sparkling eyes. She'd told him she couldn't come up with the money. Jeff, Patrick and I all excuse ourselves from the game and run over to her. She gives Jeff a long engulfing hug before wrapping her arms around Patrick and giving him a quick kiss on the cheek.

Then she turns her attention to me. "Nadi, my girl! I've missed you so much." She carefully pulls me into a light, reserved hug. She was like another mom as I grew up. The three of us were always at her house and she never minded having two extra mouths to feed.

"I can't believe you're here. Not that it is a good thing, young lady, but I tell Jeff all the time that he needs to bring you around more often. I never get to see you anymore. All I have are the boys to look after and I need a girl around!"

I give her an apologetic smile, "Sorry I haven't been around. It is so good to see you too."

"Mom, I thought you couldn't come?"

All of a sudden arms wrap around me so tightly, my arms can't move but before I can react, his voices warns me. "You hit me, and I will kick your ass."

Holy Shit. I wiggle out of his arms with a squeal and turn around, throwing my arms around my brother. "I can't believe you are here! What the hell?" He holds me tightly for a minute before letting me go. Then I proceed to punch his arm hard a few times. "Don't you know how to pick up a pen? Jerk!"

His grin is massive and contagious, I can't help but to mirror it. "Sorry. I hate writing. You know that." He gives Jeff and Patrick man-hugs, greeting them with 'what's up'.

"Okay. So now you can tell us how you both are here," I demand with all seriousness.

Jeff's mom smiles at me sweetly. "Well, I ran into your brother a few days back. With Jeff gone, he hasn't been around much, but there he was at the corner store." Jeff and Evan have the same supplier, so it's normal for them to swap product often. It also makes sense that Evan would be covering Jeff's territory with him gone. I can only hope they both decide to get out of that game.

"I was telling him about visiting day and he was so gracious as to offer to pay for our trip here. He said that he owed Jeff a favor and he really wanted to see you, anyway. It was way too generous if you ask me, but he insisted. So here we are."

"Man, I can't thank you enough," Jeff says, patting Evan on the back.

"Like I said, I owed you, which by the way means we're even."

Jeff nodes in acceptance. "Agreed."

Jeff goes to take his mom around the camp and Evan and I sit down beside our makeshift soccer field to catch up. "So how are Mom and Dad?"

He shrugs. "Dad is still pretty upset at you, but I can tell he is pretty sad you're not around. You know, kind of like he always is. I'm supposed to tell you he hopes you finally learn your lesson this time, and that he loves you. Mom is Mom. She's overly worried about you and sad you're not around. She says hi and she loves you too."

Sounds typical. "And the sisters?"

He huffs, "The same. They're all busy with their own lives. I went to see Eve in jail. She says she loves you and hopes when she gets out, we can all spend some time together." I roll my eyes. We were all pretty close as kids, but we have grown apart these last few years.

"How are you doing?" He eyes me suspiciously. "You look great by the way. Looks like you finally lost that little girl tummy you always had." He laughs and I bump my shoulder into his.

"Shut up. You had it for a long time too. It is in our genes – but seriously, I'm good. I've been working on my issues, and we work out a lot, hence my newfound figure. But get this, we have school work – and a lot of it. It's summertime and I'm stuck doing schoolwork."

He raises his eyebrow. "Sounds like torture to me."

"It isn't all bad. I mean, this isn't the worst place to be living, and I'm in great shape now. School has always been easy for me, so it isn't too terrible. At least it passes the time, and in case you haven't noticed, the hot guy to girl ratio here is in my favor."

His lips press into a line. "Any of them bothering you? I've been really worried about you." He's so serious, and it just makes my heart warm.

"I'm fine, *little* brother. I've been known to take care of myself occasionally. Besides, this place is different. There aren't groups pouncing on each other to show who is boss, or bullies who just like to go around beating up people. No colors, no drugs, it's actually pretty nice out here. The air is clean, I get along with mostly everyone, it's way better than I imagined." I can't help the grin on my face thinking about how nice it is.

His eyebrow shoots up. Damn, he knows me too well. "Um, and have any of these guys caught the eye of my little sister?" I'm not ready to tell him yet, especially because I don't want him to freak out on Aerick right here and ruin everything. He isn't going to like the fact that I'm dating an older man. Slyly, I try to play it off, shaking my head 'no', but he knows.

My eyes scan around until they find Aerick and Paulo leaning on the stage. I've noticed that Aerick has been eyeing me since Evan got here and he seems really irritated. "You want to meet my instructors? They're pretty cool for the most part."

He looks at me for a minute, evidently curious at my change in subject. "Sure." He gives me a hand up and we walk over to the stage. I purposely position myself next to a very tense Aerick to ensure I'm between him and my brother in case it happens to come out that we are dating. "Evan, this is Aerick and Paulo. Aerick is my lead instructor. Paulo, Aerick, this is my brother Evan." I can't help the grin on my face as Aerick visibly relaxes. *Who did he think it was?*

They all shake hands and say hello. "So, you guys are the ones harassing my little sis."

My eyebrows pull together. "If you don't stop calling me little, I swear I'm going to kick your ass." I'm tired of hearing that, just because I am shorter than all these guys. I'm not short or anything, they are all just tall.

"Okay, okay – younger. Man, I feel for you guys. She is a damn handful."

Aerick laughs and I eye him as he tries to hold in a smile.

"You are definitely on point there," Paulo speaks up.

"Hey! I'm not that bad."

Paulo chuckles, "Says the girl who put me on my ass."

Evan looks at me, shocked. I shake my head, not wanting to rehash that in my head now. "I – uh, some shit happened. I'll tell you about it later."

"Oh yeah. I'm sure she has all kinds of things to tell you," Aerick says with a smirk. My eyes shoot daggers at him, trying to get him to knock it off. Now is not the time to do this.

"Anyways, I am going to show my brother around. See you guys later." I start to pull my brother away.

"You guys take care of her for me. And for heaven's sake, keep her out of trouble," he says over his shoulder to Aerick and Paulo.

"Don't worry. She'll be well taken care of," Aerick says casually but as I turn back Paulo is silently cracking up and I give him one more dirty look. I mouth 'cabins' to Aerick behind my brother's back. I really want to talk to him and make sure things are okay after the whole Liz thing today.

I show Evan the dorms. He is horrified at the co-ed sleeping arrangements and expresses his dislike. Surely, if our roles were reversed, he wouldn't be so opposed to it. I also introduce him to Brand and Trent, who are in the mess hall when we go to get some coffee and talk.

It's so nice to have him here, I've missed our talks a lot. I finally get up the nerve to tell him about Jeff's suicide attempt and the discovery of his feelings for me, which I manage to do without telling him about Aerick, but I do tell him about what I did to Paulo. I run my hands along the grass where we are sitting.

"I always knew it. It was pretty obvious," he tells me. It appears I really was the only one who didn't realize it. "I actually kind of figured you guys would end up together. He's always been closer to you than anyone else outside of our family and to be honest, I wouldn't have minded you dating him."

I roll my eyes at him. "Thanks. Glad he would've been on your approved list."

"Well, when you do meet someone, he better meet my standards or he can take a hike. I ain't going to let some asshole date my sister. You need a real man that knows how to treat you and that makes you happy. I'll accept nothing less." I grin widely. *Wonder how he will feel about Aerick.* He is a man, he treats me very well, and he makes me extremely happy. I look up, realizing he has stopped talking and is looking at me.

His eyebrow is raised. "Is there something you want to tell me?"

161

Shit. I try to be cool. "No, why?" The look in his eyes tell me he doesn't believe me. I glance at Aerick quickly and then down at the ground, hoping Evan didn't just see that. Paulo is with Aerick still, so if he did maybe he won't know who. I, however, can't keep the smile off my face.

"Yeah, okay."

Luther steps out from his office. "Five minutes to the end of visiting hours."

My mood nosedives in a second. I'm not ready for my brother to go yet. It's been so nice to spend the last few hours with him. Evan jumps up and holds out his hands, pulling me up harder than necessary, making me almost fly forward onto my face. He laughs at me.

"Jerk!" I say, hitting his arm. He rubs it like it actually hurt and I roll my eyes and smile. He always knows how to cheer me up. I pull him into a hug and he hugs me back harder.

"Take care of yourself. I will see you in a few months and I expect more answers then." He releases me.

"Maybe you should try to pick up a pencil and I will write you back."

He looks at me like I'm crazy. "We'll see."

Patrick, Jeff and his mom come over. She suddenly engulfs me a hug and I'm shocked as she tightens her grip. My chest tightens a little at the contact and I'm about to push her back, until she begins to whisper in my ear. "You will always have a special place in my heart. Thank you for saving him." She lets go and gives me a loving, motherly look and I fight to hold back the tears threatening in my eyes. Everyone gives hugs and say their last goodbyes.

"You guys have a safe trip back," I manage to choke out. Jeff puts his arm around my shoulder and we all wave goodbye as they disappear between the buildings.

"You okay?" Jeff asks me as he gives me a hug and I feel Patrick wrap his arms around me too.

I hold in my tears, not wanting to cry in front of everyone. "I need some time." I wiggle out of their grasp and Jeff nods at me.

I move through mess hall and out back door to keep people off my trail. My feet move absently, around the outside to the cabins. I finally stop and lean against the wall of one of the last cabins. I'm fighting to hold in the tears, but I can't help the sinking feeling of wanting my brother back already. *Fuck, I hate this.* I hit my head on the wall several times, trying to use the pain to push my tears away.

"Stop." His authoritative voice rings out and I freeze.

I don't want him to see me like this yet again. However, I've managed to find myself where I told him I would meet him, so it is my own fault. I put my head back, still trying to hold my tears in. "I take it you and your brother are very close." I nod my head slightly and swallow down the sadness I am feeling. Aerick walks over to me. "Babe, no one is here but me. Don't be afraid to cry in front of me."

I gaze up into his beautiful eyes. "I don't need to cry. I just need you to hold me."

He gives me that knowing smirk. "That I can do." He pulls me into a tight hug, laying his cheek on my head as I wrap my arms around his waist and we stand there until my sadness subsides. When I finally feel better, I lean back and give him a smile.

"Better?"

"Much. You know how you could make me even better?"

His lips turn into an evil grin. "Now, that I can definitely do." He holds my face and kisses me tenderly first before he deepens it, turning it lustful. I forget everything but the feeling of his lips on mine. Our tongues dance around, and I pull his lip into my mouth, sucking on it. He moans and pushes me back up against the wall, continuing his assault on my lips.

I love the taste of him. I love how sexy he is. I love that he can take my mind off all the fucked-up things in my life and I love that all it takes is his touch to comfort me. I love that he makes me feel so beautiful and strong. He really is the most wonderful man. We break from our kiss, needing air, and he leans his forehead on mine. *Tell him!*

I look up into his eyes. "I love you, Aerick." He closes his eyes and smiles from ear to ear before he kisses me gently one more time.

CHAPTER NINE

(Sunday August 2nd)

MY TIME HERE seems to be flying by these days. I've made it through another week; my happiness from seeing my brother followed me into the week. I began to write him a letter telling him about Aerick but despite several attempts, haven't been able to finish it. I'm not quite sure what to say, and the nervousness of how he will react is weighing on me. I wouldn't put it past him to fly back out here and cause trouble. Maybe talking to him through Skype would be a better idea. I'd have to work really hard for the week to get the privilege. Last week, I missed it by one as Steven and Tara ranked in the top two.

Tara has started hanging out with us more and I've noticed her and Jeff sharing some glances. It would be really great for him if he finds someone he likes. So, naturally I've encouraged her hanging with us whenever possible. The more she hangs out with us the more I like her. There is a significant difference in her, now that she isn't hanging out with Leena all the time. Leena, on the other hand, just gets on my nerves more and more. Her and Joseph seem to have forgotten the whole Jeff thing and they hang on each other like two horny monkeys. It is quite irritating, especially as I am becoming sexually frustrated.

Aerick and I haven't been able to have more than a kissing session since our lunch at The Cottage. He has been working out quite a bit more this week, probably feeling the tension as well. Our little make out sessions the last few days have gotten extremely intense and he seems to really need a release. We were ready to just go at it behind the cabins yesterday as he had me pinned to the wall with my legs wrapped around him, but he was interrupted by a text from Luther. The groan that escaped his mouth was nothing less than complete devastation. I couldn't hold in my laughter, which earned me an evil look and a hard smack on my ass as I walked away, so he could calm himself before going to see Luther.

Luther reveals today's rankings and I'm in third yet again. *Damn.* I really need to stop day-dreaming during class. Aerick does the ranking. Why can't he just fix them so I'm in the top? I really don't want to cheat or get anything that I didn't earn, but I'm starting to get desperate with need.

As we fall into our morning laps, I decide to sprint the entire way, earning me a pool of stares from everyone; but I need to work out all this pent-up frustration. I push as hard as I can through our workout and by the time we are done, sweat is dripping down every part of me, and my irritations find a slight reprieve. We are dismissed, and I absently inform Jeff, who did make the top two, that I'm going to take a quick shower. Aerick's eyes shoot toward me, drawing me into his lustful gaze. What I wouldn't give to be able to have him join me – and instantly all my frustration is back. *That didn't last as long!* Aerick looks down and bites his lip with a heavy sigh. All I can do is shake my head and head off to take my shower.

Jeff, Patrick and I go to breakfast as I try not to think about having to see Liz again first thing this morning. I really wish Aerick would schedule my sessions at the end of the day so it isn't totally ruined by her. I sink into my seat with a breakfast burrito and some fruit. Aerick isn't here yet but I'm guessing he needed a quick cold shower himself. I sit and mope, eating slowly as Patrick and Royce talk about how football pre-season starts today with the 'hall of fame' game. Normally I'd be excited, but the lack of Aerick's presence has put a damper on my mood. Halfway through breakfast he finally joins us, and I attempt to hide the smile as I take in his wet hair.

My joy is cut short when Liz comes in a second later with two lattes and sits next to Aerick. "Here. I figured you could use some good coffee." She sets his coffee in front of him and slides her hand down to his leg. Aerick's body stiffens and he removes her hand quickly.

"Yeah, thanks. I will bring you the files in a few minutes, I just need to eat real quick." He sounds completely off, but not in the way I expected. He almost sounds shocked, and considering she did this last week, I'm not sure how it would be shocking.

"Okay, see you real soon." *Can she possibly irritate me any more?* Liz gets up and leaves.

"She really needs to fucking quit that shit," Aerick says quietly and I don't know if he is saying it for my benefit or his. He shivers and looks like he is trying to shake off her touch as he squirms in his seat. Paulo raises an eyebrow and Aerick just shakes his head. I want to ask him what the hell that's all about, but it will have to wait until later.

I finish up my food before Aerick, which is new, but I give him a sweet smile and follow Jeff out with a 'see you later' to everyone, but mostly for Aerick's benefit. I think, maybe if we can't both have fun later, maybe it will be possible to help him out in another way, since he did it for me earlier this week.

I head to my eight-thirty session with Liz and try to mask the displeasure on my face. As I reach for the door, it's already half open.

"Come on, Aerick, I felt your pants get tight when my hand touched your leg." I freeze. *What the fuck!* "I know you want me, and it's obvious this new thing you have isn't taking care of you very well." My blood boils with anger and irritation.

"Liz, we are not having this conversation." Aerick's voice is a little rough. *Does he want her still? Is she right?* Why would his pants tighten unless he was turned on by her touch? Explains the look Paulo gave him: he knew by Aerick's reaction.

"Aerick, baby. You know I can take care of you in all kinds of ways. Come out with me tonight, and I'll make you feel better."

I'm done listening to this shit, but this time I am not running. I open the door the rest of the way, loudly, and to my relief, he isn't standing next to her. He is leaning on the wall while she is against the desk giving him googly eyes.

His eyes shoot to mine and I don't bother to hide my anger. He closes his eyes and breathes in deeply, looking pissed as well. "I got to go Liz, and that is a no to your request." He leaves without another word or even another look to me. It pisses me off more and I suddenly feel a bit insecure.

Why doesn't he tell her to back the fuck off? I know he did once, but she obviously isn't getting the picture. Unless, maybe he does want her still, and he just doesn't want me to know about it. I move to sit down with a plop on the couch, not wanting to get in trouble for leaving.

Liz sits down with a sly smile on her face. "He sure is a wild one. I don't think any woman will be able to tame him. Even I have a hard time." I do not look up at her, and it is taking every last drop of strength for me to stay in my seat right now. This bitch is really pushing me to my limit here.

I take a deep breath to calm myself before speaking. "Maybe he just doesn't like you as much as you think. He doesn't seem to return your gestures much," I say with a fake smile on my face.

She chuckles. "Oh, trust me, that is just the facade he puts on when others are around. He is completely different when people aren't around." My fingers twitch, wanting to smack that smile off her face. "Don't worry, hon. It's not just you. He's never been able to stick with just one girl. His needs are just far too great." *She knows.*

She bites her lip and I am on my feet shaking my head. "Get a life, you dumb bitch!"

She laughs, "Oh honey. I am perfectly happy being his fuck buddy. I can satisfy his needs like no other. That's why he keeps coming back for more." *Whatever!*

Fighting everything in me, I shake my head and turn to leave. Staying her will only result in me being in jail within the hour. I head outside and Aerick is standing against the wall. He looks alarmed when he sees me and comes over quickly.

"Babe. What just happened?" He keeps his voice low.

The anger in me right now is enough to rival the depths of hell. I need to be alone. I'm pissed at him for being turned on by her and I'm pissed at her for trying to fuck my boyfriend. This is all just too much.

"Why don't you go ask your little *girlfriend* in there?"

His brows pull together. "I am looking at my fucking girlfriend and I want to know what the hell is going on."

"Well, apparently she knows it's me and is hell-bent on fucking you anyway. Since your body seems to want her so much, maybe you should go grant her request."

He visibly vibrates with anger as he struggles to keep his

voice low, "It's not what you're fucking thinking. I just got done taking a shower thinking about you naked, the only thing my body was reacting to was my need to fuck you right then."

Looking into the depths of his eyes, he's clearly telling the truth. We are so close right now without touching, it is driving me completely insane.

I move to grab his arm. "Don't," he says sternly, to keep me from making the mistake of others seeing us. "Go through the back door of the other classroom, now." My eyebrows raise in confusion. "Just go!"

With an irritated huff, I turn on my heels. I'm still pissed, but do what he says. Around the back of the building, I quietly slip into the other classroom through the back door. *What now?* I shake my head and lean up against the counter at the back.

"What the hell are you trying to pull?" Aerick's voice almost yells from the next room over.

"Come on, Aerick. I know you're fucking her. She can't keep it off her face. There is no way that little thing could possibly know how to satisfy your crazy needs." That bitch has some nerve.

"And what – you think you can?"

"I don't think Aerick, I know! I have seen it before and you will end up running to me when she doesn't satisfy your obsessive need for sex. I mean, look at you, how long has it been? A week? Two? You are already pulling out your hair in need. Let me fix that for you." My chest is screaming for me to breathe but I can't.

"Keep your fucking hands off me, Liz. You don't know me at

171

all. You're merely a toy for me to play with. Someone I can fuck and leave whenever I want, but I don't need you. I've found someone amazing that satisfies more than my hunger for sex. She reaches me on a level higher than I ever knew was possible. It makes the wait for her even more exciting and I have no intentions of being with anyone other than her. She loves me in every way possible and that is something you and I will never have. In fact, as of right now, you and I have nothing. I don't want to be with you, I don't want your friendship, and I'd be happy if I never had to see you again."

Her voice gets quiet and sad. "Aerick, you don't mean that. You need me."

His heavy boots move toward the front door. "That's where you're wrong Liz. I only need her, and you better keep your mouth shut or everyone will find out about all your fucked-up secrets." He slams the door shut as he walks out, and Liz lets out a muffled scream. *Serves her right.*

A second later, he walks in the front door of the room I'm in and closes the door, locking it behind him. He walks up to me quietly, completely focused on me, trying to reel in his anger from his conversation with Liz. "You get it. I only want you." His lips are on me hard with desperation in them and hearing his confession to Liz completely dissolved my anger, replacing it with need for him. He deepens our kiss quickly, making his intentions clear.

"The cameras," I whisper to him.

"They're off," he says quickly on my lips, almost coming out as a growl. His lips move to my neck as he presses himself against me. I can feel his need which is mirrored by my own. "You are mine and I want you right now." It isn't really a question but it's as if he is asking for permission.

"Then take me." He moans on my neck and frantically undoes my pants as I undo his.

He pulls them down quickly and I barely have enough time to kick off my boots before he's pulling my legs out of my pants. I look down at him and he stops suddenly. He gives me that smile as he bites his lip; he quickly throws my leg over his shoulder and attacks my nub with his expert tongue.

I throw my head back at the unexpected assault and bite my lip hard to hold in my moan. His tongue is relentless and in no time I'm on the edge. He slides two fingers into me quickly and his moan of pleasure at my wetness pushes me over the edge. My hands pull at his hair, trying to contain my sounds and it only causes him to moan again, sending more shock waves through me.

He stands, quickly picking me up and setting me on the counter I was leaning against. I've not fully come down from my high yet. "And I'm yours, only yours," he says roughly as he slams into me hard.

I let out a quiet moan as the smile spreads across his face and he starts to move in and out of me, fast and hard. Not having fully recovered from the first orgasm, the second one already threatens to rip through me. His bruising grip tightens as he slams deeper and deeper into me. All thoughts elude me other than how good he feels in me. So hard, so big, pushing me higher than I had ever thought possible.

"Look at me," he says, almost feral. My lids flutter open to look into his eyes as I begin to tighten around him.

"I. Am. Yours. Body. Heart. And. Soul." I can no longer contain it as he slams into me between each word, pushing me over the edge again. My hands fly up to my mouth to hold in my moans, but he catches my hands. "Let her hear."

He slams into me again, extending my pleasure, causing me to moan his name loudly. One last thrust and he follows over the edge as he buries his face in my neck, trying to quiet his own moans.

I look up and Liz is standing with the door between the rooms open just enough for me to see her. I can't help the smile that spreads across my face as he rides out his orgasm. "You are the fucking best, ever," he tells me, out of breath, still twitching inside me, and kisses me hard. The front door of the other classroom slam shut, and I know that our issue has now been resolved.

He lets out a single chuckle. "I don't think she will be a problem anymore," he says, almost proud.

I smile on his lips. "Me neither." He pulls out of me, sending welcome aftershocks up my body, and I hum in appreciation.

"Like it rough, do you?" he says with a smile on his face as he removes his condom. I'm not sure when he put that on, but I am grateful he did.

"With all my pent-up sexual frustration, I think it was a necessity," I tell him honestly.

"Glad were on the same page." He laughs, giving me a chastising kiss. "Hurry up and dress, she has another session in a few minutes.

"So, what about the cameras?" I ask him curiously as I put my pants back on.

"The cameras in both classrooms go off automatically from eight-thirty to eleven-thirty and again from one-thirty to four-thirty. Maybe we can sneak in here again sometime. It's exciting, trying not to get caught." That evil smile drives me nuts.

I bite my lip, completely turned on again, and he grabs me tight, lifting me on the counter again so we are eye to eye. "Stop biting your lip. I've not had my fill of you yet, but we are out of time.

I wrap my legs around his waist, keeping him tight to me and draping my arms around his neck. "Well, maybe you should have put me in the top two so we could have lunch together again."

He kisses me. "As much as I would love that, I'm no longer doing the rankings, Brand is." I look at him strangely. "If we're ever outed, I don't want them to say I was being unfair because you're my girlfriend. This way, I have no control over that. I told Luther I have too much other crap to do and it was a waste of my time. He agreed."

He seems to think of everything. "Well, that's smart. Looks

like I just need to work harder to get into the top."

"Please do. So I can reward a job well done."

Ugh, I am aching again. I close my eyes and push my pelvis toward him. "What's the matter? Didn't get enough of me?" His voice is incredibly low and sexy.

I repeat my actions. "You better find a way we can be alone again, and soon. I don't know if I can wait another week."

A smile spreads across his face. "I'll see what I can do." He gives me a quick kiss and lets me down. "See you later." He winks at me and goes out the front door. Damn, that man is going to be the death of me. I hear the door in the other room and hurry out the back before anything else can happen.

As we sit down for lunch, everyone seems to be in a good mood. Liz is nowhere in sight and I'm ecstatic. The pizza we are eating is mouthwatering and the guys are back on the football subject, arguing over who is going to the Superbowl this year.

"Guys, hate to burst your bubble but Seattle is going back again," Aerick chimes in, surprising me a little.

"Not going to happen, dude," Huck counters. "They totally screwed the Superbowl last year."

Aerick shakes his head, "It was one bad call, which could have led them to victory. I wouldn't call that screwed up. Now, if they had been blown out of the water like they did to Denver, I may have something else to say. Granted, they lost last year, it was one of the most interesting games ever."

Jeff laughs, "Keep telling yourself that."

"I am telling you – they're going all the way. I don't have to tell myself anything. Seriously, who do you want to win? The Bears?"

I laugh at his dig at the Chicago team. I love to watch football, but I don't have a favorite team, and have no loyalty to the home team. Aerick evidently loves the Seahawks.

Paulo sits down, giving Aerick an odd stare. "Well, don't you look like you're in a way better mood. Able to work off some of your frustrations?" He laughs and Aerick almost chokes on his food. I look down, trying to hide my face. I feel Aerick kick Paulo under the table; he just laughs. "Anyway, what's up with Liz? I just went to grab her morning session reports and she bit my head off. That one is crazy, I'm telling you."

Serves her right, the little hoe. "As far as I am concerned, that is your job from now on," Aerick says gruffly.

Paulo looks up at him. "What? Why can't you do it?"

"Because I outrank you. Besides, you're right. She's crazy and I don't want to deal with her anymore."

Paulo gets a frustrated look. "Pulling that card, huh? Whatever, man, but if she starts hitting on me again, you're going to make Trent or Brand do it." Aerick shrugs his shoulders; obviously he doesn't care, as long as it isn't him.

"You up for drinks tonight at The Brick?"

Aerick smirks and gives him a nod. He really does seem to be in a much better mood and I'm happy knowing it had something to do with me.

Royce brings my attention back to him as he asks who is up for some flag football. Everyone at our table agrees, including Aerick and Paulo. It's nice to just have some plain old fun sometimes. We all finish up our food and go out to play.

Brayden, Trent and Jake all join us. Unfortunately for Brand, he is on Dorm duty. Having some of the older guys just makes it more fun. Aerick's good mood seems to be contagious, because everyone seems happier, although he was not pleased about us ending up on separate teams. Me on the other hand, I found it to be way more exciting, since I'm quicker than he is.

By my second touchdown on a breakaway catch, I'm beat. Between pushing myself hard this morning and Aerick's rough nature earlier, my legs are killing me. "I'm out, I need some rest."

There is a series of whines, "Come on you pansy-ass, you can't quit. It'll make uneven teams."

I look at Brayden and laugh. That is the most ridiculous insult I have ever heard. "Not my problem, boys." I go over to the sideline where no one else is and lie on the grass, looking at the sky.

"I'll play." Steven stands from talking to Karen on the sidelines. "Let me run and change real quick." He turns and goes off into the dorm.

"I'll sit out for a minute until he gets back," Aerick says coming over to sit by me, but not too close. He rests his arms on his knees as he watches the guys resume the game.

"Are your extracurricular activities wearing you out?" he says quietly, a sly grin on his face. He's having one of his moments. Looking so young and relaxed.

"Yes, apparently my boyfriend likes it rough, and it was a little taxing on my delicate self."

He laughs. "I sure didn't hear any complaining; if anything, it was quite the opposite." He turns his head slightly so he can see me.

"Oh, I was in no way complaining, and would love to repeat our encounter in the near future."

"Good, because when I can finally get you alone for a decent amount of time, I would like to show you the other things I really like." He's doing that sexy, hot voice again, causing my ache to resurface.

I raise my eyebrow at him. "So, I take it you like a lot of different positions." I try joking with him, but his face gets serious and then he pulls his lower lip into his mouth, biting away the threatening grin.

"Oh baby, I have a position for everyday of the year and I would gladly show you every one of them." *Fuck!* My heart stops at his words and the look on his face.

Steven comes back out to the field and Aerick jumps up. "Something to look forward too." He winks at me as he walks away with a laugh. Argh! I finally let out my breath. How does this man turn me on so much? I cross my legs, trying to get rid of the ache, but it does no good and sitting here watching him doesn't help.

To make things worse, he comes over to the side a few minutes later, removing his shirt so I can see all the deliciousness of his upper body. He looks me in the eye and licks his lips before dropping his shirt to the ground and going back to the game. Yes, we need some quiet time, and really soon!

✳ ✳ ✳ ✳

The lights go out and my body is a pile of mush. After a little while of watching the guys, I joined back in the game again, needing to burn off the frustration between my legs that Aerick had caused. I managed to score another touchdown by slipping past Aerick, which absolutely thrilled me. We finished our game by dinner and then I was able to get my homework done, but not before our evening workout kicked my butt. I've pushed my body way too hard today and this was supposed to be our easy, relaxed day.

At least I got my work done. I really need to hit the top two this next week. I want some alone time with Aerick and he told me if I can get into the top two, he could plan something out for our lunch – whatever that meant. My mind is still buzzing, worried about how me walking out on Liz is going to work out for me this week; especially with Aerick not in charge of rankings. I'm not sure what she said about our session.

She left right after her last session without a word to Aerick or I, but something tells me this is not over. She paused coming out of the classroom at the end of the day and stared at Aerick for a minute before she headed to Luther's office. I don't look forward to having to sit down with her next week. She obviously liked Aerick a hell of a lot more than she ever let on and it seems she isn't going to just let this slide. I hope his threat to her works, and at the same time, I'm a bit curious as to what secrets he was referring to.

Aerick seems to not think much of it, but then again, he is a guy. He doesn't understand the lengths some girls go to when they get hooked on guy. They can get downright scary. I pray my feelings are wrong but in the back of my mind, I know we have not heard the last from her.

"Nadi," I hear someone whisper. "Nadi, wake up." I open my eyes, alarmed at Paulo's whispered tone.

"What's wrong?" My stomach drops. Paulo puts his finger to his lips to tell me to be quiet.

"I need you to come with me and quickly." Fear hits me but before I can say anything, he grabs my hoodie off my chair, turns, debating something for a moment, then grabs my hand, pulling me up off my bed. He pauses for a moment not letting go and looks down to me, probably to see if my normal reaction to swing is going to happen. When he's sure I'm going to, he tightens his grip as he pulls me out the door. I let him drag me along, unsure if this is real or just a dream.

CHAPTER TEN

(Monday August 3rd)

Aerick POV

"GET THE FUCK off me, Brand!"

Brand and Trent won't let me up. Stupid idiots have been holding me down on this bed in the infirmary and I've had enough. I don't need their fucking help. I'm going back there to deal with this shit. *Stupid fucking cowards.*

"Damn it, Aerick, calm the fuck down!" Trent yells at me as my arms struggle out of Brand's grip, allowing me to get off the bed again.

"I'm going to deal with those little punk asses, now let me fucking go!"

"You're beyond drunk, Aerick. Just wait until you sleep this off. Let Terrie help you." Brand pushes me back on the bed again as he and Trent each grab an arm to hold me down.

"If you don't let me go right fucking now, I'm going to whoop the shit out of both..."

"What the hell is going on?!"

Her voice stops my struggle. *What the fuck is she doing here?* She is in her pajama shorts, a hoodie, no shoes, and her hair in a messy bun. She's so beautiful, even all mussed up like this. She doesn't need to see me pissed off like this.

Fucking Paulo! I'm going to kill him. "Take her back to the fucking dorm," I order, trying to get up again.

Her hurt eyes meet mine, then fall down to my torn, bloodied shirt. Her expression changes to fear and worry. *Oh baby, don't. I am okay.* I stop struggling with Brand and Trent, not wanting her to freak out more.

"What is she doing here?" Brand questions Paulo and my eyes are glued to the expression on her face. I'm the cause of the look on her face and the feeling deep inside my stomach is sickening.

"She has an odd way of making him calm down. You guys can go now," Paulo says, completely serious, and Brand looks at him crazy.

Terrie comes in with a handful of supplies. "Brand, Trent, you guys need to get back to the dorm before Luther finds out no one's in there. Thanks for your help," she says, dismissing them.

I shake my arms out of their hold and push myself back on the bed further, looking down so I don't have to look into her sad gaze. Brand and Trent go to leave but Brand stops, giving her one last look, and I swear if he doesn't stop looking at her I'm going to kick his ass too.

"You don't have to do this. You shouldn't have to deal with him while he's drunk like this. It's not your problem," he says to her, but she doesn't take her eyes off me.

"I can handle myself Brand. Go," she says sternly. He nods at her, whispering 'good luck.'

Fucking prick, stay away from my girl! I'll show him his place, damn asshole. I jump up and Paulo steps in front of me. "Come on, man, you need to calm down and let Terrie look at you." I push him back, glaring at him so he can see I'm serious.

"I said leave me the fuck alone." *Am I speaking gibberish or something?*

As soon as Trent and Brand close the door, she is in front of me and her hand is on my face. "Stop," she says, quietly but firmly, and I freeze. My hooded eyes fall to look into hers. There is so much love there, it almost hurts to look into her deep green orbs. *How can she love me so much?* I'm no one, a failure who isn't worthy of her love, a broken man that could never be the person she deserves.

"You need to let Terrie look at you," she says calmly, her hand still on my face.

I look away, unable to stand her loving gaze any longer. "I'm fine and I don't need any help."

"Hey. You are not fine, and if you don't let Terrie look at you, I am going straight to get Luther to take you to the hospital. You hear me?" Her voice is so stern, demanding, almost mad.

She is so strong. I don't deserve her. "Lie down, please," she pleads with me, in a softer tone, and there is no way to tell that beautiful face 'no'.

My eyes squeeze shut in frustration, before I fall back on the bed like a brick. I cover my face with my arm, peeking at her from beneath it. She sighs in relief as she sits at the end of the bed watching Terrie. I bend one of my legs up so she has a little more room and she places her hand on my outstretched thigh. *I fucking love her touch.* My body relaxes under her hand.

"Now, does someone want to tell me what the hell is going on?" she says, still quiet, but demanding. She's looking at Paulo, and I laugh at her tenacity as I lean back and close my eyes. The infirmary lights are too bright and I'm starting to get a headache.

My eyes fling open when I hear fabric being cut. "Hey, I like this shirt. What the hell?" Terrie shakes her head and Nadalynn looks at me crazy.

"Aerick, your shirt is ruined. Have you not seen it yourself?" she says, as if I am crazy. Looking down, there are several rips in it already, along with a slash right across my chest and a whole lot of blood. I breathe deeply as the room spins a bit and I close my eyes again to calm myself.

Terrie peels back my shirt and Nadalynn takes a sharp breath. It must be worse than it feels, although there is an ache starting to set in. Pushing it aside, I try to focus on her hand that is still on me. I flinch, pulling away slightly, as I feel a cold stinging on my chest.

"Aerick, hold still. I don't think you are going to need stitches, but I am definitely going to have to clean it, bottles leave germs and glass." I groan as she wipes the long cut.

"What the hell do you mean 'bottle'? Aerick, what the hell happened? I am serious, I want a fucking explanation now." She gets louder, no longer able to container her anger. She's mad at me. *Good job, Aerick.*

I don't like it when she's mad at me. Grabbing her hand from my thigh, I hold it tightly as Terrie cleans the wound. She squeezes my hand back, but I still refuse to open my eyes and be forced to see her so upset.

She breathes in deeply as her patience wears thin. "Paulo, you have five seconds to start talking before I beat it out of you."

"Okay, okay. But for the record, you would not be able to kick my ass. The last time was a fluke." He begins to tell her what happened as I replay the last few hours in my head.

Flashback

"Just for a little while. I don't want to be exhausted tomorrow," I tell Paulo as we walk into The Brick Tavern.

It's much bigger than it looks from the outside. The old television show 'Northern Exposure' was filmed here back in the early nineties. It's probably the most popular bar in the area, and the one all the tourists visit. We head over to grab some drinks and then to the back where the pool tables are. I look down at the other room off to one side that houses the stage and dance floor. The DJ's music is loud and I'm surprised that it's this full tonight, even though there's no live band.

Paulo calls next game to Eddie and Sean, who are playing two guys I've never met. I greet them, and the two guys introduce themselves as Ryan and James. "So Aerick, you got a new girl, huh?" Sean says to me with a grin. I nod my head, not really wanting to talk about her with him. "So I was right about her being a feisty one?" I look at him crazy. *What the fuck?*

"Oh, come on dude. The look you had on your face when you came out of the bathroom. Either she fucked you or she gave you head." I roll my eyes and shake my head. These guys need to find their own excitement.

I look at him. "What me and my girl do is none of your business, and I have no plans of telling you what we did or didn't do in there."

He takes a drink of his beer. "Whatever, you don't have to say anything. How the hell do you get all the freaks?"

"Man, she isn't a freak."

He laughs at me. "Serious, dude? You guys fucked around in a restaurant bathroom. Pretty sure that qualifies as a freak. Bet she's fun in bed, too!" I punch him in the arm a little harder than necessary.

"We're done talking about her," I tell him, letting all my irritation out.

"Okay, okay." He turns to play his shot.

Is she a freak? I mean, we fucked outside at the top of The Lookout, down at the waterfall, and now on a counter in the classroom. She definitely doesn't mind outdoors. Okay, maybe she is a bit of a freak, and boy would I love to explore what she would do if I could get her in a bed. *Shit. Stop thinking about this.* I have to calm down before my thoughts show in my fucking pants.

I sit down at the tall table and drink my rum and coke. After the crazy day today, I need something strong. Paulo agreed to take it easy so he can drive, but only if I spill about what happened today. His excitement over my sex life is just as ridiculous as the rest of these idiots, though I'm slightly more inclined to share some of it with him over the others. I've managed to give very little detail about Nadalynn and I, but he keeps hounding me to give him 'the details'. Especially after I told him she went down on me in the bathroom. Fuck, that was hot, and completely unexpected. I would've never guessed that it was the first time she'd done that, and I didn't even have to ask. I'm hopeful that she is going to be willing to try other things; there is so much more we could do.

Paulo smacks my shoulder and I adjust my pants as he sits next to me. "Man, you really got to either stop thinking about her or tell me why you carry around a permanent hard-on all the time these days. She must be doing something right."

I laugh at the thought. "Shit man, she does just about everything right." *She really does.* She's strong, smart, and talented in more ways than one.

"That's what I'm talking about, but please start by telling me what the hell Liz's problem is."

"Dude, that could take a fucking lifetime." I raise my glass to the waitress to get another one and she nods at me.

He laughs. "Okay. How about just telling me what happened today?"

I don't normally mind discussing my sexual encounters with him, but I don't normally do the personal shit. This is the first time those two areas have ever crossed. Anything to do with Nadi is very personal. But if I have to tell someone, it might as well be him. With a shake of my head, I give in. "She figured out that I'm with Nadi. Apparently, she didn't like that I no longer want her as a fuck-buddy."

He chuckles. "That explains a lot. And the hard-on you were trying to hide from your girl?"

"Shit, I hadn't gotten any in two weeks and I just got done taking a cold shower. Then Liz grabs me inches from my dick. What the hell do you expect? Of course, Liz had to go and throw it in Nadi's face and starts talking all sorts of bullshit. Nadi got pissed off at me because of Liz's eccentric behavior again. I was done with Liz and her fucking games. I needed to prove my point to Nadalynn so I had her go into the extra classroom so she could hear me tell off Liz, and that I'm done with her completely." I pause to take a drink.

"And?" Paulo prompts. *Shit. Here goes nothing.*

"And then I went back next door and fucked her on the counter, ensuring Liz heard it. It got rid of Liz for good, and I fucked the shit out of my girl, which I had been dying to do for

189

two weeks – two birds, one stone." I shrug my shoulders but just thinking about it is making me hard again. *Fuck, what am I – fourteen again?*

"You're a shit-face liar. She didn't go along with that."

A big grin appears on my face as I down the rest of my drink. "Oh, yes she did, right after I got my dessert."

He spits out his beer. "Dude, you're fucking serious?"

Crystal brings my rum and coke and I drop some money on the table. Let him try to beat that. "For the record, I will kill you if she finds out I told you."

He takes a drink of his beer. "I swear you guys screw in the craziest places."

Yes, we do, but that is part of the fun. I guess she is a freak, but I'm not complaining. I look at him with a smirk on my face. "We really don't have much of a choice, but in all honestly it's fucking hot."

"Did Liz see you guys?"

I don't fucking know! I was too busy enjoying my girl tightening around me as she moaned my name. "I heard the door of her room slam shut, so I'm pretty certain she did. Besides, Nadi is pretty loud when I don't keep her quiet. It would be pretty hard for her not to know what was going on even if she didn't see." Paulo shakes his head in exasperation, but then his face falls.

"Speak of the devil." I follow his eyes and see Liz walking in with two of the local guys. *Great.*

"Oh God. Do me a favor and keep her away from me tonight."

I'm not in the mood to deal with her level of crazy. *Why the hell didn't she go home?* I find Crystal's eyes again and let her know I need another one, as I down the one in my hand. The guys finish their game and Paulo and I get up to play Sean and Eddie. "I break," Sean says.

By our third game I've had several more drinks. Thankfully Liz has kept her distance despite the dirty looks she keeps throwing my way. By the way she is hanging on that guy, it's clear she is trying to make me jealous. Yeah-fucking-right. There's no reason to be, nor would I be even if I wasn't with Nadi. Liz is the biggest sex freak I've ever met. Once she told me that she had an orgy with seven other people. That's pushing beyond even my boundaries. I'm not one to judge, considering her and I have had a few threesomes, but her need for sex is almost unattractive. *Almost.* Her willingness to do some of the more creative things is the only reason I keep messing around with her. She was just a distraction. Now that I have my beautiful little princess, she's all I need.

I'm not quite sure how many drinks I've had, but things are getting a little blurry. It's been a long time since I drank so heavily. Crystal comes over to me but brings me a Corona this time. I give her a strange look. "Come on, Aerick. Time to slow down a bit, sweetie." I roll my eyes at her. *Fine!* I pull out a five-dollar bill, tossing it on her tray with a smirk.

"We've got next." I turn around and see Liz's two little pony boys. *Great.* One of which is hanging all over Liz, who is in a tiny skirt and skimpy tank top. Man, she can be such a slut sometimes; but then again, who am I to judge?

"It's cool, we gotta bounce. I'm on morning shift tomorrow," Eddie tells them.

Sean comes over to shake my hand. "Take care of your sweet little thing, bro."

I chuckle at him and notice Liz giving him a dirty look as she turns, walking back to the bar. "I fully intend to." They head out as Paulo racks a new game.

I break, sinking in a stripe. I'm obviously not that drunk, as I seem to be playing fine.

"You guys work with Liz, huh?" One of the guys asks casually.

Paulo looks at me before answering, "Yeah."

Liz makes her way over back over to us with drinks for her two little friends. "Hey Paulo, Aerick, can I get you guys anything?"

"We're fine," I quickly cut her off. I came here to relax, not deal with her psychotic ass.

"Clearly," she says, all whiny. She really should stop; she looks like a child doing that.

"That's okay, sweetness. You just sit your cute little butt over there and watch us win this game," her friend says as he kisses her sloppily. I have to look away, it's disgusting. That kid has no game.

"So, what do you guys do?" The other kid asks.

"We're instructors. We teach delinquents how to behave and function in society," Paulo says, like it's a normal job.

"Oh yeah, we all know what Aerick is teaching his students these days. I wasn't aware there was a sex ed class," Liz smirks.

I glare at her. *She just doesn't give up, does she?* Paulo draws my gaze, shaking his head. She's not worth it.

"Basically, we get to work out all the time and get paid to do it. Can't beat a job like ours," I say simply.

"Plus, we get to have a little fun in the process," Paulo adds.

Liz laughs, "Seems like Aerick is adding in all kinds of personal fun, this time around."

My anger is rising at her petty comments. "Liz, fucking quit it already. You don't need to be such a fucking whiny bitch. It really doesn't suit you." Hopefully she will shut up now.

"Hey, dude. You don't need to be so rude to her." The guy she has been hanging on to stands up a little straighter.

Paulo immediately positions himself between us. "Hey man, if you want fuck her, go ahead. It's an easy score, but I suggest you back off him now."

Liz grabs the kid's arm. "What the hell, Paulo? I'm not walking on egg shells because Aerick is getting all bent out of shape over his little fucking toy."

"Liz, you need to shut your fucking mouth about her, right now," I warn her; my patience for her has ran out.

"What's the matter, Aerick? You know it's never going to work, anyway."

"You're just jealous, you little hoe, that she satisfies me in ways you never could."

The guy takes another step forward. "I said you need to fucking leave her alone."

I don't need this little shit's attitude either. "Dude, I can't help that your little date over there is too hung up on my shit. Don't be surprised if she calls out my name when you're fucking her later," I laugh; he lunges at me but Paulo catches him and pushes him back.

"Bad idea," Paulo tells him.

"Fuck you, I ain't afraid of some muscle-bound asshole that has no respect for women."

My chest rumbles hard. "Oh, I have respect for women, but she is no woman. Hoe, maybe!" Swallowing down the rest of my beer, I move toward the door. "Clearly this idiot is delusional. Let's go, Paulo." We go outside and I stumble a little as we go along the curb. Maybe I'm a little more drunk than I meant to get.

"Shit dude, I left my jacket in there. I'll be right back," Paulo says. I give him a nod and lean against the stop sign.

I look up at the stars, remembering holding my Nadi in my arms while we both enjoyed the sparkling night sky. God, she invades my head almost every minute of every day. *What the hell has she done to me?* I close my eyes and her beautiful green eyes are looking up at me with that megawatt smile on her face.

Oh fuck! I am stumbling forward. I turn around to see who the fuck just pushed me. It's the bigmouth and his friend. "What's the matter, asshole? Can't fight your own battles?" he says to me. His friend is standing behind him, drinking a beer and enjoying the show.

"Trust me, you don't want this. Go back in to the little hoe. Don't worry, she'll give it up to anyone."

He lunges at me and I let him hit me once to get my adrenaline flowing before I push him back on the ground. He jumps back up and hits me in the side. *Damn, this alcohol is making me slow.* He hits me again in the same spot. I focus as the adrenaline starts flowing and he lands another in my other side. *Fuck, this kid actually hits pretty hard!*

I concentrate and let loose on him, punching him in the face. He is down after two hits, but I keep going. *Teach this little fucker to mess with me.* His buddy suddenly tackles me from behind, sending us both flying. I get up quickly and he looks at me as he picks up the bottle he dropped and broke on the ground. *Is this fucking kid for real? This is a scene straight out of a movie!*

He tries to hit me with it and misses. I see Liz coming out of the bar and running over to her friend on the ground. It distracts me just enough that the kid swings and I feel something warm on my chest, pissing me off more.

I kick the bottle out of his hand and land one that connects perfectly with his jaw. He falls back on to the sidewalk and Paulo grabs me before I can go after him. "Aerick, stop. Come on."

I shake him off, pissed off that this fool had the nerve to pull a broken bottle on me. He cut me with a fucking bottle, stupid motherfucker. "Get the hell off me. This asshole wants a fight, I'll give him one. Think I'm going to pussy out because there's two of you? Bring it on." A few other guys coming out of the bar get in my way. I know them, but I can't think of their names, all I know is those two fools over there need a lesson in ass-whooping.

"Aerick, man, enough. They have had enough," one of the guys holding me says, but I'm not ready to quit; they started it, but I'm definitely going to finish it.

"Get him in my car," Paulo tells them as he helps the guys drag me and put me in his car. "Paulo, let me out of this fucking car, I'll show them who the fuck they are messing with. Who do they think they are?" He starts up the car and quickly pulls away before my hand can pull the door release.

"Dude, you need to calm down. We need to get you to a hospital." He is speeding down the highway.

"Don't you dare take me to a hospital, I'm fucking serious. They'll call the cops and I'm not doing that shit. Just let me out here so I can go back to deal with those dumb-asses."

"No way, man. If you won't let me take you to a hospital, I'm calling Terrie and you're going to at least let her look at you." He pulls out his phone and calls her.

"I'm fucking fine. Let me out of this car, Paulo, right fucking now!" He ignores me, mumbling something about Trent and Brand. My adrenaline is still pumping and I just want to go back and finish teaching those kids a fucking lesson. *No one fucks with me, no one!* I will fucking walk back from camp, they can't stop me.

We pull into the camp and Brand and Trent are outside. "Paulo, you asshole! I'm fine and I can deal with this shit myself." I get out of the car, moving toward one of the SUVs.

"No, you can't, you're drunk and not thinking straight. Let's go inside."

"Are you deaf? I don't need to. I'm perfectly fine, now leave me the fuck alone." Brand and Trent grab my arms. "I said get the fuck off me." They are dragging me backward to camp. Twisting and pulling, my arms knock into them, throwing them on the ground, and I almost getting away until Paulo joins in, dragging me into the infirmary.

"Keep him here!" Paulo yells as he takes off, mumbling something to Terrie on his way. *This is crazy, they can't keep me here!*

End Flashback

At least Paulo kept his word, skipping over our conversation about her. Terrie puts a large bandage over jagged cuts that have to be at least six inches long. Now that the alcohol and adrenaline are running out of me, I'm starting to realize how stupid all this was. This is why I don't get really drunk. *Shit.* I never wanted Nadalynn to see me like this. I am ashamed of myself. This is the old Aerick.

"There you go. You need to take good care of that for the next few days," Terrie says and I nod. "Cameras are off in here. Stay as long as you need, I'm going back to bed."

I look up at her. She lays a hand on Paulo's shoulder and they share a look before she walks out.

"You good, man?" Paulo asks.

"I'm good. Sorry about tonight." He shrugs. It isn't the first time I've gotten into a fight and had to have him pull me away. He knows me pretty well. It just took some time for me to calm down and come to my senses.

"I'll be outside if you need me." He leaves, closing the door.

It's only us now. I chance looking up at her and she is staring down at the bloody shirt that is on the bed next to me as she chews the inside of her cheek. She must be thinking she made a mistake being with me. This is my past coming back to bite me in the ass. *I am a fucking monster.* We sit here in silence for several minutes until it's no longer bearable. My body is aching to hear her voice.

"You mad at me?" I ask her.

She finally looks at me. "Mad at you, no." *Really.* "I am more sad and upset that I wasn't there to beat her ass myself."

I shake my head. "It's illogical for you to want to be there, but I'm sorry that I am yet again the reason behind your sadness. I told you that I'm not good for you."

"Aerick, stop. You're drunk. Some guy got on your nerves, you walked away, and they came at you, you fought back. Geez, one tried to cut you open! How the hell is this your fault?" My mind is unable to form a good response to that. "We all have weaknesses, remember. Hello, have you read my file of why I'm here? It's just when I came in and saw you like that, I got...anxious, and I don't like feeling that way. I didn't know how bad you were hurt, and I was worried that you may not be okay."

She gets up and comes to sit next to me at the top of the bed. "Aerick, I don't want to lose you. I don't know what I would do if something happened to you. I love you."

My eyes scrunch closed at her words. This is my sweet, sweet girl. Hearing her say 'I love you' is the best thing in my world. My heart rate picks up and I get that warm fuzzy feeling again. I wish so much that I could love her back the way she deserves, but my mind and heart don't know how. I didn't even realize it was possible to care about someone so much until I met her. My body is begging to hold her.

"Come here." I pull her down to lie with me, draping my arm over her stomach. "I don't want to lose you either. I know I don't deserve you, but I never want to lose you."

"Aerick, don't say that. You deserve someone that will care for you and love you. If anything, I don't deserve you." My arms wrap around her, hugging her tight to me while trying to ignore the pain that shoots across my chest.

Why does she never see herself as the beautiful, loving, smart women she is? "Stay with me babe, please."

I close my eyes, suddenly overcome with exhaustion and I hear her whisper as I fall into a dreamless sleep. "Always."

CHAPTER ELEVEN

(Wednesday August 5th)

"CODE RED. ALL cadets remain in the dorm. Camp is on lock down until further notice. Code red. All cadets remain in the dorm. Camp is on lock down until further notice. "

My entire body startles awake at a screeching robotic message from my alarm clock speaker that is repeating the same massage over and over. "What the hell?!" I whine loudly. *It's too fucking early!* I sit up in bed and look around, confused, as does almost everyone else. The numbers on the alarm clock show it's just after four in the morning; if it were possible, the stupid clock would be in pieces across the room already.

Paulo and Aerick come running through our dorm half-dressed in their pants and boots, both pulling their shirts on as they come to a stop. "They're all here – it's not them. Do not leave this dorm!" Aerick shouts as they run through the door leading outside. *Really?* He says it as if the annoying message playing through all our speakers isn't conveying that already. I'm not sure what's going on, but when Aerick's eyes flashed in relief at the sight of me, it gave me an inkling of what's happening.

"What's going on?" Jeff asks, rubbing his eyes, as the annoying message finally goes quiet, only to be replaced by Patrick's insistent snoring. *How the hell is he still asleep?*

"Well, my best guess is someone got out. Though I'm not sure how that happened, unless they found a way to get the bracelet off. Honestly, the two I really care about are still in bed on either side of me, so I'm going back to sleep." I flop back down on my pillow just as Royce comes in.

"Hey! Is John in here?" There is an echo of no's and our question is answered. "How the hell did he get out?" Royce asks no one in particular. No one answers, but I am sure we are all asking ourselves the same question. *How?*

I've played with my tracker a few times and there's no way to get it off. The first week here, I pulled at it with all my might and it didn't even budge. Jake has been very diligent in making sure it is nice and tight every week. He's had to tighten mine several times as my body has changed.

It's become clear to me over the last few months, John is extremely smart. He doesn't say a whole lot but when he does, you can tell he knows what he's talking about. He mentioned once about getting in trouble for hacking a police server. He's here on an assault charge but my guess is that this was the first time he got in trouble for assault. If someone found a way to get it off, it makes sense that it was him.

Royce comes over and sits at the foot of my bed. *What the hell?* I groan, giving him a hard look, but he ignores me. Sleep is calling my name, but everyone from the other dorm begins trickling in, making themselves comfy in various spots around the room. Royce tells us that Brand and Trent came in and all he heard was cursing from Brand as he took off. It kicks off a cluster of conversations discussing how he might have accomplished it.

* * * *

Two hours later Aerick plods in through our dorm while everyone is still just sitting around talking. He's drenched in sweat, covered in dirt, and has a gash on his forehead near his hairline. "All of you – get your asses dressed and be outside in five minutes." He seems extremely pissed and doesn't even look at me on his way through the room. My curiosity is piqued, but his cold tone is concerning. Everyone is quick to follow his command and it only takes a few minutes for us to be lined up in front of the stage.

Trent and Paulo are the only ones on the stage and they look like they've already had a work out. It's probably a good bet they were all chasing after John. *How would they even know where to look?* The property is huge and there are about fifty different trails. We have only covered some of them, but Aerick told me there are tons more that we'll never see because they rotate which ones are used based on the season. There's no way to know which way he went.

UNSTRUNG

Is there?

There's still see no sign of Brand and it's doubtful Aerick is going to make an appearance. We line up and Paulo gets up on stage. "Obviously this hasn't been a typical start to our day. In the early hours of our morning, John took it upon himself to try to leave without permission, and more important, rudely waking me up from my beauty sleep. Only an idiot would be foolish enough to think we would only rely on your trackers; the trackers just make our jobs easier. Remember this, cadets: we have back up plans for our back up plans. Anything you could possibly think of has already been prepared for. If I have to give this speech again, you will all be sorry. Each of you will run fifteen laps and only then will you be excused for breakfast. If you don't finish by breakfast time, you're shit out of luck for the morning. Trent, track their laps." Trent nods at him, leading us all over to the path, where we do a few stretches and start running. It sucks being out of the loop. I make up my mind to sprint all fifteen laps. If I can beat everyone back, there might be a chance to catch Aerick alone and find out what's going on.

With all my extra running lately, I easily finish my laps way ahead of everyone. Trent looks at me funny when I count off my final lap to him and he dismisses me to the dorm. Inside, all is quiet. Hearing the shower running, I tiptoe into the bathroom and decide to peek into the instructors' dorms. The door is cracked open and I spot Paulo sitting at his desk with his back to me.

"Is there something I can help you with?" Aerick scares the

shit out of me as he comes out of the shower. I'm so wound up I didn't even hear the water turn off. His voice is low, clearly still pissed off. My eyes find the cut on his head and it looks deep. As I begin walking over to him, he grows tense, stopping me in my tracks still several feet away. *Fuck. The cameras!*

"What do you need?" he asks coldly.

"I, uh – just wanted to be sure everything was okay."

He rolls his eyes. "It's fine." He's oddly closed off, completely out of character for him when we are alone. Well, the last few weeks, anyway. My eyes flit back to cut on his head.

"There is nothing you need to know, cadet, so go about your business." *Ouch. What the hell did I do?* He's been under a lot of stress lately and this morning must be pulling him, but it doesn't make his words sting any less. He takes a deep breath, his pissed-off look not breaking, before walking around me into his dorm.

After a few deep breaths to even out my own nerves, I decide on a quick shower before breakfast to clean off the sweat dripping down my back. There's still plenty of time so I won't even have to rush. Yes, a relaxing hot shower sounds perfect right now; it's been a long morning.

Aerick has seemed a bit off since his drunken escapade. After he had fallen asleep, Paulo came in to check on him. He told me that although Aerick has a reputation around town for being a fighter, the fight wasn't his fault this time. He didn't have to try to convince me. My instincts told me when they explained that he had tried to do the right thing, that they were telling me the truth.

It was frightening, walking in and seeing his blood-soaked shirt. My stomach was in my throat at the realization that he was injured. At first, I was pissed at Paulo for not taking him to the hospital, but when Terrie said he was okay, the anger ebbed away and only my concern remained. The police showed up the next day and questioned him. One of the guys had been hospitalized with head injuries and his friend insisted that Aerick had done it unprovoked. Luckily for Aerick, there was another witness that saw the other guy start it. The police merely had to confirm the witness's story.

Luther was furious at Aerick for not telling him before the police showed up. When the police left, he called Aerick into his office and ever since then Aerick has had this edge that seems to have him teetering on some unsaid emotions. The problem is putting my finger on what exactly they are. Today seems to have just amplified it. This man has more mood swings than a menstruating woman.

Our times alone the last few days have been few and far between, but when we have managed, he seems different. Finally getting fed up, I pressed him yesterday to find out what was going on. For a moment, as he looked deep into my eyes, I thought he was going to tell me, but instead his lips found mine and he kissed me breathless, causing me to forget my line of questioning. Clearly, there is something he isn't telling me, but I don't want to push him – he'll tell me when he's ready. I just need to be patient with him.

Jeff, Patrick and I head off to breakfast and after getting our plates, we take a seat in our normal spot. Paulo and Trent join us but Aerick is nowhere in sight. Paulo's mood seems just as sour as Aerick's, but he tends to have a friendlier demeanor, so I take a chance. "Hey Paulo. Is everything okay?" His big brown eyes find mine and I pray he sees the concern that I only allow to show in my eyes.

"It's fine." Argh! *Is that all I am going to get out of them today?* I look around, trying to collect my thoughts, and then back at my food.

"So, what happened to Aerick's head?" Thankfully it comes out sounding like pure curiosity, but when I look back up I can't keep the worry off my face.

Paulo takes a deep breath, the wheels turning behind his eyes before answering. "John took him by surprise and tackled him to the ground. They rolled down a shallow ravine. Aerick is usually much more aware. I don't think I've ever seen someone take him down like that. He put it to an end to it quickly, but he is pretty pissed at himself. He's been distracted lately, and it's affected his performance."

Distracted... as in, me. Shit. This is my fault. He's not concentrating on his job because I'm distracting him. That explains his coldness toward me earlier. My appetite disappears with this revelation and I quietly excuse myself from the table. Paulo's lips tighten into a line and Jeff turns to me, concerned. He offers to join me but I refuse, letting him know I want to be alone.

He nods but the apprehension remains on his face.

Outside, John is running laps while Aerick stands in the center yelling at him that he will be doing this all day. John is sporting a bruise on his cheek and I wonder if Aerick did that to him, or if he got it when he tackled Aerick. Aerick's eyes find mine but the emotion in them is unreadable. After a second, he goes back to barking at John.

I head back to the dorm and grab my iPod before going out to the bonfire pit. Turning on my music, I try to work this shit out in my head. For the first time, I'm thinking Aerick and I should rethink our relationship while I am in here. We have to hide it just to keep him from getting in trouble. Now he is not doing his job effectively because I've become a distraction. *What if John had really hurt him?* He could have had a weapon or something and Aerick might not have come back. I couldn't live with myself if something happened to him because of me.

My chest tightens at that thought. It never really crossed my mind until the other night when he was all bloodied in the infirmary, and now for the second time in three days he has gotten hurt. Maybe we should put our relationship on hold for a few weeks until I'm done and out of here.

It's not something I want to do, and my heart is aching just with the thought, but it wouldn't be fair to just think about me. It would be selfish; this is Aerick's livelihood, after all. *How would he feel toward me if he lost his job because of me?* Maybe he needs to focus on himself for a while. As much as it hurts, it's what is best for him and what happens to him right now is more important than my feelings. I have to do this, for him. *This is what is right.*

* * * *

Aerick has spent the better part of the day making John do push-ups, sit-ups, sprints, and run laps. Honestly, it's amazing John hasn't collapsed by now. He has had Aerick yelling in his face the whole time; dragging him up, pushing him down, going all morning and afternoon, only stopping for him to drink and eat. Aerick even missed his classes and lunch. Somehow he still looks just as pissed as he did this morning.

I slink down into my seat at dinner, trying to figure out how I'm going to tell Aerick we should take a break so he can focus on his work. Something tells me he isn't going to take it very well. Just as Paulo is about to sit down, he gets a text and leaves the dining hall, leaving his tray on the table. I watch out the window as Paulo walks over to the middle of the court yard where it looks like John is laying on the ground. I see him and Aerick both pick him up and carry him toward the infirmary, but he still seems conscious. *Wow, a little harsh isn't it?* He ran him into complete exhaustion.

Paulo comes back a few minutes later, shaking his head as he sits down and begins eating his cooling food. I'm tempted to ask him, but after a second look at him I decide against it. Aerick catches my eye walking past the mess hall. He must be going to the gym, which means he is still upset. I didn't eat much for lunch and haven't eaten any of my dinner but I'm not hungry anyway.

Silently, I get to my feet and put my tray away before heading to the gym, grateful that Jeff doesn't question me.

Aerick's already pounding away at the bags. Heavy thuds with each strike at the bag make it evident he's still pissed – making me more resolved that it's the right thing to do. I put on a pair of gloves and go over to join him. As I position myself next to him, he pauses for the briefest of moments, before resuming his ruthless blows to the bag. My fists begin to move, attempting to find their rhythm on the bag next to him, while I take in deep breaths to get up the courage to do this. It takes several minutes before it's possible to form any words and my chest is tight.

"Aerick, are you okay?" I keep my voice low with the hope that the camera doesn't pick up our conversation. He keeps punching but his eyes close for moment.

"I'm fine. I fucked up and just need to figure this shit out."

That's the final confirmation I need. *I have to do this.* "Aerick, I think we should take a break." My voice comes out barely a whisper and if wasn't for him freezing mid-punch like I'd just paused a video game, I'd have thought he didn't hear me.

"Why would you say that?" he says quietly, but without turning my way.

My chest rises, taking in as deep a breath as I can manage. *Do it!* "I'm not good for you." My staggered breathing is almost unnoticeable but the tightening within me is getting worse. That isn't what I mean to say, but it works just the same.

He turns to me with shock on his face and speaks, anger

dripping from each word. "You're joking, right?"

With a heavy sigh, I stop punching and face him. "Look, we both know your work is suffering and it's because you are distracted."

He huffs. "And you don't think I don't know that. I've heard that shit enough lately? Surely I don't need you throwing it my face, too."

So, he isn't denying it. "It's because of me, and I refuse to be the cause of it."

"What the fuck are you talking about?" His voice is still low, but he is slowly rising with each outburst.

"Look, I care about you, Aerick, and I'm not letting you throw away everything you have for me. It's not worth it. I'm not worth it."

He stands, stunned. Turning around, I start to leave, needing some space between us before I lose control over the tears threatening to spill over. He runs over to me and catches me before I can walk through the door. "Don't I get a fucking say in this?"

There is no way I can look at him. I'll lose all my resolve. "No." I shake his hand off my arm, leaving him there frozen in place. *He didn't deny it.*

Outside, I work hard trying to draw air into my lungs, but it isn't helping. My chest is being crushed from the inside out. My feet sprint toward the fire pit and I collapse on the logs. *I did it – the right thing. This is the right thing!*

I punch the log, but I still have the gloves on – not helping a goddamn thing. I remove them quickly and hit the log hard several times. The pain in my hand is a welcome pull away from the pain in my heart.

I've never felt pain like this in my life. *Breathe.* All the physical pain I have been through and none of it even comes close. *Breathe.* My fist finds the log several more times. Pulling in the air through my nose and out my mouth between each hit, using the pain to get through the horrible pain in my heart.

He didn't come after me. He must know I am right. *I am right, I'm not worth it.* I put in my earbuds and drown my thoughts away.

✳ ✳ ✳ ✳

We are almost through evening PT and I've managed not to cry, but my hand is killing me. I'm having a hard time doing up-downs, and push-ups were nearly impossible. Aerick pushes all of us harder than normal as he shouts out to us from the stage. He's still pissed off and his cold stare keeps finding mine. Everyone probably thinks it is because of John but it's not. My eyes avoid him at all cost, but the few times they find him, the tightening comes back.

"Everyone except Nadi is dismissed," he barks out and everyone leaves, exhausted. *Shit.* Why does he insist on doing this? I stand still, shoving my hands into my pockets, and look at the ground until I feel him right in front of me, his boots coming into view. "What did you do to your hand?" he questions me coldly and I'm suddenly grateful that I subconsciously was trying to hide it from him.

"I'm fine," I say, deciding to give him a bit of his own medicine.

"Nadalynn, you just struggled to do a workout I know you're more than capable of keeping up with. Don't fucking lie to me." He hisses at me.

"It's no longer you concern." My voice is low, trying to fend off his anger. I hate this; I want to look at him so bad but can't.

I hear him huff, "No matter what, I'm your instructor, and it is my concern. Now tell me." *Or what?*

I continue to just stand there until he suddenly yanks on my wrist, pulling my hand out of my pocket. "Ahhh!" I can't help the yelp that escapes my mouth and my teeth clench as pain shoots up my hand.

A sharp in-take of breath comes from his mouth. He examines my hand gently, turning it in his own. It's completely black and blue and my swollen knuckles are all bloody. His breathing picks up. "What the hell is wrong with you?" he whispers. *Everything.*

I don't answer. "Answer me!" he shouts, making me jump at his sudden outrage. I squeeze my eyes shut; he stops and I hear him take in a deep breath.

"Fucking hell. Go see Terrie, now – that's an order." He's furious. He releases my hand, fixing his at his side as I head off for the infirmary before he can say anything else.

I hear him growl quietly to himself and sneak a quick glance back to see him pulling his hair, staring at the ground.

In the infirmary, Terrie is at her desk. She looks up at me as the door opens. "Hey Nadi," she starts to say cheerfully, but her expression falls when she sees my face. The door to the next room is closed. "What's up?" she asks carefully.

"I was ordered to get my hand looked at." I show her my hand.

"Ouch. Come sit."

We go over to sit on the couch. She begins to feel around my hand, making me flinch several times as she applies pressure. "So, what did you hit and why?"

My eyebrows pull together. "How do you know I hit something?" I ask skeptically.

She looks at me sharply. "You don't have any broken bones. It's likely a boxer's fracture. It's what happens when you don't punch with proper form or you punch too hard. So, what was it? Because it sure did a number on your skin."

"The log out at the fire pit."

She gets up and opens a cabinet. "I'm going to need to clean up your hand. Do I get to know why?"

I shake my head. "I don't want to talk about it."

She gives me a long hard look as she comes back over and sits down. "Fine, but if you need someone to talk to, I'm here – okay?" I nod my head and she seems satisfied for now.

She hands me two pills and water. "Ibuprofen. You need to come see me to get some more. I can give them to you every six hours. If it's bothering you after lights out, just ask one of the instructors to come get it for you. I'm going to clean these cuts now. Sorry, but it's going to hurt."

I shrug my shoulders and take the pills, then let her clean my hand. It hurts like a crazy, but I don't care. When she's done, she wraps my hand. "Take it easy with your hand for the next few days. And come see me anytime." I give her one last nod and then go back to the dorm.

Immediately, I go for my sweater and throw it on even though it is still warm out. The last thing I need is for Jeff to see it, but my luck sucks and he walks in from the bathroom just as I'm putting it on, catching a glimpse of my wrapped hand. I turn and go right back outside, not really sure where to go. I instinctively head toward the fire pit, which is becoming my sanctuary. He follows me out and stops me by grabbing my arm as we reach the path.

"What the fuck did you do?" He's pissed too. *Great.*

"Jeff, I'm fine, just need some time to clear my head." He shakes his head, he isn't going to let me off easy like normal.

"Bullshit. This," he grabs my arm and pulls back my sleeve to expose my hand, "is not fine. What the hell happened? You haven't hardly eaten all day, and you've just been sitting out at that fire pit. You wanted alone time, I gave it to you. Now it's time to explain."

"There is nothing to explain. Just let me be." I try to turn and walk away but he pulls me back.

"No, not this time. Nadi, hurting yourself isn't the fucking answer. I am not going to watch you start doing this shit again."

Great. He had to throw that in my face.

It pisses me off and I huff at him. "Says the person who just opened up his veins." That was a really low blow, but right now I just want out of here. I turn and walk away and he just stands there, stunned. That is the second time today I've left a man I care about speechless.

I don't make it far before Jeff's shout fills the air. "What the fuck did you do to her this time?"

I turn around and see that Jeff has approached Aerick, who must be on his way to the gym again, and is getting up in his face. *Shit.*

"Who the hell do you think you are talking to?"

Holy Hell! I can't let this happen. Turning around, I rush back to them.

"I'm talking to the asshole who obviously did something to piss off my best friend to the point she is hurting herself again," Jeff spits out before I can reach them. Aerick body goes rigid and a confused look crosses his face. It's clear this is going to end badly. After a moment he takes a step forward, closing the small space between the two of them.

"I didn't fucking do anything to her. She's the one who flipped out." He pushes Jeff and just as Jeff goes back to push him, I jump in between them, placing a hand on each of their chest.

"Christ! That's enough." Aerick stills under my hand and my heart leaps out of my chest. "Jeff, let this shit be. I'm a grown-ass woman."

He looks at my injured hand on his chest and looks up into my eyes. "Clearly," he says between his clenched teeth. He moves around us and walks back toward the dorm. I look back toward Aerick without looking at his face. Both his hands go to grab mine, still resting over his heart, but I drop it immediately, making him freeze again. I hesitate for a moment then walk toward the field without another word, and again he doesn't follow.

✻ ✻ ✻ ✻

I wake up sweating and out of breath, my skin still crawling. Another nightmare. At least I didn't wake anyone this time. I drag myself up against the headboard, grabbing my legs and pulling them tight to my chest, trying to calm myself down. A noise from the bathroom door draws my attention. Aerick is standing in the doorway. I look back down at my knees. I want nothing more than to have him come sit with me but it's not right. I have to stick with my choice.

He walks over and sits at my feet. "Here." He tries to hand me some pills that I'm fairly certain are Ibuprofen. I shake my head. "Nadalynn, stop being difficult and just take them." He sounds almost sad. The throbbing pain my hand is almost unbearable, so taking a deep breath, I put out my good hand. He sets them in my hand, letting his fingers linger on my palm a second more than is needed, and then gives me a glass of water.

I take the pills and hand him back the glass. I avoid his eyes and try not to move. My body wants to jump into his lap right now but I have to do the right thing. I have to be the stronger person.

He attempts to hold my uninjured hand, but I pull it back. "Aerick, don't. I need to go to bed. Please just let me be." I barely get it out and hate that it sounds like I'm begging him. He takes several deep breaths and then stands, walking back to the door. Tears start pooling in my eyes.

He stops, "I don't know what the hell is going on, but when you're ready to talk, I'm here." He sounds so defeated and the tears begin streaming down my face watching him walk out.

For the first time since making up my mind, I wonder if this is the right thing to do. How can something that is so right, hurt so bad? *No!* I'm strong, and I have to be strong for him. I can't let him throw it all away, not for me. I lie down and silently cry myself to sleep.

CHAPTER TWELVE

(Sunday August 9th)

FUCK! THE HORRID nightmares are back as vivid as ever. My shirt is soaked in sweat and sticking to my clammy skin. Breathing in and out deeply, I attempt to slow my heart rate. They have been coming every night since I broke it off with Aerick. He is back to being cryptic and has gone from moody to downright pissy twenty-four-seven. It's starting to irritate the shit out of me.

He seems to have lost common sense, as he now stares at me all the time, not caring who sees him. The tension between Jeff and him has returned with a vengeance and is suffocating. I've tried to explain to Jeff that this was my choice, but he doesn't seem to believe me. On a good note, Aerick has given me my space, but it isn't stopping Paulo, who has tried to talk to me several times. I blow him off, telling him it is between Aerick and I, and to mind his own business; but he's made it clear he's not happy about it.

UNSTRUNG

The alarms go off and I take a deep breath before getting out of bed and getting ready. Aerick has been projecting his antagonistic attitude ever since Wednesday. Yesterday we had extra PT because someone's bed wasn't made 'properly', so today I make sure we all do it to his standards.

My hand still hurts but it's hard to heal when I don't take it as easy as I should – mostly due to the welcoming pain that it provides. Last night, I unwrapped it to give it a little air and the coloring is still pretty bad. It crossed my mind to leave it unwrapped, but quickly changed my mind when I caught a glimpse of Jeff's pissed-off face. It was the first time he'd seen it since I hurt it. The less he has to see how bad it is, the better off I am. He's back to sticking close to me, but he hasn't hidden the fact that he's pissed with me.

We line up in front of the stage and Luther starts talking. *Blah, blah, blah.* The rankings come up and I'm at the top. Internally I cringe because I was working hard for that, but for a purpose that no longer exists. Luther takes his leave and we start our workout. Irritated as ever, I push myself hard, trying to keep from wincing at the pain in my hand as we go.

My eyes scan the group and find John. He seems to be struggling as well. He spent most of the evening and night in the infirmary on Wednesday, just to have Aerick work him again until he collapsed on Thursday. Though it only took him until lunch to collapse and return to the infirmary; I suppose Aerick wanted to make a point. He finally joined us again on Friday morning, looking completely ragged.

We talked for a while yesterday evening while we were doing our homework. He told me Aerick threatened another two days if he tells us how he got the bracelet off. He also explained how he made it several miles outside of the main camp before they caught up to him. He figured the only way he was getting out was to take down Aerick – probably not his brightest moment. It wasn't very well thought out, and the one punch Aerick made to his face knocked him out. He doesn't remember anything else until they were dragging him back into camp. He has a new bracelet on now, and something tells me no one is trying that again.

We finish our workout without any issues, but my hand is aching so bad I'm debating on whether to go to the infirmary for some ibuprofen. Aerick calls Mike and I up to the front and dismisses everyone else. Jeff hesitates beside me for a moment, protective as ever. "It's okay, Jeff."

He looks from me to Aerick. "Fine, but I will be right inside.' I roll my eyes at him and he walks away as Aerick glares him.

He lets Mike pick first, and he picks the iPod. Several of us have them now, so they have become a common thing around camp. Aerick dismisses him after he tells him to come by later to pick it up. He hands me the list and my eyes immediately fall to the Skype session. *My brother...* Suddenly, I want to talk to him more than anything. Maybe he can help me feel better. Aerick is chewing the inside of his cheek, looking down at my injured hand

"I want to Skype my brother, please," I tell him quietly,

handing back the tablet.

He lets out a sigh. "I'll get it cleared," he says sounding almost disappointed. I turn and leave quickly before he can say anything, and to keep him from seeing the threatening tears that are blurring my vision.

✳ ✳ ✳ ✳

"Nadi, your brother is on a call for you." I look up to see Paulo standing in front of me. My lips tug up in a half-smile as I gather my books off the grass from where I'm working beside Jeff.

"Tell him I said hi," Jeff tells me.

"Me too," Patrick chimes in.

"Sure." I follow Paulo into Ayla's office, which also doubles as the main office.

As we walk in, Aerick is sitting in front of the computer. "Here she is," he says to the monitor before getting up and walking out, his eyes not meeting mine.

"You've got thirty minutes. I'll be back when your time is up," Paulo tells me. I him a tight nod, and he leaves as I move to the desk.

My brother is on the screen with a cheesy grin plastered on his face. "Taking your time, aren't you?" he says, and I force a smile on my face.

"Hey kid. How are you doing?" I ask.

"Same shit, different day. Nothing has really changed much since I saw you, but I hear you have been busy."

My eyebrows pull together. "Really? Where did you hear

that?"

"So, is that what you were avoiding telling me when I was there?" *Aerick did not tell him. Seriously! Why would he do that?*

"Did you talk to Aerick before I came in here?"

He pauses for a second. "I did... and he told me something that I would have much rather heard from you."

I give him an apologetic look. "Sorry. I just didn't know how you would react. You've always been really protective. I started to write you a letter a few times, but I figured this may be a better way. Obviously, someone beat me to the punch." I can't keep the irritation out of my voice. I can't believe the nerve of Aerick. *Why would he do that, when I broke things off?*

"Honestly, I'm kind of excited in a weird sort of way. I was beginning to wonder if you liked guys at all." He looks at me pointedly.

"Ha, ha, ha. You're hilarious."

"Seriously. What is going on though? He said you guys were happy and then you just broke it off. Why would you do that, sis? Were you not happy? Did he do something to you?"

"No, it wasn't like that." I stop his thoughts right there before he gets mad. "I was really happy." My eyes begin to blur a little.

"Why, then? I don't get it. You deserve to be happy. You know that, right?"

Taking a deep breath, my eyes fall down to my hands. That pain in my chest I've been beating down, is starting to surface again just thinking about it. "I know, and I want to be happy, but not at his expense."

"Care to explain?"

"He was risking everything by being with me. He lives for this job. It's the only accomplishment in his life he's actually proud of. It's not right to let him lose it because of me." I glance up to see his face is dripping in disbelief.

"Something tells me he doesn't quite see it that way."

Huh? "Why? What did he tell you?"

"He wants to be with you, Nadi. Maybe you should actually talk to him. It seems he really cares about you."

I shake my head. "He tell you that, too?"

He gives a quick huff. "He didn't have to. It was clear there was something between you two from the moment I came to visit you. His eyes were shooting daggers at me from the moment I hugged you. At first, I thought maybe he just liked you, but when I saw the look you gave him and the way your eyes always seemed to find him when he was around, it was pretty obvious it was two-sided. I was just waiting to see how long it took you to tell me; you always do in your own time. It's pointless to push you into things before you're ready."

My lips press together. "You know me too well."

His laughter fills the room. "Which is why I am telling you, just talk to him! If you have a chance to be happy, then you have to take it."

This is not the advice I want or expected to hear. Can't he just agree with me and convince me I'm doing the right thing? "So that's the only advice you have?"

"What? That's not good enough for you?"

A giggle escapes a second before my gut catches up with my thoughts. "I'm just not sure if I could live with myself if I end up ruining his life just so he can be with me."

He taps on the screen, bringing my eyes back to him as soon as they begin to fall down to my hands. "You just need to think about it from all angles. You are a smart girl, start acting like it."

"Fuck off, douche. I'll think about it." That's enough talking about this. "Anyways, Jeff and Patrick say hi. Business must have picked up for you in their absence. I sure hope you're being careful. The last thing I want is to come home and see you in jail."

He smirks at me. "I'm smarter than that… no offense to them. Anyway, I got to get going. I have some things to attend to." Hesitation cross his face.

I smirk, realizing for the first time, I don't recognize the background. "Something, or someone, since you are clearly not at home."

He looks off screen; his eyes shoot up before he looks back to me. "Hey, you're not the only one looking for happiness."

"Yeah, okay. Love you, bro. See you soon." He gives me a quick wave and a devilish grin.

"Love you too, and I hope to see you in a better mood next time. Bye, sis."

An unforced smile grows on my face, "I'll see what I can do. Bye kid, take care."

The screen goes black. I feel a little better, but still don't know what to do about Aerick. *What else there is for me to think about?* I pick up my stuff and go back out to join Jeff and Patrick. Aerick is sitting outside the gym watching me, but I ignore his gaze.

"How did it go?" Jeff asks as I sit back down next to him.

"Good, he says 'hi'." He didn't really, but I want to be polite. Jeff beams at me as I settle in to get my work done.

* * * *

Begrudgingly, I head to my session with Liz. Nervousness is wracking my body; not because I'm afraid of her, but because I am afraid for her. The shit she pulled last week is still at the forefront of my thoughts, putting me on pins and needles. I walk in and she doesn't meet me with her normal greeting. Moving over to the couch, I sit and try to keep my cool. Feigning disinterest, I focus on my nails, absently picking at them.

"Hello, Nadi," she says smugly.

"Liz."

"So... how's Aerick?"

My eyes fly up to meet hers. "Do you think you are being funny?"

She shrugs, "It's not like I meant for him to get hurt. I had no idea my date was going to do that."

I can't help but roll my eyes. She really is a dumbass. "So, I ranked first today. Why didn't you say anything about me walking out on you last week?" I've been curious about that all morning.

Darkness flashes in her eyes. "I didn't have much of a choice."

"Just like you don't have a choice now." I turn, hearing Aerick's voice as he stands in the door way, clearly a little pissed. Looking back at Liz, her eyes light up at Aerick. *Get a clue, you damn idiot.*

"Liz, go next door, I need to talk to Nadi."

Her eyebrows shoot up. "You're kicking me out of my session with her, so you can screw your girlfriend? Hell no!"

Aerick's gaze turns icy cold. "Liz, you have five seconds to leave this fucking room before I throw you out." His voice sends chills down my spine.

She seems to ponder it for a second. "I swear if I have to listen to you two again, I'm going straight to Luther."

"Get out!" Aerick roars. She jumps up quickly, finally getting it through her thick head, and goes through the door to the other room. He follows her, closing the door securely.

I stand up, trying to decide if it would be better to just leave or see what he wants to say. "Aerick, I don't want to talk."

"You can't just keep ignoring your problems, Nadi," he says angrily. *I don't ignore my problems.* Choose to bury them deep inside maybe, but I don't ignore them. I shake my head and start toward the door.

His deep sigh reverberates throughout the room before his heavy footsteps cross to me. Large warm hands wrap around my waist. I freeze at his touch and he lets me go quickly, leaving a burning sensation where his hands touched my stomach. His boots move a step back, but my body is still tingling at the nearness; I'm frozen in place, unable to turn around to face him.

"Please just talk to me. I need to understand why you are so upset. This is killing me here." I flinch at his choice of words.

He takes a half-step closer to me and I can feel his body heat radiating off him. "I miss you," he whispers in my ear without touching me. My heart implodes and tears pool in my eyes. "I need to know. Give me one good reason and I'll leave you alone, I swear."

My brother's words replay in my head. Maybe I owe him at least that much. "Aerick, I'm screwing up your life," I murmur to him.

He huffs behind me. "That's a bunch of bullshit, right there."

But it's not. No longer being able to resist, my body turns to face him. "Aerick, before you met me this was your life. This job, you love this job. It was all you had, it was what made you happy."

His lips press together. "Yes, I like this job and it made me happy to be here. It was the first time I felt accomplished; I've told you that much. But that was before I met you."

"I'm no one special, Aerick. I can't ask you to give up your whole life for me."

His eyebrows pull together and he breathes deeply. "For fuck sake. You are the most frustrating woman ever. Do you not see how much my life has changed since I met you? I don't wake up thinking about work, I wake up thinking about you. You are the only woman I've ever wanted to actually be with. How can you not understand that you make me happier than anything else in this world?"

"Aerick, I want you to keep your job; you're happy with it. I don't want you to have to choose between me, who you just met, and a job you love, that you have been at for years. And it's not just that, I'm a distraction. You got hurt because of me."

He throws his hands in the air and raises his voice. "Are you not listening to me? I don't fucking care about this job, I care about you – only you! I'd gladly march into Luther's office right now and quit if it meant I could be with you again. Do I need to do that to prove it to you?"

He looks into my eyes for a moment and then moves toward the door with intent in his eyes. I grab his arm and electricity shoots through me. He turns back toward me, "Dammit Nadalynn, I fucking need you." He grabs my face with both of his hands. "What do I have to do to make you understand?"

My resolve is faltering. *Maybe I was wrong. Maybe he needs me as much as I want him.* I close my eyes in a sad attempt to hold back my tears.

"Please babe, be with me," he whispers, and I feel his lips mere inches from mine. I can't hold back anymore. Closing the distance, our lips meet as my tears begin to flow. He wraps his arms around me tight, pulling me as close to him as possible as he deepens our kiss. I have missed this so much. His touch electrifies me, sending shock waves throughout my entire body. Our tongues knot around each other until we are both breathless. He leans is forehead against mine.

"I don't want you throwing your life away just for me Aerick; I'm not worth it."

His chest rises and falls against me, "Babe, stop being so self-deprecating. I'm not throwing my life away. I know I've been struggling lately, but I'm just trying to find a balance in my life. Just give me a little time to get it figured out." *How many times have I asked that same thing?*

A smile tugs at the corner of my mouth. "Take as much time as you need. Just please, please be more careful. It kills me to see you get hurt."

He nods and pulls me into a suffocating hug. "Yeah, I know the feeling."

"No fucking way!" Liz shouts, coming into the room, and instantly my mood is soured. "What makes this skank so special, Aerick? After everything we have done together. Why her?" She looks utterly furious and devastated at the same time.

"I told you before Liz, she reaches me on a level you never did – or anyone, for that matter."

"And you would give up everything for her?" she spits.

He shrugs, his lips pulling up at the corners. "Yes. Yes, I would." She turns and stomps out of the room.

I chuckle. "Something tells me this isn't the end of her tantrum. You know that, right?" I stare up into his eyes, but he doesn't seem to care.

"Will you meet me behind the cabins after dinner?"

I look at him curiously. "Or we could just go now?"

He shakes his head at me. "You haven't been eating much; you need to eat. I've been so worried about you the last few days." There is a deep sadness in his voice as he runs his fingers down my left arm to my injured hand.

I close my eyes, taking in his touch. *Why do I always screw up everything?* I almost let go the best thing that has ever happened to me and all because I had some stupid notion that he didn't need me in his life. "Okay, I will meet you after dinner."

He pulls me into another crushing hug, nuzzling his face in my hair. "I got to go. Luther called me into a meeting. Please go eat, okay?" I nod in agreement and he pulls me in for one more gentle kiss.

* * * *

I lean back against the cabin, waiting for Aerick. I tilt my head toward the sky and close my eyes. It is amazing how much lighter and happier I am. It feels good, it feels right. My brother was right, I was being stupid. If our roles were reversed, I would choose Aerick over a job any day. Suddenly my body tingles, feeling his presence. His arms wrap around me and he pulls my chin around a little so his lips can meet mine. "I have missed that," I tell him.

His chest vibrates against me. "Me too." He gives me another peck on my lips and then suddenly I'm being pulled down in his lap. *What the hell?* He is sitting cross legged and I am sitting in his lap with my back to his chest.

"Um, what's going on?" I turn my head to the side to look at him.

"I thought maybe we could talk."

"Talk about what?" I ask suspiciously.

He breaths deeply. "What are your plans after you are done here?"

I shrug. "I don't really know. It's not something I've thought about it; but I figured we would need to talk about it eventually."

"Would you want me to move to Chicago?" He sounds completely serious and a heaviness spreads across my chest.

I glare down at my hands. "Aerick, I just broke up with you because I don't want you to throw this job away. You're happy here. I don't want you to quit because of me."

He hesitates for a moment. "Would you consider moving here with me?" His voice is barely above a whisper. His body is tense, waiting for my answer.

I love him, and I want to be with him; the answer comes immediately, so quick and so sure I'm caught off-guard for a moment. "Yes."

His whole body relaxes and his arms tighten around me as he whispers in my ear, "Good." *Was he worried I would say no?* If we stay together it would have to go one way or the other.

"I don't know what I'd do here, though. There aren't a lot of jobs that would consider hiring someone like me."

He chuckles. "I think we can figure it out. What about working here? We work kind of a crazy schedule which sucks, and we don't really have too much of a social life."

I shrug my shoulders. It wouldn't be so bad to work here, out in nature. "Where do you live when you're not working here?" We don't talk about his life much and his real home never came up.

"I have a condo in Des Moines, on the Sound."

"Des Moines? In Iowa?" I have no clue what 'the Sound' is!

He chuckles. "No, it's just south of Seattle, on the Puget Sound."

Wow. "That must be nice. You live on the water?"

I can hear the smile in his voice. "Yep."

"Kind of expensive, isn't it?"

I feel his chest rumble under my back. "This job pays pretty well, and half the year I don't pay for clothes, food, or utilities. The other six months I work at Amar's gym when he needs me to. I've actually built up quite the savings."

My mind is swirling in a thousand directions, but one question is screaming in my ear; I need to hear it. "Do you want me to move here?"

"I've never wanted anything more in my life, but I want you to be sure. Leaving everything behind isn't easy. I want you to be happy, and I really hope you want to be happy with me." He kisses my head and my heart warms. "So, will you move here with me?" He is holding his breath again and a grin pulls at the corner of my lips.

"Um, we'll see," I joke with him.

He pokes me in my side, making me jump. "Hmm, my little

princess is ticklish." I immediately try to jump out of his arms, but he attacks my sides and it takes everything in me not to scream.

"Aerick, stop!" I say in an uncontrollable giggle but he's relentless. Soon I'm on my back and he is half lying on me. He stops to let me catch my breath.

"Come on. Tell me you will stay with me." His eyes look deeply in mine.

I smile at him. "Always." He tightens his grip and leans in to kiss me deeply.

"Finally!" I jerk my head back, hearing Paulo. "You know he is a real pain in the ass when you two are having your lovers' quarrels!"

"Fuck off, Paulo," Aerick tells him, irritated. "You need to disappear. Your virgin eyes won't be able to handle what I am about to do to her." My face turns bright red and I hit Aerick on the arm, making him and Paulo both laugh.

He kisses my nose. "I'm just playing, Princess. That's for my eyes only!" The roughness in his voice is making me feel a bit shy. He places a tender kiss on my lips. Paulo clears his throat.

"I thought I told you to get lost," Aerick murmurs on my lips.

"Sorry man, Luther is looking for you. Figured it would be better I found you first." He lets out a sinister laugh and walks away.

"Fuck. I can't wait to get you alone where we won't be interrupted."

I nip at his lip. "Soon enough!" He growls and slides his hand between my legs and begins to massage me through my pants as he kisses me brusquely. A hard ache springs to life between my legs. Then suddenly, all his contact is gone. My eyes fly open and he is standing above me with an evil smile.

"You better get in the top two next week," he growls at me, before helping me up.

I laugh at him. "Calm down, tiger. I'll do my best."

He raises his eyebrow at me then gives me a quick kiss. "See you later, Princess."

CHAPTER THIRTEEN

(Sunday August 16th)

I'M SLOW TO get up this morning, as is everyone in our dorm. We were up until the wee hours talking. It was cool to reminisce about the old days. We spent a lot of the time talking about Jeff, Patrick and me. When we were kids and what it was like growing up in our neighborhood. The nights we would sneak out and hang out drinking or go walking around downtown all night long. We really had some fun times.

There's a smile on my face as we line up, even though I'm barely awake. Aerick stands on the stage wearing a smirk on his face as he looks around at us. Something tells me he sat up listening to our conversation. A big part of me wishes he could have come in and joined our little late-night group. At one point we did get a little loud, laughing at Mike's hilarious jokes. A half-awake, crazy-haired Brand came in telling us to quiet it down and get to sleep, which just making us laugh harder when he walked out.

Aerick's face suddenly shifts, getting serious as Luther gets up on stage. Aerick got in a bit of trouble last week and has been trying to be on his best behavior. When Paulo interrupted us last week, Luther had been looking for Aerick to talk about what happened earlier in the day. As it turned out, Liz complained about Aerick interrupting her sessions to give her paperwork, and some bullshit about only having a limited time with the cadets.

That is what she told Luther, anyway. We know that she was really pissed that Aerick interrupted our session to confess his feelings for me, but she's still not willing to tell Luther what's going on. Aerick is under strict orders not to enter the room during her sessions anymore. He was pissed at her bullshit claim, but played along. On top of all the other things that Luther has been coming down on him for, it was the last thing Aerick wanted to hear.

We talked about telling Luther, but he told me he is enjoying our little bubble and he isn't ready to give it up yet. He assures me he will, though, and that he has heard there may be an opening at the camp soon. I've tried to pry it out of him what that meant but he said I would find out all in good time. It sucks not being in the loop. Other than the one conversation, we really haven't talked any more about me moving to Washington, but I can't help but notice we are going into the home stretch here. There's only a little over a month before we finish and are home free.

I'm momentarily astonished that the time has gone by so quick. In the beginning it seemed to drag by and now here we are: I am happy with Aerick; my best friend is doing much better, carrying around a smile all the time; and I'm deciding my future. In the next few weeks, I'm going to have to make some life-changing decisions, but I am getting more confident about them.

"Here are this week's rankings," Luther says, bringing me out of my thoughts, and my smile grows from ear to ear. My name is in the second spot this week, right under Patrick. I glance at Aerick and his lips twitch up ever so slightly before he composes himself and starts off with our workout. Our workouts have been getting harder now that the routine has changed a little. Aerick explained that it is normal, since our bodies have gotten use to the exercise, that we've changed it up to continue to push our muscles. Apparently, that is why he is so ripped. Although I'm sure it has something to do with the fact that he works out seven days a week and usually at least three times a day. My own body has become amazingly defined. My arms, legs, stomach have all become much more lean just in these last three months.

We finish up and even though there is a dull ache in my muscles, I feel great. Patrick and I go up to claim our prize. Patrick takes the Skype session and I say the lunch without even looking at it. Aerick's façade almost slips but he manages to hold in his smile.

✳ ✳ ✳ ✳

Lunch time arrives, and I happily go to meet Aerick out front.

It's a blessing that my counseling session today is the last one for the day. The longer I don't have to deal with her today, the better. Plus, spending some time with Aerick will put me in a better mood before having to put up with her psycho ass. Out front, Aerick and Paulo are waiting for me – Aerick looking like a delicious underwear model standing against the car.

He smirks, "Congrats on getting into the top again."

I give him a wink before turning to Paulo. "Coming with us again, Paulo?"

"Damn straight, little sister. Let's go, I'm starved." I raise an eyebrow at the nickname and Aerick just shakes his head, opening the back door for me.

"Little sister, huh?" I ask when he starts up the car. I notice that Aerick is not driving this time. *That's new.*

"Well, yeah. You're dating my brother, which makes you my sister, right?"

I giggle at his playfulness. "Okay. If you say it, then it must be true."

Aerick roll his eyes. "Babe, don't encourage him." Whatever, it's funny!

It doesn't take long for me to see we are not going the same way to the restaurant. "Where are we going?" I ask, a little curious.

"Oh, don't worry your pretty little head. Your boy over here has got a little surprise for you," Paulo laughs.

Aerick punches his arm and then turns back, giving me an evil grin. "We'll be there soon babe, just relax."

Hmm, yeah that's not happening. Now my stomach is all twisted in knots. *What does he have up his sleeve this time?*

We pull onto a long driveway through a canopy of trees and after a minute it opens up to reveal a huge two-story cabin. My eyebrows pull together. *We are going to hang out at someone's house?*

We come to a stop and Aerick gets out, then opens my door. I give him a questioning look and he ignores my stare, waving his arm for me to get out.

"You kids don't have too much fun, now. I'll be back in a bit," Paulo chides.

"Bite me," Aerick tells him but his tone is almost giddy. Paulo drives off as soon as the door is shut.

"He isn't staying?" I look up at Aerick.

"Nope. He is going to get our lunch. Come on." We walk up onto a huge wooden porch and the front of the house is nearly all windows on the bottom floor. He reaches above one of the decorative shutters and pulls down a key.

"Is this your house?" I question curiously, and he lets out a chuckle.

"No, this is my friend Casey's cabin."

That sounds familiar. "As in, Liz's friend Casey?" He looks at me, confused. "She mentioned it when I overheard you guys talking *that day*."

He looks down, pursing his lips. "Oh yeah. Well, Casey is a mutual friend. He lives over on the other side of the mountain, near Seattle, and often lets his closer friends use his cabin. As long as we don't trash the place, he's cool with us using it." I bite my lip.

"What?" he asks, seeing my hesitation.

"There's no chance that she is going to show up here, is there?"

He laughs, "I talked to Casey earlier. He said she didn't ask to use it this weekend so no, she shouldn't be showing up." He gives me a big smile and pulls me into the house.

This place is the poster board for what a bachelor pad should look like. It has an open floor plan and you can see everything when you walk in. To the right there is a hug flat-screen TV equipped with an Xbox One and a PlayStation Four. A top-of-the-line stereo flanks the TV and there are tons of couches. On my left there is a pool table and mini bar. The log cabin exterior has been brought inside and adds to the masculine feel. Like the front of the cabin, the back wall is all glass and has the most beautiful view looking out to the river.

Aerick pulls me toward the back wall into the kitchen area. He gets into the fridge, pulling out two bottles of water, and hands me one. I immediately open it and take a big drink as my mouth seems real dry suddenly.

"Wow, this place is beautiful." He smiles at me but doesn't say anything, just looks at me, leaning against the counter. His stare sends a bolt of electricity through my body and pools between my legs. My weight shifts to the other foot as the ache appears. "So, what are we doing here?" I ask, although by the look on his face there is no question what's on his mind.

He shrugs his shoulders. "I thought it would be nice to spend some time alone, without interruptions, or having to worry about who is around. We can just be ourselves. Come, let me show you around."

He takes my hand in his, lacing his fingers between mine. We go out the back door onto a huge party deck. This place is really quite amazing. We are surrounded by giant trees and the river rushing close by adds to the character of the house. I lean over the railing slightly and admire the view.

"He likes to have a lot of weekend parties up here."

I grin, trying to hold in my laughter, "Let me guess, rich and unmarried?" This place screams 'playboy with a lot of cash'.

Aerick comes up behind me, wrapping one of his arms around me while the other pulls back the hair on the side of my neck. "You are very observant," he whispers into my ear as he brings his lips to ghost over my neck. "Is that how you like your men, rich?" I close my eyes at the amazing tingling sensation that is shooting down my body.

"Honestly, I haven't really met anyone rich. It makes no difference to me. Just having someone that can touch me is enough."

He nips at my neck, making me moan, and I feel him smile on my neck. Just when I think he is going to keep going, he pulls back, leaving me wanting more. "Let me show you the rest of the house." He takes my hand and we go back inside and up the stairs. He opens the first door and it's a massive theater room with twelve oversized recliners stair-stepping down toward the front of the room. *Geez, this guy must be loaded!*

I sense the rumble in Aerick's chest as he sees my reaction. "Maybe he's a little rich. He owns a few businesses that are doing really well. This place is awesome to watch movies. It's got a sound system that would rival any movie theater. Maybe we could take advantage it some time when we are not restricted by time."

"Sounds fun."

We go out and down the hall further. He opens a door to a good-sized room with the same look out toward the river as down stairs. "And this is what I've been waiting for."

I bite my bottom lip and he pushes me up against the wall, kissing me hard and desperate. He pulls back. "I've been waiting to get you to a bed."

"You don't count the infirmary?" I joke.

"Nope, not one bit." He grabs me under my ass and I wrap my legs around his waist, letting out a giggle of surprise. His kisses move to my neck and I tilt my head to the side to give him better access.

"I like hearing you giggle," he mumbles on my neck. His lips feel incredible. He turns us and walks us over to the bed, lowering us both down so he is lying on top of me my legs hanging off the edge of the bed.

He looks into my eyes. "You are so beautiful." He kisses me lightly on my lips. "And smart." He moves down to my jaw. "And selfless." His lips trail down to my neck. "And brave." He bites at my collarbone and my ache becomes uncomfortable. "Nadalynn, I need you."

"Then please, satisfy that need. Along with my own." My voice is weak but that is all the encouragement he needs. He sits me up and removes my shirt before kissing my neck again, pushing me back down. His lips feel so good moving across my skin. They kiss and bite their way down my stomach. He has my pants unbuttoned before his mouth reaches the top of them and he bites harder at my hip bone. I buck my hip up and moan at the intense pleasure it causes. He peels my pants and underwear down, pulling them off after quickly removing my boots and socks. He takes my foot in his hand and locks eyes with me. He bites softly at the top of my foot while dragging his thumb nail down the bottom, sending shivers up my body and a whimper escapes me as a grin crosses his face.

He slowly kisses up my leg until he hits the apex of my thighs and I can't help but squirm under him from the anticipation. I squeeze my eyes shut and lay my head back. He blows between my legs, causing my loud moan to fill the room.

"That is the most wonderful sound in the world, and here you don't have to hold back. No one will hear you but me." He quickly runs his tongue along my folds and I let out a louder moan. "That's right babe, let me hear you."

He begins his assault on my sensitive spot, circling it slowly at first, and then picking up speed. The deep pull appears quickly and I know it will not be long. His tongue moves with expert care, not stopping as I feel his fingers slide into me. He groans and the vibration pushes me closer to the edge. "Always so wet for me Princess."

He begins sucking and running his tongue round and round as his fingers begin pumping in and out. The intensity is almost unbearable. I start to buck my hips, but he pushes me down with his free hand, holding me in place, forcing me to absorb the intense feeling. "Let go Nadalynn. Let me taste your sweetness," he mumbles and then hums hard, causing powerful vibrations, pushing me over the edge as I cry out his name.

That was so unbelievable, there are no words. I sense him crawl up next to me. After another moment, I manage to finally open my eyes to a beaming Aerick as he runs his fingers lightly down my side. "You okay, Princess?"

I hum my approval, still not ready to speak. "Speechless? That has to be a first." There's pride on his face and I can't help but smile. He sits up, pulling me up and wrapping his arms around me. "You taste absolutely incredible." He kisses my neck. "But I am not done with you yet," he whispers in my ear.

He pulls his shirt off; then he removes my bra, leaving me naked. My instincts kick in and I try to cover myself, but he grabs my hands, shaking his head. "Don't hide from me. Trust me, you really are perfect in every way." He kisses me lightly on my lips before moving me so I'm lying up on the pillow. He removes his pants and boxers in one quick movement, allowing himself to spring free. His impressive size always seems to take me by surprise and I take a deep breath at the sight of him before me.

He crawls across the bed, kissing me everywhere as he moves up, settling between my legs. He stops for several moments to tease my nipples with his tongue, causing my need for him to return. As he reaches my mouth, he kisses me deeply and he pushes his hardness against me, teasing my already tender sensitive spot.

He lowers his mouth to my ear. "Thank god you're on the shot because I fucking hate condoms." He pulls his face back to look into my eyes, and just as I wonder how the hell he knew that, he slams into me hard before he stills.

I close my eyes tight at the sudden fullness that fills me and hearing his sweet groans drive me even crazier. After a moment, I begin to move my hips up toward him, needing relief, and he complies, beginning to move in and out of me slowly.

"Holy hell, you feel amazing." He starts to pick up the pace and I meet each thrust as I'm driven higher. My hands pull at hair as I get close to my release and there is a rumble in his chest as his mouth attaches to my nipple, sucking and nipping. It's incredibly intense, making me a little afraid to let go. I moan his name, unable to make a coherent thought.

"Come for me, Nadalynn!" He slams into me again and I lose myself, calling his name over and over, just as he does, and we ride out our orgasms together.

His weight shifts off to the side of me as I try to slow my

breathing. "You still coherent, babe?"

I smirk at his playfulness. "Nope," I say in between my labored breaths and he laughs.

"So you approve of beds, huh?"

"Definitely have their advantages. Much more comfortable for sure."

Once I'm breathing normally again, I bite my lip, looking at him shyly. "So how did you know I am on the shot?"

He turns on his side, propping himself up on his elbow, and smirks at me. "Terrie told me she gave it to you when you were on your period." My cheeks flush; he can be so blunt sometimes.

"Hmm, I love watching you blush," he says, and he leans down to kiss me.

A hand slides up, cupping my breast; I arch my back, pushing myself into his hand. "It's amazing that your breast fits so perfectly in my hands." He teases my nipple and I moan into his mouth.

"It's been too long, and I haven't quite had my fill of you just yet, babe. We'll make this easier for you. Turn on your stomach," he whispers in between his kisses. He breaks our lips and I do as he request. He climbs over me and pulls my legs off the side of the bed so I am standing on the floor again. The height of the bed allows me to comfortably rest my stomach on it. He positions himself between my legs. "Aerick?" I say not quite sure about what he is going to do.

He rubs his hands over my bottom and I feel him hard against me again. "Don't worry babe, I promise not to take things too fast." He slaps my ass, leaving just a slight sting, and then slowly glides into my wetness, then back out and in. His hands hold my hips incredibly tight as he continues at an agonizingly slow pace until I whine his name.

"What, Princess? What do you want?" I'm not sure if I can say it. I'm too shy when it comes to this stuff. "Tell me, Nadalynn. Do you want it faster? Do you want it harder?" His words are so rough and raw, hitting me right in the stomach. I hum, hoping he will accept that as I try to move my hips against him. His grip tightens. His slow pace is driving me crazy. "Tell me, babe, or we will be here all night."

"Yes," I manage to get out.

"You want me babe? Only me?" he growls, resonating in his chest.

I moan at the excruciating need inside me. "Yes!"

He lies down across my back, biting my shoulder lightly. "That's what I want to hear." He begins to move faster, rougher, but it is a very welcome feeling. His fingers grip my sides so hard there are sure to be marks tomorrow, but the slight pain feels so good. An arm around my waist holds me to him tightly as he continues pounding deeper into me. He slides his other hand around in front of me and begins to massage my sensitive spot. My body begins to tremble uncontrollably.

"All mine." I hear him whisper in my ear and I'm lost in the clouds. I faintly hear him mumble a string of curse words mixed with my name as he pours into me.

When my thoughts finally become coherent again, he has moved me up so am fully lying on bed and he is lying on his side next to me, running his fingers lightly across my back. The feeling is amazing on my sensitive skin. He kisses my shoulder lightly. My eyes are so heavy, but I open them so I can gaze at the perfect man beside me that is mine.

"Welcome back." He has a wonderful glow to him as he smiles down at me. I need a nap; my eyes close again in complete exhaustion.

"We really need to whip you into shape so these little sessions don't wipe you out." I let out a chuckle. "I take it you are well satisfied." He continues running his fingers over me and it feels absolutely amazing.

"There are no words," I murmur, and laughter rumbles through him.

"As much as I would love to stay here and nap with you, Paulo is going to be here with our lunch soon, and we have to be back by two." I sigh and let out a whine of disapproval. "I know babe, I know. Rest a few more minutes and then come downstairs. There is a bathroom right across the hall, and don't worry about the bed, the maid will be here later. She'll put some clean sheets on."

My eyes fly open and my eyebrows shoot up. "Really?"

He laughs and kisses me on the temple. "Don't fall asleep." He gets up, smacking my bare ass and making me yelp. When I look at him, he's biting his lip, lust still hinting at his eyes. Wow, didn't he get enough! I watch as he quickly slips his boxer brief and pants on and grabs his shirt and shoes. He kneels on the bed, giving me one last kiss on my temple. "I'm serious. Don't fall asleep."

"Or what?" I question.

He huffs, "Or I might decide to show you how rough I can be." His low, uneven voice sends shivers down my body and I feel him laugh in satisfaction. Then he is gone.

Holy shit. If this is how it is always going to be, I may choose never to leave this bed. My man is amazingly talented. For a brief moment, I wonder how many women he's been with, but I quickly push the thought away, not wanting to ruin the amazing feeling coursing through my body right now.

After lying there for longer than I probably should have, I scoot toward the edge of the bed and stand up slowly. Wow, it's like I just ran a marathon. My fingers reach toward the ceiling, stretching my overworked muscles, before I dress myself, getting lost in the lingering feeling of his hands on me.

Going across the hall, I find the bathroom. I'm flushed and have a permanent grin plastered on my face. Unfortunately, my hair doesn't agree as much. I take out the hair tie I slipped in my pocket this morning; thankfully I always keep one on me. With no brush, I quickly throw my hair up into a messy bun before going down stairs. Aerick has turned on the music and has racked up the balls on the pool table. I raise an eyebrow.

"Do you like pool?" he asks curiously, and I nod my head. We used to play all the time at the billiards hall by my house. It was something to do without drawing in unwanted attention. He walks over to me, giving me a gentle kiss as he wraps his arms around me. "Good, you break." He shrugs his eyebrows at me.

He watches me intently as I bend over to shoot. "Damn, that is a mighty fine sight. If we had more time, I'd consider taking you right there." He grins evilly at me.

His boldness makes me laugh, "Down tiger. We'll have plenty of time to have all kinds of fun."

He saunters up behind me and leans down, nipping my ear. "I'm counting on it." Just then the front door opens.

"Okay, enough of that shit, unless you want me to join in!"

Aerick tenses behind me. "My eyes only, asshole," he growls, and I grin at his possessiveness.

"Bro, I was joking. Lighten up."

He sets some to-go plates up on the mini bar and I'm suddenly starving. "What did you get me?" I ask as I walk over to him.

"I got you the same you got last time, and Aerick and I got country fried steak."

He is so awesome. "You're a saint. I'm starving."

"I thought we were going to play?" Aerick whines, and I can't help but laugh at his pouty face.

"You can stare at my ass later, handsome. Right now, I need to replace all that energy that has magically disappeared." I send him a playful smile and bite my lip.

UNSTRUNG

"Aerick, better watch out for this one," Paulo grins.

Aerick strides up to me, holding my eyes with his intense stare. He wraps his arms around me, pulling me tightly to him, and leans in to bite my ear softly. "Fine, but if I get a chance, I'll be helping you work it off again." He makes no attempt to be quiet and I know Paulo heard him, making my face to bright red as he pulls away with a satisfied look on his face. "Let's eat before we have to get back." I turn around toward the bar and his hand drags down the length of my side before he takes the seat next to me.

"Wipe that shit grin off your face, asshole," Aerick says, snapping my attention back up.

"Hey, it's just nice to see you so happy."

He shakes his head before opening his plate and digging into his food, but Paulo is right, it is nice to see him happy.

✳ ✳ ✳ ✳

I head over to my session with Liz. I was able to get in a quick nap beforehand and feel completely happy and relaxed. Not even her shitty attitude can ruin my mood. I go inside and head straight for the couch. *I will sit here in silence for the next thirty minutes and I will not let her ruin my mood.* The first thing I do notice is that she looks pretty pissed off, but who really cares? *Not me.*

She doesn't waste any time. "So, he took you out to Casey's cabin, huh?"

How did she know that? I glare at her with disbelief. "You're spying on us now?"

She looks at me like it was a stupid question. "I have my ways

251

of knowing things, too. Besides, he takes all of his little booty calls up there." I shake my head. I'm not going to let her get to me. "You know, Aerick and I have spent many weekends there." I cross my legs and look at her, letting her know I could care less. "That huge log bed is quite comfortable, isn't it?"

I'm slightly irritated to know they have been there too, but I am not sure what she is talking about. The bed we were on was not a log bed. He must have taken me into another room. Thank goodness for small favors. As much as it is frustrating to know he has been with her, I will not let his past ruin our relationship. I have one fucked up past of my own.

I look down, shaking my head. "I know what you are trying to do, Liz, and it isn't going to work. I don't care about his past."

"Oh, is that right? Did he tell you how many people he has been with, or how many *at once?*" My composure breaks momentarily, and my eyebrows pull together. *Shit. I don't care.* I take a deep breath and look back at my hands. Liz continues, "I already told you, he has an uncontrollable need for sex, and there is no way you will be able to satisfy that. He needs a real woman, someone who knows how to satisfy him in every way possible."

I stand and clench my teeth as my anger starts to get the best of me. "You're just jealous, bitch," I seethe.

She lets out a small chuckle as she stands, getting in my face. "Of what? You? You're just a temporary distraction for him. He will come around when his infatuation wears off. I have seen it before. You aren't special, and soon enough he will forget all about you."

I've had enough of this skank. I tilt my head and put my hand on my hip. "No, I think you have it wrong. You weren't special, and you're just pissed because you want him, but he doesn't want you. Did you fall for him, Liz? Did you actually think you were special enough to hold him down? He doesn't want some hoe that puts herself out there for every man to get off on like you. He doesn't want a whiny, weak cunt that doesn't know how to say no."

The anger in her face grows more and more with each of my words. I secretly hope she actually hits me so there is a reason to hit her back. I take a step forward and she takes one back. "You are not special. You will never be able to be with him. He doesn't want your nasty ass, and you're just jealous that his large, hard, satisfying cock was in me earlier. And you know what, Liz, I loved hearing him scream my name as he came violently inside me. He will NEVER be yours. HE. IS. MI..."

A searing pain rips through my stomach, cutting off my words and stealing all the air out of my lungs.

Looking down, a shiny metal letter opener is sticking out of my stomach. My eyes fly up in disbelief and all I see is hate. All my anger, all my hatred, shoots through me all at once. Everything I have ever felt for her, and all my rage for what she has done to Aerick. All the pain and heartache she has caused both of us. I send a single blow hard to her temple before I even know what is happening. She drops to the floor in a confused daze. *I'm not done with you yet, bitch.*

I fall to my knees, grabbing her head, and start banging it on the ground over and over and over until she goes limp in my hands. *STOP!!!* My internal voice screams and I freeze, letting her body fall to the ground one last time. I try to catch my breath and calm down as I stare at her unconscious body. My whole body is still shaking in anger.

My eyes are drawn to the blood beginning to pour onto the floor under her head. *Fuck! Did I kill her? What did I do? Fuck!*

Sudden dizziness hits me like a ton of bricks and I barely catch myself from completely falling to the floor. The pain rips through me again, reminding me of the object sticking out of my abdomen.

"Aerick?" I try to yell, but it comes out only as a small whine.

I have to get outside, now. Black spots are beginning to cloud my vision and I try to stand but quickly fall back to the floor – my adrenaline is used up. "Shit."

I crawl, using one arm to scoot across the floor while I try to keep the object sticking out of me from moving. Pain shoots through me each time it's jostled and the black tries to close in. *I can't give up. I have to see Aerick one last time.*

If I am going to die, his face is the last one I want to see. I drag myself closer to the door, trying to keep the blackness at bay but I'm running out of time. *Come on Nadi, Move!*

I reach the door and the handle seems like it's ten feet tall. I stop, taking several deep breaths. *Do it.* If I don't, I'll never see him again. *Aerick.*

I squeeze my eyes closed and reach up, trying to ignore the pain that rips though my body. My body falls forward as the door gives way, swinging outward, spilling me onto the small platform outside the door. I barely catch myself with my forearms. Excruciating pain ripples through my whole body.

"Nadi?" I hear Jeff's confused call from the court yard. My eyes flit upward but I can barely see past the blur in them. *Jeff!*

"Nadi!" he yells as he jumps up and runs toward me, while everyone stares at him in confusion.

Then my eyes lock on Aerick's as he comes out of the dorm. He smiles at me sweetly for a moment before his face contorts into horror. I can't hold myself up any longer, the weight becomes overwhelming. I collapse to my side and look down. There is so much blood. There are shouts all around me, but it's impossible to focus on them. I'm trying to breathe, trying to keep the darkness from taking over.

"Nadi, what the hell happened?" Jeff asks as he looks me up and down, not sure what to do. He looks back to my stomach, "Oh my god! Who did this?" My voice is mute. It is taking everything I have to stay conscious. I focus on my short, labored breaths. Jeff goes to grab me.

"Don't fucking touch her! Don't move it, don't do anything." His voice is my single spark of happiness and my tears begin to spill over.

"This is not fucking happening." He looks me over as he kneels next to my head. "Babe, I'm right here. Hold on dammit, just hold on." He carefully scoots his legs under my head, brushing my hair back. There is so much going on around me but it's hard to focus. "Brand, where is the fucking ambulance!" He shouts, and I hear the panic, the same panic I've heard before. *He knows.* I'm not going to make it. At least I will die here in his arms.

Luther is next to me a second later, picking up my hand. "Nadi, who did this?" It's getting harder to breathe. Sliding my hand out of his, I point toward the classroom and horror builds in Aerick's eyes as Luther stands and goes in.

"Hold on, babe. You can do this, you're strong. I need to you to hold on." The sirens fill the air but I'm not sure I can hold on much longer. Beside me, tears are falling down Jeff's face. *He knows too.*

"Paulo, she is out cold. Get in there and restrain her hands before she wakes up again," Luther says as he kneels next to my legs. "Hold on, kid. It's going to be okay. Do you know why she did this?"

My gaze finds Aerick and I see him trying to hold himself together. "It's my fault." He says softly, with so much regret in his voice. "She did it because of me." I shake my head, staring into his eyes. It isn't his fault, it's mine. I pushed her to this.

"What the hell do you mean, Aerick?" Luther demands but Aerick ignores him.

He cups my cheek in his hand as my tears continue to fall. *Say it, before it is too late.* I take the biggest shallow breath I can manage. "I love you, Aerick."

He shakes his head and takes a deep breath, bringing in his strength. "Don't you give up on me, baby. Come on, I need you to fight. They're here. They're going to help you. Fight just a little longer." I see him look toward the front. *It's okay, babe.*

The heaviness bares down on my weakened body. I drag my hand up, placing it over his, and turn my head slightly to kiss his hand. I can no longer keep the blackness from closing in and my eyes close.

"Nadi. Nadalynn. No! Fucking fight baby. You have to fight. You promised you wouldn't leave me – now fucking fight!" he shouts.

He breathes in deeply as I feel him move and then feel his lips on mine. "I love you, Nadalynn. Please, please stay for me." His voice is so soft, so sad, so hurt. My heart breaks at the sorrow in his voice. I don't want to go, but the darkness wins.

CHAPTER FOURTEEN

(Day?)

I HEAR VOICES, but my body is unmoving despite my effort.

"How is she?" Luther's voice fills the room.

"She's stable but she's still in a serious condition. I was able to repair most of the damage, but she's lost a lot of blood. She's extremely lucky. The next forty-eight hours will be crucial; she isn't out of the woods just yet." He must be talking to the doctor. "Let me know if you need anything, the nurse is right outside."

"Aerick?" *He's here?*

I feel a hand tighten over my own. "I told you Luther, I'm not leaving her."

"How long?"

"A few weeks. After her birthday. Luther, please just give me some time." He sounds so defeated.

"Okay, son, but we will have to talk about this."

The blackness pulls me back down.

* * * *

"She is going to pull through this, man. She is strong, stubborn. Just like you."

"It's killing me seeing her this way, Paulo. She's hurting and I can't help her. This is all my fault." *Aerick, this isn't your fault.*

"Man, I love her, and it took her dying in my arms to tell her. I don't even know if she heard me." His voice is so quiet and I feel him bring my hand to his cheek. The weight of the movement makes it feel like bricks are being piled on my chest.

"You seriously love her?"

"Yeah, I'm pretty sure I do. How fucked up am I? I didn't even realize that it was love that I felt for her. But when I was holding her and I realized she might die... Christ, I thought I'd never see her again, never hear her say she loves me again, it felt like I was losing part of me, like my heart broke in two. I never thought I could love anyone." *Oh baby, I love you too!*

"She'll come back to you man. I just know it. She loves you too."

I try so hard to open my eyes, but the blackness takes me again.

* * * *

There is a loud noise and I feel my bed shake. "You piece of shit. What the fuck did you do?" my brother shouts and I hear the sound of flesh hitting flesh, and again, and then another struggle.

"I'm so sorry, I never wanted this for her." *What is my brother doing here?*

"Evan, that's enough!" *DAD!* The room falls silent.

"I'm sorry, but you need to take this outside or I will ban all visitors," a woman's voice hisses.

"Evan, take a walk. Now!" Footsteps storm out of the room. "Sorry, ma'am. That won't happen again." My dad's voice full of authority and shoes squeak out of the room.

It's quiet again for a moment. A hand grabs mine tightly. "You better take your hands off my daughter and start explaining before I finish what my son started." My dad's voice is so controlled but so threatening, it chills me to the bone. *Dad please. It's not his fault.*

He releases my hand. *No.* "Sorry, sir. My name is Aerick, I'm her boyfriend."

"She was supposed to be at boot camp and you are clearly much too old to be there with her. How the hell did you two meet?"

"I *was* a cadet at the camp four years ago. But I straightened out my life, worked hard, and now I'm the head instructor there." Aerick's voice is surprisingly steady.

My father huffs. "So, you thought it was okay to take advantage of my daughter." Although he is calm and collected, I know he's pissed.

"I swear to you sir, it's not like that. I tried to stay away from her, but she is... stubborn." I hear my dad grumble something too quiet for me to out. "I care for her deeply and never meant for any of this to happen. She doesn't deserve this." His fingers drag down my cheek lightly.

"What the hell happened then?"

"Liz is my ex-girlfriend, who is also the camp's psychiatrist. She was jealous. As far as we could tell they got into an argument during her weekly session and Liz stabbed her. Nadalynn, being the fighter she is, laid Liz out before crawling out of the room so we could see her." He takes my hand again.

"And where the hell were you?" My father is getting more upset which is never a good thing.

"I was doing my job," he growls. *Calm down Aerick!*

"If you were her boyfriend, it was your job to fucking protect HER!"

Aerick sighs heavily. "I know. Christ knows I failed her." He kisses my hand. "I'm so sorry, Princess." The defeat in his voice is heart-wrenching.

"You're touching her. She doesn't like people touching her." My dad clears his throat, "Does she let you? That is, when she's awake?"

"Yes, and I know that's extremely rare for her."

There is a long deafening silence. "Do you love her?"

"Yes sir, I do." Aerick releases me and the heat of his body disappears.

A new hand grabs the opposite one that Aerick released. "You better hope she wakes up. Because if she doesn't, I'm holding you responsible and you will be finding yourself on a date with my forty-five." He squeezes my hand. "Fight this, Nadalynn. Be strong and fight this." He squeezes my hand and kisses me on my forehead. *I love you dad!*

Back into the darkness.

✳ ✳ ✳ ✳

My entire body is absolutely exhausted. My throat is so dry, it feels like it's on fire. It's quiet except the beeping that has sped up just slightly. I attempt to open my eyes and find they move with great effort. It takes a moment for the blur in them to clear, but at least they opened. I'm in a stark white room and the lights are dimmed. Out the window there is only darkness. *It must be night time.* I try to move my hand but it's being held down. Turning my head slowly to the side, I see Aerick sleeping, lying with my hand folded between his and his head resting on top. He looks all mussed up like he has been through hell and back. I guess maybe he has.

I use my other hand, which is hooked to an IV, to push his hair off his forehead and I notice a bruise below his eye. As I run my fingers along it, he stirs. He looks confused for a moment until his gaze meets mine. "Oh, thank God baby, you're awake!" He jumps up and closes the distance to place a soft kiss on my lips as he takes my face in his hands.

"Where-" I clear my throat, "Where is Liz?"

His eyebrows pull together. "Hey, don't worry about her." He picks up my hand and kisses it as he sits next to me.

"Aerick, please just tell me."

He breathes deeply. "She's being released later today to the Kittitas County Sheriffs. She had a concussion and some bleeding on the brain, but she has mostly recovered and has been cleared for the transfer." Damn, I was hoping I damaged her more than that.

He closes his eyes tight and takes a deep breath. "Fucking Christ babe, you scared the shit out of me. You know that? Don't you ever try to leave me again."

"Aerick, I would never leave you on purpose. I can't believe that stupid bitch actually stabbed me! As mouthy as she is, I figured she was a stupid coward. She is lucky she got me so good or I would have killed her."

He shakes his head. "Babe, you're lucky you made it, and for the record, I thought several times about going into that hospital room and killing her myself."

I see the anger in his eyes. "Hey, it's fine. I'm okay." I reach up to grab his neck and flinch at the pain that shoots through me.

"Hey, don't move. Let me go get a nurse."

He goes to move but I catch his hand. "I love you, Aerick," I tell him, with all my heart. He smiles and pulls my face gently with his hands so that our lips are barely an inch apart. His eyes are so full of emotion. "I love you too!" he says as he closes the space and kisses me, allowing me to feel his declaration.

I hear someone clear their throat and we both look to the side. My brother is standing there. Aerick kisses me on the forehead. "I'll go get a nurse." He gets up and gives me a wink before walking out.

My brother walks over to me. "What the hell did I say?" He asks, trying to act angry.

I shake my head at him. "Well, I've never had to worry about psycho ex-girlfriends before. Sorry if I'm a bit out of practice. And what's the big idea of punching him for it?"

His eyes scrunch together. "How did you know that was me?"

I roll my eyes. "Who else would it have been?" I think I remember hearing them fighting, but it's all a bit hazy.

"Well, when I saw the guilt on his face, I knew one way or another, this was his fault. Might I mention, I was right."

I shake my head at him. "It isn't his fault that he has a crazy ex. It was my fault for egging her on and underestimating what she might do in return."

He grunts. "Of course, it was your mouth. It always is."

"Fuck off. Where's Mom and Dad?" It's coming back slowly but I remember hearing my father as well.

"Dad is sleeping out in the waiting room and just to warn you, he has been acting really weird. Mom's at the hotel. Dad convinced her to go take a shower and sleep for a few hours."

I bite my lip. "So, they met Aerick?"

He nods his head. "He refused to leave the room. He explained what happened to me and Dad."

"Yeah, after you punched him, right?"

He gets a sheepish look. "Well, I was right, it was his fault."

"Hello, Nadalynn. How are you feeling?" the nurse asks as she walks in and starts checking things, Aerick following her in.

"It's a little hazy and my throat feels like the Mohave. Can I get some water?" She adjusts the blood pressure cuff on my arm and pushes a button on the monitor, bringing it to life.

"You're on a morphine drip for the pain, which may make you feel a little hazy and tired. Water will make you nauseous, but I can give you some ice chips until the doctor gets here to examine you."

"Thanks." I give her a smile.

"I'm going to get Dad and call Mom." I give Evan a nod and he leaves. Aerick is standing near the door with an unreadable expression on his face. Evan pauses to pat him on the shoulder and whispers something to him before he walks out. Aerick just rolls his eyes.

"Alright, Nadalynn. Can I get you anything else?"

"Actually, it's Nadi. The only two people that call me that are the big lug over there and my dad." I smile at Aerick and he smirks back at me.

She laughs. "I'll be back with some ice chips." She leaves and Aerick comes back over to join me on my bed.

"My brother gave that black eye, huh?"

He chuckles, "Well, according to him, he whooped my ass, or at least that is what he just apologized for. Considering I didn't fight back, it doesn't count."

My eyes narrow. "Why would you let him do that?" I say, chastising him.

"Babe, this is my fault. She did this because of me. As far as I'm concerned, I got off light." He looks down at my stomach.

"Aerick, if you don't stop saying that, I'm going to whoop your ass." His eyebrows shoot up as he looks to my eyes. "This is not your damn fault and that is the last I want to hear of it."

He stares at me for minute. "Okay, okay." Something tells me that isn't the last of it.

"So how long have I been here?"

"It very early Wednesday."

Wow, almost three days. "My brother said that you haven't left."

He looks down again. "I had to be here when you woke up," he says quietly.

"Have you eaten?"

His lips press in a line. "Luther has been visiting. He brought me some clothes and some food."

"So, he knows, huh?"

Aerick nods. "I sort of told you I love you when you passed out in my arms. Everyone heard me. I was too focused on you, but Paulo told me that he has never seen Luther frozen with shock. Then I grabbed the keys and followed the ambulance here. I couldn't talk; I just left. It kind of gave him all the proof he needed. He's a little pissed at me and I haven't talked to him about what is going to happen yet. Honestly, all I care about is that you are okay." He squeezes my hand. My eyelids are getting heavy. "You should get some sleep, babe. I will be here when you wake up." I nod at him with a smile. I turn at the curtain moving and see my Dad, his face full of relief.

"I'm going to go get a coffee," Aerick says.

I raise my eyebrow. "You're going to drink coffee in the middle of the night?"

He chuckles leaning forward to kiss me on my forehead. "I'll be back, Princess." He gets up and leaves as my dad walks over to me.

"Hey, sister." He hasn't called me that in years.

"Hi, Dad." I am really struggling to stay awake. "I'm going to be fine, Dad. Don't worry about me."

He rolls his eyes, "I never doubted you, kid. Fighting is in our blood. I knew you would pull through."

I grin. "Thanks, Dad."

He looks at me pointedly. "So… that's your boyfriend, huh?"

I suddenly feel a little nervous. "Um, yeah."

He looks into my eyes. "Does he treat you good?" *Always protective.*

I start to chuckle but stop as soon as the sharp pain shoots through me. "Yes, Dad, he does."

"Well, he better or he is going to see just what I have in my safe."

I shake my head. "Dad!" I can only hold my eyes open half way.

"Get some sleep, sister. I'll bring your mother by in the morning. Love you, kid."

"Love you too, dad." He kisses me on my head. "Night Dad." My eyes close without my permission and I give into the exhaustion.

CHAPTER FIFTEEN

(Wednesday, August 19th)

THE NURSE SNEAKS in again to check my vitals. *How are people supposed to sleep here?* She's been in here every hour like clockwork. It's rather annoying, even though I only half wake when she comes in; it feels like I haven't gotten any sleep. Aerick is sleeping on the chair next to me with his hand holding mine. It's eight in the morning, so he must not have been sleeping or he'd have been awake hours ago.

Deciding that I'm not going to be able to sleep, I stretch out, trying to loosen up my stiff muscles, but wince half way through my stretch.

"The doctor just got here. He will be in soon to talk with you. There's also a detective that would like to talk to you this morning, whenever you're ready."

The nurse looks to Aerick, keeping her voice low so she

doesn't wake him. "Difficult one you got there. He hasn't eaten and hardly slept the whole time you were out. I tried to get him to eat a sandwich a few times, but he just sat there holding your hand, ignoring everyone's attempt to help him." My face falls. *Aerick.*

"Make sure he eats something when he wakes up. Don't want to see him end up in here, too."

"I will. Thank you." She turns and leaves. As she walks out, I look back toward Aerick. Something tells me life with him is going to be interesting. I still have to figure out how to tell my family that I am moving here. My brother isn't going to be happy about it. It's kind of scary to think about, but I know Aerick will make sure I'm okay.

It feels a little surreal that he told me he loved me, but his actions make it impossible to ignore how much he really does care about me; and now my parents know about him, too. Not exactly how I planned on telling them, but what's done is done. Hopefully they will feel better about me moving out here now. I must be out of my mind moving here with him after only knowing him a few months, but I've never done things the normal way. It will be interesting to see his actual home. *Our home.* It's a weird thought.

Suddenly the lights come on and a doctor walks in. Aerick is startled and on his feet in a second. I smirk at him. "Morning, sleepy head."

He composes himself quickly and gives me a kiss on my head. "Morning, Princess," he says softly and turns to the doctor.

"Well Nadalynn, glad to see you awake. My name is Dr. Cross, I'm the doctor who did your surgery. As I told Mr. Stephens here, the surgery went well. I was able to repair all the damage and you should be back to normal in a few short weeks."

"I have to stay here for a couple of weeks?" My voice comes out a little higher than I meant.

He laughs, "No. The camp you're at has a certified nurse. We will be able to release you to them. We would just like to monitor you for a few more days to make sure no complications arise from your surgery. But it will be very important that you ease back into physical activities and not take on too much, too quickly."

I take a deep breath. "Good. No offense Doc, but I'm not a fan of hospitals." Aerick squeezes my hand.

"None taken. I just need to check you over really quick while I'm here." With my nod of approval, he starts poking at me and looks under the bandage covering my stomach. It doesn't look like much now, but there is a lot of bruising around the stitches. He finishes up and pulls my gown back down and Aerick covers me again with a blanket. "Get some rest, I'll check in again with you tomorrow."

"Thanks." He turns and walks out.

"How are you feeling, babe?"

I shrug my shoulders indifferently. It's not terrible, as long as my body stays still. "It would be better if I could sleep for more than an hour at a time. How about you? What is this shit I hear about you not eating? You going to make a habit of lying to me?"

"I said Luther brought me food, I never said I ate it."

My eyes roll upward in irritation that he isn't taking better care of himself. "Well, you better eat this morning."

He gets a smug grin his face. "Oh yeah, and what are you going to do if I don't?" That sexy, playful grin does crazy things to me.

"I don't know. Feed you myself," I challenge.

"Oh babe," he says biting his lip, "I'd enjoy that entirely too much, but you need to take it easy for a few days. So, I promise I'll get something to eat." He kisses me roughly on the lips and the beeping on the monitor starts to go crazy.

He breaks our kiss far too early, looking at the monitor, and disappointment runs through me, but it only lasts a minute. It's not like we can do anything here anyway and I'm still exhausted.

"Good," I say with a yawn, unable to hold it back any longer.

"Get some sleep, Princess. You're going to get a lot of visitors today." I look at him confused and he shakes his head. "Just get some rest." After another yawn I relax back into the pillows and let myself fall asleep.

✻ ✻ ✻ ✻

There are voices, but somehow I still don't feel any more rested, so I don't bother opening my eyes.

"And how is that supposed to work?" My brother is here.

"I want her to move here with me."

"You're joking, right? You want her to move out here? After what just happened to her? You have got to be kidding me."

Someone touches my leg.

"It's up to her. If it makes you feel better, I asked her if she wanted me to move to Chicago first, but she said no."

"Of course she did. She'd never ask someone to give up their life for her, or did you already forget why she broke up with you?"

"I don't think it's just that. I think she's looking to get away. I've only known her for a few months, but I know that she's had a rough go of it." A silence fills the room for a minute.

"Why can you touch her? Why doesn't it bother her like it does with anyone else outside our family?"

Aerick tightens his grip on my hand. "You know, I've been asking myself that same question. Ever since she freaked out in class, I have been trying to make sense of her actions, but she's one confusing woman."

"Freaked out? What class?"

"It was self-defense class. We were practicing getting away from an attacker. She was okay at first, although they seemed to be talking heatedly about something. When she switched places with Jeff to role-play the victim, her body language changed like she was nervous. Jeff was nervous too, but she seemed to push him and then she completely freaked out. My first instinct was to push her further, which is what we typically do. You know, test the cadet's limits."

"Kind of a dick move, dude," my brother huffs out.

"It's my job! It's important to know how far we can push them," he tells him forcefully, before taking a deep breath and continuing quietly. "But I didn't do that to her. When I walked up to her and saw the look on her face, I just couldn't do it. It took everything in me not to wrap her in my arms and just hold her until she was okay. I have no idea why I felt so protective of her. None of it made sense in my head." *That made two of us.*

"I spent the next several weeks trying to get that look she had on her face, out of my head. My mind screamed at me to stay away from her, but the harder I tried, the more she drew me back in. I began noticing little things about her. Her withdrawn attitude, the way she always kept an invisible shield around her. I wanted to help her, to find out why she freaked out every time she was touched. It sort of became my life's mission. After all, part of my job is to help these guys, or at least that is what I kept telling myself."

"Did you ever find out the cause of it?" *Oh God, don't say it, please.*

"You don't know?" I concentrate hard, trying to continue to breathe evenly. Maybe it's time he knew. As much as I don't want Aerick to tell him, maybe it's time my brother knows.

"No. She was fine until she went off to summer camp when she was younger. I didn't go that year because my uncle flew me out to Texas so I could help out on his ranch for the summer. Nadi wanted to stay with her friends, which was different because we always stuck together, but I understood. My cousin had died a few years earlier, and my uncle had grown resentful toward Nadi. I think it was because they looked so much alike." His long pause fills the room with deafening silence.

"She was never the same after that summer. She started flinching when people touched her, even us, and she always wanted to be alone. We live in a small, two-bedroom apartment. Back then my parents had one room and the girls had the other. I slept on the couch. Often, I'd hear her crying late at night, or rustling around in her sleep like she was having a nightmare. Sometimes she would sneak out for hours and come back early before my dad got up for work. I asked her about what happened that summer, but she would never tell me."

"The only ones she let close were Jeff and Patrick. I asked them a ton of times what happened, and they insisted they didn't know, but I knew Jeff was lying. The way she clung to him after that – I just knew. After a while I got the hint that it was probably something really bad. I didn't want her to have to rehash it before she was ready. I decided to do everything to protect her after that, and figured she'd tell me in her own time..." He takes a deep breath and I hear Evan speak again.

"After that summer, no one was able to get close to her other than family, Patrick and Jeff, but even then she's still reserved. That is, until she met you." He pauses for another minute. "I have always wondered if things would be different if I'd stayed." I doubt it would have. It may have even made it worse. Something else for him to use against me. "Did she tell you?" Aerick doesn't speak his answer but I suspect he nods in reply. "Really?"

He sighs. "I kind of tricked it out of her. It was an asshole move, and afterward I felt like a piece of shit. I don't know everything, but I know enough. I'm sure she will tell you when she is ready but trust me, you're better off not knowing. It was bad, it changed her as a person and now she just needs to move past it. I'll do everything in my power to help her do that."

"I don't know, man; I mean, maybe moving out here will help but I don't like her moving away from me. She's trouble with a capital T."

Aerick huffs. "Boy, you can say that again." *Hey, fuck off!*

"I have always been around to protect her, to get her out of things. Trust me, without me around, she would have been in jail, or worse, a long time ago. She has absolutely no control of her anger."

"She's actually getting better at that. She hasn't really got into any fights since a few weeks into camp."

"That's because everyone knows now not to mess with her."

Aerick laughs. "She did do a bit of damage, but that's not it. I think being around me has helped. Not to sound arrogant, but she seems to be calmed by me. For whatever reason she lets me touch her, and it calms her too. Maybe it's the touch itself, I'm not sure, but I've seen it. She is different around me, more relaxed, comfortable instead of always on edge. It's hard to explain."

"Sounds like you are very observant." My brother doesn't sound happy.

"What can I say? It's hard not to stare, she's hot." I can hear the smirk on Aerick's face.

"Okay, fuck-face. That is my sister."

Aerick laughs again. "Sorry. She's just a very interesting person." He hesitates for a moment, "Can I be honest with you?"

"By all means."

"I've been with a lot of women – a lot," he says quietly, and I can feel his gaze on me. I must be a sadist because damn it all to hell, I want to hear what he has to say.

"Not inspiring a lot of confidence, dude."

"Let me finish. I used to feel so alone. My upbringing was pretty screwed up. My parents believed that emotions, other than the drive for power, were for the weak and useless. I was driven to be the best at everything and even when I achieved it, it still wasn't good enough. It created a need in me that I continually tried to satisfy. Those women were just a way for me to escape my fucked-up thoughts and needs. They were nothing to me."

"Still not inspiring confidence here."

"My point is that she changed all that. I think I was drawn to her just as much as she was drawn to me. Naturally, we both fought it. Her stubbornness mirrored mine and we have spent a lot of time pushing each other away. I hate to admit that I've hurt her." My brother's hand tenses on my leg. "Not physically, I swear," Aerick spits out quickly. "But emotionally. I was trying to push her away. My feelings were throwing me in a thousand different directions. I was confused, distracted, all I wanted was be around her and it took everything in me not to be. I've never felt like this about anyone. After a while, I finally gave in and then she pushed me away. Trying to do the right thing, I gave her the space she wanted. The last thing I wanted was to push her into something she didn't want." He quiets.

"But you obviously ended up together again. So, what's your point?"

"My point is, she isn't just a distraction to me. I think she has changed me just as much as I've changed her. I swear to you, this isn't a game to me. I truly care about her. If she stays here with me, I promise you I'll take care of her – I'll protect her. I swear to you, I won't let anything happen to her again."

Wow. My heart swells so much, I feel like my chest is going to burst. My body is buzzing, but I stay still. I don't want him to know I've been listening. "Well this better never happen again, or I won't stop at a single punch."

"Fair enough."

The door latch clicks. "Son." My mom's soft voice breaks into the room.

I decide now is the time to 'wake up'. I let my eyes flutter open and smile. "Hey Mom, Dad."

"Good morning," Aerick gets up from beside me. I look at him and smile. He kisses me on the cheek. "I'm going to go get some breakfast while you catch up with your family." He nods to my mom and dad then winks at me as he leaves the room. *Yep, no way I am leaving now.*

✽ ✽ ✽ ✽

My body is heavy with exhaustion, again. I spent the last two hours trying to explain to my parents that my plans are to move here. I figured they deserved to hear it in person. My father was less than happy. It wasn't so hard to convince my mom, but my dad was a whole other story.

Although he didn't say it, I have a feeling it's because he realized his baby girl was going out on her own and it's probably even harder knowing it's so far away. He's just concerned for me and wants the best for me; but this is what is best for me – I just wish it were easier to explain why.

Our conversation ended when I shouted in frustration that 'I love him' and that seemed to stop him in his tracks. After a long hard look, he said 'fine' and that they had to leave tonight to get back home, then quickly told me goodbye. I know it hurts his feelings, that he only left to show his disapproval, but I'm going to be selfish for once and think about my happiness.

There was understanding in my mom's eye as she said her goodbye, which made me feel a little better. My brother told me not to worry about it. That if it makes me happy, then it's the right thing to do. At least he seems to support my choice now that he and Aerick have talked.

Aerick magically shows up as soon as they all leave. I'm still upset at my father but seeing the smirk on his face makes my anger fade away quickly. Something tells me he heard at least some of the conversation between me and my parents.

He comes and sits on the bed, giving me a long, gentle kiss. "So it's official? You're moving here – with me?"

I give him a shy smile. "Yep. You're stuck with me now."

He kisses me again. "I wouldn't want it any other way. Although the way your dad looked at me when he walked out... if looks could kill, I'd be dead a thousand times over." He laughs.

Luther walks in, interrupting us. "Hey, you two." We both say "hi" in unison and then laugh. "Glad to see you're okay," he tells me.

"Thanks." Suddenly, nervousness wracks my body. Aerick hasn't mentioned what is going to happen to him now that Luther has found out. I don't want him to lose his job or be punished for being with me. That is not fair for him. "Look, Luther, this isn't Aerick's fault." He goes to speak but my words spill out quickly, trying to explain. "I'm the one that started this and it isn't fair for him to get in trouble because me. I am a grown woman and I can make my own decisions. He didn't push me into this, it was all me." When I finish, Aerick is trying not to smile, but Luther doesn't hold back his laughter.

"Well, that is good to know, but if I could speak now." He pauses and a sheepish grin burns my face.

"Sorry."

"I was going to say that I don't encourage personal interaction between my instructors and the cadets. It obviously isn't good for business. However, I've known Aerick for some time now and while he pretended to be content, he was clearly unhappy for most of that time. Since he met you, I've noticed a big change in him. I have been coming down on him hard, thinking he was just distracted by his old issues. It was to get him to regain focus; but as it turns out, I was actually creating more problems. Something was up with him, but I didn't know what. Never in a thousand years would I have guessed this was the issue." His lips turn up slightly. "I'm glad to know now. However, it's disappointing Aerick didn't say something to me sooner."

Aerick tenses up. "Luther, I was going to."

Luther holds up his hand, stopping Aerick. "It was smart you gave up your duties over her rankings to avoid conflict of interest, but really, it's still there just by you being her lead instructor."

Panic begins to drum in my chest. "Luther, you can't do this to him. He loves this job."

"Just listen, Nadi." My lips tighten into a line to refrain from continuing into another rant.

"I was just going to say that you and Tara will be switching lead instructors. You will now be under Paulo. Aerick will be Tara's lead instructor." I smile at him and he returns it.

"So Aerick gets to keep his job?"

Luther lets out a chuckle. "Of course he does. I'm really happy he has found you. I was tired of him being a miserable bastard." He smacks Aerick hard on the shoulder, making him jerk forward slightly.

"Fuck off, Luther," Aerick says, without any conviction.

"But with all honesty, you really should have told me. I'm extremely happy for you, but it better never happen again. I don't like being left in the dark and if I'd known sooner, I could have...

I don't know, done something." He shakes off the sadness that has seeped into his face and turns to Aerick, looking very serious.

"Aerick, I need your word that Nadi will not affect your judgment going forward, or I will have to put you on leave until she's done. This means, not distracted, not disappearing at inappropriate times, and above all, you need to maintain a low profile while she has finishes out her time here."

"You have my word, Luther."

"Good. I've already endured enough grief from her parents, but they've agreed to drop it be since she is legally an adult." He rubs the back of his neck, showing how much tension has built up. My father is a very intense person and I could only imagine how that conversation went.

"Nadi, I need to know if anyone at camp creates any more problems. It's imperative the rest of this session go off without any other issues."

"Will do, boss man." He gets a sly smile on his face.

"Good. Don't make me regret this decision. Now Nadi, there is something else I would like you to think about. Assuming you past your final testing, Aerick has made me aware you will have enough credits to graduate."

My eyebrows draw together in confusion. "What do you mean?"

"Well, this camp is certified as a summer school, and the work that you do here gets you high school credit. It's one of the reasons our curriculum is so exhausting and focuses on core classes. It helps those who have gotten in trouble to catch up, since usually they are behind by the time they make it here. I have been over your school records and you only needed four and a half more credits to graduate, which isn't surprising. You're far from our typical cadet." Aerick laughs silently beside me. *Jerk.*

"Anyway, each of your educational classes qualifies for a half a credit; that is three credits in total. In addition to that, your physical classes get you two more credits, which go toward physical education and occupational credit. That gives you five credits. You will have enough to graduate early. You should really be proud of yourself." My mouth falls open in shock – I don't know what to say. Looking to Aerick, his face shows nothing but pride.

"We have a position opening and I would like you to consider taking it. I would prefer to have Aerick stay here, and it's clear you will be the key to that. I'd like you to consider taking the position, if it is a career path you think you would enjoy," he says with his eyebrow raised. Aerick doesn't seem surprised; he clearly knew about this.

"What is the position?"

"This needs to stay in confidence for a little while longer, which means you'll need to keep this to yourself for the time being."

I shrug my shoulders. "Okay, I can do that."

"As it turns out, Tia is six weeks pregnant. She would like to resign so that she can stay home with her child. Her and Brand have been looking to buy a home up here and he will stay on as an instructor, other than the three months he's taking off when the baby is born. I'd like you to take her position."

"Wait, really!" I say, shocked, and Aerick face mirrors Luthers' but with a hint of surprise. He must have known this was coming but probably hadn't discussed it with Luther yet.

"Yes. We would need to get you certified, which is going to be a lot of work for you. It would be through a fast-track program, which means a lot of CLEP exams. If you pass them, will get you automatic credit to cover your core college classes and then you'll take the remaining classes online at the local college while you train under Tia. She will stay on as our teacher until she gives birth, and you can become certified. In all honesty, I believe you would be excellent at this position. You are very smart. I don't think you will have a problem getting through it."

I am ecstatic until realization hits me. "Wait, I have no way of paying for college. There is no way for me to come up with that kind of money."

"Don't worry. You likely qualify for Federal Pell Grants that should cover the majority of your cost. I also provide my employees with tuition reimbursement. There will be very little cost for you to cover, and we can figure that out when the time comes."

Aerick huffs beside me. "No need, I'll take care of it."

"Aerick, I can't let you do that," I interject.

He glares at me. "Funny, I don't remember asking for your

permission. I said I'll pay for it. End of story." I roll my eyes, not in the mood for this argument right now. I press my lips into a line, showing my disapproval, but see he's not going to back down on this.

"Fine. You can loan me the money." I look away and back to Luther, continuing before he can argue. "I'd love to take the position Luther."

He smiles widely, though I'm not sure if it is from my defiance toward Aerick or if he's happy I said yes. "Great, we can go over the details later, but please remember what I said. I do not want any more problems arising from your relationship." We both nod at him, but Aerick is still tense next to me. I'm sure we are not done talking about that.

"Now Nadi, if you don't mind, I need you to handle a situation for me." I look at him, once again confused, and so does Aerick.

"Your friend Jeff has been causing quite the problem for us. More like, he has been raising hell. We had to sedate him the day it happened and ever since then, he has been a royal pain in my ass. My agreement with the courts is you guys cannot cross out of the city limits of Cle Elum unless there is an emergency, so I can't bring him here. I need you to talk to him and get him to calm down."

"Wait. Where are we?"

He pulls out his phone and sends a text. "We're in Ellensburg. Cle Elum only has a small clinic. They weren't equipped to handle your situation. Same reason Jeff was brought here when he was taken to the hospital." His phones rings and he answers it quickly.

"Thanks Brand, put him on." Luther hands me his phone and I take it reluctantly.

"Hello?" I say, a little timid.

"Jesus Christ, you're okay! I was about to risk trying to jump ship to come see you. What the hell happened?" I refrain from rolling my eyes at Jeff's shouting on the other end of the phone.

"A psycho bitch stabbed me, obviously," I say with a little laugh, but Aerick clearly doesn't think it is funny as he shakes his head slightly and nearly bites a hole in his lip.

"I know that, but why the hell did she do it?"

It's probably not the best time to get into this conversation. "Jeff, I will explain everything when I get back in a few days, okay? Until then, can you stop giving everyone such a hard time. You are going to end up on mess hall duty for the next month, you dumbass." I can almost hear him calming down at my smart-ass remarks.

"Fine, but you're really okay, right? That was some pretty gruesome shit."

No shit, Sherlock. "I am okay. They're releasing me in a few days and I'll explain, okay?"

"Yeah, okay. Has Aerick been there with you? I haven't seen him since it happened."

I look up at Aerick and he's watching me intently. "Yes, he's been here. My mom, dad and brother are here, too."

"Okay. I suppose that makes me feel a little better, although Luther is an asshole for not letting me come there to see you. And I swear if that nurse sticks one more needle in me, I'm going to break her arm. I hate that shit."

"Jeff, you better not. They have rules to follow just like us. I said I'm good. Now man the hell up and deal with it until I get back. Understood?" Luther and Aerick try to stifle their laughs as Luther mumbles 'yep, she'll fit in great'.

"Whatever, bossy. See you in a few days."

I huff. "Better. I'll see you soon. Love you." Aerick's eyes fly to mine just as I realize what I said.

"Love you too, brat. Take care." Brand gets back on the phone and I hand the phone to Luther, who starts talking and walks away from the bed. Aerick's eyes are still on mine but I can't read his expression.

I'm assuming he was not happy hearing that out of my mouth. I breath in deeply and take his hand. "Don't even think it. You know the love I feel for you and the love I feel for him is different. He's a very close friend, like a brother. I need you to be comfortable with that and know I would never do anything to hurt you. Ever!"

He holds my gaze for a moment longer and his expression shifts as he leans down to kiss me hard before pulling back. "You are mine and I don't share." His voice is so low and full of authority.

I want to laugh at his possessiveness but think better of it.

"Calm down, killer. I'm all yours." I take his face in my hands and kiss him lightly and then draw back to look directly in his eyes. "Just yours," I say softly, putting all my heart into it, and kiss him on the tip of his nose, with a smile.

His chest rises and falls with a sense of relief. "Good."

Luther rejoins us, saying his goodbyes, and I get settle for a much-needed nap. Aerick turns on the TV to a rerun of the Sons of Anarchy, and I fall asleep as he traces a figure eight on the inside of my wrist.

✳ ✳ ✳ ✳

I'm awoken yet again by a nurse. She informs me they are transferring me out of the intensive care unit, to the progressive care unit, which means I might actually get to sleep tonight. The downside is I will be losing my morphine drip and they will be putting me on pills. At least I'll finally be able to eat a decent meal again.

Aerick sits next to me as the nurse lifts up my gown to look at my wound, checking it for signs of irritation. Even with the morphine, it hurts a lot. Aerick looks away as soon as she lifts the bandage, which seems a little odd. He did it when the doctor looked at it, too. It isn't like he's squeamish.

She moves it around slightly and I try hard not to flinch. Aerick tenses beside me and tightens his grip on my hands, trying to comfort me. She covers it up again with a nod of approval. She tells me they will be moving me sometime in the next hour, then leaves again.

288

Aerick continues to look down at my hands that cover his. "Are you okay?" I ask gently. His eyebrows pull together. He still feels guilty. "Babe, stop it. It wasn't your fault." He looks to me.

"Excuse me?" We both turn to see a man in a pair of jeans and a nice blazer standing at the door.

"Hello, Detective Raines," Aerick greets him, and the gentleman nods in response before addressing me.

"Good afternoon, Nadalynn. Good to see you are on your way to recovery. I am Detective Raines. If you don't mind, I need to speak to you about what happened."

Out of the corner of my eye, I see Aerick glare at the man. "Is this really necessary?" There is a substantial amount of anger in his voice, which is odd. He's usually composed when he needs to be.

"I am afraid it is." Aerick bites his lip and looks at me. *What now?* He's uncomfortable about something.

"Nadalynn-"

I stop the detective by putting my hand up. "Please call me Nadi."

"Yes, ma'am. Can you please tell me in your own words what happened?" *In my own words? Whose words would I say?* He takes out a tape recorder. "Do you mind?" he asks, seeing my gaze on the recorder.

"No, it's fine." He presses the button and then says my full name and the date and time.

"Please continue," he says to me.

"Well, I was having my weekly session with Liz. She had her choice words to say about Aerick. I responded by defending him and she got in my face and then stabbed me. I fought back before she could do anything else and then I crawled outside to get someone's attention before I could pass out and bleed to death."

"Why would you ladies be talking about Aerick?"

Aerick gets more tense beside me. "He's my boyfriend, but he used to be with Liz. She wasn't too happy about that."

"And you never threatened her?"

My eyebrow shoots up. "No. Why would I do that?"

He looks to Aerick, "Would it be okay if Aerick steps out for a few minutes?"

"Absolutely not," we both say at the same time.

Hesitantly he continues. "Did you ever feel threatened by her that Aerick was cheating on you with her?"

"What?! No, of course not. He's not like that." I look to Aerick, and he is shaking his head slightly with his eyes closed. *What the hell?*

"Did your boyfriend tell you about his colorful past with women?"

My anger is starting to rise. "His past is just that, his past. I don't care. I'm his future, period!" A slight smile tugs at Aerick's mouth. "Why does it even matter? That stupid bitch stabbed me."

"Well, ma'am," he says as he stiffens, "she's claiming she did it in self-defense. She says she only stabbed you after you hit her and slammed her head into the ground out of jealousy."

Fuck me. "You've got to be kidding me." I say exasperated. "That is a complete crap."

"I agree," Aerick chimes in. "I have no feelings for Liz. I really never did, and she was pissed about that."

"That's funny, because she told me that you recently got into a fight at the local bar because you were jealous that she was there with someone else."

Aerick's face turns red in anger. "That's bullshit. I have witnesses, I tried to walk away. He started that fight."

"Well, this will be something you both will need to take up in court. The judge has granted her bail and a hearing has been set for thirty days from today. Until that time, she's not to come within a thousand meters of either of you. I have talked with the owner of the camp and he has let her go, requesting she not return. Until the hearing, Nadi, you will remain at the boot camp, since your sentence is not up yet. My suggestion is that you get a lawyer, seeing how you are already in there on assault charges. Good day!"

He turns around and walks out. *What the hell just happened? How did this get turned around on me?* My mouth hangs open in shock.

"They don't believe me!" I seethe. "I'm a fucking criminal and she is an upstanding citizen. She's going to get away with this. This is bullshit!"

Aerick leans down, hugging me to comfort me, but his body is vibrating with anger. "She is not going to get away with this babe,

I promise you. No one believes the shit that just spewed from his mouth. We'll figure this out."

CHAPTER SIXTEEN

(Saturday, August 22nd)

"COME ON, LUTHER. Please?" I whine.

"Nadi, I said no. You just got back here a couple of hours ago. You need to rest." I scrunch my face at him.

"Seriously, Luther, I've been confined to a hospital room for a week."

He chuckles. "You were comatose for half of it."

"Yeah, but it has been a week since my surgery, and I need to get up and move around. Especially since I'm to be cooped up in an even smaller room for the next week. Aerick, will you help me out here?"

He looks at me like I'm crazy. "Sorry, Princess, but I have to agree with him on this; you need to rest."

Ugh, I thought at least he would be on my side. "Luther," I say, getting very serious, "I can make the next week either really easy or really hard. You know I can. All I am asking is for a few simple things."

He breathes in deeply, looking a little defeated. "Fine. How about we compromise. I'll allow you to begin going to the mess hall for meals starting tomorrow, and to your educational classes on Monday. Other than that, you are in this infirmary, got it? If you can behave for one week, I'll let you move back into your dorm. However, I strictly forbid all physical activities for two weeks. That was the doctor's orders."

At least I got something. He was going to just keep me confined here for the next two weeks, but I'm already itching to get out and move around. The idea of being stuck in here for two weeks makes me want to pull my hair out. "But I get to go tonight, right?"

He sighs and throws up his hands in frustration. "Fine, but Aerick is to escort you to and from the bonfire, and he's not to be staying in here with you at night. You need to recover, and he needs to get back into his duties like we talked about." My face lights up and there's a hint of a smile on Aerick's mouth.

It isn't everything that I requested, but I'll take it. I would have much rather gone back to the dorm and got back into the normal routine. Of course, I would have taken it easy with the physical part, but Luther immediately shut me down, and seeing the look on Aerick's face, he agreed with Luther.

"Thanks, Luther."

He rolls his eyes and purses his lips. "You're definitely going to fit in here. Another pain in my ass." Aerick and I both laugh at him. "Now Aerick, she is fine. Get out of here and start getting your shit caught up. I expect at least two of your reports done by sundown and on my desk before you take Nadi to the bonfire."

"Sure thing, Luther." He come over to me where I'm sitting on the bed against a bunch of pillows. "See you later, Princess." He gives me a quick kiss on the top of my head and Luther scoffs as he says 'princess' under his breath. Aerick leaves and Luther looks at me.

"I'm serious. He needs to focus, and you need to behave. I won't tolerate insubordination. This only works if you to do what you are supposed to do. You need to show me you guys can handle this."

I nod my head. "Thanks again Luther, for everything."

He chuckles, "I was serious, he used to be a major pain in the ass. Hopefully things will get better for him now. It's all I want for any of you – to be happy." He turns without another word and leaves me alone.

My body relaxes into the pillows. The trip home from the hospital was a little exhausting, not that I would admit it out loud. It's weird how just a car ride can make you tired. It seemed like overkill when the hospital insisted I be wheeled out in a wheelchair, right up to the waiting car. It made me feel weak and I don't like that, but now I understand.

I'm happy to be back at the camp, as crazy as it sounds. Aerick's constant hovering was actually getting a little irritating.

Always asking what I needed, or how I was doing, or if I was in pain. Always walking me to the bathroom or picking me up to set me on the chair, treating me like a fragile piece of glass that might break at any moment.

Even when he kisses me, it's reserved. Anytime I tried to deepen the kiss he immediately pulls away. My sexual frustration is off the charts right now. He feels it too. I've teased him a few times and felt his excitement. But instead of acting on it, he just gives me an irritated look and excuses himself from the room to calm down.

Sometime really soon, I'm going to need some kind of relief. I am getting all achy just sitting here thinking about it. Taking several deep breaths, I lie back and eat the food that Aerick brought me for lunch. For now, a good nap will do me good so I'm ready to go later tonight. It will be nice to be around everyone again.

Jeff was waiting for me this morning when we arrived. Luther looked a little irritated and I thought Aerick was going to beat his ass when he hugged me so hard I yelled out at the pain that shot through me. Of course, Paulo, Brand and Trent all stopped in to say hi, but so did just about all the staff. Brayden was also a little too excited when he plopped down on the bed, sending more shooting pains though my body. Aerick hauled him up by his collar and threw him against the wall a little harder than needed. It would have been funny if I wasn't so scared for him.

The whole Liz situation still has my nerves tied in knots.

Luther has offered to get me a lawyer since I was injured in his camp. He also said the lawyer was good, and that there isn't anything to worry about, but my mind just won't let it go. Instead of her going to jail for attempted murder, I may get yet another assault charge, and this time it would be two to five in prison, because of all my past criminal record.

That's what scares me the most. It's doubtful Aerick would wait around for me for that long. At first my fear was just going to prison for that long. Minimum security was usually for non-violent crimes. My record would easily land me in a medium security prison that's full of sexual predators and violent offenders

Of the two, my bigger fear is losing Aerick. My feelings for him still scare me a bit. It still floors me that love can be so strong, but as each day passes, I realize more and more that I don't want to ever be without him. Even when he irritates me, the draw to be near him is so strong.

Over the last few days we did nothing but talk. It was like we missed the whole phase of 'getting to know each other' in our relationship. There is so much I've learned about him. We talked about everything, from the stupid little things like our favorite things to do, to the deep things he said he's never shared with anyone. He told me about his childhood, which wasn't the happiest. His dad sounds like the biggest asshole and his mom is in a class of her own. I couldn't imagine growing up like that. It really made me appreciate my parents so much more. He explained he hasn't talked to them in more than three years and has no intention to in the future.

Caught up in one of our conversations, I admitted to him that I heard his and Evan's conversation. He wasn't surprised, and already knew because my heart beat had picked up. He explained that what he said to my brother was just as much for me to hear as him. He wanted me to know that he only cares for me, that I'm special to him. Though I already knew that, it was still nice to hear.

After finishing my food, I reluctantly take the pain medication Terrie left for me before scooting down on the bed. I flinch and suck in a quick breath at the pain as I try to get comfortable. The Percocet and Ibuprofen only help with some of the pain. The closer it gets to the time to take my next dose, the more painful it gets; but I can deal with this. It will be important to show Luther I'm okay, so he will lay off me a little; being confined to this room sucks. Putting in my earbuds, my finger pushes the volume up button and my eyes finally close.

* * * *

"Ready?" Aerick comes in to the room. Terrie just helped me get into my shirt, since I still can't lift my arms above my head without an absurd amount of pain. She was kind enough to give me a little extra pain medication, but she warned this was a one-time favor.

"Yep," I say, a little to sweetly. He hands me one of his sweaters.

"Thought you might like one that smells like me," he says as he wraps his arms carefully around me, making sure to avoid my cut. As he leans down to kiss me, the smell of alcohol on his breath assaults my senses; whatever he's been drinking is strong. As he kisses me again, there is the distinct taste of whiskey. At least it seems to have loosened him up a little. That was the most passionate kiss I've gotten in a week. I give him a mile-wide grin.

"What?" he asks, trying to be all innocent.

"What kind of whiskey are you drinking?"

He chuckles. "Black Velvet. We had a pre-bonfire get-together. It's a normal thing for us." I bite his lip softly, letting him slowly pull it out of my teeth.

"It tastes delicious. Especially tasting it on you."

He bites his lip, clearly turned on, and kisses my nose. "And if you weren't taking those Percocet, I'd offer you some, but too bad for you." His laughter fills the room. He sounds so carefree tonight, which is a breath of fresh air after being so uptight and tense all week. I'm glad he finally gets to relax.

"Well, I expect you to share at the next one," I tell him, trying not to smile but failing miserably.

"You got it, Princess. Come on, we got a date with all your friends, who are dying to spend some time with you." He grabs his sweater out of my hand, gently putting it over my head, and patiently helps me get my arms in. Once it's on, I breathe in deeply. He is right, it smells deliciously of him. I love the smell of the cologne he wears, mixed with the smell of his Brut aftershave.

He laces his hand in mine and I look at him. Luther told us to keep a low profile. "Luther said it's okay, don't worry. Holding hands is okay, at least for tonight while everyone is here." I raise my eyebrow questioningly at him. "He allowed Shauna, Jack and Laura to come, since Tia is going to make her announcement tonight. Besides, half the camp heard me tell you I love you. It isn't like it's a secret anymore." He kisses me on top of my head. "Let's go."

We slowly walk out to the fire pit. By the time we get there I am breathing heavily and Aerick looks at me a little worried. We sit down on a log together as he continues to look at me. "I'm okay; stop freaking out," I scold, not wanting to draw attention to myself.

He looks down. "I'm not freaking out, only making sure you're okay," he says grumpily. It's so cute when he pouts.

"Why don't you get me a water?" I say, poking him in the side. His smile returns.

"Yes ma'am. For the record, I'm supposed to tell you that you are not to get up from that seat all night, or I have to take you back. So don't move that cute little ass of yours. I am rather looking forward to spending this time with you, and I won't be happy if Luther makes me take you back." His tone is stern but there's a smile threatening at the side of his mouth.

"Okay, fine, I promise to stay right here."

He goes over to get a water and grabs out a soda, too. He opens it and guzzles some before handing it to Paulo. I'm momentarily confused until I see Paulo pull out a flask. *Interesting.*

I smile as he comes back to join me with his drink and my bottle of water. "And what, might I ask, is so amusing?"

"You know that is how we hid our alcohol from you guys during our first bonfire?"

"I figured. It hasn't been that long since I had to hide my alcohol," he chuckles. "Looks like your boy found a little action of his own." My eyebrows pull together in confusion and he nods his head to the side of me.

My gaze follows his and I see Jeff is kissing Tara. *Wow.* That was unexpected. I know she likes him, but I didn't realize he had returned any of those feelings.

They break their kiss and Jeff's eyes catch mine. I give him a big smile and he looks down a little shy, but he wraps his arm around her waist. Good for him. "I am happy for him. He deserves to be happy."

"At least I don't have to worry about him around you, anyway." I elbow Aerick in the side and I'm suddenly glad he sat on the opposite side of my wound. "I know, I know, but it is hard to get past the fact that he crushed on you for years."

I roll my eyes. "Well, get over it, because I am not giving up my best friend because of jealousy."

He shakes his head. "Okay, Princess. Whatever you say."

"Princess? I think you may have hit your head," Huck says as he sits down next to me. "So, this explains a lot." He points to our joined hands.

"It's a joke between us," I explain. "And what do you mean 'explains a lot'?"

He shrugs, "How you got into the top so many times," he says, and I see the smile he is holding in.

He is only kidding, but Aerick has gone tense. "I had no control over her rankings, asshole. I gave up that responsibility a few weeks in." He's downright pissed and I put my hand on his thigh to keep him in his seat.

"Dude, chill out, I was just kidding." He looks at him a little crazy, almost afraid.

"He knows that, Huck. He just isn't used to your uncanny charm." I grin at Huck and give Aerick's leg another squeeze.

"Anyway, welcome back," he smiles and leaves to go talk with some of the others.

"Aerick, you need to relax a little." He takes a long swig of his drink, but is still tense. As he goes to take another drink, I move my hand up the inside of his leg, causing him to almost choke on his drink. "I could help you work off some of that tension if you want."

I feel his groan as much as I hear it. "Nadalynn, behave," he says quietly.

"What if I don't want to?" I squeeze the inside of his thigh harder; he jumps a little as he quickly grabs my hand and sets it back in my own lap.

"Behave or you will go back to bed," he says roughly as he adjust his pants quickly and I hide my smile.

"That could be fun!" I bite my lip, hoping it will work. I'm absolutely aching for him right now.

"Alone," he says, deadpan, and I purse my lips.

"You're such a party pooper."

"We will have plenty of time for that, babe. Just be patient," he says, trying to soften the blow.

"Easy for you to say!"

"I'll make it up to you later," he whispers in my ear, sending another thrum of aching between my legs. I cross them, trying to get a little relief, and he laughs at me.

"Keep laughing and I will show you how funny it is," I say, completely serious, but it just makes him laugh harder.

"Asshole."

He gets that incredibly sexy smirk on his face. "Never said I wasn't."

Trying to ignore him, I take in my surroundings. Everyone is here, laughing and having a good time. This is so what I needed. Luther shows up with Ayla and Jack and our s'more supplies.

Aerick sees me eyeing the table. "You want one?" I nod at him. The hospital food was atrocious, making all food look even more delicious. He squeezes my hand and gets up to make me one.

Royce and Mike come over to say 'hi' and to welcome me back. Royce sits rather close to me, while Mike just stands next to us. We sit and talk for a minute until Aerick comes back, handing me my s'more, and sits next to me, placing his hand on my thigh. I notice Royce's sour face seeing Aerick's hand resting on my thigh, which I'm fairly certain he did to make sure Royce knew to stay back. We talk for a few minutes and they move on to talk to Jeff.

"Aerick be careful, your jealousy is showing," I say sarcastically.

"I wasn't being jealous, simply touching my girlfriend." I try to think of a retort but Tia stands and asks everyone for their attention. Brand stands near her and looks a little nervous.

"Well, I have some news for everyone. Actually, I have two things, now." She is absolutely glowing. Luther look at her, confused. "The first thing is... that Brand just asked me to marry him." He holds up her hand to show a ring on her finger and everyone erupts in cheers.

I feel Aerick huff beside me. "It's about time. I was starting to think he would never ask her," he says quietly. I look at him questioning but he just shakes his head and shouts, "And?"

Brand gets a smirk on his face as everyone quiets down to listen. "And," he places his hand over Tia's stomach as she blushes. "I'm going to be a dad." The staff members all yell at once and quickly converge on them, the guys knocking Brand around and the girls all placing their hands on Tia's stomach.

Luther picks up a bag that was at his feet and Ayla starts handing out glasses and filling them with champagne. "He's letting us drink!" I look at Aerick surprised and he laughs.

"Yeah right, it's sparkling cider." *Damn.*

Everyone gets a glass and then Luther gets everyone's

attention. "Congratulations, Brand and Tia. Your friends and I wish you two nothing but happiness as well as good health to your little one. To Brand and Tia!"

He raises his glass and everyone shouts in unison, 'Brand and Tia!' I stare at them smiling and I can't help but wonder if that will be Aerick and me someday.

Aerick grabs my hand and brings it up to his lips, gently kissing my knuckles. "One day, babe," he murmurs against my hand.

Holy shit. Did he really just say that? My freaking heart is racing. I don't say anything because I want to remember tonight just like this. I smile at him shyly and he mirrors it.

He stands and pulls me up so we can go congratulate Tia and Brand. I give Tia an odd, side hug since Aerick has refused to let go of my hand, and nod at Brand. "Great news, you guys. I'm so happy for you. Congrats to you both."

"Brand, you finally grew a pair. 'Bout time, Congrats." I elbow Aerick in the stomach.

Brand just laughs and looks at our joined hands, "Apparently so did you." I press my lips together to keep from laughing.

"Oh, trust me, that was never the problem," he says, biting his lip and looking down at me. I blush, looking away from him. He has definitely never been shy about asking me anything.

"Thanks, guys," Tia says, trying to stop the pissing match going on in front of us. "Nice to see you back, Nadi. You sure do have your hands full. Good luck with that one."

We both laugh. "Thanks," I say and pull Aerick away before he can say anything else.

We sit, and the night continues to pass quickly. Just about the whole camp has come over to say hi, and my eyes grow heavy with exhaustion. I lay my head on his shoulder and Aerick lays his head on top of mine as he wraps his arm around my waist. "Getting tired?"

My eyes gaze up into his eyes. They are so warm and loving right now. "Just a bit."

He smiles down at me. "Come on. Let me put you to bed."

We walk in silence back to the infirmary. I notice he is staring at the stars again. It's so cute that he does that. We get into the room and I tighten my grip on his hand. "Lie with me until I fall asleep?"

He smiles at me. "Sure, babe. Let's get you ready for bed." My body really wants him right now. I'm feeling a bit high from the pills Terrie gave me, and it's making the feeling all the more intense.

I grab out my shorts and I'm suddenly happy I'd already put my tank top on. He doesn't need to see the bandage on my stomach. His hands gently help me take off my sweater and then my tee shirt.

I swear I feel his pants twitch, telling me he is just as horny as me. He takes a step back and pulls out his phone. I look at him, a little confused. "Just making sure the camera is off. I'm not supposed to be staying in here with you tonight, even if I am only staying for a while. I don't want to get in shit from Luther." I grab my shorts off the bed, shaking my head. Works for me, since I'd totally forgotten there was a camera in here. Turning my body away from Aerick, I slowly slide my pants off down to my boots and then untie my boots slowly.

"Good," he mutters right before I hear him breathe in deeply. I'm sure he just caught slight of me bent over in front of him. My smile spreads. I slip off my boots and remove my pants. I stand up and turn back around. He jerks his face away quickly, looking like he just got caught with his hand in the cookie jar. His pants are beginning to bulge, making me bite my lip in excitement.

"Behave!" he tells me sternly.

"I don't know what you are talking about," I feign with an innocent, toothy grin.

"Get into bed, Nadalynn." He's definitely frustrated and have to hold in a laugh. I start to walk around the bed.

"With your shorts on," he says as an afterthought.

Crap, I'm caught. I comply, slipping them on quickly, and then lie on my side, patting the bed next to me. "Come on. Come lie with me, I'll behave."

He pauses for a second and then sits down, taking his boots off. His body slides in next to me and I rest my head in the crook of his arm, wrapping my arm around his waist. With one arm under my neck, he puts the other on my waist. He starts to run his fingers up and down my side, but doesn't go down to my wound. The contact, even though is so little, turns me on so much. "I love you Aerick," I whisper.

He kisses my forehead. "Love you too," he says, as his arm tightens around me slightly.

I begin drawing circles on his stomach. I can feel his muscles though his shirt. Damn, this man is so fucking hot. His breaths start to even out. He has been sleeping in a hospital chair for the last week and is surely more tired than he's let on. His hand relaxes on my waist and I'm fairly certain he's fallen asleep. I smile as a plan slowly forms in my head.

My hand moves down his stomach and very carefully undoes his belt, and then unbuttons his pants. The little hairs from his happy trail tickle my hand as it moves down to his pants. Slowly, I unzip his pants, trying not to wake him up just yet.

My hand slip into his pants and under the waist band of his boxers. Touching him lightly, I freeze as he moves just a little. When I'm sure he is not awake, I begin rubbing him slowly. He begins to harden under my hand and a moan escapes his lips. He's not quite awake yet so I continue stroking him a little faster as he hardens beneath my hand.

Suddenly his eyes fly open and his hand covers mine. "What the hell are you doing?" I squeeze him and he breathes in sharply. "Babe, we can't do this. No strenuous activity, remember." I feel his hips push up just slightly and apparently his body isn't agreeing with his brain.

"It's just my hand Aerick. It'll be fine." His hand relaxes just for a second and I begin to move mine again before he stops me.

"Please baby, I need you," I beg; I'm dying here. I squeeze him again. He turns his head to look me in the eyes. I pull at him once more, trying to get his mind over the edge he's teetering on.

He closes his eyes for a moment and then turns onto his side so his whole body is facing me. "Lie on your back," he says, sounding defeated, and I've won. We move over slightly on the small bed so I can lie on my back. "We are not having sex tonight, but I'll relieve a bit of that pressure for you if you promise me you stay still. If you move around, I will stop, okay?" I nod.

He leans down and kisses me. He deepens it quickly as he slides his hand down my shorts and into my underwear. As soon as he touches my bundle of nerves, I let out a loud moan and push my hips up into his hand.

He freezes. "I said stay still." He takes his hand out of my shorts and grabs my leg, hiking it up so it is bent and leaning against him, then slides his hand back in to my pants. "Absorb the pleasure, babe," he whispers into my ear. "And for fuck sake, stay quiet before we get into trouble." He starts kissing down my neck and begins to massage me again. It's like I've been waiting weeks for this, but he needs to be satisfied too.

I slide my hand down into his pants again. He pauses for just a moment as I stroke him. I feel the shiver go up his body and then he continues. It takes all my strength not to move anything other than my hand. When he slides his fingers into me, I let out an involuntary moan. He quickly covers my mouth with his. "Always so wet for me," he mumbles and then picks up the pace, sliding his fingers in and out of me while circling my nub with his thumb. I stroke him harder, trying to cope with the intense feeling building in me and he moans into my mouth.

As I'm getting close, my legs involuntarily try to pull together, but he uses his arm to keep my leg pinned against him. "I said absorb it." His voice has gone very low and rough. I pick up my pace as my hand tightens around him because that is the only movement I'm allowed. The pleasure is almost getting painful and he pushes his fingers into me deeper, hitting my spot, and my body begins to tremble and I tighten around his fingers. I squeeze him hard in response.

"Ah, fuck." He breathes in in deeply between his teeth and I pause. "Oh God, don't stop," he begs and I do it again, once, then twice and I feel the warm liquid begin to spill from him.

He groans and bites me on the sweet spot on my neck as he continues with his fingers, causing my orgasm to go longer. It feels fucking amazing. We both continue for a minute until our orgasms run their course.

That was crazy intense, and I feel a hundred times better. He rests his forehead against mine as he tries to catch his breath. "You never cease to amaze me." I hum, not able to speak just yet. "Feeling better, Princess?" I hum again. "Is that all I am getting out of you tonight?" I smirk and hum one last time. He laughs as he reaches over, grabbing the box of tissues, and begins cleaning off my hand. "Looks like I'm going to have to come give you a sponge bath tomorrow," he says with a wicked grin and then gets up to wipe down just above his waist band.

He buttons and buckles his pants before lying back down with me. "Now, go to sleep." He kisses my nose and I snuggle into his chest. I can't wait to fall asleep like this every night.

"Night, baby."

"Night, Princess."

I close my eyes and fall quickly into a deep sleep.

CHAPTER SEVENTEEN

(Sunday, August 30th)

I AM SO relieved to take a real shower. Body wipes are no comparison to a good ol' shower. It feels so good to relax under the hot water and wash away the residue from the wipes. Another plus is being able to dress in normal, everyday clothes again, instead of the sweats and tee shirts that I've been forced to wear all week. More than that, I'm happy to be back in my own crappy bed.

The infirmary bed is even more uncomfortable than the beds in the cabins. The only advantage to being in there is the privacy, which does absolutely no good, because the only person I'd like to be alone with is still treating me like a porcelain doll. I've tried to get Aerick to mess around with me all week to no avail.

Apparently, the alcohol was the only thing that loosened him up last week or I'd be even more sexually frustrated. Right now, my sexual appetite probably rivals a man's, always wanting sex. It's like I'm literally becoming addicted to it; or maybe I'm just addicted to being passionate with him.

As if he's reading my mind, Aerick comes strolling into the dorm. I've just finished putting my stuff away and was going to go outside to join everyone in the court yard. Problem is, I really don't have homework left to complete. Being stuck in the infirmary all week and not being able to participate in physical classes has given me plenty of time to get it all done throughout the week. He comes over to me and kisses me on the head. "How you are feeling, princess?"

"Okay, I guess."

He raises a questioning eyebrow. "Just okay? I thought this would make you happy. You have been itching to get out of there all week."

I look down at my hands before standing up in front of him. "Don't get me wrong, I'm happy to be back in here, but there are other needs recently neglected and I would much rather they were satisfied." I peek at him through my lashes and his eyes narrow at me.

"I would be happy to satisfy that for you," he says with a smirk on his face.

Thank goodness. I pull his face to me to kiss him, but he pulls away far too soon with an evil grin. "As soon as the doctor clears you for physical activity."

Stupid ass. "Come on Aerick, I'm dying here!" I whine at him, making him chuckle. *What the hell?* This is like punishment at its finest. Of all the men in the world, it figures the one bad boy that actually has self-control is standing in front of me.

"Sorry, but we are following the rules on this one. I refuse to be the one responsible for you hurting yourself. I'm not blind. You've been holding back how you're truly feeling." He's right. I've cut out my medication even though there is still quite a bit of pain, but today it's better than it has been since being released from the hospital.

"I'm fine." Irritated, I push him away and sit back down.

Suddenly he pushes me back on my bed, putting just enough weight on me to hold me down. My eyes fly to him with shock, hoping he is doing what I think he is doing. He kisses me softly.

"Suck it up. We shouldn't rush back into things." He kisses me again, trying to soften the blow.

"Well, I think you should stop treating me like a doll and satisfy my raging needs!" I say firmly. I've gotten bolder around him, but I'm not sure if it's because I feel more safe with him, or if he just makes me feel stronger. Maybe it is both.

"Babe, it isn't that hard. Only one more week," he tries to soothe me.

"Easy for you to say, my hormones are exploding here and it is all your fault."

He tries to hold in his smile. "Easy is definitely not the word I'd use to describe it." He pushes down his hips, allowing me to feel him hard against my thigh.

"See? All the more reason to take care of our frustrations now." He is quiet for a moment, an internal struggle silently raging in his head, and I secretly hope he gives in because the aching is getting unbearable, especially with him lying on me like this.

"Hey, Aerick." I groan at the sound of Paulo's voice and look over to see him standing in the doorway to the bathroom, frozen in shock. "Um, sorry. Didn't mean to interrupt anything."

Aerick quickly jumps off of me, looking the opposite way to Paulo while he adjusts his pants. "No, it's fine, Paulo. What's up?" His eyes shoot up and he looks at me.

"You know, Paulo, you have great timing." It's pointless to try to hide my frustration, as I squeeze my legs together, trying to dissolve the ache. He chuckles and I turn a little pink at my brazen attitude toward him.

"Sorry sis, duty calls."

"And it would be nice if you would fucking get to the point of why you came in here." It appears Aerick may have been leaning on the side of just satisfying our needs.

"Sorry, man. I need you to review this and sign off on it ASAP. Luther wants it on his desk in twenty minutes."

Aerick purses his lips and turns back to me. "Sorry babe, like he said, duty calls. I'll see you later and for heaven's sake, take it easy, okay?" I roll my eyes at him as he leans down, kissing me again quickly before he goes to join Paulo, who has already turned around and left.

I've really got to find a way to loosen him up. There is no way I'm lasting another week, and after what just happened, it's not likely he can either.

I head to my counseling session with the new psychiatrist. We did my session in the infirmary last week, but it was fairly boring. He basically asked me about what had happened and my feelings on the situation. He seems like a fairly nice guy, and had apparently worked here several years ago before Luther hired Liz.

Aerick explained that he decided to open his own practice down in Seattle and was doing quite well for himself. Of course, he was very cute, in his late-twenties, with a very handsome smile and an extremely hot Australian accent.

"Good morning, Nadi," he greets me at the door.

"Good morning Christian." We shake hands as we go sit down.

"How was your week?" I let out a sigh of pure frustration. "That great huh?" He obviously observed the sarcastic look on my face.

"Well, let's see: mostly confined in a small room for an entire week, only leaving for small amounts of time, and that is only after spending a week confined to a hospital bed. So, let's just say I have been ridiculously bored, with nothing to do but think about things."

"What kind of stuff have you been thinking about?" He seems genuinely curious, but I'm not crazy enough to explain my sexual frustrations to a hot guy that, at a stretch, is young enough for me to date. He tilts his head to the side as if prompting me for an answer and I blush at the thought that just crossed my mind. "Well, I definitely have all kinds of theories about what you are thinking but I'd much rather hear it from you."

Great. Does he really know what my thoughts? I rack my brain quickly for something to say. "Um, I'm mostly worried about Liz and the hearing." It isn't exactly a lie – my brain has been working overtime thinking about it; it just isn't what I was thinking about a minute ago.

"Why are you worried? You told the truth, right?"

"Yes, of course, but I'm afraid that her reputation far exceeds mine and there are no witnesses to prove my side of the story."

He writes something down. "So, if there was a witness, would you be afraid?" I'm a little confused by his question.

"No. It happened exactly as I said it did. I didn't touch her until after she stabbed me." His questioning is starting to get me on edge.

"And why would she say it happened differently?"

Seriously. "I don't know. Maybe to cover her own ass?"

He looks at something he has written down. "Luther tells me that he has hired you an attorney. What does he say?"

It's true. I met with the attorney, Simon, last week. He was a very nice guy and was very patient. With a little encouragement from Aerick, I explained everything exactly as it happened and everything that happened leading up to it. Simon assured me he would only use what was necessary, so I explained everything, from her little hints to me, all the way up to the argument that happened right before she stabbed me.

After our lengthy conversation, he said there wasn't anything to worry about. That he would work on getting information to corroborate my story, which basically was Aerick and Paulo, since they were the only two that knew what was going on. Although, to me, that isn't much to go on.

"He told me not to worry about it, but it isn't just something I can forget. This could mean going to jail for assault; not something I would be too happy about."

"Yeah, I can understand that, but what I don't understand is why you always seem to think the worst is going to happen."

I bite my lip. "Maybe because bad shit is always happening to me." My quiet confession is out before I can stop myself.

His eyes are intense as the wheels in his head spin. "Just playing devil's advocate here, but you are the one who has been convicted of assault four times. Are you saying that it was never you fault?"

"No, I didn't mean that. I'm not denying all of those things, but it was a reaction, and that is the bad luck part. Being put in the situation to begin with." I stop short of saying the reason out loud.

"A reaction to being touched."

I look at him confused, "How do you know that?" His lips tighten into a line. "I have been given permission to go over Liz's session notes. Just as with her, this information will remain confidential."

I'm curious to know exactly what was in those notes. "Really, and what else did those notes say?"

"Well, the notes in your file seemed to be a little emotional, and only the first couple of sessions actually had reliable notes. Most of the early notes bring reference to your problem with touch. Since you have been here, have been several incidences in which you were touched, and you reacted violently to it." Of course, this couldn't just be an easy few sessions where we restart and don't have enough time to get to the actual culprit.

"Let me guess, you want to know why?" It shouldn't be surprising, but my hope was he was different.

He smiles. "Well, typically your condition is caused by one of two things. Either you suffered a great traumatic event, or you were born with a condition causing it. Now Liz, had already deduced that this was something you developed in your youth, meaning there must have been a traumatic event causing the issue. I am sure you know what it is, and it is likely that you do not like to talk about it. Since we don't have a lot of time to delve into it, I'm more interested in trying to help you to learn to deal with it. How does that sound?" I like this guy already.

My lips turn up in a smile. "That sounds like a good idea."

"Good. That is what I like to hear. We will need to start out with the basics. Are you able to handle touch from anyone?"

I pull my bottom lip between my teeth. "Yes," I say simply, not sure how much to reveal. He stands up and comes to sit close to me, without touching me. Every nerve in my body stands at attention. *Please tell me that he is not going to try to touch me.* My emotional well-being cannot handle this shit right now. I feel my chest tightening and I try to discretely wipe my sweaty hands on my pants.

"Are all of those that are able to touch you, people that were in your life prior to your traumatic event?" I clench my hands, trying to stay calm, but it isn't working too well. *Why can't I just get a normal person, instead of all this mess of craziness?*

"All but one," I breathe, trying to focus on the question. He moves his hand toward me slightly and my whole body becomes stock-still. *Please don't fucking let this shit happen.*

Then all the sudden he stands and walks back to sit where he was, his expression completely impassive, like nothing just happened. "Sorry, I don't want you to feel uncomfortable." I gaze at him dumbfounded. *What the fuck did he just do that for?*

"Please don't be upset with me. It was important for me to see how strong your reaction would be. It helps me know how bad the problem is."

I shake my head, trying to calm down. "You could have just asked!"

"Actually, I needed to see it in an unstaged environment."

I wipe my hands off again on my pants, trying to regain my composure. "What would you have done if I'd hit you? I'm sure you are well aware that it is my natural reaction."

He chuckles, "Yes, that is a risk, but I am short on time, and again, I apologize for making you nervous like that. So, can I assume that the one person that can touch you is your new boyfriend, the one all the fuss has been over?" He sounds genuine and it's hard to stay mad at that annoyingly cute grin on his face. I breathe in deeply as my body begins to relax a little.

"Correct, Aerick is the one that can touch me."

His smile grows as if he just had a major breakthrough and he writes down something before looking at his watch. "Well Nadi, we got a lot accomplished today, so you can go now. I really want you comfortable when we talk, and I have upset you, which I again apologize for." I'm not sure how much we actually accomplished, since very little was said. "I look forward to our next session." He walks me to the door but keeps his distance and his hands to himself. *Smart move!* "See you next week."

Once out in the fresh air, I feel a little better. He does seem sincere about wanting to help me, even giving me some space after pushing my limits. Maybe this guy will be better than the other ones I've seen. In the past, they always wanted me to talk about what happened, and that is something I don't want to do.

✳ ✳ ✳ ✳

At eight-thirty I head to the infirmary. During dinner, Aerick had slipped me a note telling me to meet Terrie there at eight-thirty. It was a little odd, but I figured he just wants us to have some alone time. It wasn't a horrible idea either, after the day I've had. Alone time with Aerick is never a bad thing.

The day had become cloudy and windy, prompting everyone

to move indoors, and gave me a perfect opportunity to escape without question. The guys thought nothing of it when I mentioned going over to see Terrie. After being stabbed a few weeks ago, it didn't seem that out of the ordinary to them. They probably assumed she needed to check it or that I needed some medicine to help the healing process.

She took out my stitches yesterday, which wasn't painful, but felt extremely odd. It probably had something to do with the pain medication she had me take while I waited for the hot, wet hand towel she put on it to soften up the stitches.

As I walk into the infirmary, Terrie smiles at me. "Hey, what's up?" I question, glad to finally find out what is going on.

"You up for hanging out for a while?"

I shrug my shoulders. "Sounds good."

She locks up before we leave, walking around to the outside perimeter of the buildings. My curiosity has piqued, but I keep quiet. There is a mist of rain coming down and the clouds have darkened the skies, making it seem later than it is.

"How are you feeling today?" she asks, breaking the silence as we round the back of the mess hall.

"Good, actually. It was really nice to get to take a normal shower." It was the highlight of my day.

She smiles. "Yeah, I think that would have driven me nuts, too."

Finally, it is too much for me to take. "So where exactly are we going?"

"We are going to my cabin. I thought maybe we could hang out for a while. It's normal for staff to gather in the cabins in the evening just to relax and wind down from the day. Since you will be working here soon, I thought you would like to join us tonight."

I look over to her in surprise. "I didn't know Luther had told anyone yet."

"He didn't, Aerick told Paulo, so naturally I found out. I think it's awesome. You seem cool and I think we will get along great."

"Thanks." My lips turn up in a smile. It will be nice to have another girl to talk to. I don't tend to get along well with other females. My lack of anything feminine and hatred of all drama doesn't make me a great option for a girlfriend. Then again, I've never had the need to talk about men with anyone else. She has a little insight on Aerick, making her the perfect female to become friends with.

We walk into her cabin just as the rain really starts to come down. The inside is bigger than it looks from outside. It reminds me a lot of a dorm room, only slightly larger. Bright colors peek out of a small bathroom through a door to the right. Two beds, two dressers, a small couch and a small round table with four chairs take up a good portion of the room, but there is still enough room to comfortably move around. Aerick, Paulo and Brayden are sitting at the table playing cards.

"You guys start without us?" Terrie asks, and Aerick looks up from his cards and smiles at me as he waves me over to him. I walk over next to him and he wraps an arm around my waist, using the other to pull me down by the collar of my shirt to kiss me.

"Hey, you," he greets me and I smirk sweetly at him but realize quickly everyone is looking at us. I'm not use to him being so open with our relationship.

"Hi," I say quietly.

Terrie walks over to a mini-fridge with a microwave perched on top of it and pulls out a bottle of Corona. She looks at me with an apologetic look. "Sorry, Nadi, but letting a cadet drink in my cabin is grounds for termination. It's bad enough I turn a blind eye to Brayden drinking in here."

I shrug my shoulders, not upset at all. "It's fine, no offense taken. The last thing I want is for you to get in trouble." Aerick already gets into enough trouble because of me. Guilt from anyone else getting in trouble is enough to quell negative feelings.

Terrie smiles as she sits down at the last chair. My eyes scan the room and there's no other chairs for me to sit in, so I debate going to sit on the couch. Aerick must feel me tense at the thought and quickly pulls me down to sit in his lap, wrapping his arms around me so he can hold the cards in front of me. I melt into him, loving the protective feeling of being in his arms.

"What are you guys playing?" I ask curiously.

"Poker," Aerick tells me. "Terrie, buy-in is forty bucks. You in?"

"Of course. I love taking you guys' money." She pulls out two twenties and gives it to Paulo, who hands her a stack of poker chips.

"So, this is what you guys do to relax at night – play poker and drink?" One of Aerick's hands moves down to my leg.

"Sometimes. One instructor has to be in the dorm during free time, so we trade-off; and sometimes we do other things." As he says the last part his hand moves up my leg. My body tenses a little and I feel him smile on the back of my neck before he kisses it. Damn prick, he knows what he is doing.

"So where is everyone else?"

"Andi, Tia and Jake are over in Tia's cabin. Brand and Trent are in the dorm."

"Where is Ayla?" I know that Terrie shares a cabin with Ayla, but she's not here.

Terrie looks at me. "Oh, Luther and her usually go out for drinks on Sunday nights."

Well, that is kind of nice. "Do you guys ever all hang out at the same time?"

"No, not usually. The cabins are pretty small, and Brand and Aerick don't get along. But occasionally we have a poker party in the instructors' cabin so that we can all play and hang out together. Especially during football season," Terrie tells me as she deals out a new hand.

I look to Aerick, "Why don't you get along with Brand?"

He presses his lips tightly together. "Brand is a dick."

I chuckle, raising an eyebrow. "Why is that?"

Paulo speaks up before Aerick can. "Brand is still pissed at

Aerick for trying to steal Tia away from him."

My mouth hangs open momentarily. "What?" I say, a little higher than I meant.

"It isn't like that princess. Brand is just a cocky motherfucker. I didn't like Tia, but I knew he did. I just wanted to prove something to Brand. He's always thought he was better than everyone else, but I know otherwise." He takes a deep breath as he feels me relax a bit.

"Besides, I helped the fucker. After I kissed her, he got up the balls to finally ask her out. If I didn't do that, he probably would have never have done it. Look how long it took him to finally propose to her, and he probably only did it because she's pregnant." I can't help but be a little surprised by his admission, but it really doesn't bother me.

"Aerick, be nice," Terrie scolds him.

We spend the next hour just relaxing and talking. It's a nice change to what I have been doing lately. Aerick continues to move his hands around me, touching lightly in different spots, my thighs, my sides, my arms. Occasionally he kisses or nips at my neck; it's so normal, almost comforting to feel him in a relaxed environment. I get the feeling it isn't a normal thing, either. Several times I catch the others sneaking peeks at us and grinning.

Nothing would have made my night more than if we could have gone back to the infirmary, but that is no longer a possibility. Not that I think he actually would have, anyway. He is a good thirty dollars up when he says it is time to go.

"Lights out is in five minutes, so I got to get her back to the dorm," he tells everyone.

I shrug, "It's okay. I'll walk myself back. You stay here and play."

He smirks at me, "Now what kind of gentleman would let you walk back to the dorm in the dark by yourself?"

Suddenly Terrie laughs hard and Aerick turns to glare at her. "Maybe Paulo should walk her home because never in a thousand years would I ever call you a gentleman, Aerick." I chuckle under my breath.

"Fuck off, Terrie." He stands up, pushing me up as he goes. I don't know how he can stand still, after I just spent over an hour sitting on his lap.

He stretches. "Paulo, count me out and bring my money when you come. Come on babe, let's get you back." He takes my hand, grabbing his sweater from the back of the chair and I say 'bye' to everyone as we walk out the door.

Once we are outside I realize it's still raining. Aerick stops me before we can get out from under the small porch outside the door and puts his sweater over my head, coaching my arms through the sleeves.

"Don't let them fool you. I can be a gentleman. I just have never seen the need to show it before I met you." He is so damn cute sometimes. He wraps his arm around me and we walk the short distance to the dorm, stopping outside as we reach the door.

"Now that I have walked you home, do I get a goodnight

kiss?"

I grin, loving his playfulness, as I grab the back of his neck and pull him down. "I think I could at least do that much for such a fine gentleman." He smiles and I close the distance between us, kissing him passionately.

CHAPTER EIGHTEEN

(Sunday, September 6th)

Aerick POV

FUCK! I AM really getting tired of waking up this way. Soaking wet from my own sweat with this achy feeling in my stomach. I dreamt about *that day* again. The dream is always so fucking vivid. I always wake up and have to convince myself it didn't happen like that.

When Liz got there that morning, she gave me this odd look that sent chills down my spine. It was hard to ignore the feeling that I shouldn't let Nadi go see Liz by herself. I was so tempted just to get her to skip her session, but quickly changed my mind. Luther had been breathing down my neck, and Nadi and I had just had such a great afternoon. Instead, I decided to finish the paperwork Luther had been hounding me about, letting her go to her session. I've should have known better than to ignore my gut and have tortured myself with replaying it in my head over and over again.

Flashback

I sign off on the last daily log and grab the folder with the paperwork to take it to Luther. *Wow, that didn't even take fifteen minutes, so much for trying to occupy my mind.* I walk through my cadets' dorm just to check whoever happens to be in there. It's empty, of course, since it's a nice day; everyone is outside. I stop for just a moment at Nadi's bed. It's so crazy how I ended up here.

Never in a thousand years would I have thought I'd find someone I cared about so much. I've been conflicted about some of the feelings I have for her. Paulo told me it sounds like I love her, but that's ridiculous; I've never felt love before. Certainly, there was never anyone who loved me until I met her. It was shocking when she told me, but is it possible that I love her too? I just don't know. Taking a deep breath, I decide to take the forms over to Luther and then maybe just sit out on the stage until she is done.

Grabbing the door handle to the dorm, I hear Jeff yell her name. Maybe she got pissed and walk out of Liz's session. I smile at the thought as the door swings open, my eyes locking with hers. She is propping herself up on the small platform outside the door and Jeff is running over to her. *What the hell is going on?*

Then I see the blood. My whole world slows down as the papers in my hand fall to the ground at the same time she falls to her side. I see Brand is just coming out of the other dorm.

"Brand, get a fucking ambulance RIGHT NOW!" I yell at him as my legs take off running, not waiting for him to respond, but he grabs his phone out of his pocket quickly. *This is not happening, this cannot be happening. Not her, please not her.*

Several more people begin to converge on her. As I reach her, Jeff is about to touch the shiny thing sticking out of the side of her stomach. "Don't fucking touch her! Don't move it, don't do anything." I scream at him in a panic.

Pulling Mike out of my way, I kneel down by her head. "This is not fucking happening. Babe, I am right here. Hold on dammit, just hold on," I tell her, seeing the tears stream down her face. My own tears begin pooling, blurring my vision, but I have to be strong for her.

I pick up her head as carefully as possible, trying not to move the rest of her, and slide my knees under her head. I need this contact as much as she probably wants it. My fingers gently move her hair out of the way so I can see her face. The life is slowly draining out of her cheeks.

God, please don't let this happen, I beg silently as my heart tries to beat its way out of my chests – I need her. "Brand, where is the fucking ambulance!" I shout over my shoulder as I begin losing control of my emotions.

Luther is at her side a second later. "Nadi, who did this?" he asks, and I see her point in the classroom.

Fuck. It clicks in my head; Liz must have done this. *Oh shit, I let her go in, I let Liz do this to her. My gut told me something was wrong, and I let her go anyway.*

Her breathing is getting staggered and another wave of dread washes over me. "Hold on, babe. You can do this, you are strong. I need to you to hold on." I don't know if I am trying to convince her or myself, but I hear the sirens and they are close.

She looks over to Jeff and he's crying; she tries to smile at him. She is always trying to make everyone feel better, she is so selfless. "Paulo, she is out cold. Get in there and restrain her hands before she wakes up again," Luther demands as he exits the room.

My mouth falls open. She fought back and knocked her out. *Christ. Fucking Christ, always so strong.* Liz better hope Nadi doesn't die because as lucky as she got, I will kill her if she does – in fact I might do it anyway.

Please Nadi, hold on, I need you babe, please. I just keep repeating it in my head, hoping my silent prayer will be answered. I've never been one to believe in God but right now he is the only hope I've got.

Luther talks softly as he kneels beside Nadi. "Hold on, kid. It's going to be okay. Do you know why she did this?" Nadi looks up at me.

"It's my fault," I say before I can stop myself – because it's true. "She did it because of me." She shakes her head at me and I can see in her eyes she doesn't believe my words, but it's true. I pushed Liz to this and I should've known she would do something stupid.

"What the hell do you mean, Aerick?" Luther demands but I

can't speak, I just stare into her eyes. Her tears fall over my hand and I feel like my heart is breaking. She is struggling to breathe and it's clear she's slipping away from me.

"I love you, Aerick," she says, with a finality in her voice. She is giving up. *NO! You can't give up dammit.* I hear the ambulance. She has to hold on just a little longer.

"Don't you give up on me, baby. Come on, I need you to fight. They're here. They're going to help you. Fight just a little longer." I look toward the front and see Brand running in between the buildings.

She brings her hand up over mine and kisses it before closing her eyes. *NO, please don't give up on me baby, please, please.* " Nadi. Nadalynn. No! Fucking fight baby. You have to fight. You promised you wouldn't leave me – now fucking fight!" I yell at her, not knowing what else to do. I can't lose her, I just can't live without her, I need her.

I fucking need her, please. I have to tell her, she needs to know. I bend down, kissing her softly, praying that is not the last time I get to kiss her. "I love you Nadalynn. Please, please stay for me," I beg. Her body goes completely limp as the EMTs move in and start assessing her condition.

I'm frozen in place, my head hovering above hers as a single tear runs down my cheek. The EMTs are shouting stuff back and forth. "Sir, we need you to move back."

I shake my head. "I am not leaving her," I tell them, but I feel disconnected.

"We need you to move so we can help her."

Luther jumps up, shouting orders, but I don't care.

"Come on, Aerick, let them do their jobs," Paulo says as he pulls me back, but as soon as I'm a few feet away I shake him off me. I sit down on the grass, my elbows on my knees and my hands pulling at my hair. I'm losing the only person I have ever truly loved, and it is all my fault.

I watch on as they put her on a stretcher. I know people are trying to talk to me, but I can't do anything but look at her as they begin to take her away. The most incredible girl who came into my life and stole my heart, and now it will die with her.

End Flashback

I shake my head. I've had that dream many times in the last few weeks, but instead of me watching them take her away in the ambulance as I follow, in my dream, the EMT turns to me and tells me she is dead. His words echo in my head as I wake up breathing hard, covered in a pool of my own sweat.

Finally, my breathing evens out. My head falls to the side to look at the clock and it is almost four-thirty in the morning. Might as well get up and shower.

Before I go turn on the shower, I look through the door to her dorm. She is sleeping peacefully. Looking a lot like she did those first few days after her surgery. There were a few tense times when we weren't sure if she would make it. Late on the day after her surgery, she developed a fever which they believed was due to an infection. They had to give her stronger antibiotics than the

334

ones she'd been already been given.

I sat there all night just watching her, thinking about how much I needed her and how I couldn't live without her. A lot of really dark thoughts crossed my mind over those few hours. By morning, her fever had broken, and they told me that everything looked promising, but we had to just continue to wait and see. It was torture not knowing what would happen. I continued to pray for days that if there was a God, he would spare her life.

I go over to the showers and turn the water on as hot as possible, hoping it washes away the lingering feeling of dread that woke me. She's alive. She's okay, and I will never let anything happen to her ever again.

Once dressed, I've mostly shaken off my nightmare and I get ready to go out and start the day. The guys are all dragging themselves out of bed and pulling on their workout clothes. We only have two more weeks of this session and then our wrap up week. The bus leaves to take the cadet back to Chicago on the twenty-first. Luther has already filed paperwork for Nadi to be released directly from here.

Luther also offered Jeff an assistant instructor position, which he accepted. I'm not quite sure where that leaves him and his new girlfriend, but I know in my heart, he is staying to protect Nadi. I don't think he will try to steal her away from me, but what happened to her affected him almost as much as it did me. I think he understands now what she must have felt when she found him. He'll never stop caring for her, but I have come to terms with that.

At least if something ever happened to me, he would look out for her.

She has been getting more and more nervous as her court date gets closer. She has to be in court on the eighteenth. I have already spoken to the lawyer and been told I'll likely have to testify against Liz regarding her behavior leading up to her attack on Nadi. He told me that he was working on some confidential stuff with Luther, but I couldn't get him to elaborate. He asked me not to worry Nadi with it, but I really wish I had something more to keep her from worrying so much. I hate seeing her upset about it, even as much as she tries to hide it.

The guys and I go out to the stage and Brand gives me a nod. I am a little curious as to what that is all about. I wouldn't say we are friends these days, but things seem to have relaxed between us since he proposed to Tia.

The cadets start filing out of the dorms. As Nadi comes out, my eyes find her immediately and I give her a quick wink before composing myself. This is the first day she is allowed to participate in PT since she was cleared for physical activity yesterday, but she is under strict orders not to work too hard, and I will make sure of that. I let Brand know he will be leading today so that I can roam. I know her, she will push herself hard to prove she is okay. She has already been doing it all week.

The sexual tension between us is so thick right now, it's suffocating. Cold showers have become a daily thing for me, but I'm determined to make sure she is okay first. Terrie gave me the okay last night, so I will definitely be taking advantage of that sometime today, no matter what it takes to get her alone.

She has been egging me on for weeks. There was a momentary lapse of judgment the night of the bonfire, mainly because I was so drunk, falling asleep just to wake up to her massaging my shit. It's still hard to believe she did that.

Luther gives his little speech and the rankings appear on the screen. I look up, realizing I didn't check them last night after Brand put in his report. Nadi is first. Suppressing the smile on my face, I look at Nadi, who is grinning from ear to ear. She has been working hard to bounce back, and it appears Brand has noticed it too.

Luther departs and Brand starts us off. There isn't much need for the extra instructors anymore. We shout out a few comments every once in a while if someone is being lazy, but more the most part, the cadets are in really good shape; they know all the exercises and don't have a hard time keeping up. Brand calls out to run laps.

Usually Nadi and I would take the lead, but I grab her arm, letting everyone else take off first. "Ease back into it," I say sternly. Ranking first must have put her in a good mood because she rolls her eyes but listens. We run quietly together in the back of the group. It's clear she is having a hard time keeping up since she hasn't worked out for the last several weeks other than the laps she walked around the courtyard this week.

I have to remind her to slow down a bit during the rest of the workout, but she makes it through even though she's quite winded. I call her and Tara up to collect their prizes for ranking in the top two and dismiss the rest of the cadets. This is the first time Tara has made it into the top and she looks ecstatic. She chooses the iPod and I dismiss her. I go to hand Nadi the tablet, but she looks at me with a raised eyebrow. "I already know what is on the list."

I smirk at her. "And your choice?" I try not to laugh, but her enthusiasm is making it difficult.

"I would like to go out to lunch." My eyes fall to the ground and I bite my lip. Luther has already talked to me about this.

"What?" she asks, sensing my hesitation.

"Um, sorry babe, but Luther said you can't go out of camp for the next few weeks."

Anger creeps over her face but she takes a deep breath. "Why exactly is that?"

I know her anger is also part of the disappointment of not getting to spend the afternoon with me. "Sorry, Princess. He doesn't want to chance you running into Liz. If it makes you feel any better, I'm not allowed to go out either until this is over with. He's just being cautious."

Her bright eyes dull out a little as her gaze falls to her foot, which kicks the ground. Well, he said she couldn't leave, not that we couldn't have lunch here. "How about we have a quiet lunch here?"

She peeks at me through her lashes. "Really?" She says softly and making me wish I could wrap her in my arms right now.

"Don't worry, I'll figure out everything, alright?" She bites her lip, making me twitch in my pants.

"Okay. I will see you later." Giving me a beaming smile, she heads back to the dorm. It takes a moment before I finally pull my gaze from her and head off to make some arrangements.

* * * *

My morning has been extremely busy. Luther keeps pestering me for the weekly logs and to get all the physical assessments done for all the cadets for their files. Things always get crazy during the last few weeks of camp. After asking Tia to go get Nadi and have her meet me in Terrie's cabin, I hurry to drop off the paperwork to Luther.

As I exit Luther's office I see Tia and Nadi waiting for me. It's as if my legs can't carry me across the courtyard quick enough. I'm suddenly a little nervous and I'm not sure why; this was my idea. Terrie and Ayla were gracious enough to let me use their cabin for a quiet lunch, but of course Terrie had to go overboard, going all out once I explained why I needed it.

She had Andi make some of her delicious chicken fettuccine, and garlic bread. There is probably more, but Terrie told me not to worry about it. Knowing her, there's a five-course meal waiting for us on the table. She also had Paulo tell me if we fuck on her bed, I better change the sheets. I almost doubled over laughing since it hadn't really crossed my mind at the time, but it sure as hell sounds like a good idea. I could just see the look of disgust on

Terrie's face telling that to Paulo. I'll really have to thank her for letting us borrow the cabin.

I reach the girls and Tia gives me a little smile. "Thanks, Tia." She doesn't bother to linger, just nods as she walks away. "Hey, babe." I greet Nadi with a kiss her on her cheek. "Hope you're in the mood for pasta."

She does her little shy smile and I grab her hand, pulling her into the cabin. I'm momentarily shocked to see that the table is all set nice and pretty, with a few flowers and lit candles, while soft music plays on the stereo in the background. *Terrie.*

I quickly compose my face and look at Nadi. Her shock is much more apparent as she just stares at the table. I don't look away while I wait, letting her get her bearings. She looks at me with a huge grin after a few seconds. "Wow!" is all she can say.

My lips find her cheek again and I pull her over to the table that has two place settings next to each other. Reaching for the gentleman in me, I pull out her chair for her, before taking a seat in the one next to her.

There isn't a five-course meal but we have pasta, a salad, a basket of garlic bread and one large piece of chocolate cake, which I assume we are to share. There is also a bottle of New Zealand Sauvignon Blanc wine. I'm not even sure I want to know where she got this.

"Well, I think my little joke of calling you Prince Charming may be rubbing off on you," she says smiling over at me. I bite my lip at the slightly sarcastic tone. She knows it wasn't all me. "So, who helped you out putting this together?"

I try to look shocked. "Who says I didn't do this myself?"

She laughs and I have to bury the embarrassment trying to creep onto my cheeks. "Well for one, the radio is playing Journey. Not so much your listening style." She knows my play list and she is correct; not my style at all.

"And second?" I prompt her.

"And second, I have been watching you all morning running around like a chicken with his head cut off. You were way too busy to put this together." She is always so observant, and she is also right again.

I give in. "Okay, so I asked for Terrie for a little help, and she went a little overboard." I grab the bottle of wine which is already opened and pour us each a glass. "But with that being said, she did a great job." I'll give credit where credit is due. "Here is to excellent lunch date." I tap my glass against hers and take a large drink. Excellent choice of wine, I have to admit. "There is one thing that has to change, though," I say as she takes a drink of hers.

I get up and pull my iPod out of my pocket. Attaching it to the radio, I scroll to Nadi's play list and press play, but I keep it low in the background. She laughs as she tells me, "Much better."

I sit down and put my napkin in my lap. The food smells delicious and I pick up my fork before noticing Nadi is staring at me. "What?" I ask, a little worried something is wrong. Taking in everything around me, it all seems perfect.

She takes another long sip of her drink. "You know..." She

stands and slides quickly between me and the table, sitting on my lap facing me. She takes another sip of her wine before setting it down on the table and wrapping her arms around my neck. "Ever since Terrie cleared me for physical activity, I've been waiting to be alone with you."

Her hunger for sex drives me fucking wild. It takes about two seconds for me to get hard beneath her. Her lips look good enough to eat and I want to feel them on me right now. I bite back my need for her for just a moment. There is an excitement stirring in me with her taking control like this, and I wish to let her play it out.

"Is that so? And why is that?" I question, barely holding in my smile.

She leans down and runs her teeth across the side of my jaw back to my ear. "Come on, Aerick. I know how difficult it's been for you." She rocks her hips and I breathe in deeply. She gently bites my earlobe. "You're already hard under me, baby. Are you going to sit there and say you don't want it?" *Hell yes, I do!*

"Hmm, maybe." I try to play it off, rocking my hips a bit as my pants start to get uncomfortably tight. She kisses down my neck to my shoulder before she bites down and I let out an involuntary moan, grabbing her hips to keep her from moving. I want her so badly in this moment. If she had a skirt on, I wouldn't let her move from this spot – I'd be buried in her already.

"Sounds like you want it to me. Do you want it, baby?" she says against my neck. My hands tighten on her, but I am not done teasing her.

"Don't you want to eat your lunch, Princess?" My voice is much more raw than I intended.

She brings her face up to look me in my eyes. "Fuck lunch, I want you in me now." Her voice so full of need.

My eyes close as her words sink in and crush my lips to hers hard. It has been far too long, and I need to feel her around me. "Good," I say, breaking our kiss briefly before grabbing her tightly to stand us up.

She is momentarily caught off guard by my quick motions bringing her over to the bed. I'm glad I locked the door when we came in. I rid Terrie's bed of its cover and carefully lower us both onto the bed, not wanting to hurt her. I move over her, only lying half on her, making sure to not go to the side of her wound.

I'm way to excited already, I need to slow this down or I'm going to come undone in my pants. I soften my kiss a bit as I slide my hand under her shirt and bra. She moans into my mouth, making my body heat up even more. She is so reactive to my touch, I love it.

She needs to be close, and quickly, before I lose my shit. I slide my hand down to undo her pants and I quickly slide my hand down, inserting my fingers as she gasps. *Holy fuck!* She is so damn wet already, making me let out a low growl. She pulls my hair hard as I quickly work my fingers in her. It only takes a minute before I feel her body starting to tense, but I am fairly shocked.

Doesn't she play with herself? No way she went this entire time without relieving her own need for an orgasm. She has been all over me for weeks, so she had to be aching for it.

I remove my fingers quickly and she whines my name, but I want to feel this with me buried deep in her. I remove her pants and underwear as she kicks off her boots. I have my pants off in record time. I position myself between her legs but I see her shirt is slightly bunched up and I see the still red line on her stomach. I lean down and kiss it softly before I roll over, bringing her up so she is straddling me. She shrieks in surprise as I turn.

I don't want to be worried about hurting her. After her moment of surprise passes, she positions herself over me. She sinks onto me painfully slowly, moaning the whole way down, and I feel her tight wall flutter around me slightly. She feels even better than I remember. I hold her in place for a moment until I am sure I won't end this too quickly.

I breathe deeply and I can feel her trying to tug as I hold her hips in place. "Slow," is all I can get out as I loosen my grip. She begins rocking against me slowly and I put my head back as I take in the most wonderful feeling in the world. As I start pushing my hips up to meet hers, she picks up the pace; I can't hold on much longer as she moans my name again. She feels so amazingly good and I love hearing her call out my name.

She begins moving even faster and I feel her muscles get tense, tightening around my extremely swollen cock. "Babe, come for me now," I say roughly because I know she is on the edge and I can no longer hold on; without fail her orgasm hits her extremely hard. I pull her forward one more time as her orgasm squeezes me unbelievably tight and I spill into her with unimaginable force. "Fuck, Nadalynn," I try to say but it comes out in an odd broken form as I continue to move her against me so we can ride it out together.

Finally, she collapses on my chest. "Christ woman. Did you miss me?" She hums into my chest. "You are amazing," I tell her as I kiss the top of her hair. She hums again and I smile, remembering her having the same reaction at the cabin.

I sit up, bringing her with me, and she smiles as she looks up at me. I could get lost in those beautiful green eyes. "Come on, our lunch is getting cold." The look she gives me makes it clear that lunch isn't what she wants, but she needs to eat.

Kissing her on the forehead, I lay her down beside me so I can get up. I put my pants back on but remove my tank top and tee shirt since they're now sweaty. I pick up her pants, removing her underwear from them and throwing them at her before depositing her pants back on the floor.

She gives me a confused look and I sit back down next to her. "Is this your way of telling me you want to have lunch with me in just my underwear?" She jokes with me, but I just put on a serious face.

"I'm not done with you yet, and I want unimpeded access." I see the lust making its way back into her eyes. "But first I need to get some food in you, so you have the energy to keep up." She giggles and it is so fucking adorable. I kiss her again and go sit down at the table, filling up our wine glasses.

She joins me a few seconds later. This probably isn't the right time to ask, but I need to get this out. "Hey babe?" She looks at me as she grabs a piece of bread. "Christian stopped me earlier." She stops and looks at me in wonder. "He wants me to join your session today."

She looks down, a little nervous. "Why would he ask that?"

"I told him I would only do it if you were okay with it." She bites her lip and I know she is debating it. I take a bite of my food giving her time to think it out. I don't want her to be uncomfortable. Taking a deep breath, she finally answers me.

"It's fine. I don't mind."

I look up, a little shocked. "You're sure?"

She nods her head. "Yes, I don't mind." If I knew any better, I would swear she is trying to convince herself. I really wish I knew what was going through her head right now, but I don't want to push her.

I reach over and squeeze her thigh and feel as she presses them together. I smile as I would love to take her again right now, and it seems she would like that, but I want her to eat. She hasn't been eating very much again. She always gets food, but she mostly pushes it around on her plate while she talks with everyone.

I have hard time eating because I can't keep my eyes off her. Her bare legs, her lips as she takes slow bites. I am getting more and more impatient to have her again. I sit back after a few minutes of us eating in a comfortable silence. Grabbing my wine, I just watch her. I am one lucky sonofabitch. I still can't believe she is mine.

After a minute she realizes I am watching her. "Like what you see?" she asks as she licks her lips, and I hit my breaking point. I grab her hand and pull her out of her seat, over to me. I scoot my chair back a little and pull her to sit on my legs.

"Princess, I could look at you all day."

She blushes and she leans down to kiss me. "I could say the same about you." She runs her hand down my bare chest. I love feeling her touch. Inspiration hits me. "You know, I think I am ready for desert." She gives me a questioning look. I reach over to the cake, scooping some frosting on my finger as I use my other hand to pull her hair back off her neck.

"I think this may taste better on you." I put the frosting in a streak across her neck. I see her close her eye for a moment before she catches my hand in both of hers. She looks me in my eyes as she pulls my finger into her mouth, sucking off the remaining frosting. *Damn, that is hot.*

My chest rumbles as I feel the shiver that runs down me. I wrap my hand in her hair, pulling it to the side so I have plenty of room. She closes her eyes and I attack her neck. She lets out a moan and I can't help the thought that this frosting really does taste better on her.

I want to know if my thoughts from earlier are right. I grab her hand and begin to pull it down between her legs. She pulls her hand back. "Aerick?" she whispers but I don't stop licking and biting her neck.

"I want to feel you play with yourself." I bite at the sensitive spot on her neck and she moans again.

"I don't know if I can do that," she whispers. I pull back a little to look at her, raising an eyebrow. "Are you telling me you have never played with yourself?" She looks down immediately and her embarrassment shows on her face as she shakes her head 'no'. *I knew it.* It's still kind of shocking. That must take an enormous amount of self-control. I lift her chin so she will meet my eyes. She tries to look down. "Don't be embarrassed babe, I will show you." I still see the hesitation in her eyes. I kiss her gently to relax her and, after hesitating for a moment, she kisses me back. I lock my fingers over the back of her hand and move it slowly down her stomach.

As we get to the bottom of her stomach, I flatten my hand over hers and move it over her underwear. She swallows hard but she doesn't stop. I move her underwear aside and coax her fingers to circle her nub. She moans into my mouth.

"Don't stop," I mumble to her as I rest my head on her shoulder and look down, removing my hand from hers. As I watch her play with herself, I'm hard as a rock. "That is so fucking hot. I need you now babe. Stand up." She complies and I quickly undo my pants again, releasing myself.

I pull her forward, so she is straddling me. Moving her panties to the side, I pull her down, sliding into her. It takes no time before she starts moving. She feels absolutely amazing, tight and hot around me. I swear if I died right now, I would be the happiest man on the earth. We get lost in our rhythm as I alternate kissing her lips and her neck. When she begins to get close I move my hand down and use my thumb to circle her sensitive spot. "That's right baby, let go." Her orgasm hits hard at my words and I let myself follow as she moans my name.

✳ ✳ ✳ ✳

I head over to her counseling session, which is the last of the day. I stayed behind in the cabin to clean up the table and change the sheets. Terrie had left some at the foot of the bed. I am really going to have to do something nice for Terrie. That was the best lunch date ever and spending alone time with her was what we really needed. Only a few more weeks and I can have her all to myself, for more than a few hours at a time. *I can't wait.*

I walk into the classroom and she is already sitting there. She looks a little nervous as Christian waves me in and I take a seat next to her. "Hello, Aerick. I was just explaining to Nadi that I would just like to get another person's perspective on things. You likely have been the most observant of her during her time here."

"Okay." I smile at her to try to get her to relax.

"I really want to get down to the difference in her reactions," he says, and I am curious what he is getting at. "I have several reports that show incidences here at the camp. Once she reacted violently and immediately, while the other one was after a minute. Would it be fair to say she seems to just react when something takes her by surprise, whereas when it is something slow and deliberate, she reacts out of anger?"

I think back to all the times I have seen it, both in person and on the surveillance videos that I am embarrassed to say I watch a lot. "Yes, that seems to be the case."

"Have you ever seen her not react?" I look to her and I really don't want to say anything she doesn't want me to.

"Yes, when she was practicing self-defense with her childhood friend. She just froze." I keep a close eye on her reaction, but she remains still.

He turns toward her. "So, this is a friend prior to the event, correct?" She doesn't answer or even look at him, just nods her head, and I can tell that she is uncomfortable. "So, you have the ability to control it, then." He says but it isn't really a question.

She looks up at him. "But that is only with my friends, like Jeff."

"That isn't true. You held back when I did it." My eyes snap up to his and my anger is through the roof.

"You did what to her?" I seethe and his eyes get wide.

"Calm down Aerick, I never touched her. I simply wanted to see her reaction and if she could restrain it. I needed to see how bad it got." She puts her hand on my leg and I take a few deep breaths, trying to calm down. "The point is, she didn't attack me out of anger, which is her normal reaction, but it did put her into a panic attack." He smiles. "Nadi, why did you hold back when I threatened to touch you?"

She shrugs. "I was determined not to get in trouble again. I am hoping to stay here as an employee." He writes something down before turning back to me.

"Aerick, has it ever seemed like she was intimidated by you?"

I think about that for a minute. "Maybe a little, but she seemed to fight it, determined to prove me wrong." She smiles and I wonder what she is thinking about.

"So Nadi, I think the key to helping you is to teach you to control your emotional reactions. Learning not to let people catch you off guard, learning to not let your anger take over, but above all, using your determination to overcome your issues. Then it is a matter of learning some breathing techniques to help you work through the panic attacks." I am shocked, but his reasoning makes sense. She must think so too, because she is smiling.

"Aerick, thank you for coming by. I would like to finish up with Nadi one on one."

I hesitate for a second before I turn and kiss her on the temple, before standing up. I look back at him. "Christian, in the future, keep your distance," I tell him as a warning. He just laughs at me.

"Aerick, he is trying to help me," Nadi scolds me. I take a deep breath and make my way toward the door.

"See you at dinner," I say, and she smiles at me sweetly

"Looking forward to it." I leave and head for my dorm to shower.

I really need to control my own emotions. I trust her, I just worry about her. Trouble always seems to find her.

CHAPTER NINETEEN

(Saturday, September 12th)

WOW, IT'S ABSOLUTELY incredible! I cannot believe we only have one more week of camp. Time here has flown by and so much has happened. I almost lost my best friend, I fell in love, and then I had to deal with a crazy ex-girlfriend that almost killed me.

Aerick told me there is usually one or two crazy things that happen each session but this time around, it seemed to be a lot crazier. I turn and smile at him as we eat breakfast, and he puts his hand on my knee, squeezing it lightly. We have been trying hard to behave ourselves and don't touch much unless we are alone. It is not always easy to do, and occasionally Aerick will find reasons to touch me in class, but other than that he behaves rather well.

I still haven't stopped worrying about the court date this coming Friday. Both Simon and Aerick have told me over and over to stop, but I can't. However, we do have exams this coming week, which will hopefully be a welcome distraction.

We have our final exams Monday, Tuesday and Wednesday for all our educational classes, and tests for our physical classes on Thursday, Friday and Saturday. That is what I will be focusing on for the week. I need to make sure to do well on them so I can get my credits. I honestly hate school and didn't want to go back to school anyway. Jeff was excited to find out that Washington State has high school online, so he will be able to finish up his schooling here.

This is almost becoming bittersweet. It will be sad not to be around these guys anymore. I have become really good friends with just about everyone, even Leena, though still she gets on my nerves occasionally. We have been wrapped up in this bubble for so long, it's going to be weird going back to the real world.

For me it's going to be even more weird, because I am not going back to my old life, I'm starting a whole new one. New home, new job, new city, it's all kind of a big leap. I'm staying here at the camp for a week after everyone goes back to Chicago. Aerick has to do his post week wrap-up at camp, and the staff will be bringing me up to speed on different things. Jeff is going back with everyone but will be back the week prior to the next session in November.

Everyone seems excited today. Not only is it Jeff's birthday today, but we found out this morning we are playing capture the flag tonight with paint balls. It is a tradition to do it the Saturday prior exams to help blow off some steam before we have to really study. It sounds like a lot of fun and my excitement is through the roof. *What could be more fun than chocolate cake for dinner and paintball after lights out?*

Most of the male staff will be setting up in the large field for the majority of the day when they are not in class. Since Aerick has the second class of the day, he gets up, telling Trent and Brayden it is time to get to work and with a wink to me, he leaves. I hate waiting; too bad we can't play now, but it will be more fun at night. Plus, in our afternoon class, instead of hiking, we get to practice shooting the paintball guns.

I only wish Paulo was with Aerick's group for that class, but I don't mind Paulo. He is incredibly funny and is always dropping ridiculously inappropriate comments when others aren't paying attention. I have recently learned he is a lot like an older version of Brayden. It's hilarious finding out all the things that happen in the background at camp. Brayden and Trent are quite the pranksters. They have pissed off Aerick several times the last few weeks and I get the feeling some of those irritating days he had in the beginning of camp had something to do with them.

* * * *

I make it to our hiking class, which we are using to practice shooting paintballs today. We are lined up behind the mess hall, where there are human shaped targets that have been put up along the wall. Paulo has us all pick up a paintball gun and then he shows us how to shoot them, along with the proper stance when standing still and when moving. When he is done, he has us line up for practice.

These guns are similar to the small assault rifles I've shot before, except they have a ball catch attached to the top, and are lighter. They are definitely nicer than the worn paint ball guns I have used before. Personally, I love to go paint balling with my brother and his friends. We don't get to do it much, but we have a lot fun when we do. In fact, my brother and I aren't allowed to be on the same team when we go because we always win when we do.

I line up and it takes me just a few minutes to get the hang of the gun. After I hit the center ring that is on the target's chest and head, I continue shooting in rapid succession until they are completely covered in yellow paint.

"Damn, you're good," Royce says to me.

I shrug my shoulders. "What can I say? I like to shoot guns. My dad taught me from an early age." He nods his head and keeps practicing. "You really should open your stance just a little, and then take a breath, freeze and shoot." He follows my instructions and his aim improves significantly.

"You trying to take my job now, Nadi?" Paulo says behind me.

"Not yet, but if you want to keep it, you better start teaching these guys to shoot better," I smile and laugh at him as I line up to take another shot. I squeeze the trigger just as he kicks my foot, throwing me off balance, and my shot hits high up on the wall.

"You better be careful, or Luther is going to have you painting the wall," he laughs as he continues down the line.

"Butthead!" I yell to him, but he ignores me and keeps walking.

* * * *

We all gather out at the stage at ten, just as the lights turn off in the dorm. Aerick came around a little while ago and gave us all padded vests to wear. They are supposed to help soften the hit with the paint balls.

Luther, Ayla, Aerick and Brand are all on the stage. Luther and Ayla look odd, wearing all-white outfits that seem to almost glow a soft blue color, instead of their normal black clothes.

"Alright, listen up. This is a basic game of capture the flag. If you are hit, sit down and remain there until the end of the game. No discharging your weapon, and no helping your team. Luther and Ayla will be floating around to referee the game," Aerick bellows out so we all can hear, but is cut off by Luther.

"And a word of warning; shooting at the head is off-limits and if either Ayla or I are hit, you will be running laps for an entire day."

He looks back to Aerick, who nods his head and continues. "The first team to grab their opponent's flag, wins. Any questions?"

"What do we get if we win?" Joseph asks.

Aerick turns to glare at him. "The pride of saying you won! Sometimes that is worth more than any other reward you can get." Joseph looks down and shrugs his shoulders. "Alright. Brand and

I are captains. Shall we start with the cadets?" He looks to Brand but Brand waves to Aerick to choose first.

Aerick smiles and looks down. "I'll take Nadalynn." He still insists on calling me by my full name, and I have to say, I don't mind anymore when it is coming from him.

"I'll take Jeff," Brand says quickly, and they continue splitting up the rest of us and then the staff. When they were done, Aerick's team includes me, Patrick, Mike, Royce, Karen, John, Paulo, Brayden, and Andi. Brand's got, Jeff, Huck, Tara, Steven, Leena, Joseph, Tia, Trent, and Jake. Poor Terrie. She wanted to play but she told me she has to sit out in case someone gets hurt.

Luther yells out to everyone, "Okay. Follow your captains to your side of the field and come up with a strategy. The game starts when you hear the gun shot. You've got ten minutes."

We follow Aerick as we go out to the left side of the field. There is a glowing green flag in the corner of the field and in the opposite corner, a red flag. Both of them are atop something tall, but I am not sure what. There are only shadows of objects all over the field.

As we gather behind our flag, I observe that there are stacked wooden boxes that stair-step up in a triangle to the top where the flag sits. It's like a life size version of a geometry math problem. They must be all those boxes that were stacked behind the gym and mess hall. I had always wondered what they were for. It seemed weird to just have them stacked back there.

Aerick hands us all four green light sticks on strings and tells us to clip them on to the shoulder of our vest so two hang down the front, one on each side, and two down the back. I quickly take mine and making short work of it as I find the clips to attach mine Once we are done, he directs us to each grab the already-loaded guns at the foot of one of the wooden boxes.

"Alright, cadets. What do we do?" We all look at him for a second. "What is the best strategy? This is an exercise for you guys. The staff are just here to have a little fun," Aerick says, smirking at us. "But be warned, I hate losing."

"Well, we can take a sports stance to this. We can have an offense and a defense. Half of us stay and defend, the other half go try to get their flag," Mike spits out quickly.

I hide my smile as I answer him. "That is a good idea, except that Huck is all about sports, and it is likely to be their stance as well." I see a smile tug at Aerick's mouth in the low light.

"What if we just leave one person to defend, and the rest of us bull rush them?" Brayden says.

"I don't think that is going to work, Brayden," Andi pipes up, and that is when all common sense goes out the window as everyone starts talking all at once. I listen for about fifteen seconds before my frustration hits, but it helps me develop an idea. I don't bother stopping the current argument going on, I just walk away.

I go over to the wood boxes and with a sigh of frustration at our group, I set my gun down on the ground. Suddenly, I feel Aerick behind me. "Penny for your thoughts?" he asks quietly.

"Recon," I tell him, and he gives me a big smile.

The boxes are each about four and a half feet tall, and the ones in our corner are stacked three tall. "Here, let me," he says but I shake my head.

"I can do this, Aerick. I'm stronger than you think." It's irritating that he doesn't think I can do it.

"Relax, I just wanted you to save your energy, Princess. No need to get hostile. I know you are plenty strong enough. I was merely being a gentleman. Here," he grabs me by my waist and basically thrust me up onto the first box, and I am able to stand easily.

"Thanks," I say sweetly to him as an apology, and then I climb the next box and peek over the top of the third box where our flag is sticking out. It is hard to make out the people, but I can see their light sticks fairly easily. I can see they are splitting themselves into two groups. I quickly look around the field and notice the scattered boxes. There is just enough moon light that I see the darker shadows of them. I note their positions and quickly climb down, allowing Aerick to help me down from the last box. He takes the opportunity to grab my ass as he sets me down.

"So much for being a gentleman, Prince Charming," I smile at him, then walk over to our group.

Everyone is still bickering, and we are running out of time. Thankfully Aerick breaks in, "If you all want to shut up for a second, I think Nadi has something that will help."

I'm almost shocked that he used my nickname. Everyone quiets down quickly at his commanding tone.

"Thank you, Aerick," I say, once everyone is looking at me.

"Hey, just because you are the boss's booty call doesn't mean you call the shots," John says rudely. *Oh shit.*

Aerick starts to move toward John so I step between them, lightly pushing back on Aerick, but he stops right behind me. "First of all, John, if I was just a booty call then I would have slept with you when you kissed me months ago thinking you could get some; so stop being a jealous dick. Second, I can't help that I was smarter than you and actually decided to do a little recon before we made a plan. So back the fuck off." I hear Patrick try to hold back a laugh and Aerick's chest rumbles against my back.

"Now, if you are done being a pain in my ass, I would like to tell you all that they are forming two teams. Also, that the boxes in the field are formed into a diamond shape with four different layers. We are at one tip of the outside diamond and they are at the other tip. My suggestion is that we break up into three teams. One stay and defend, while the other two attack from opposite sides. One hides while the other attacks, drawing all of their defensive group to one side, and the others sneak in behind. They will likely assume we are in two teams like them."

John just looks at me, dumbfounded.

"Um, yeah. Anyone got a problem with her plan?" Paulo asks with a little sarcasm in his voice, and it gives me a natural high that he approves of my plan. Some shake their heads 'no' and the others just keep quiet.

"So how should we split up?" John finally asks.

"I say Karen, Royce, Andi and Patrick stay to defend, setting up two on each side, one on each corner of the flag wall and one out on each side at the outside box. Brayden, Paulo, John and Mike go to the right and draw the fire, Aerick and I will go to the left and work our way on the outside of the diamond. And before you can say it, John, I'm saying Aerick and I because we are probably the best shooters here. We can defend ourselves best if we run into trouble."

Royce steps forward. "She isn't lying, man. You should have seen her at practice today." Patrick nods his head too. He knows I grew up shooting guns.

John looks at me. "Actually, I was going to ask why not three people?" It is a valid question.

"Because we need to stay as hidden as possible. The more people we have, the more likely we will be seen, since we can't remove or cover our lights. With more people to the attacking side, they will think it is all of us."

He shrugs his shoulders. "Okay."

A loud, single gunshot echoes in the night.

"Does everyone understand our game plan?" Aerick asks everyone, and they nod their heads.

"Make sure you give us enough time to get over there," I say to Paulo. He nods and we start moving out.

Aerick and I stay back a little, letting them all move away from the flag before we move out to the left, staying low behind the outside boxes. I lead as we quickly move from box to box.

Once we round the corner half way down the field, I feel Aerick grab the back of my vest just before I'm about to run to the next box.

I'm confused and look back as he pulls me to the ground so he is laying over me and we are tight against the box. I am about to ask him what is going on when I hear whispered voices. We stay still for another moment and they pass us right on the other side of the box.

As soon as they pass I lean up in Aerick ear. "Let's go."

When I pull back there is a huge grin on his lips. "You know. This is super hot, you being all in-control and shit." His voice is full of lust.

I laugh quietly, not able to keep it in. If he only knew how hot it was to hear him say how hot I am. "Good to know. We win this thing and I will personally give you a reward in private."

He kisses me hard and I let out a quiet moan into his mouth as I feel his hands grab my hips tightly. "Let's fucking do this then," he whispers on my lips. "I lost to Brand last year and I am not going to do it again. Not to mention, I would love to get that reward."

We get up and start moving again quickly from one box to another. When we are only a few boxes away I can see there are two figures behind the boxes leading up to the flag. "There are two people guarding the flag behind the wall."

He pulls me behind him so he can peek around the corner. Suddenly we hear a flurry of activity and a bunch of shouting. "It's working – they are all going to that side, but Jeff and Brand are staying put." He pauses and I see the wheels turning. "This is what we are going to do. You stay behind me, as soon as you hear me shoot Brand, you shoot Jeff; use me as a shield if you need to and then get your fine ass up there and get that flag."

He is so damn cute, but I also know he wants to take control, so I let him. "Ten-four, captain," I joke with him.

He tries not to laugh as he crouches. "Stay low and don't let go of the back of my vest until you get him." I give him a nod and we start to move. Brand and Jeff are at each corner, but both are turned mostly toward the other side where there are a bunch of people shouting and all you can hear are the puffs of the paintball guns. We are almost there when Brand, who is closes to us, turns quickly and I hear two shots at the same time. I quickly release my shot, hitting Jeff square in the back.

"Fuck," I hear all three of them say in unison as they all sit down.

I laugh quickly, jumping up onto the first box. "Sorry boys, looks like this is a job for a woman."

I jump up on the second box and I hear Jeff say jokingly, "Better go get one, then." I turn to see Aerick stretch out and punch him in the arm. "I was just kidding, man," Jeff whines as he rubs his arm.

Suddenly I see paint splatter right in front of me on the box. Someone must have seen me up over the box. I duck down quickly. "Oh shit. That was close." I take a deep breath and stand, grabbing the flag and pulling it off the pole before giving a louc whoop.

"Hell yeah!" Aerick hoots behind me and I look over to the other side of the field to see that they were fighting over on the other side too, but I got to the flag first! Luther blows a whistle and announces Aerick's team has won. My team on both sides o: the field start shouting out their hooray's.

I climb back down quickly and Aerick gives me a quick kiss before anyone else comes into view. "Good job, Princess," he says as the part of our team that was our decoy comes rounding the back side of the boxes. Paulo and Aerick look at each other before each grab one of my legs and lifts me up on their shoulders. I yelp in surprise and Paulo quickly shouts for me not to hit him. Laughing, I raise the flag, shouting of our victory as everyone starts walking toward the fire pit in the middle of the field. I am on the top of the fucking world!

CHAPTER TWENTY

(Friday, September 18th)

I AM EXTREMELY nervous, sitting here waiting for Luther to come get me. I have to be in court in a little over an hour. Luther has excused me from my classes today, and he and Aerick will be taking me to Ellensberg, where court will take place.

Everyone wished me good luck as they left to go to their first class. Now I'm just sitting her on my bed, all alone with my thoughts. Terrie was gracious enough to lend me a conservative long, black skirt and a blue button-up blouse, since I only have uniform clothes. The fit is a little snug, but it isn't too bad. At least the long skirt hides my boots, because they look more along the line of combat boots instead of dress boots, and my feet are too big to fit into any of the girls' shoes. I hate having bigger feet.

Aerick walks in and gives me a smile. "You ready?"

I nod my head and smile because I know my voice will betray

me. He stops me in front of him, wrapping an arm around my waist and using his other hand to force my head up to look into his eyes. "Don't worry. Everything will be fine. I promise, I won't let anything happen to you." He leans down, kissing me gently before grabbing my hand, which I happily take, and he leads me to the front of the camp.

"Good morning, Nadi. Ready to go?" Luther says, way too cheerfully, but I can tell his smile is forced. I nod at him and Aerick opens the rear door for me before going around the passenger side to get in the front seat. He really can be a gentleman. I smile slightly as he gets in and looks back at me. *How did I get so lucky?*

We drive in silence and the closer we get the more my stomach turns into knots. Aerick was very displeased when I refused to eat my breakfast, but I really think it is for the best. It's likely my nerves would have it all coming right back up anyway. It's stupid to be so nervous. I've been in a court room a dozen times before.

Maybe it is because this is the first time it will be in adult court, or maybe it is because Liz will be there. I've literally been talking to myself to remain calm instead of instantly jumping up to kick her ass. Probably wouldn't go over too well, considering she is claiming what she did was in self-defense. *Stupid cunt.* Just to be safe, I explained to Aerick how I felt about seeing her. He promised he would stay between the two of us and would keep me from doing anything stupid.

We pull up at the court and find Simon out the front waiting for us. "Any word?" Luther asks him and he shakes his head.

"Good morning, Nadi," he smiles and nods to me. "I just spoke with the prosecuting attorney from the District Attorney's office and as of now they have not been able to come to an agreement with Liz, so this is going to go forward."

I look at him, confused. "What do you mean 'go forward'?"

"I will explain it all to you after we are done. I'm still not sure of all the facts, since we have to wait for the judge's decision, and we have to see if Liz is going to maintain her self-defense plea. We really should be going in. I would like to introduce you to the prosecutor who is in charge of this case."

Again, I am confused. "If he is the prosecuting attorney, then what are you? I apologize, I'm just a little confused here."

He smiles at me. "That's okay. I am your attorney, I'm here for you, basically representing the victim, which is also why you have not had to meet with him yet. He has been meeting with me, and I'll make all decisions to make sure it is in your best interest no matter what that may be. The district attorney's office is who filed charges on the government's behalf against Liz and will be the prosecuting attorney in this case. Does that make sense?"

I nod my head now that I think I understand this a little more. "Okay. Please, if there is anything you need to say, let me know quietly at any time. Do not speak up, try not to even make a face at her. We do not want to give her any fuel for the fire."

I take a deep breath. "Okay. Let's do this." He nods and we head inside.

After going through security, we head to a courtroom off to the side. The moment we walk in, my eyes immediately find Liz sitting at a table in front of the divider which separates the benches from the front of the court room. There are several people just standing around.

I freeze as she turns her head back, finding my eyes. She looks all nice in a fitted woman's suit. If I didn't know any better, she almost looked like she was one of the lawyers sitting around her. Aerick puts a hand on the small of my back to coax me forward.

"Breathe," he whispers in my ear. What he probably doesn't know is that I am holding my breath out of anger, not fear. All I want to do right now is beat her until she can no longer move.

By a miracle from God, I manage to keep my face composed as we walk to the very front bench. Aerick moves me away from Liz toward the other side where there is another table and three men standing behind it. Aerick makes an attempt to move so that Liz is no longer in my view.

Simon greets the men, shaking hands with each. "Nadi, this is the prosecuting attorney, Brian Leeks. Brian, this is Nadalynn Reese."

The man smiles and shakes my hand. "Nice to meet you, Ms. Reese. Nice to finally meet you."

"Call me Nadi, please. It is nice to meet you as well." He nods at me.

"All rise." I look over his shoulder as the bailiff bellows. "The honorable James T. Smith presiding." As he is speaking, an older man enters the court room and proceeds to the judge's chair.

"You may be seated," the judge says, once he has sat down. We sit in the benches and Aerick rests his arm behind me on the bench. Liz gives me a cold look before her attorney gives her a nudge and she turns around toward the front.

"Your honor, this is case 15-965896, The State of Washington versus Liz S. Wilkins, all parties are present," the bailiff says to the judge then steps back to his spot, and the judge nods.

"Mr. Leeks, I have read over the papers and see that no agreement has been made at this time. Is that correct?"

He looks over at the prosecutor as he stands. "Correct, Your Honor. We have been unable to reach any agreement in this case." He sits again as the judge writes something down before turning to Liz's table.

"Mr. Edwards, for the record; would you client like to maintain her 'not guilty' plea on count one, assault in the first degree and on count two, assault with a deadly weapon?"

Her attorney stands and nods. "Yes, your honor."

"And I assume that you have made your client aware that if convicted she would face a minimum of ninety-three, to a maximum of one hundred and forty-seven months in prison and a fine of up to fifty thousand dollars?" I swear Liz's face goes two pale shades lighter.

"Yes, Your Honor."

"Okay. I will set the trial date to begin December twenty-first, with jury selection to begin on December fourteenth. Is there anything either of you would like to add?" *What? I thought this was going to be the trial! What is going on?*

The prosecutor stands quickly. "Your honor, we would like to request, due to the violent nature of the crime, Ms. Wilkins' bail be revoked, and she remain in custody until the trial."

Liz's attorney jumps out of his seat. "Your Honor. Ms. Wilkins has no prior record and maintains this was self-defense. She is an outstanding member of society and we believe that revoking her bail is excessive. There is no other evidence that she will be a danger to anyone, including Ms. Reese. In addition, her roots are here in this state. She poses no flight risk."

The judge looks through his papers before looking at the prosecutor. "Mr. Leeks, I see there is a restraining order filed on behalf of Ms. Reese against Ms. Wilkins. Is that correct?"

Mr. Leeks breathes in deeply. "It is, Your Honor."

I know the answer before he even says it. "In this case, I will have to deny your request, Mr. Leeks. There is a protection order in place and I do not believe there is enough cause to keep Ms. Wilkins in custody. With that being said," he looks at Liz, "Ms. Wilkins, you are not to leave the state at any time prior to the trial. In addition, any violation to the protection order will immediately revoke your bail, and you will remain in custody until the trial. Is that understood?"

She stands, looking suddenly confident. "Yes, Your Honor." He nods and she sits back down.

I knew it! They look at her like she is some educated little princess who does no wrong. I know enough that reputation does plays a part in criminal cases. She is being charged with assault on the word of a person with questionable reputation, who has been convicted of assault several times.

"Alright, I will see everyone back here on December fourteenth for jury selection. Good day to everyone," the judge says as he picks up his folder and leaves.

"So, what the hell does that mean?" I ask both Simon and Mr. Leeks. Liz gets up and follows her attorney, giving me a smug smile. I go to jump up, but Aerick grabs my shoulders tightly, holding me in my place. "Stupid bitch," I mutter under my breath.

"Calm down," Aerick hisses in my ear and I take a deep breath. I turn to Simon, waiting for an explanation.

"That means the trial has been set for December twenty-first. This is what they call a pre-trial hearing. We were hoping to get some more evidence which would convince Liz to take a plea deal, but we have not been able to obtain it."

My stomach drops. "This isn't the actual trial yet?"

He presses his mouth in a line. "No. Today is more of a formality in which parties try to avoid trial, but obviously that didn't happen. When this goes to trial, we will help prep you to take the stand as a witness, and you will explain your side of the story."

"But she gets to remain out of jail until the trial. So she is free to do whatever she likes, right?" Aerick's hands tighten on my shoulders again. I know I need to calm down a bit but I'm furious.

"We tried to get her bail revoked, but it didn't work," Mr. Leeks says apologetically. "However, she is still banned from coming near you or speaking to you."

I laugh, "And what is that going to do? It is a stupid piece of paper. It doesn't do shit. Just ask my dead neighbor back home who was stabbed to death by her stalker ex-boyfriend. Can a paper stop a knife coming at you, or a bullet, for that matter? You and I both know that paper does absolutely nothing. It's a fucking joke that gives a false sense of security."

Aerick looks at me in shock. I don't think I have told him about that, but right now, I don't care. I am so angry that Liz is out running free after what she did to me.

"Not to mention, how this is going to look in front of a damn jury when they bring up my multiple assault convictions? It's like trying to charge someone with raping a woman whose profession is a fucking prostitute."

"Nadi, you have to calm down," Aerick warns me again, now that I am practically yelling. I glare at him for not backing me up on this, but inside I know he is right. I take deep breath, slumping back in my seat, and lean my head back on his arm.

Simon finally speaks up. "Nadi, I'm in the process of trying to get your juvenile record sealed. Unfortunately, I can't file it until you're finished with your sentence, which doesn't end for a few more days. I'm working to get an expedited hearing and if we can get it done prior to trial, they will not be able to use that against you or even bring it up during the trial."

"That is a pretty big 'if'," I murmur, feeling defeated.

"Please do not worry about this Nadi. Let us do our jobs and it will work out. Everything points to her guilt," Mr. Leeks says.

Taking another deep breath, I stand up. All the guys automatically stand with me and I do my best to keep my voice low and controlled. "You know, you all keep telling me not to worry, but no one seems to able to offer me any assurances or to tell me I'm wrong when I bring up all the shit they can use against me. Good day, gentlemen." I turn and walk away quickly, with Aerick stumbling to catch up to me.

I walk to the car in silence with Aerick right behind me, but he remains quiet. When we reach the car I just wrap my arms around myself and lean my forehead against the side of the car. Aerick's hands wrap around me and he kisses the back of my hair. "I have a bad feeling about this Aerick. Nothing ever goes my way."

He tightens his grip. "That's not true," he says simply.

I turn in his arms to face him. "How is that not true? Everything in my life has been one fucked up mess. Ever since I was a kid, my life has been nothing but bad luck and heartache."

"Your forgetting one thing, Princess." I look up at him and he has a slight smile on his face. "You found me. Prince Charming, remember?" He is so adorable. My lips tug up slightly. He leans down and kisses me lightly as Luther walks up, clearing his throat.

"Come on. Let's get back to camp." Aerick opens my door and

to my surprise he tells me to scoot over as he slides in next to me. I think Luther is a bit surprised as well because he freezes but after a moment, he gets into the driver seat. We spend the ride back in silence as Aerick holds me tight to his side.

My mind is racing the entire time, but I am pulled out of my thoughts when Luther goes into town instead of camp. "We don't have time to get lunch at the café, but we can get a quick lunch at the fast food place. Lunch is almost over at camp."

Aerick sits up a little straighter, coming out of his own thoughts. "Sounds delicious," Aerick says to Luther, then turns to me. "What are you hungry for, babe?" I shrug my shoulders; I'm still not hungry. "You didn't eat breakfast. You have to eat lunch." I let out a huff at his demanding demeanor. He doesn't leave much to argue with as he climbs out of the SUV, pulling me along into the dining area.

"Welcome to Burger King. What can I get for you today?" the cute guy behind the counter asks, staring right at me despite my two escorts.

"I'll have the double whopper with cheese meal, large, with a chocolate shake. What about you, babe?" Aerick asks me as he drapes his arm over my shoulder. I laugh a little at his show, but it works. The guy's eyes fly over to Aerick, who smirks back at him.

"I'm really not that hungry," I say carefully. My stomach is still in knots.

"Babe, please just eat something. For me?"

After a moment, I sigh, giving in, and look up at the board. *Something light.* "I will get the chicken apple-cranberry salad and a small tropical mango smoothie."

"I guess that is something," Aerick says quietly. Luther tells the guy his order and pays for our meal.

While Luther waits for the food, Aerick guides me over to a booth, his arm still around me. I really think Aerick just wants me away from the other guy. It doesn't matter right now.

"Maybe having you in a skirt isn't the best thing," he says, looking a little smug.

"What is wrong with what I am wearing?" I prefer pants, but I'm curious to see what his excuse is. I really don't need to ask, though, because that smirks tells me before he says it out loud.

"Well, nothing really. You look extremely beautiful right now. In fact, it is making my pants quite uncomfortable. The problem is that little piss-ant that was just starting at you like you were a piece of meat; I noticed that, too."

I roll my eyes. "Really, Aerick? You have no reason to be jealous."

His eyebrows pull together. "I'm not jealous."

I laugh out loud. "Aerick, if you were any more jealous, you probably would have just jumped over that counter and beat his ass."

"That is not true. I was simply showing him that you were not available. I was helping you out!"

I shake my head. "Okay, keep telling yourself that."

Luther joins us with our food and we begin to eat. "So Nadi your trial will be during our next session. I will make sure tha your schedule is clear." Aerick looks at him with a raised eyebrow and Luther stops. "Aerick, I cannot have both of you gone for ar extended amount of time."

Aerick gets tense. "She needs me there, Luther. I won't leave her there by herself."

Luther thinks for a minute. "I will give you a few days, bu that is all I will promise you, Aerick. Anyway, we will make it work. Until then, I want you both to be careful. I know you are going down to Aerick's condo after the wrap-up week. Make sure you look out for yourselves, alright?" We both nod our heads.

"When does the next session start?" I ask Luther, trying to get my head away from the issue of Liz.

"Well, we have two sessions a year. We typically refer to them as the summer session, which is the one we are currently in, and the winter session. This year the winter session will be starting November twenty-third. You will be expected to report one week prior to the session, and when it ends March thirteenth, you will be required to stay one additional week. There is typically a lot of paper work that has to be completed and filed with the courts and educational board."

I stop eating and stare at Aerick, who is dipping his fries into his chocolate shake. Luther notices and stops talking, but it takes a second for Aerick to look up at me. When he does I raise my eyebrow. "What?" he asks, confused.

"Are you, like, five or something?" I ask him, laughing.

He nudges me with his arm playfully. "For the record, this is the best way to eat fries. You know, the whole sweet and salty thing." I shake my head and his whole-body changes, almost sinking in on itself. "Besides, my parents would never take me out for fast food and if I dared to do this, I probably would have gotten an ass-whooping for not eating properly," he says quietly. *Wow.*

Luther takes a deep breath and continues. "Tia is due April twelfth, so by then she will be very pregnant. You may be asked to take over toward the end of the session if she is having any issues." I nod my head at him.

"What about sleeping arrangements? I mean, she is staying in her dorm for the wrap-up week, but what about next session? We don't have any more beds in the cabins," Aerick says with a sly smile.

"She isn't sleeping in your bed, Aerick. Nice try, but I was serious. Your relationship stays between you two, except the few times during the session that it is allowed. Don't make me choose like I did with Trent and Shauna, because I will."

"What happened with Shauna and Trent?"

"The cadets caught them fucking in the instructors' dorm," Aerick replies.

I raise my eyebrow. "That's it?"

He laughs, "And the gym, and the field. Luther finally had enough when the cadets complained they heard them having sex on the lookout camping trip. That is why couples aren't allowed to go together up there anymore." I try to hide my smirk, thinking of all the places Aerick and I have been and by the look on his face that is what is going through his mind too. Luther just looks extremely uncomfortable, listening to what is coming out of Aerick's mouth.

"Anyway, I don't want a repeat of that from you two. Got it?" We both nod. Guess we will still have to be careful. "Back to the original subject, I will have sleeping arrangements settled when you guys get back."

"We better head back," he says as we finish up our lunch. Nadi, you'll still have time to make your archery class for your test, if you want to. That way you won't have to make it up. But if you want to wait, that's fine too."

I grab my smoothie and Aerick takes my garbage, throwing away my half-eaten salad as he silently protests with a grimace on his face. "I think I'll go. I already have to make up the self-defense fight and the timed wall climb tomorrow. I'd rather get this over with today."

I breathe deeply as we get back to camp. Two more days until the end of the session! *Wow!*

CHAPTER TWENTY-ONE

(Sunday, September 20th)

I TRY TO tear my eyes open as I hear the alarm go off. *I thought they said we were done.* Today was supposed to be a truly free day, or so Aerick told me. Everyone is supposed to just hang out and relax today. I look over at the clock and see that it is six in the morning; we got to sleep in for a whole hour.

The speaker in our alarm clocks come to life. "Get dressed and be outside in formation in ten minutes," Aerick's voice says, and I can't say I'm too upset now. At least he gave us ten minutes. Maybe it wasn't such a good idea to stay up all night talking. We all went to bed somewhere around three this morning, thinking we would be able to sleep in. Apparently, we were wrong, and we are still doing PT this morning. I get up slowly, throw on some pants and grab my hoodie because it feels a little chillier today.

We get outside and lined up, but it is different. It looks more like our first day here. The entire staff is outside at the stage, piquing my curiosity. Once everyone is lined up, Luther steps forward on the stage.

"Good morning, cadets. It seems like not so long ago, you all were standing in front of me, a bunch of misfits from Chicago. Today, you stand in front of me better men and women. Despite what you may think, you all have come a long way in the last four months. All of you passed your classes, and the average GPA between you is a three point three. That is a 'B' average, which is a huge accomplishment for some of you." Tia starts walking around and handing each person a piece of paper.

"I hope you have all learned a lot here and take it with you, practicing it in your everyday life. Each and every one of you can become more if you are willing to work for it. Just remember, nothing in life is free, but if you are willing to work for it, the possibilities are endless. This program has a re-offense rate of less than five percent, which is almost unprecedented. The staff here mostly consists of previous cadets who made the choice to become more. Others have gone on to be everything from doctors, to lawyers, to business owners. Let them be an example of what you can do with your life. It is up to you to make your future."

Tia hands me my paper and I peer down at it. The paper is basically our report card for all the classes we have taken. I am shocked as I look down at the scores.

Nadalynn Reese
DOB: 06/27/97
Grade: 12

Cumulative Semester GPA – 3.9
Total credits earned – 5.0
Courses/Grade/Credits (credit type):
English – 98%, 0.5 Credits (English/Elective)
Math – 100%, 0.5 Credits (Math/Elective)
Science – 97%, 0.5 Credits (Science/Elective)
Social Studies – 97%, 0.5 Credits (Social Studies/Elective)
Nutritional Health – 95%, 0.5 Credits (Physical Education/Elective)
Technology – 99%, 0.5 Credits (Career Education/Elective)
Archery – 100%, 0.5 Credits (Physical Education/Elective)
Knife throwing – 98%, 0.5 Credits (Physical Education/Elective)
Hiking – 100%, 0.5 Credits (Physical Education/Elective)
Self Defense – 96%, 0.5 Credits (PE/Career Education/Elective)

Wow, I didn't even feel like I tried very hard! I mean, a lot of it was just a welcome distraction, or a way to deal with extreme boredom. I hear everyone start talking, but they quickly get quiet again. Luther has continued talking, but I have no idea what he is saying because I am still stunned from my report card.

"These are the overall standings." I look up at the screen behind Luther.

1 – Nadi
2 – Jeff
3 – Steven
4 – Royce
5 – Karen
6 – Huck
7 – Tara
8 – Patrick
9 – John
10 – Mike
11 – Leena
12 – Joseph

"Nadi and Jeff, please join me on the stage." I look over to Jeff and we make our way up onto the stage. When we are both up there, Luther stands between us. "Based on the rankings, it is clear that these two have worked extremely hard in every aspect of this camp, and hard work deserves to be rewarded. At the end of each camp, I always offer the top two cadets positions at the camp. want to officially announce that both Nadi and Jeff have been offered positions here, which they have accepted. They are the next generation of leaders here, and we are proud to welcome them." Everyone claps for us and my eyes meet Aerick's. His face shows pure pride. Luther excuses Jeff and I; we go back down to stand with everyone else.

"Again, I want to thank all of you for yet another successful camp. As a parting gift, since I made you throw out your god awful clothes when you arrived, you will find a gym bag with your graduate clothing for you to take back home, along with few other items I would like you to have, when you get back from breakfast. Please enjoy the rest of your day, but be aware your bracelets will not be removed until you get on the buses tomorrow morning. I request you spend today having fun." Everyone's faces instantly turn into smiles.

"All items you have earned here should be put in your bag once you receive them, so you do not forget them. Please leave all other camp property at your bunk and they will be cleaned out after your departure. Staff will be on mess hall duty today, but please be sure to attend your final counseling session. You must sign off on your counseling report so it can be filed with the courts, since it is a requirement. Failure to do so will result in your sentence being reported as incomplete, and after all your hard work, that would be a shame. Enjoy your final day here. Buses will leave here tomorrow morning at seven a.m. sharp. You're dismissed."

Everyone looks around at each other. It is a little surreal. Several people come up to congratulate me, including the staff. "So how did he know Jeff and I would be in the top two?" I ask Aerick as he walks up and smiles at me, but does not hug me. I guess technically I'm a cadet until tomorrow morning, so hugging would be inappropriate.

"You and Jeff have been out in front of the overall rankings for a while. Plus, Tia can usually get a good estimate of how well you would do on your testing based on your last four months of work. Normally Luther would have waited until the end of the last week to offer the positions, but he was fairly certain how it would play out, especially you. You excelled at just about everything you did. You were at the top of both your educational and physical classes. You overcame every obstacle that was put in front of you, and for you that was a lot in the last four months. You always pushed yourself to be the best, even when you really weren't trying to. That is a quality Luther greatly admires, among others you have shown. Bravery, honesty, selflessness, kindness, and to be smart are the values this camp is built on. You showed all of them. Weren't you listening to his speech?" he scolds me.

I'm a little embarrassed, "I kind of got caught up looking at my grades and tuned him out."

He looks at me with a smirk. "Yes, it was very impressive. Your GPA is the top of the class. You did really well here. I couldn't be prouder, of you babe," he says a little quieter so others don't hear him, and I blush in response. "I will see you later at breakfast," he tells me with a wink and turns back toward the dorms.

After breakfast we decide to go back to the dorm and clean up a little. Well – at least I want to clean up a little. It is one of the things I do when there are too many emotions running through my head. I thought about going for a run, but I don't want Aerick to worry; it would be a red flag. He has learned a lot of my ticks in the last few months, so physical activities are out.

When we get back to the dorms, not only are there nice black gym bags on each of our desks, but there are also small crystal tablets with uneven edges. As I get closer, there are plaques of completion. Picking mine up, it's quite beautiful, and has my name on it, along with 'Ranked #1'. *That's awesome!*

I look in the bag. There are two sets of black track suits with a blue stripe running down the side, several tee shirts, hoodie and jacket, all with the Donnelly Bootcamp logo on it. There's also a lanyard, key chain and a few other small objects with the camp name and logo. I guess it's good advertising.

Suddenly there are two unfamiliar hands on my waist. I immediately freeze and tighten my fist before taking a deep breath. "Remove your fucking hands before I break them."

Whoever it is moves away from me quickly. I turn around, pissed off as all hell, and see Mike with his hands up like I'm going to shoot him.

"Please don't hurt me. Christian asked me to do it. He promised me you wouldn't hit me," he whines. Boy, he is lucky I've been working on my issues! Nodding my head, I let him know he meant no harm, but he'd better hope Aerick didn't see that.

✻ ✻ ✻ ✻

"So Nadi, how are you feeling today?" Christian asks.

"You mean besides having Mike put his hands on me?" I can tell he is holding back a smile.

"You didn't hit him, did you? Luther and Mike will not be too happy with me if you did." I hold in my smile and try to seem irritated.

"No, but if Aerick sees that camera footage, I can't promise he will show the same restraint."

He laughs, "I will have Luther talk to him, but it worked. Instead of reacting out of panic, you paused for a moment before you acted. Correct?"

"Yes. I almost kicked him in the balls, but instead I focused on taking a breath, pushing through the tightening in my chest, and reminding myself that I'm a different person. It gave me enough time to assess the situation before I reacted."

He smiles widely. "Good. You are learning. For the record, I knew you would be okay, or I wouldn't have asked him to do it.

So besides that, how else are you feeling today?"

I shrug. "Happy, sad, scared."

He nods his head slightly like it's nothing. "These are all normal feelings. Can you explain how they relate to you specifically?"

"Well, I'm happy that I have completed this camp, and for being at the top of the class. I'm happy I finally met someone that I am totally in love with. Happy that I have a new job already. But then, I'm sad that this is over, if that makes any kind of sense. Over the last four months, this has become like the normal and it has become comfortable. I'm going to miss all the people I have met here, and I am going to miss my old friends as well."

He smiles. "An answer I completely expected. How about being scared?"

"Well, there is quite a bit for me to be scared about. I'm moving here from Chicago based on a relationship that is only a few months old, starting a new job, expected to go through fast-paced schooling, and on top of all that I still have to deal with the whole Liz situation. Not to mention working on all the things we have been over the last few weeks to help me with my anger and panic attacks."

"Yes, but you have done extremely well. And it isn't something that is going to change overnight. You will have to continue to work at it, but you will be able to get past this. I have all faith in you. Have you considered my offer to continue seeing me once a week? My office is in Seattle, not too far from where you will be living."

I take a deep breath. I've thought about it, and I really do want to, but I don't know about the money. "Christian, I really think it would help, but I'm not sure what my money situation will be able to accommodate that." Technically, I won't even be making a paycheck for a couple more months, and I'm not even sure how that will work.

"I am sure we can work something out. I'm going to be here for the winter session as well while Luther looks for another replacement. Maybe I will just work it into his cost."

"Sounds like a plan; although, Luther has already done so much for me. I'm starting to feel like I am taking advantage of him." My mouth has become entirely too loose around Christian. Since when do I just admit my most pressing thoughts? It seems he too has found a way in; not too deep, but there all the same.

"Don't. Luther does this to gives back to the youth. To give you guys the second chance his son never got. It makes him feel proud to see you succeed, just like you are his own kids."

My mouth hangs open at his statement. Luther never has said anything about kids. "Luther has a son?"

He takes a deep breath. "He *had* a son, but that is something you would have to speak to him about. It is not my place to discuss that with you. It is a touchy subject, so please approach it gently if you decide to." I nod.

We continue to talk about my progress and the different techniques to help both my anger and my panic attacks. When we

are finished, he gives me a statement to read which jus
summarizes my known issues and how they have been dealt with
It also details the further actions that he has written about during
the session. I sign the statement and feel almost as if this is a
closing point – like this is really the end.

My mind feels lighter as I leave my counseling session. I wall
out into the center of the court yard and sit down. I take a deep
breath and look around me. I've been through so much, not jus
in the last four months, but over my entire life. I have beer
through things no one should have to go through, but I can't let
those things dictate my life. It's time to put my past life behind
me. Tomorrow is the beginning of my new life, and I am
determined to make my future better than my past!

Coming later 2019…

UNSTABLE
Book Three in
the Donnelly Bootcamp Series

About the Author

Danielle Leneah is a person with limitless aspirations. Whether she is working full time to help support her family, designing web sites for fun, or writing books to calm her mind, she always puts her heart and soul into her work.

Her reading and writing ambitions started at a young age. By sixth grade, she was reading full Stephen King novels and writing short stories. Her first publication came when she was in high school. Her work was accepted to be published in a well known poetry book. Even though her dreams of writing were temporarily halted as she began to build a family, it eventually drew her back.

As she began writing, she remembered the peace and joy it use to bring her. In astonishing 50 days, she had the rough draft of the first two books in her new series completed.

In her mind, if she can make just one person happy with her stories, it would have been worth it.

Danielle was born and raised in the suburbs of Seattle, Washington where she still lives with her husband and children.

To get the latest news and stay up to date, visit her website at:
www.DanielleLeneah.com

Made in the USA
Coppell, TX
28 May 2021